In memory of friends:
Alok Roy, Vikram Malhotra and Anuradha Chopra

CONTENTS

HOUSING PROBLEM

Agastya was so enervated by his life in the city that ever so often, when he was alone, he found himself leaning back in his desk chair or resting his head against the armrest of the lumpy sofa in his office that served as his bed, shutting his eyes and weeping silently. The cry generally made him feel better.

His office was his home, so hard-working a civil servant was he. Just a week ago, he'd been placidly content in his position of a Joint Commissioner, Rehabilitation (on Leave Not Granted and Without Pay), snugly afloat on the unplumbed murk of the Prajapati Aflatoon Welfare State Public Servants' Housing Complex Transit Hostel in the country's capital. As an illegal occupant of flat A-214, he had felt in those days cocooned and distanced from the swirl around him. Marathon power cuts in summer, a cleanish Municipal swimming pool a minute's cycle ride away, great dope, no sex though—all in all his life on leave had been okay-minus. Then out of the blue—Personnel always moved like lightning when it wanted to fuck somebody's happiness—he'd received his transfer orders to this fifteen-by-fifteen boarded-up section of veranda on the fourteenth floor of the New Secretariat in the western province's capital city.

The grimy, once-orange, lumpy sofa was for V∞IP visitors. His predecessor had won it from Protocol and Stores after a stimulating five-week struggle. Beneath the windows lay the plain wooden bench that Agastya had stolen from down the corridor. It was his kitchenette; on it stood his kettle, cafetière, electric stove and tea things. Beside the door, on a desk, sat a personal computer swathed in dusty dust sheets—the Ultimatum System Configuration Module 133 Mhz Intel Processor 8MB RAM 1 GB HDD 1.44 FDDSVGA Megachrome Monitor Skylight 99 was entitled to air-conditioning, so it had to remain. The windows of his section of veranda offered a breathtaking view of the world's largest slum undulating for miles down to the grey fuzziness of the Arabian Sea.

Agastya spent three to four nights a week at Daya's, a forty-five-year-old divorcee whom he'd met on the luxury coach that he'd caught out of the Transit Hostel on the occasion of his transfer. They'd found themselves sitting side by side at the rear of the hot and crowded bus. Luxury simply meant that its tickets cost more. Daya was bespectacled, and had been dressed in a whitish salwaar-kameez. Agastya had been in his valedictory present from the staff of his Rehabilitation office, his new blue jeans. After eight years in the civil service, he'd come to dread farewell gifts chosen by subordinate office employees; after the tearful speech-making, they'd routinely, on each occasion, given him a clock.

'So that even though time flies, you'll remember us,' they'd explained when they'd felt that he hadn't looked grateful enough. At the Rehabilitation Commissionerate, therefore, he'd summoned the Office Superintendent and asked:

'Do you plan to collect some money for a farewell present for me? Yes? How much will it be? If you don't mind, I'll accompany whoever's going to buy the thing . . .'

The long last seat of the bus had been intended for six bums; eight had been a disgraceful crush. Agastya's right thigh had virtually fused with Daya's left; thus the ice had been broken. The heat had helped too.

She'd taken off her glasses rather early in their relationship.

She had large, tired eyes and a wide mouth. Agastya had immediately yearned to go to sleep with his face restful between her ample, firm breasts. Only repressed homos, his soul had pointed out to him then, long to fuck women old enough to be their mothers, especially when their own mothers are dead. Ah well, que sera sera.

She'd wanted her sunglasses and some tissues from her travelling bag and he'd got up to take it down from the overhead rack when he'd noticed an uneven dark blue strip running down the outside of the thigh of her whitish salwaar, like a ribbon down a bandmaster's trouser leg. His new blue jeans had been shedding colour like a snake its skin. Destined To Fade, ran their ad; they were called Eff-Ups. He'd died of embarrassment for four seconds, then had plonked down with her bag on his lap, determined not to get up till journey's end, or till she lay down on the floor of the bus, wriggled out of her kurta, peeled off her salwaar, sighed and begged him to gnaw off her panties with his teeth—whichever was earlier. Hadn't she noticed how he'd touched her up? Ahh, her spectacles were off. Ohh, the blessings of imperfect sight.

'Where in the city will you be staying?'

'Oh . . . at the Raj Atithi State Guest House.' Daya had looked blank, reminding him that the world of the city encompassed much more than the universe of the Welfare State. 'That's on Pandit Samrat Shiromani Aflatoon Mahamarg.' She'd continued to look blank. 'On Cathedral Road, between the Secretariat and what must be the world's largest garbage dump.'

Her face had cleared. 'Ah. The Secretariat was a splendid colonial structure before they boarded up those verandas and installed those Freedom Fighter statues.'

The Raj Atithi Guest House was a fourteen-storey building crawling with low life. A five-foot-high wall separated its compound from the world's largest garbage dump. Atop the wall stretched four rows of barbed wire, from various points of which sagged torn polythene bags of diverse colours. These contained human shit in different stages of decomposition. They'd been flung, of course, at the dump and hadn't made it across the wall. They in fact looked pathetic, like POWs in a Hollywood movie ensnared in a vain attempt to escape from a concentration camp.

'Hmmm ... breathe deep, my dear, this fragrant, invigorating air,' said Agastya to himself as he crossed the covered car park towards the stairs.

Amongst—and in—the twenty-odd white Ambassador cars there nested the low life with its charpais, kerosene stoves, lines of washing and racing children. It included some of the drivers, peons, bearers, attendants, cooks, orderlies and sweepers who worked in the Guest House and the Secretariat. Like a million other servants of the Welfare State in the city, they faced a housing problem. They'd got themselves enrolled in the list of those needed for Emergency Services and in almost every other list for priority housing that they'd heard of, namely, Priority Housing List, Top Priority Housing List, Chief Minister's Quota, Housing Minister's Quota, Scheduled Castes Percent, Scheduled Tribes Percent, Backward Classes Segment, Other Backward Classes Segment and Depressed Groups Reservation. They collected receipts, notifications, stamped documents, resolutions and photocopies of illegible forms as a kind of substitute for brick and cement; nobody had either land or houses for *them*.

On the first floor, Reception was a noisy ceiling fan, a decolam-topped counter with an abandoned dinner thali on it, a flickering tubelight, a vacant armchair, and behind it on the floor a snoring maid in a blue sari. Agastya rapped on the counter, and '*Koi hai?*' he hollered in his we're-the-Steel-Frame-that's-kept-the-country-together voice. The maid snorted and briefly opened one eye. She stopped snoring.

A taciturn bald clerk with crimson eyes had no room for Agastya. Agastya showed him a photocopy of his illegible room reservation form. The clerk belched explosively. With a 'tch' of exasperation, the maid got up, adjusted her sari and left. 'Look here, I've been posted here as Deputy Secretary.' (*I'd rather sniff a eunuch's pussy than bribe you, you shaved arsehole.*) 'Look here, I'm a girder of the Steel Frame, okay?' After a twenty-minute discussion, a yawning lackey accompanied Agastya in the groaning lift to a room on the twelfth floor, from where, in the morning, through the birdshit, the crud and the whitewash droppings on the window panes, he could enjoy a spectacular view of both the garbage dump and the slum.

The room had two separate beds. The second bed had been unoccupied when he'd nodded off, thinking of Daya's blue thighs and—regrettably—smirking. He awoke early and abruptly to discover two men in the second bed and two women and a third man on the floor, all asleep. While he blinked at them, the loo door opened and a fourth man came out with a bottle-green towel around his neck. He and Agastya stared at each other sullenly and silently. Agastya watched him cross over to the jute bag on the table, rummage in it and return to the loo with a shaving razor.

Once in the Secretariat, insecure, disoriented and unhappy, he wanted to meet the Housing Secretary to discuss his housing problem. He couldn't because the Housing Secretary was too senior. He'd joined the Civil Service before Agastya had been fathered. On alternate weekdays, only Joint Secretaries and above could call on him, and only between three and five p.m., to plead for solutions to their housing problems. The others could go fuck a duck. Ditto for Joint Secretaries and above after they'd pleaded.

His PA told Agastya to go and call on Menon, the Deputy Secretary (Personnel Housing) instead. Menon wasn't in his room; Agastya could finally meet him two days later. Eight years ago, they'd been posted together in the district of Madna and had pleasantly disliked each other.

'Hi, Menon! Long time no see, great to see you, have a nice day . . . look, are you in charge of the Raj Atithi Guest House? . . . I share my room with six strangers and I'm not used to it. When I return to my room in the evenings, one or two of them are sprawled out on my bed . . . Yes, they do get up when they see me . . . naturally, Steel Frame and all that . . . they're quite inoffensive, actually, and the younger woman, when aroused, would, I'm certain, make the earth move . . . but, I say, the point surely is: what about the prestige and the perks of the Steel Frame? . . . because of that horde in my room, I haven't been able to exercise in the morning ever since I've arrived . . . I've had to work out in my office room, and some bugger downstairs on the thirteenth floor came up to check on all that thumping and interrupted my spot run, so I had to stop, chat with him and start all over again after he'd left . . . shit, I'm sick of my life here . . . I don't see why you fart around in a three-bedroom two-thousand-square-foot flat by the sea while I've to moulder in a cloak room with a gang that for all I know could be a nomadic criminal tribe . . . how long did *you* have to wait before you could allot yourself the flat you're in?'

'Three years,' simpered Menon.

'Oh.' Long pause. 'They've placed their gas cylinder and burner right next to my bed, eyeball to eyeball with my pillow, practically . . . the most sullen of the men apparently follows some special diet and can't eat even carrots and tubers in general because they grow underground and don't get any direct sun while growing, and therefore are full of germs instead of being full of—well, goodness . . . I've begun to breakfast and dine with them . . . I decided that on the second day after my first meal in the Guest House Canteen . . . as the British would say, my word! . . . I went to complain about them to the Reception counter . . . their reservations are just as valid as mine—more, actually, because their booking's apparently for ever, whereas mine's for a mere ten days . . . so what's going to happen when my time runs out? is what I asked Reception . . . in reply, all of a sudden, it simpered so wickedly that my heart really bobbed up and down for seconds, I swear it . . . my room- and loo-sharers are guests of gun-loving Makhmal Bagai, Honourable scion of the ex-Chief Minister . . . they're on their way to some place to do a job for him, probably beat up some innocents . . . what a wicked world . . . what're their women for, then? I asked, and they gave me a Look . . . one cooks, the other's for fun . . . some people truly travel in style . . . Look, every time I leave the Guest House in the morning, I don't know how many strangers'll be floating around in my room-loo when I return, and whether they'll let me in . . .'

Menon asked him to fill up some forms and, simpering, added that he'd see what he could do about his position on the waiting list, which was 1294. 'Unless,' he smirked, pushing across a second set of off-white, cyclostyled papers, 'you want one of these more recent, sub-standard houses.' Agastya picked the sheets up with reluctance.

4/Applications/SS/TAB/84-92
The Welfare State
Regional Commissionerate of Estates
Allotment Type 'A'(B)

Dated:

Memorandum

Subject: Invitations for Applications for Unclassified Sub-Standard Houses of Type A

The undersigned is directed to state that the servants' quarters and outhouses (of the erstwhile Imperial Barracks) that do not have any modern amenities and were originally intended to be demolished and that would *have been brought down had it not been for the*

stay order from the High Court that has been obtained in this regard by the Heritage Preservation Trust are therefore now available to those Category A government servants already enrolled on the Emergency Accommodation Shortlist. A list of available locations of these servants' quarters and outhouses is at Annexure A.
It may kindly be noted that only those officers who drew a pre-revised salary of Rs 950 per month or above on 1.1.87 and who entered service on or before 1.1.81 are eligible for the above accommodation. Grade III (pre-pre-revised) Short Service Staff are also deemed to be eligible in this regard. The application form is at Annexure B . . .

'What does "do not have modern amenities" mean?' Agastya wished to know before he decided. 'No jacuzzi or no craparium?'

'It probably means an early-morning squat on the beach, with salt water tickling your bum, alongside a hundred thousand of your fellow citizens from Bhayankar. It's quite good fun, I'm told, after one loses one's initial middle-class inhibitions—rather liberating, lots of fresh air early in the day, no stink. The waiting list for the sub-standard houses stands at 379.'

'I can't decide whether 380 is an auspicious number for me or not. Let me first explore other avenues and the apartment blocks on them.'

On the phone, Daya sounded happy to hear his voice. After the preliminaries, he got down to business. 'Hi, Daya, do you smoke dope?'

She didn't falter at all. 'No. Why?'

'I'm new to the city. I mean, I've been here before for meetings 'n things, but I haven't stayed here for more than a couple of days at a time. Do you know anybody who can tell me where I can buy some good dope without being harassed by some cop? Either grass or charas? I'm old-fashioned.'

'I'll have to phone you back.'

She did, at about seven that evening, while he was vegetating in his office room, observing a tiny mouse scamper about from corner to corner, wondering i) how to extract a TV set for his office out of Protocol and Stores before the World Cup started, and ii) whether, since mice were cute and rats loathsome, it followed that compact men and women were more likely to enjoy better sex than jumbos, other things being equal.

'There are pushers everywhere in the city, one per streetlight, i.e., for every thirty metres of road length. I understand that they usually sell lizard shit to novices. However, I do have a couple of friends of my age who still make believe that the sap gushes just as strong in their veins. They *order* their charas from Golinaal and Megham—so I gathered. One of them is here from Madna with the latest on the plague; he's never been without dope in the twenty-seven years that I've known him. If you're desperate, you could join us for a drink—or him for a smoke, I should've said.'

Agastya was elated at the prospect of meeting Daya again. If her spectacles are off, that's a sign that God too thinks that I should sleep with her this month. By this weekend. Tonight. He returned to the Guest House to find his room empty and an eviction notice taped to his pillow. It declared that the Executive Engineer (State Housing) hereby gave the legal occupant of Bed No. 1 in Room No. 1206 five days' notice to vacate the said bed and to remove his/her belongings from the said room, failing which action as deemed fit under Section 63c(ii) sub-clause 41d of the State Immovable Properties (Maintenance, Protection and Preservation) Act would be initiated against the illegal occupant ('So help me, God,' murmured Agastya). Details of that action as deemed fit had presumably been too ghastly for the cyclostyling machine to bear, for the rest of the notice was a muddle of lines wandering off in unexpected directions, lurching over one another, often ambling back on themselves.

He prepared for war by threshing about all night in Bed No. 2, drafting in his head letters of resignation from the Civil Service. It had been one of his favourite pastimes in the last eight years. 'I'm sick of the pointlessness of the work I do and the ridiculous salary that I get for it, you fuckfaces,' was what he, by three a.m., finally settled on; he repeated the line till dawn like a litany just to check the rhythm, its fall. At eleven, fuzzy, unwashed, unexercised and rebellious, he showed up in Menon's anteroom to learn that Smirker'd buzzed off for a week to attend, with the Housing Secretary, a seminar on Alternative Housing and The Coastal Regulation Zone.

'I see. Where've they gone?'

'The Seychelles, sir.'

'So what should I do about this eviction notice? Should I sit on my arse and rotate until they return, and maybe tickle my balls with it while rotating?'

Menon's PA pooh-poohed the idea. 'The standard practice, sir, has been to avail of the shelter of the landmark judgement of the Supreme Court in the case of Bhootnath Gaitonde and Others Versus The Welfare State, wherein the Honourable Court has decreed that the need for shelter, though not a fundamental right of the citizen, nevertheless is so basic a necessity that it ought to be one of the Welfare State's primary objectives, that is, if the State considers itself a Welfare State at all. The Honourable Court has demanded, sir, very pointedly, though rhetorically, *How is one to distinguish the Welfare State from the Police State?* It aptly quotes in this connection Tirupati Aflatoon quoting Kautilya: *Only the Rule of Law can guarantee security of life and the welfare of the people.*' Menon's PA paused for a moment for the exasperated look on Agastya's face to change. 'Sir. Bhootnath Gaitonde was one of the two million inhabitants of—' he gestured towards the grimy, frosted glass of the window '—Bhayankar, which, as you know, is the world's—' his voice quivered with pride '—largest slum; it covers over two hundred and fifty hectares. Bhootnath Gaitonde was an advocate's clerk, a quiet, well-behaved law-abider, a worm yet to turn, a model citizen but for his address.

'Early one June morning, the Municipal Corporation showed up at his door. It had decided that week to clean up his part of Bhayankar—a routine exercise that it undertakes every month in different parts of the city, to tear down the shacks of those without clout, harass all who do not bribe to devastate the property of the unprepared. Under the noses of the police and the demolition squad, however, Bhootnath Gaitonde waved a stay order from the court. The worm had turned—and moved like lightning.

' "Me-laard," argued he before the judge, "I don't *want* to stay in this slum, I didn't *choose* to live surrounded by several varieties of excrement, used sanitary napkins, the rotting refuse tossed out every day by a thousand neighbourhood eating-houses, soiled bandages, broken syringes and bottles chucked out by clinics, dispensaries and hospitals, the rubbish of a thousand and one shops, cottage industries, backyard factories, workshops—and rats, stray dogs and vultures—I didn't select them as my neighbours. Of course, I had no choice; in any other city, with my salary, I would have been staying in a two-room flat in a lower-middle-class area with trees, a playground and perhaps even a municipal school—but I work in this city, and I'm one of the millions that make this city work. We're all here in Bhayankar, me-laard, we clerks, taxi-drivers, autorickshaw-walas, bus-conductors, peons, postmen, delivery boys, shop assistants, waiters, porters, cleaners, dhobis, telephone linesmen, electricians, plumbers, painters, cobblers, tailors ... If the Welfare State is the driving force, me-laard, then we are the wheels, and each one of hundreds of thousands of us stays—each with seven-to-ten members of his family—in a ten-by-ten tin-and-jute box; we all troop out and crap every morning amongst the vultures and dogs. Our women queue up at the water taps by four a.m. We shell out five rupees a bucket to whichever hoodlum's taken over the taps.

' "I've been in Bhayankar now, me-laard, for twenty-two years, in which time the Welfare State's done nothing for me for free—which is as it should be. I'm not a freeloader, and I'm not complaining. I've paid in bribes for my ration card, my photo pass and my electricity metre. I've been bribed in return for my vote—but that's all fine, it's the proper procedure. Self-interest is the only commandment—naturally—of the Welfare State, the rest is waffle."

'Bhootnath Gaitonde, sir, held forth in court for weeks. He reasoned that if the Welfare State was at all humane, it wouldn't dishouse him just before the monsoons, which, as me-laard well knew, could be awesome in this region. Me-laard agreed completely and at the end of a forty-four-page judgement, ordered the Municipal Corporation to not even dream of going near Gaitonde's shack till the winter.'

'Oh you bewitching storyteller, may I cuddle up in your lap like a rapt grandchild, tickle your navel and ask you what happened next?'

'No thank you sir. Instead, you could with profit cite the Gaitonde verdict in your appeal against your eviction notice. The cases are very similar, the same city ward, seven-to-ten persons per room, versus a heartless Welfare State, the same season of the year, give or take a few months. On the coast, one really can't tell winter from the monsoon ... You should submit your application quickly, sir, to the Housing Secretary.'

'At once. Tomorrow, anyway. I shall draft it tonight

during Night Duty. Can you check it . . .?'

'With pleasure, sir, I'll be honoured. Who knows what the future has in store for us? Bhootnath Gaitonde, for example, sir, abandoned Bhayankar long before that winter. He became an active member of the New Vision Democratic Party at the Centre, so enthused was he by his performance in court.'

Night Duty was in the Secretariat Control Room. Up and down the sixteen floors, out of the Annexe and into the East Wing, withdrawn from the New Extension and eased into the Old Basement, over the years, the Secretariat Control Room had changed venues in the manner of a file being tossed about from Home Affairs to Labour to Finance to Employment to Personnel to Home Affairs. When Bhanwar Virbhim had been Chief Minister the first time, the idea of a Control Room in the Secretariat had been suggested by his Principal Secretary to 'convince the electorate, sir, that yours is a government committed to delivering the goods.'

The Secretariat Control Room was supposed to monitor and sift the information relayed to it by the thousands of Police-, Earthquake-, Flash Flood-, Cyclone-, Typhoon-, Fire-, Landslide-, Other Acts Of God-, Communal Riot-, Festival Mishap-, Special- and General- Control Rooms located all over the region. To show that the Bhanwar Virbhim government was serious about the Secretariat Control Room, they set up the first one on the sixteenth floor itself, within the Chief Minister's Secretariat, just a few doors away, in fact, from his suite of rooms. After three months, however— 'It's a security risk,' opined the police on the basis of the evidence that began to be discovered there in the mornings: an empty bottle of Old Monk Rum, a couple of used condoms, a page or two of adult literature. It was then decided to shift the Room to the Ladies' Lunch Room on the third floor; the Ladies' Lunch Room sank into the basement to dislodge the

Court Receiver of Smuggled Goods, who trudged up to the eighth floor to evict the Controller of Cattle of the Dairy Development Commissionerate, who in turn drifted onto the ninth floor of the Annexe to unhouse the Joint Chairman of the Committee for the Welfare of Nomadic Tribes . . . and so on. At any point of time, at least one Department in the Secretariat is transferring one of its offices from one room to another; since movement is action, a permanent housing problem is itself proof that the government works.

The thousands of Control Rooms in the region had been instructed to inform the Secretariat Control Room of anything important that happened in their areas. But what was unimportant? Naturally, nobody could tell. Thus it was that the two phones in the Secretariat Control Room were kept permanently off the hook. The Night Duty staff could therefore better concentrate on the telly. The staff comprised one Deputy Secretary, one Desk Officer, one clerk, one peon, one bearer and four cops. For all of them, the bearer provided dinner (pooris and dal) and snacks (pooris and tea).

Being English-speaking, the seniormost present and a man of the world, Agastya strode up to the TV and switched to BBC. The Look that the others gave him turned his insides to jelly. From eight to eight, he too then watched, in fits and starts, four-and-a-half benumbing, cacophonic, brutal, gormless Hindi films—and a sluggish rat that he'd spotted beneath one of the almirahs and that was plainly invisible to the other TV-watchers.

In the wee hours, when he was in a catatonic trance on the settee, skull twitching to the thwacks, thuds and shrieks from the TV, God pointed out to him that his housing problem'd been solved, hadn't it; all that he had to do was to smuggle in, in his file boxes, his clothes, his tape recorder, cassettes, his books.

By Friday evening, he'd begun to feel at home in his boarded-up section of veranda. Being slow and secretive, he told nobody—not even his PA or his peon—that he'd moved into his office room. He knew that nobody cared where he stayed as long as he didn't formally inform them or ask for permission. 'Say No till Kingdom Come, then deflect to Finance' was a guiding principle for Personnel.

He was shocked to discover that the Secretariat had neither showers nor bathrooms. He had to bathe in the loo with a bucket and plastic mug. In the mornings, therefore, after his traumatic Canadian 5BX workout, he began to dress appropriately for his journey down the corridor, in once-white sleeveless vest and blue-and-green striped, loose drawers. Swinging his red bucket in one hand, whistling and humming sixties' Hindi film tunes, he indeed felt like his assumed role—a carefree carpenter or plumber who'd been up all night toiling away somewhere in the Secretariat and was now going to refresh himself after a job well done.

He breakfasted, lunched and dined at Krishna Lunch Home, a dreadfully crowded two-storey eatery on the fringe of Bhayaṇkar. Fanatical account-keeper that he was, he'd calculated that on his disgraceful salary, in that frightfully costly city, he couldn't spend more than a hundred rupees a day on food. With its thirty-rupee thalis, Krishna Lunch Home suited his budget. So did its atmosphere him. Women, for example, both young and of a certain age, dined singly there without attracting even a second glance, leave alone being harassed by leers, salacious suggestions, obscene gestures or sudden lunges. The waiters too were uniformly pleasant, usually adolescent, with ready smiles. Their shorts, though, tended to be tiny and tight, making them reveal many inches of thigh and strut more than walk.

Booze was swigged only upstairs at the Lunch Home. The ground floor hall, a forty-by-thirty crush of tables, customers, waiters and food, was for those madly pressed for time—a soup, two idlis, an uthapam, some halwa, a coffee and away. The first floor was smaller, windowless, always tubelit and cosier despite the cold white light, quieter, with a quarter bottle of gin or rum on almost every decolam top. Single customers generally shared a table with lone strangers. Conversation was not obligatory, but sharing the pickled onions, chillies and mango was. One could strike up a romance if one wanted to fall in love with, say, a bald fat man with bulldog jowls and yellow teeth who looked as though he planned to drink himself to death, alone.

Or one could hang about a bit to see whether one got a seat opposite a human being. Thus it was that two evenings in a row, Agastya sat across from a very beautiful, thirtyish woman with open, shoulder-blade-long jet-black hair. He hadn't known that hair dye could be that black. Throughout both evenings, she pecked at veg chowmein, soaked up rum 'n Pepsi and wept silently. While fashioning her face, God had contemplated shaping a stunning pink pig; seconds before the finishing touches, however, He'd plainly been called away. Ah well. In her jade-green salwaar kameez, she looked like a radiant emcee from an outlandish Zee TV set; she spoke Hinglish too in a charming Zee TV-Puppie way. Agastya'd never piled on in his life before to anyone in Hinglish. It was rather a challenge, like trying to babysit an unfamiliar infant of another race.

Never before either had he sat in front of anybody who'd snivelled in this manner two evenings running. And he hated food being wasted, particularly in a developing country. On Thursday, therefore, while waiting for his order, he reached over and began helping himself to her chowmein. Quite tasty. Her smallish eyes focused and flickered a bit. Almost mechanically, she pushed the pickled onions across to him.

'No thanks, we're to utter sweet breath tonight.' He waved to Thaïs and, when he strutted over, asked him for cigarettes, Wills Filter Navy Cut.

He felt stuffed by the time he'd finished with her chowmein and his own chholey-bhaturey, keema dosa and alu-pooris arrived. 'Developing country,' he explained to her as he attacked the keema dosa. She smoked a cigarette. 'As in a marathon, one must pace oneself in life, with people, with food,' he clarified to her as he pitched into the alu-pooris. 'Anything is possible at the right speed.'

She rose unsteadily from the table. He beamed enquiringly at her. 'Looking at you, I want to vomit,' she mumbled in Hinglish and lurched off towards the stairs. As her first words, they didn't augur well for their romance.

He was torn between her and his chholey-baturey, between sex and food, love of woman and love of country. Hating her for winning, for making him waste both money and nurture, he followed her.

The world's largest slum had its virtues. One could, for example, puke anywhere and you couldn't tell. When he emerged from Krishna, a voided Kamya had her arms wrapped around one of those wizened mongrel trees that abound in the city, that survive against awesome odds, that offer neither shade nor flowers or beauty, the trunks of which are too flinty for the nails of advertisers' boards, dour, self-centred, enduring without growing.

'Are you all right?' he asked in Hinglish—'*Aap all right hain?*' While waiting for her to unwrap herself, he realized that he liked the rhythms of Hinglish. It was a genuinely national language, as truly mirroring the minds of the people as Benglish, Tamilish, Maralish, Punjlish and Kannalish. He told himself that when he returned to his boarded-up veranda, he should note in his diary the following items as food for thought: i) Why can't Hinglish be the Official Language of the Welfare State? and ii) Why don't you translate into Hinglish or Benglish some of your favourite English poems? *Jhe Alphred Pruphrock-er Laabh Song?* And *Shalott Ki Lady?*

'I stay right here.' He pointed vaguely in the direction of the Secretariat. '*Main right here stay*—'

'*Main English follow karti hoon, thank you.*' She was tall. '*Hmmm, so aap right here stay karte hain.*' Her eyes had widened and brightened with interest.

At the gate of the Secretariat, he advised her. 'If the guard asks, just say, Night Duty. If he acts tough and argues that women are exempt, scoff and enlighten him, New Policy, Women's Quota.'

She liked the room. She drifted about in it, touched the kettle and his skipping rope on the wall, gazed out of the window at the night lights and asked how come. Feeling safe with her, he explained how he'd solved his housing problem. She was more impressed than amused. '*Ek dum top-class idea, Tiger,*' she lolled on his lumpy sofa, now covered with a brightly-patterned counterpane, '*Ek dum top-* . . .' Her head slumped to one side as she fell asleep.

I should unhook her bra as a *beau geste*. Then, feeling old, lonely, morose, washed out, tired of his own jokes, he too bummed around the room, brewed himself some tea, flopped down behind his desk, now and then watched her breast rise and fall in sleep, and finally bedded down on the jute matting between his computer and his kitchenette. I should get married now to any one of those decent, horny Bengali dullards from Calcutta that Manik Kaka's been dying to line up for me for the last eight years. Enough of this hepness of being single. After a while, one just felt sick of books and music and cinema and being boss of one's time; one wished instead for human company and the warmth of another body in bed, for everyday domestic clutter and social completeness, for the outward tokens of an ordered life—a sofa set in the drawing room, a washing machine, a magnetic remembrancer on the fridge.

A little after six, he woke abruptly to find himself alone in the room. He waited for a minute or two. Then he crawled over to the sofa and nodded off again in the faint aroma of perfume.

The preceding Thursday. Daya's flat had been a fifteen-minute walk away from the Secretariat. Upmarket, downtown, one of the backlanes behind the new steel-and-glass Stock Exchange. The backlanes were quieter, greener, pseudo-colonial and comprised some of the world's costliest real estate. One square foot of flat cost eighteen thousand rupees, i.e., more than twice Agastya's monthly salary. It could cost more if, from it, one could glimpse a corresponding square foot of the sea. 'Not worth it, honey,' he cautioned himself as he crossed the street to avoid a knoll of garbage that stank—whew! like a government permission—and to which had been drawn a zoo of cattle, pigs, curs, cats, crows and rats.

Daya was on the third floor and her doorbell a sexy chime. She took some time to answer it. He heard her trill to somebody, presumably the dope-provider, 'You're barking up the wrong tree,' before she opened the door. She looked like Ageing Raw Sex Incarnate. No spectacles. She'd touched up both eyes and hair. She wore an itsy-bitsy, teeny-weeny yellow polka-dot—a luxurious peacock-blue-and-amber salwaar kameez. She beamed at him and offered him her cheek (facial) for a peck. He was a bit taken aback at how happy he was to see her.

'I'm so glad that you don't have your blue jeans on, otherwise I'd've had to smother the entire flat in dust sheets . . . I didn't notice how you'd fouled up my salwaar till I came home that evening . . . for a while, I couldn't even figure out what'd happened . . . and then I imagined that you'd done it on purpose, for some perverted reason . . . was it your way of making a pass? . . . I even fancied that you might've been a sort of walking ad for a, you know, detergent or something . . . that'd've been clever . . . or an anti-depressant . . . Don't spread the blues . . .'

A spacious, lamplit living room, French windows at the far end, a veranda beyond. Arty, uncomfortable furniture, bric-à-brac, tribal statuary, richly-coloured rugs on the floor that Agastya kept tripping over and apologising for; white bookshelves with sleek tomes on Modernism, Reductionism,

Margaret Mead, The Death of Tragedy, Russians in Exile, Rilke; a colour TV before a settee, on, on the settee a tall, darkish, handsome, hairy, bespectacled, generally groovy man with long, wavy salt-and-pepper hair who rose with a commanding smile to shake his hand.

'Rajani Suroor.'

'How do you do.'

The telecast was a recording of the inauguration of the Festival of Russia. Gymnastics, the human pyramid business. The camera closed in on one of the saps in the bottom row. It shouldn't have, the bugger was *dying*, but in the cause of better relations between the two countries.

'So you're a dope-smoking civil servant. Do you bring to your work a new perspective?' Groovy Suroor apparently knew a lot about the government. From his kurta pocket, he pulled out a metal cigarette case and a silvery Yin-Yang box and while rolling a joint, dropped names in a well-bred way. Agastya decided to 'sir' him while sharing the smoke, to try and discompose him. The camera had abandoned the Russians and zeroed in on the V$^{\infty}$IPs in the front rows, beanbags all in starched, billowy white, a white Gandhi topi atop each like a blob of icing crowning a cake, snugly shapeless in white armchairs and sofas. 'Ah, our dear, dear Minister-to-be, the Jewel of the Deccan Mafia,' murmured Groovy as the TV showed bald, bespectacled, obese Member of Parliament Bhanwar Virbhim of the heavy-lidded eyes licking the toenails of Jayati Aflatoon, the wife of a cousin of the Prime Minister.

'That isn't fair, Rajani,' objected Daya, handing Agastya a glass of watermelon juice. 'If you can't stand even the possibility of his appointment, you should stop sucking up to authority. My favourite commandment from the *Reader's Digest* goes: If you don't like what you do for a living, quit. If you can't quit, shut up.'

Then folk dancing, by what Agastya presumed were

Taras Bulba and Co. Just watching them tired one out, their never-ending extreme form of the Canadian 5BX, and grinning all the while too, or were those rictuses of agony? Next, Groovy Suroor, after a long drag on the joint: 'For you, Daya, everything's always been either black or white. In my world, the pros outweigh the cons, but that doesn't mean that the cons don't exist.' He beamed avuncularly at Agastya. 'Does this not-so-young man have any opinions on the service of the Welfare State?'

'Yes. I feel weird. I ask myself all the time: How do you survive on your ridiculous salary? And *why* do you survive on your ridiculous salary? At the same time, I feel grossly overpaid for the work that I do. Not the quantity, which on certain days can be alarming, but the quality. In my eight years of service, I haven't come across a single case in which everybody concerned didn't try to milk dry the boobs of the Welfare State.' The dope was first-rate. 'But I suppose that's what the boobs are there for.

'In my earlier office, on the ground floor of the Commissionerate, alongside the stairs, stood a kiosk that we'd leased out about a decade ago, for a rupee a month, to a privileged underprivileged. He was Backward Caste, Depressed Class, Physically Handicapped—his right leg petered out at the knee—Mentally Zonked—his file had a photocopy of an illegible four-line note from some Assistant to the Head of the Department of Psychiatry of the Trimurti Aflatoon Welfare State Hospital—and Utterly Black and Angry. The clerk who used to deal with Handicap's file would say that the Hospital note merely certified that he, Handicap, periodically needed to have his head examined.

'The kiosk wasn't that small—about eight-by-eight—and he'd set up a photocopying machine in it. A sound business prospect because the Commissionerate shares its compound with the Sessions Court, the Registrar of Births and Deaths and the Deputy Tribal Commissioner. Handicap's photocopying machine, of course, had been funded by three separate Welfare brainwaves: i) The Rural Poor Self-Employment Generation Scheme, ii) The Physically Handicapped Economic Self-Sufficiency Project, and iii) The Depressed Classes Financial Independence Plan. The three loans had to be repaid over twenty years—it came to a little over four hundred rupees a month.

'A lot, isn't it? Handicap certainly thought so—particularly after he stopped feeling grateful. To get hold of the loans in the first place, he'd forked out nearly five thousand rupees in bribes—under The Welfare State Public Servant Economic Regeneration Grant, or so he called it. Four years ago, when a new government took over, Handicap petitioned anew the Rehabilitation Minister. Under the Minister's Discretionary Write-Off Quota for Semi-rural Economic Incentives Programme, Honourable exempted Handicap from the loans—after accepting a contribution of five thousand rupees, of course, to his wife's Non-Governmental Organization for the Creation of Viable Employment Alternatives for Backward Caste Semi-rural Women.

'Within days of my joining the office, Handicap applied anew for permission to instal in the kiosk a public phone with both National and International Dialling Facilities. He'd been beseeching us for a couple of years and we'd ping-ponged his request about—call for the comments of Telecom, the No Objection of the Municipal Corporation, ascertain the views of the Parent Department, that sort of thing. I don't think that any of the clerks was specifically angling for a bribe; it was just that nobody knew how to deal with his application because it had no precedent.

'I did a terrible thing. I decided the case. In his favour, but that was secondary. You must know how weird, how spooky it feels to actually—to use officialese—take a decision in any government matter. Boy. You see, I'd begun swimming by then at the Municipal pool and that very morning, I distinctly remember, I'd finally figured out the leg movement of the breast stroke. Oh what a feeling. Life therefore was a long song—a bit like Julie Andrews screaming and haring around amongst green hills in *The Sound of Music*—by the time I showed up at my desk. I took decisions in several files that day. It was horrible.

'Handicap sub-let the kiosk for two thousand rupees a month to a guy with no legs. Legless wangled the phone through some Scheme or the other. Sometime in the middle of last month, Handicap slipped in a proposal for starting up a Cooperative Society For The Physically Handicapped beneath the stairs; the kiosk will certainly have to be enlarged.'

'May I ask what percentage of our civil service is corrupt? I mean, I know that my ex-husband was—is. But whether *every* public official is dishonest?' Daya spoke loudly from the kitchen. 'Or am I being too naïve?'

Swan Lake on the telly. The ballet frock, decided Agastya, was the kinkiest, the horniest dress that he'd ever seen. *Swan Lake* would have been even better had the chicks not worn any panties—they could've had their frilly frocks start at the nipples and extend fanlike till the navel; from the navel till the knees could've stretched a fecund expanse of pussy, fat, lush, many-coloured. However on earth could Tchaikovsky and Bhanwar Virbhim connect? Fecund pussy was much more Bhanwar's scene, and yet there he was, furrowed head propped up on forearm, an attentive and discerning member of audience. Unless he too was seeing pussy instead of pantie. 'I'm dishonest, but not corrupt. I use my office phone to make personal calls—that's, strictly speaking, being dishonest, but I haven't yet had my palm greased. I have received a box of mithai at Diwali and a bottle of Scotch at Christmas, though.

'I did try once to milk a lakh or two of rupees out of the Welfare State:—' Agastya here turned to an intelligently-smiling Suroor—'it was out of that dairy farm, the Department of Culture and Heritage. It had two mindblowing Twelfth Plan Schemes of doling out lakhs of rupees to any bearded pseud documentary film-maker to shoot Our Endangered Tribal Heritage and The Jewels of the North-East. A friend of mine and I'd mapped everything out—we'd lug a Handycam down to the dhabas by the river, behind the Tibetan Monastery on Mall Road in the University area, and film ourselves smoking dope with the pushers there. But at the last minute, our middle-class pusillanimity and squeamishness spiked our plans.

'Many moons ago, when I was a babe in these woods, I'd imagined that People Like Us—i.e., those who've grown up on Richmal Crompton and the Rolling Stones, and who speak English more often than any other Indian language—we just aren't corrupt, we can't be, constitutionally. Fortunately, these silly notions evaporated pretty quickly in these woods—as soon as one grew up, really. How worthless one's upbringing's been when it's come to facing one's own country! Ah well.'

Daya'd joined them by then; she looked a little alarmed at these confessions but clearly felt that they could still serve as a topic for drawing-room conversation. 'Why then did you become a civil servant in the first place?'

'Because within the civil service, one is likelier to know somebody who knows somebody who knows somebody who knows a cop. Or so I believed eight years ago. Now that I'm wiser, I know that the government can fuck you up bad even if you're part of it—unless you suck, suck, suck. The civil servant can fellate with the best of them. I say, sir, can we roll another joint?'

'But why don't you quit, then?' Daya was correctly puzzled.

'But I like it here! And quit and go where? The more years one spends in the civil service, the more competent one becomes to remain in it.'

'Don't be silly. I'm sure you could find a job more to your taste. Cynicism is a waste of a life. Why, I could give you a job if you wanted.'

He glanced at her. She laughed and answered, 'Because I like you, Peter Pan.'

Just at that moment, however, on the TV screen a close-up of Suroor himself, looking deadly in a silk kurta, head intelligently bent to peep at the boobs of a gorgeously-painted middle-aged woman who was seemingly tonguing his ear. 'Ooooh . . . who's that?' trilled Daya in theatrical envy.

'Why, that's me . . . oh, the woman . . . don't you recognize her? . . . Rani Chandra, the capital's new Culture Czarina . . . they change every three months . . . she too shed her caste-revealing surname somewhere on the way up the ladder . . . but she'll learn, sooner or later, that the single factor that works in every corner of this country is caste . . . a Brahmin vibes best with a Brahmin, a Thakur lends a hand most often to a Thakur . . . her surname must've been Saxena or Katoch—something simply not arty enough . . . at that point, she was breathing into my ear that coitus these days is totally out of fashion because nobody has the time . . . at best a couple of minutes off for a quick grope and feel . . . the only way in which she unwinds is in her Toyota Lexus, listening on her Walkman to a tape of a male voice thinking aloud about what he longs to do to her body . . . very hot stuff, no holds barred . . . the tapes are a by-product of her husband's electronics mega-company . . . she gifts the tapes to her closest friends . . . they're rather well-composed, actually . . . very little music . . . there are four sets of tapes . . . Man-to-Man, Woman-to-Woman, Man-to-Woman, Woman-to-Man . . . her brainchild, apparently . . . I gather that she presented a box set of CDs to Kinshuk Aflatoon at Diwali and that he and

Jayati listen to nothing else . . . in the capital, amongst the Gur Baoli Farmhouse jetsetting crowd, Rani Chandra Cassette parties are nowadays all the rage . . . RCC get-togethers, they're called . . . she plans to diversify soon into a separate range for paedophiles . . . the sky's the limit for those blessed with enterprise . . .' Now that he'd seen himself, he rose and switched off the TV just when, after surveying the audience, its camera returned to *Swan Lake*.

He stretched, yawned and smiled at Agastya. 'Why *aren't* you venal? How *do* you survive on your ridiculous salary without being dishonest? . . . Some six months ago, they'd been planning a Roving Festival Of Tribal Arts for South-East Asia. A Cultural Delegation from Japan, Malaysia and Singapore'd visited us and I'd escorted them when they'd called on the Heritage Secretary, Harihara Kapila—he's just returned here, hasn't he, to Regional Personnel? The delegation was headed by a TV mogul from Singapore. We'd sent them off to Jalba, Agrampada and Sindhyachal and they'd predictably returned with heatstrokes and the shits.

'However, they still had questions to ask—about the Heritage budget and the Archaeological Survey and transport bottlenecks and Buddhist monuments and overseas funding and local initiative and the Preservation Trust. Then, after a lull and out of the blue, "Mr Secretary, may I enquire of you a personal question?"

'Kapila, whose wit's given the world some of the deadliest headaches that it's ever known, beamed and quipped, something like, "Oh, fire away," said he as he snapped away his cigarette and faced the firing squad, inscrutable to the last.

' "What, Mr Secretary, is your basic pay?"

' "I cannot invoke the Official Disgraceful Secrets Act against our honoured guests . . . Eight thousand."

' "Dollars US?"

'Kapila chortled, not the sweetest of sounds. "No . . . rupees, my dear sir."

'A gasp from a lady member of the delegation; then, after a pause, "How is that possible, Mr Secretary? After over thirty distinguished years spent in the top ranks of the civil service of the world's largest Welfare State, how can it be that you earn merely about sixty dollars US per week? Sir, please do not misunderstand our questions. We're neither civil servants nor diplomats and yours is a bewildering country in more ways than one. One cannot argue that you are a poor nation because from this magazine—" the TV mogul drew out from his camera bag a fat, slick *The State Today*—"I learn two facts germane to this issue, i) that in the last five years, an enterprising stockbroker of Navi Chipra has filched from the system more than three thousand crore rupees, which is almost one billion dollars US, and in those five years, the system didn't wince even once, and ii) that within the last two years alone, eleven billion dollars have been laundered away from here to the US alone, and the system hasn't hobbled even a step—how can the country therefore be poor? You also enjoy one of the severest tax structures in the world, so one cannot plead that you are a rich country with a poor government."

' "Oh no, I'd instead assert that we're a rich country, a rich government and a poor civil service . . . We've now touched upon a subject as old as Plato, namely, How can you entice the best brains of a country to take on the onerous task of administering that country disinterestedly and well? Answer: By getting them, the administrators, to tell themselves and one another, all the time, that they *are* the best brains, the cat's whiskers, the absolute cream of the scum mainly because they perform their onerous task so disinterestedly and well. And who gets them to swallow their own gobbledygook? God, without a doubt. God is a first-rate bureaucrat, one of the best. In all matters, He sees the truth, but is yet to take a decision. We have high regard for Him. In almost all the homes of civil servants, you'll find a puja room devoted exclusively to Him . . . Doesn't it amaze you to learn that over three hundred thousand hopefuls sit for the Public Service Examination every year, of which just about a hundred are selected for the top slots? Ergo, there must be something in it! Job satisfaction is my salary! We get by on plain living and low thinking."

'Kapila stopped without warning, as was his wont, but continued to beam at them. The delegation clearly would have preferred him to go on discoursing instead. His beam was winning when the TV mogul tried for the last time, "A rich country, a rich government, at least one fabulously rich Navi Chipra stockbroker, and a poor civil service: who then, Mr Secretary, manages all that money?"

' "Some of it goes down the drain, of course—we being a Welfare State. Some of it goes—with the blessings of the Almighty—to a good many bank accounts located in several tax havens. The balance we leave to the guidance of God."

'The delegation's Escort Officer from External Affairs was a bespectacled blob of oil, a disciplined envoy-in-the-making. I could read on his face an increasing concern for the sanity of the Heritage Secretary—to whom nothing happened, of course, for shooting his mouth off, or for losing his marbles, in front of a foreign delegation. Some sub-caste network shielded him, I gathered.

'What do *you* think, my dear Agastya, of the hordes of bureaucrats who go off their rocker in the course, and because, of their official duties, and who consequently indulge in diverse kinds of conduct unbecoming of a civil servant? Is nobody, as you mandarins say, seized of the problem? The system—the work they do, doubtless—is to blame; the strain, the tensions, together with the futility, the absence of direction, the triplespeak, the bottomless greed of our middle classes, certainly produce a lethal blend—but my point is, it is the civil servant's preposterous salary that is at the heart of it! My God—if you're honest, on your savings you can't take your family of four out to dinner more than once a decade and you can't fly them, say, Navi Chipra—the capital—Navi Chipra, on a holiday more than once in your lifetime, and you definitely can't do both, if you're honest.'

Agastya wished to contribute his views. 'I too have examples of plain living and low thinking. The plain liver is my Assistant Director friend who turned vegetarian because he couldn't afford meat. The low thinker is my cop acquaintance, a Station House Officer who was dementedly corrupt because he contended that he had four daughters to marry off with dowries of over five lakhs each. Speaking of which, why doesn't the Welfare State legalize dowries for the civil servants of its Steel Frame? It could then stop paying them salaries altogether.'

'Are you married?'

'No, not yet.'

'Why not? You aren't that young. Are you gay?'

'No, not yet. But tomorrow is another day.'

'You should marry early. As one grows older, one becomes increasingly reluctant to share one's toilet with someone else. What's kept you from marrying so far? Haven't you yet found the dowry of your dreams?'

'That's it, exactly. My expectations're always being thrown haywire by inflation and the new economic policy. Eight years ago, I'd more or less settled on marrying a Kelvinator fridge, a Videocon colour TV with remote and a Maruti 800 Deluxe car, red, with a.c. and stereo. How naïve I was! A noble savage, a rough diamond. Now, of course—I'm happy to say—that sort of simple-mindedness is a thing of the past. But today's decisions suffuse me instead with a modern disquiet. A Peugeot diesel 309 or a Mitsubishi Lancer? The Samsung TV or the Whirlpool Washing Machine? The BPL three-door fridge? A mobile phone? These tides that've to be taken at the flood—they're upon me, I feel it in my bones. I'll certainly invite you to the wedding.'

Smiling intelligently, Suroor departed soon after for dinner with his dear friend the Governor. He sweetly left behind for Agastya his Yin-Yang dope box. 'You look as though you need it, friend.'

Despite the Hindi Top Ten sort of music that drifted in through the French windows, the apartment, all at once after Suroor's departure, began to feel cosy and restful. His nervous energy disturbed others; it clamoured all the time to be the centre of attention. Agastya followed Daya into the kitchen for a refill of watermelon juice. She was busy with the ice bucket when he held her by her shoulders and lightly kissed the nape of her neck. She paused to smile at him before returning to the drawing room with their drinks. He felt a bit silly.

Gingerly, he sat down beside her on the sofa and grinned at her with stagey bashfulness. 'I need to improve my style.'

An exhausting night. No dinner till three in the morning. After the watermelon juice, Daya had without warning bobbed up and vanished into her bedroom. A few minutes later, through the closed door, Agastya had heard some terrible Shirley Bassey kind of music. Then the door had opened and she'd called him. He'd all at once felt nervous, as before a job interview. With reason, boy, he'd realized at the doorway. For the room was dark and Daya naked, legs crossed, in a rocking chair by the window. Serves you right, fucker, for trying to be so cool.

'Please shut the door, Agastya and take off all your clothes . . . Could you leave your shoes outside, please? . . . Thanks . . . you could put away your jeans etc in that almirah on your right . . . there are free hangers in it . . . hmmm . . .

could you please wash yourself, Agastya, as a courtesy to me? . . . thanks . . . the light switch—no, up . . . up and left . . . no, you can leave the door open . . . ahh, come, come . . . now lie down . . . the sheets are cool, clean and blue . . .'

He continued to feel nervous and depressed as he adjusted the pillow beneath his neck. You deserve this, you Dildo King, he told himself again as he watched her toss her hair off her shoulders and straddle his stomach. He'd generally lived his life according to two dictums: Finish what you start, and Don't start what you can't finish. He couldn't quit his job, for instance, because of his dictums, just as because of them he now had to swallow whatever this middle-aged bomb was going to dish out. He was nervous because he would have preferred to be in control. Couldn't she've asked him first whether he'd relish being suffocated by her pussy? Wasn't he too a human being, with feelings? She wriggled about a bit till her vagina was split wide and tight against his solar plexus. She then began to ride back and forth, slowly at first, then with gathering momentum, lazily but irrevocably sliding up over his chest towards his face. With her hands, she fondled her breasts, teased her armpits, kneaded her stomach, played with her hair, adjusted the sound from the stereo by the bed. Rhythmically, she groaned and gasped, deep but subdued, and licked her upper arms, her breasts. By the time that she'd crossed Agastya's nipples, his spunk was flying all over the room like Casper the friendly ghost. You don't even know the surname, Arsehole, of this juggernaut who's pussy-lathering your neck. Now that he'd spent himself, he would have liked to relax a bit, smoke a cigarette or something, but *she'd* just finished warming up. He made a move to rise but quick like a cat, she slid up and clamped her pussy down on his face. She then began to bloody gallop. Soft whoops of near-hysterical rapture, thinnish Casper in half an hour, the creaking bed marking time, quickening rhythm, his jaws unhinged, till at last from her a succession of deep, slow, sated moans, wrenched out, as it were, from the bowels of the earth. From where she'd last squatted, Daya, now drained through and through, abruptly flopped back and lay down on her lover, writhed about a bit to make herself comfortable, her hair a ticklish, silken tangle about his loins, crooned a few bars along with the Shirley Bassey type and miraculously fell asleep. He palmed her breasts, idly wondered whether she'd ever get up and allow him to go for a piss and then dropped off too.

He awoke at two. He was alone in bed and the stereo was mercifully off. A blue night light above the bathroom door. Daya, still naked, sat crosslegged on a rug on the floor, arms outstretched, back of wrists poised on her knees, her index fingers forming circles with her thumbs, the other fingers pointing down at the floor; she was meditating. He sleepily watched her till he nodded off again. At three, hunger and a bursting bladder dredged him up out of sleep. She hadn't stirred an inch from the floor. What about damn mosquitoes? he wondered. Her fridge stocked only grim health food. Zonked, not believing what he was doing, he chomped on a carrot and some sprouted thing in a bowl, and slurped down a jug of buttermilk.

In the morning, radiant, renewed, she explained to him that for the last decade or so, she'd meditated in different yogic postures instead of sleeping. 'Are you at all familiar with Yoga?'

Agastya, who felt as though every pore in his skin had been buggered non-stop for a year by some bleak, unforgiving Jehovah type of person, said, no, not beyond the occasional magazine article.

'Oh dear . . . The loss of innocence, I believe, more than anything else is the loss of sleep. One can't regain innocence, of course, but one can *accept* its loss. I don't try to empty my mind—that's virtually impossible—but I relax, lie down or sit, stock-still—and allow whatever it is to enter my head. A free for all! Anxieties, fantasies, dreams, longings, plans, images of the day—the doors remain wide open for all, all the clutter. Sooner or later, however—after half an hour, perhaps—the clutter decants, settles down. I then begin to see what is of worth, to separate the salt from the litter of my life. Over the years, I've noticed that whenever I've succeeded in focusing on the essential, in meditating on the truly important, I've achieved it. Are you with me?'

'What about mosquitoes? The ringing of the telephone? . . . And don't you at least eat eggs? There are none in the fridge.'

He in part solved his housing problem by spending three to four nights a week at Daya's. Strange nocturnal assignations, redeeming, releasing, with the blurred, magical quality of a dream, as though he wore spectacles by day and routinely left them behind in the Secretariat for the night. They never met by day—for lunch or for a film, somehow never. They fell into a pattern—crazy, gruelling sex that began at the door and lasted till Daya'd finished with him; then dinner, not enough conversation, followed by a numbing sleep for him in bed, alone. Early in the morning, he'd awake exhausted, with cold aching joints.

His constant, silent wide-eyed bewilderment at her taste in music and food led her to relent a bit. The Shirley Bassey types gave way to Gordon Lightfoot and Warren Zevon, whom he unwound with after Casper had flown round for a while. Daya postponed dinner till after midnight because he was with her only as long as he didn't sense any food; once he began to stuff himself, the single other thing that he could think of was sleep. Indeed, on certain evenings, the two were separated only by one stupendous burp. Dinner started to vary—dates, almonds, grapes, honey—but only up to a point; in Daya's kitchen were forbidden frying, baking, stewing, roasting, even liquidizing.

'But what about palak paneer and masala dosa—don't you miss them?'

Their attitudes to their affair differed. In her own way, she wanted a romance—a lover, some music and conversation—whereas he simply wished to get rid of his day. Yet they were happy together—and the surroundings, the atmosphere of the flat, encouraged happiness. Through the open French windows of the bedroom, for example, through half the night, they could hear the occupants of the other flats in the building converse with one another from their verandas about their daily lives. One female even played Hindi film songs on her recorder for the others on request. Now and then, she hollered for Daya to pop out to her veranda to yell back her choice of song; Daya'd even obliged a couple of times, leaving the bed, pulling on a robe, cursing under her breath, shoving her head past the curtains and politely, embarrassedly, asking for the song *Ek Do Teen* from the film *Tezaab* because Agastya liked it.

'How can you not drink tea in the mornings, Daya? I'm zapped.' So she began to stock tea, Lipton's Green Label. 'How can anyone not read a newspaper in the mornings? I mean, Daya, where did you grow up?'

'Bombay.'

'I ought to have guessed.'

She refused to subscribe to any newspaper for him. 'You don't love me,' he concluded bitterly. She maintained that she'd managed very well without newspapers for forty years. She worked in—headed, in fact—a small, arty and successful ad agency. He started to bring along with him *The State of the Times* and the crossword from *The Statesman* and pore over both over tea the morning after. He was more enthusiastic than successful with the crossword. He devoted most of his attention to an old addiction of his, the Wanted ads.

'There's a vacancy for a Junior Technician (Electrical) in the Regional Engineering College at Roorkie. I say, Daya, should I apply? . . . And the other interesting one today is:

"Wanted two Hair Stylists for a Star Hotel at Cochin. Apply with references Box 345 etc." Does that mean prostitutes or not? I'd like to write in.'

His tea lasted till Daya was ready to leave for work. Her chauffeur-driven air-conditioned Cielo dropped him off at the Secretariat. Agastya looked rather scruffy in comparison to the chauffeur. 'If I join your ad agency, what'll I do, precisely?'

'Oh, you could be Senior Vice-President, Client Servicing . . . ha ha . . . if you're serious about accepting the offer, then give me a couple of days to mull it over.'

It seemed that everyone in Softsell, Daya's ad agency, was a Senior Vice-President. Agastya was invited to become one too and handle the Public Affairs portfolio. He'd be given a three-bedroom apartment downtown, an air-conditioned car, a chauffeur, a salary of thiry-five thousand rupees per month, a bonus of about two hundred thousand rupees a year and a domestic servant. Further, the ad agency would pay his electricity, petrol, car and cooking gas bills.

He became so suspicious that he immediately knew that he wouldn't be joining them. He'd always travelled light—a grip, an overnight bag, a cassette recorder—ready to escape in a wink from one life to some other. With the years, however, flitting had become increasingly difficult. The baggage of age—self-doubt, caution, a contempt for impulsiveness and the drag of the allure of material goods—had slown him down. 'Now let me see . . . this sounds great . . . my resignation from the Civil Service will take some time . . . believe it or not, it'll have to be accepted by the President of the Welfare State . . . what fun . . . I'll draft a letter out tomorrow . . . positively by the end of the week . . .'

The very next morning, in his office, he'd actually begun composing a letter of resignation—namely, had written down *Dear Sir* and crossed out *Dear* when his PA informed him that Housing Deputy Secretary Menon wished to see him. Agastya rushed.

The Seychelles hadn't pleased Menon in the least. 'There was too much sun,' he complained, 'I had to wear a hat everywhere, even to the bloody loo.' Losing his pinkness would've been as catastrophic as—and tantamount to—losing his caste. He whined for a while to dissolve Agastya's envy, then slipped in a googly. 'Where're you staying now, by the way?'

'With friends. Why?'

'This is you, isn't it?' Menon heaved a thin file across to him. Its root was a thank-you letter addressed to The Sweet Officer Who Lives in the New Secretariat, Fourteenth Floor, from Ms Kamya Malhotra, Senior Vice-President (Public Affairs) of TV Tomorrow. The notes that preceded the letter marked its sluggish, tortuous journey within the Secretariat:

What's this? Sd/- Secretary (Administration General)

Please speak with previous papers. Sd/- Deputy Secretary (Administration)

Is this ours? Please forward with compliments to Home Affairs. Sd/-Under Secretary (Desk VIII)

'This is a Government Buildings matter. Pl fwrd cmplmnts to Public Works. Sd/- Deputy Secretary (Home Affairs)

Missent. Pl fwd to Information and Public Relations. Sd/- Deputy Secretary (Public Works IV, Watch and Ward, Additional Charge)

Redirect to Housing. Sd/- DS (I&PR)

Agastya tried to beam with calm intelligence at Menon. 'Let's say that I've done more than my share of Secretariat Control Room Night Duty.' From the letter, he jotted down Kamya's telephone numbers.

'You'd better move out of the Secretariat ... what if a terrorist blows the place apart or some clerk, warming up his lunch rotis on the electric heater in his room, sparks off a devastating fire? ... searching for scapegoats in the post-fuckup Clean-Up-the-System scenario, won't we just love unearthing you on the fourteenth floor! ... tell you what—cart your bags back to Raj Atithi Guest House, I'll order them to book you in as Deputy Secretary of a different Department. You'll then technically be a different person. If you can show them pieces of paper to prove that you're being transferred about every ten days, you should be able to hang out—or in—there for a year or so . . . find a good locksmith—there are about a thousand in Killi Galli in Bhayankar—and periodically change the lock on your door . . . and also get a stay order from some court . . . that should be foolproof . . . for the sake of form, however—to ensure that the file doesn't sort of lose its momentum—I'll have to issue you a Show Cause Notice Why the Welfare State Shouldn't Take Disciplinary Action Against You for Your Conduct Unbecoming of an Officer of the Civil Service and for Trespassing on Welfare State Premises After Duty Hours . . . but it'll be purely routine . . . write us back some bilge . . . and we'll close the file.'

Agastya returned to his room peeved at his own impotence and amused by how powerless even his resentment was. His letter of resignation would have to wait until he voided his spleen in a reply to the proposed Notice. Which, since it was intended to fuck somebody's happiness, arrived within the hour. He meanwhile phoned TV Tomorrow and left a message for Kamya in Hinglish with a female retard.

> *Reference your Show-Cause Notice No. Soandso dated Soandso, it is humbly requested that the undersigned cannot be accused of indulging in Conduct Unbecoming of an Officer because it is respectfully submitted that the undersigned is* not *an Officer. Had he been an Officer, he would have been treated like one and provided accommodation worthy of an Officer. May kindly see please.*

A non-Daya evening, Krishna Lunch Home as usual at seven, he ordered the thali of the day and watched the off-duty female prostitutes drinking up and gobbling down at the other tables and the on-duty male prostitute waiters strutting about, displaying their wares. Feeling safe, he smoked some of Rajani Suroor's dope and desultorily struggled with *The Statesman* crossword till Kamya breezed in, dazzling like a searchlight, grinning from ear to ear, at ten-thirty. Her teeth scintillated like large pearls, a bit like being gagged by a necklace.

'Hello dear, sorry *main late hoon* . . . *shooting thi* . . . how are you? . . . *aap ne my letter receive kiya?* . . . *baap re!*' Agastya'd risen to his feet and kissed the necklace.

She couldn't, however, accompany him back to the Secretariat. She laughed embarrassedly at the notion, as at a disagreeable memory of adolescent foolishness. She had a carload of soul mates waiting downstairs, for one thing . . . she wouldn't've turned up at all because the retard hadn't given her Agastya's message till about an hour ago . . . the retard couldn't really be blamed for the mix-up because there were three Kamyas in TV Tomorrow and Necklace Kamya's official, real name wasn't Kamya, but (grimace) Sunita . . . a few years ago, she'd renamed herself Kamya after her all-time idol in *Hum Log* . . . she couldn't quite believe that Agastya didn't know *Hum Log*, the mother of all epic TV soaps . . . he apologized and asked whether she'd rather join him later at the Secretariat.

She giggled at the idea but she couldn't because of her Friend . . . he owned the car waiting downstairs, was a Gujarati venture capitalist ('That sounds like a buccaneer, Kamya, what is it?'), had two flats downtown and was thus the solver of her housing problem.

Oh. That sounded like the end of a chapter. 'But don't you have a family? Parents?' Just for something to say.

Yes, she did. They stayed in the—she sobered up here, even paled a bit—suburbs; she journeyed to meet them whenever she could, about once a month. It wasn't that she didn't get along with them, but, you know, the suburbs, well . . . she had to be off then . . . nice to've met you . . . 'bye . . . 'bye.

In office the following afternoon, Menon was in a great mood because he'd successfully intrigued all morning for Agastya's transfer. He hadn't enjoyed in the least the rejoinder to the Show Cause Notice. He took a dim view of wit when it wasn't his own. When it was all settled, he couldn't resist sending Agastya an Unofficial Reference that would fuck his happiness for a while.

> *I'm dashing off this UR to let you know that the powers-that-be weren't overly pleased with your reply to the SCN. There are plans afoot to pack you off to the boondocks. Not in itself such a ghastly idea since it'd definitely solve your housing problem!*
> *In brief, I learn from the grapevine that you're going as Collector, Madna to fight the plague on a war footing. We couldn't find any other fat cat for the rats. Congratulations.*
> *If you blanch at the prospect, rush to your godfathers before the transfer orders are issued and grovel right right now. If you don't have any, see if you can make do with me.*
> *Your choice is to push off to the Centre as Special BOOBZ Officer, snug in the lap of Finance. Aren't you excited, you lucky thing, you!*

CONDUCT UNBECOMING OF A CIVIL SERVANT

In different parts of the country, people reacted differently to the news of the plague in the district town of Madna. In Madna itself, for example, the Chief Revenue Divisional Commissioner and Agastya's boss-to-be, on scanning the headlines in *The State of the Times*, merely said 'Hmmm' and focussed with more intensity on the Love-Like-Hate-Adore game that he was scratching out on the side on a memo pad. Whereas fourteen hundred kilometres away in the capital, in marked contrast, Miss Lina Natesan Thomas, Junior Administrator (Under Training) in the Ministry of Heritage, Upbringing and Resource Investment—and eventually Agastya's subordinate-to-be—submitted, on the subject of the plague, a thirty-page memorandum to the Head of her Department. To each his own, particularly in a vibrant democracy.

Love-Like-Hate-Adore isn't as well-known a game as it should be. It is a splendid time-killer because while squandering away one's most precious resource, it permits one at the same time to rove from one object of one's lust to another to gauge whether—and to what extent—they reciprocate one's affections—and indeed, deep in one's heart, what one oneself truly feels for them. It—LLHA—also encourages one to spell correctly. On a piece of paper, one writes the name of whoever one is idly itching for at that moment, or on that day. For instance:

LINA NATESAN THOMAS

Beneath the line that one draws under the name of the lustee, one writes one's own:

LINA NATESAN THOMAS

BHUPEN RAGHUPATI

One then sifts through the names and strikes out the letters in common. Thereafter, on the letters left over, one bounces, in order, the choices of Love, Like, Hate or Adore. The sentiment at hand at the end of the name is what the person truly feels for the other below or above the line. Emotionally, it is, so to speak, the bottom line.

L~~INA~~ N~~ATE~~SAN T~~H~~OMAS like

BHUP~~EN~~ R~~A~~G~~H~~UP~~ATI~~ adore

Lina Natesan Thomas likes Bhupen Raghupati. Bhupen Raghupati adores Lina Natesan Thomas. Vexed, the Chief Revenue Divisional Commissioner, groping for loopholes, wondered whether she—Bunswali—spelt 'Natesan' with an 'h'. Wouldn't that transform the outcome? He would've so liked the stumps of both names to nucleate to Adore, to skim, like a flat stone across water, past the choices Love, Like and Hate, and swoop jubilantly down on the last, somewhat like a buxom, burly, imperious woman, the chairperson of his thoughts of the past eight weeks, descending on her timorous adorer. Whenever both the names climaxed in Adore, he felt that the deities had beamed refulgently on his itch of the month.

L~~INA~~ N~~ATE~~S~~H~~AN T~~H~~OMAS like

B~~H~~UP~~EN~~ R~~A~~G~~H~~UP~~ATI~~ hate

His visitor, Rajani Suroor, cleared his throat for the second time. The Commissioner transferred his blank, baleful stare from his memo pad to him, to his modish, beige kurta, his wire-frame spectacles, the golden bracelet on a hairy wrist, the black-and-white, wavy, dreadfully groovy hair that Suroor, narcissistically, fondled without pause, the sardonically respectful, damn annoying half-smile. This fool, the Commissioner felt, should massage him, long and slow, glisteningly, with mustard oil; when he'd been sated, he'd lumber up off the mat and with his belt, thrash Suroor into hushed rashers of crimson flesh; then he'd come all over whatever remained of his smirk.

For Lina Natesan Thomas, the plague was altogether a graver subject.

Confidential
By Registered Post

From
The Junior Administrator (Under Training)
In the Ministry of
Heritage, Upbringing & Resource Investment
New —
Dated: December 9, 19—

To
Dr Harihara Kapila
Secretary to the Welfare State
(BOOBZ and Official Grievances)
In the Ministry of Heritage, Upbringing and Resource Investment, Aflatoon Bhavan
New —

Subject: General administrative difficulties faced in the functioning of the above-mentioned department

Sir,
I must record that I was surprised to receive yesterday a State Order directing me to report, within three days

of its receipt, at the Office of the Municipal Commissioner, Madna, for emergency duty to combat on a war footing the plague that has been raging there for the past two weeks. If I fail to comply with the order, I understand that the severest disciplinary action will be contemplated against me. For ready reference, I enclose at Annexure A a copy of the State Order (No. SUS/Plague/ Crash-FCN, signed by D. Sengupta, Desk Officer, Home Affairs Disaster Management Cell, dated December 5, 19—).

Upon receipt of the said order yesterday, I sought appointments with your good self at 10.30 a.m., 12.45 p.m., 3.15 p.m. and 5 p.m. On the fourth occasion, your Principal Private Secretary told me to put down in writing any items for discussion with you that I might have. I pointed out to him that had he informed me at 10.30 a.m. of these instructions of yours, he would've saved the Welfare State one full working day of a Junior Administrator which, when computed in time and money, must surely amount to something. I don't think that your PPS understood my point. Had I known Punjabi, I would have spoken it and he might then have followed me. I have not known him to speak any other language. In fact, in your office, one gets the impression that Punjabi is the official language of the Welfare State.

This present application is handwritten because I do not have any stenographer or typist attached to me—that is to say, to the post that I occupy. In fact, ever since I joined this Department two months ago, I haven't been assigned any personal staff—no Personal Assistant, no peon, no clerk. I have failed to understand why. Representations in this regard have been made periodically to the Deputy Secretary (Administration), Joint Secretary (Administration), Additional Secretary and your good self (reference may be made to Annexures B, C, D, E, F, G, H, I, J and K). It will not be out of place to mention here that when I first arrived in this Department, in lieu of my own desk and office room, I was offered a seat on a cane sofa in the chambers of the then Deputy Secretary, Shri O.P. Chadha. I had at that time complained in writing that it was neither possible nor proper for a Junior Administrator (Under Training), a lady officer, to function out of the chambers of the Deputy Secretary (Administration), a satyr. My complaint, which can be perused at Annexure L, had inter alia noted that Shri Chadha had verbally proposed to me at that time that if I did not care for the cane sofa, I could work sitting on his lap. I had requested him to make me the same offer in writing, but I received no response from his seat. My complaint (at Annexure L), like all my other complaints, has been ignored.

Since I have no personal staff, I will have to go myself to the railway station to book a berth on the train to Madna. My trip to the station itself will be a waste of the time and money of the Welfare State unless it is clear beforehand precisely what I am scurrying off to Madna for. Desk Officer Shri D. Sengupta of the Disaster Management Cell will have no idea because he's one of us. Between cups of tea, he'll blink and sign whatever is placed before him.

Which he does, invariably. A characteristic of his that Lina Natesan can vouch for since they, once upon a time, for a couple of weeks or so, actually shared a room—with five other officers, fortunately of comparable rank—in Aflatoon Bhavan, housing being one of the more acute problems in the Welfare State.

When she had refused Deputy Secretary O.P. Chadha's offer to function from out of his lap, he had arranged for Miss Thomas one chair and one half of a desk in a fifteen-by-fifteen room on the fourth floor between the Gents' Toilet and the canteen of the Department of Mines. The smells from the toilet and the canteen had been her faithful companions week after week, had mingled in her consciousness and at their most potent, had every now and then blended to make her swoon.

One half of a desk means that she sat on one side and Under Secretary Shri Dhrubo Jyoti Ghosh Dastidar occupied the other side. She made it clear to Shri Dastidar from the very first day that he was welcome to the visitors' side of the desk. To his credit, he didn't seem to mind, either then or later. Nothing upsets him much, unless it be the sight of work.

The room therefore, to begin with, had four desks and seven officers. Apart from Under Secretary Shri Dastidar, Desk Officer Shri Sengupta and her good self Miss Natesan, there were Assistant Director Dr Srinivas Chakki and Assistant Financial Advisor (Housing for Cultural Luminaries) Mrs Minu Tutreja, who faced each other, and Assistant Heritage Advisor (Pending Parliamentary Questions) Mr Govindarajulu, who shared his desk with Additional Counsellor (Delayed Pensions and Republic Day Parade) Mrs Govindarajulu. As per norms, each officer had been assigned one large Godrej steel almirah, one three-tier open wooden file rack, one heater, one wooden teapoy for his or her official water jug and glass, and a second teapoy for his or her telephone. At Annexure M of her memorandum, Miss Thomas has provided for the reader's perusal a fairly accurate sketch of the room as it stood two months ago.

The sketch makes it clear that to reach the door from their seats, both Shri Sengupta and Mrs Minu Tutreja had to squeeze through between the wall and Miss Thomas's chair. Shri Sengupta always preferred to rub his private parts against her shoulder while Mrs Tutreja liked Miss Thomas's upper arm to knead *her* buttocks *en passant*. We all have our quirks. Miss Thomas complained in writing (Annexure N) about both the private parts and the buttocks. They were consequently removed. Then there were five. Miss Thomas has always believed in the power of the written word to move mountains, what to speak of buns.

For the record—and for a clearer picture of the room—about a week before the plague, Shri Govindarajulu went to hospital and hasn't returned yet—not at least to his old desk. During lunch hour one day, Mrs Govindarajulu reached across the files that they all found so convenient to use as table mats and whammed her husband on his skull with her steel lunch box. The others present couldn't glimpse much of Shri Govindarajulu's face, because of all that curry and blood. Domestic discord, no doubt, spilling over into officc hours. A couple of days after, Mrs Govindarajulu availed of the Leave Travel Concession facility and undertook an apparently unending religious tour of the South. Then there were three.

Dr Srinivas Chakki's sudden disappearance from the room was effected by the Disaster Management Cell. He left for Madna on plague duty. Then there were two. To quote from Page 26 of Miss Natesan's memorandum:

> *Dr Chakki is also my neighbour in the Prajapati Aflatoon Welfare State Public Servants' Housing Complex Transit Hostel near the Pashupati Aflatoon Public Gardens. Does your good self know the Transit Hostel? Twelve hundred one-room fully-furnished flats built at breathtaking speed by the Ministry of Public Works four years ago for the* International Man, Woman and Child in Nature *Conference that was eventually held at Djakarta? Anyway, I stay in B-318 and Dr Chakki in C-401. We have been meeting almost every morning at six for the last four years or so because we both go and buy milk at about that time from the local Mammary Dairy booth. It was while we were returning from the booth on the morning of*

November 27 that Dr Chakki revealed to me that he had received orders to join the Central Team of Experts that was being Rushed to Madna that very day.
I should add, to place matters in perspective, that he is an Assistant Director in the Ministry of Public Health (and thus, according to pay scale, half a rung senior to the undersigned).
He returned from Madna on December 7 with the plague and both a red alert and the police out for him. As one of our national newspapers puts it, he is truly the hero-villain of the Prajapati Aflatoon Transit Hostel. He is a hero for having gone to Madna to fight the dreaded disease and a villain for having returned with it.
He is an entomologist by profession. Entomology is defined as the science dealing with insects of public interest, much like a litigation. Dr Chakki has over twenty years' experience in the field. He is a veteran of the Menugunta Typhus Epidemic of 1973, the Gaurangabad Malaria Scare of 1976 and the Phatna Encephalitis Rout of 1979. His open letter to four national newspapers, on which I rely heavily, is at Annexure V for ready reference.
After two days of intensively combing the plague-affected areas of Madna for insects of public interest, he contracted high fever and a cough. He attributed the first to the heat of Madna and the second to his cigarettes, and continued working till on the third day, his associates Miss Shruti and Miss Snigdha insisted that he consult a doctor. He snarled and pointed out to them that he was one himself. His sudden display of choler—for he normally is one of the mildest of men—convinced Miss Shruti and Miss Snigdha that something was seriously amiss. Abandoning him and their combing, they fled to the Office of the Municipal Commissioner and returned with a couple of fierce-eyed constables. Your good self will no doubt be aware that the police

and para-military forces are all over the place in Madna. Nothing in our country moves or happens without them—naturally—we being a Police State as much as a Welfare State. In Madna, they have enough work to keep them occupied till their retirement. They track down and force the absconding Municipal sweepers and scavengers to return to work, they then protect them from the wrath of the citizens of the town, they guard the abandoned houses in different wards and the clinics of the doctors who have fled, and the persons of those who've returned, they prevent suspected plague patients from escaping from the hospitals and they defuse potential rebellions amongst the overworked, stressed-out medical staff.

It took six policemen two days to locate and cart to the Bhupati Aflatoon Memorial Hospital a comatose Dr Chakki. He was found sprawled in an alley beside an enormous garbage dump, clutching a fat dead rat in his outflung right hand. He took a day to come around. Then, to quote from his open letter, he 'had a look at the conditions in the hospital and promptly relapsed into unconsciousness because then I felt safer.'

Not everyone from the capital who happened to be in Madna that week had been brought there by the plague. Naturally not, the officially-unconfirmed outbreak of the epidemic being neither new nor anything more than a sideshow in the complex life of the nation. Rajani Suroor, for instance, last seen seated and smirking before a balefully-aroused Chief Revenue Divisional Commissioner, was visiting for purely cultural reasons (almost-purely; since everything is partly politics).

He, to quote part of his visiting card, is a theatre activist. He discloses easily in conversation that he is wholly committed to Total-, New Broom-, Intimate-, Alternative-, Street-,

Militant-, Contramural- and Inadmissible Theatre. His troupe is called *Vyatha*, or Pain. His detractors call it *Gand Mein*, or In the Arse. *Vyatha* procures, under the programme '*6493: Promotion and Diffusion of Demotic and Indigenous Drama and Other Such Forms of Self-Expression*', handsome quarterly grants from the Ministry of Culture, Heritage, Education and Welfare. When Bhuvan, the nth prominent Aflatoon, became Prime Minister, he changed its name to the Ministry for Heritage, Upbringing and Resource Investment—HUBRIS, in brief. At a subsequent Press conference, he asserted that the new name was more affirmative, focussed, thrustful and forward-looking. These adjectives were chosen for him by his Information Advisor, one of his New Men, who were mostly youngish and greedy, mostly from his old school (where, they recalled fondly, he'd been a complete duh), mostly Oxbridge, mostly homosexual. They mostly wore white or off-white Indian clothes. In a sparkling response to a vapid question from *The State Today*, the PM had added that further, translating the new name of the Ministry would at last give the Department of Constitutional Languages some work. He—God bless him—was generally devilishly witty at inopportune moments. The ministerial change of name cost the taxpayers of the Welfare State twenty-one lakh rupees in stationery and nameplates alone. The Press conference cost just four lakhs.

Rajani Suroor had been seven years junior to Bhuvan Aflatoon at school. Traffic-paralysing street theatre has brought him and *Vyatha* to Madna. They intend to perform, outside the Mall Road Gate of Aflatoon Maidan, on Wednesday, Thursday and Friday, roughly between 12.30 and 2.30 p.m.—when several schools release their charges, the shops haven't yet shut, the drones outside the cinema theatres and the hawkers haven't yet dissolved into the afternoon—a play, a skit scripted by Suroor, the first of a venturesome quintet on a rather grand theme. He has titled the skit *Baahar Nikal*,

Ashleel Jaylee; that is his translation of Shakespeare's phrase, 'Out, Vile Jelly.'

The play depicts an event that occurred in the town some eight years ago, at the Hemvati Aflatoon Welfare State Home for the Visually Disadvantaged. With a hot ladle, an infuriated attendant had gouged out the right eye of a blind girl just because at breakfast, she, like Dickens's Oliver Twist, had asked for a second helping of gruel. The gruel had been, as always, an uneven mixture of hot water, a trace of sugar dust, wheat dust, much true grit, some cockroach shit. An appalled Directorate of Welfare Homes had forthwith suspended the guilty attendant and initiated against him both criminal proceedings and an Official Enquiry. So Karam Chand the deft ladle-wielder was ordered to skip work for months, and paid just half his salary, poor thing, for doing so. Before the Enquiry Committee, he deposed indomitably, denied the accusation, contended that he was a victim of the caste politics of the Home, and emphasized that there weren't any credible witnesses against him, for however could the testimony of eleven blind juveniles be considered sound?—and that finally, when all was said and done, the episode wasn't that horrifying, was it, because after all, in the first place, the girl had never had any eyesight to lose, had she? The Enquiry Officer, a spiritless Welfare official, took five weeks to conclude that since the matter was *sub-judice*, the Directorate should await the outcome of the criminal case before awarding a final penalty, and that of course till then, the punishment of suspension should continue.

For the seventeen months that Karam Chand stayed away from work, he stitched undies for men and women and hawked them on the footpath of Junction Road, a.k.a Prajapati Aflatoon Marg. He and his tailor colleagues called them wearunders. He made about sixty rupees a day—not bad, considering that it exceeded his take-home pay—namely, his salary plus his Dearness Allowance plus an Additional Dearness Allowance plus his Regularization of Pre-Revised Pay Scales Emolument plus an Advance Increment plus his House Rent Allowance plus his Uniform Allowance plus a Festival Advance minus his Standard Provident Fund Subscription minus his Group Insurance Programme Contribution minus a Compulsory Security Plan Payment minus a House Construction Loan Instalment minus a Bicycle Purchase Advance Part-Settlement minus his Standard Provident Fund Loan Repayment minus no taxes. Karam Chand's income was beneath being taxed by the Welfare State. A standard welfare measure, no doubt—one doesn't snatch at the earnings of the almost-submerged four-fifths, particularly when one pays them chickenfeed in the first place. But Karam Chand—and most of the rest of the hundreds of thousands that compose that only-just-floating four-fifths—aren't overwhelmed by the bounty of the Welfare State. We earn chickenfeed, they grumble—with misgivings for the Zeitgeist darkening their brows—hence we aren't obliged to work hard.

Not at our jobs, anyway. In Suroor's skit, the Karam Chand character whoops out a rather peppy song while sending up A Routine Working Day in the Life of an Attendant. Whose shift officially starts at eight every morning, but who never shows up at the Home before nine—which is when he shakes hands with the other Karam Chands, drinks with them several cups of tea, signs the Attendance Register, ungrudgingly tastes the breakfast of the day, dispenses it to the inmates, shakes hands once more with the other Karam Chands, lopes off to Junction Road to hawk his wearunders, returns to the Home for lunch at twelve, and then at two, slips back to the footpath for the rest of the day. The other duties of his post he's disregarded for years, indeed, has all but forgotten—and like his colleagues, he steals for himself and his household whatever he can from the stores of the Home.

Whenever his Superintendent'd remind him of one of his effaced chores—'Can you please fill up the water cooler in my room, yaar?'—Karam Chand would snappily point out, 'Room coolers are not on my list of duties, saab . . . I don't know, saab. I do my own work to the best of my ability, and I don't poke my nose in other . . . I don't know, saab. It is not my duty to know by heart the lists of everybody's duties . . . I don't know, saab. It could be the duty of the peons or the junior orderlies, the dafadars, senior bearers, jamadars, sweepers, the night watchmen, chowkidaars, assistants Grade IV, malis, or daily wagers . . . No, saab, why should I have a copy of my list of duties? It was never given to me . . . I don't know, saab. You should make a reference to the Directorate . . . Arrey, suspend me, saab! But for what, for not doing someone else's duty! . . . Control your tongue, saab! We've suffered a good many Superintendents like you, okay! . . . Ohhhh! You're doing politics! You're insulting my caste . . . I'll make a complaint to the higher authorities! . . . I'll make a representation to the Kansal Commission! . . .'

Tackling Karam Chand requires tenacity and cunning, the doggedness to prod the Welfare State to move its mammoth, immensely sluggish arse. One maddened Superintendent, as a first step towards fixing the attendant, did in fact make a reference to the Directorate of Welfare Homes.

The Hemvati Aflatoon Welfare
State Home for the Visually
Disadvantaged

Date, etc.

Subject: Official List of Duties of Post of Attendant Type II in the Above Organization

Sir,

With reference to your letter No. Nil dated Nil, it is requested that the above subject is not readily available in this office. May kindly send two copies post-haste and oblige.

Yours sincerely,
Etc.

No reply, of course. A reminder after five weeks. After a further six weeks, a second reminder, this time on flesh-pink paper, to underline the fact that it was a second reminder. Then the Directorate replied that with reference to your letter No. DTY 1093/LST 163/89/A dated etc., a reference had been made (copy enclosed) to the Ministry Of Heritage, Upbringing and Resource Investment and that their reply was awaited. May kindly see please.

In his skit, Rajani Suroor does not present Karam Chand entirely as some unmanageable monster. On the contrary, he is also portrayed as a duteous family man—for whom not even the most openhanded pilfering from the stores of the blind will suffice to sate the underfed mouths at home; a concerned father of four nubile daughters, a survivor of abysmally cynical inertness whose refrain is: Not even the Almighty can divine how I plod on. His obviously symbolic significance is further emphasized by the umpteen references of the narrator-persona of the skit to Karam Chand's strategic drifting in and out of the other plays of the quintet. This persona—stout, jovial, tumid-eyed—like those raconteurs who doubt that their audience has grasped the point—also, every now and then, pounces on his spectators with posers like:

How much did it cost you taxpayers to have the eye of a blind girl gouged out by an employee of the Welfare State in the course of his official duties?

After much farcical calculation, he himself estimates, 'Rs 17.45 per second, and a grand total of Rs 469318.35.'

All the five skits comprise knockabout money-talk of this kind. Karam Chand's salary, for instance, is debated by a bunch of boisterous characters; each Allowance, Emolument, Increment, Advance, Subscription, Contribution, Payment, Instalment, Settlement and Repayment is a persona clothed in greyish-muddy kurta-pyjama; the dismal hue is meant to convey the colour of the Welfare State file covers. These players clamber onto one another's shoulders to suggest ceiling-high stacks of files in a typical office cubicle; they hide behind one another to mimic files getting lost, they slink out when the narrator-persona pockets a bribe; one stoops and bears another spider-like on his back to convey both the oppressive load of the work and the inconsequence of the subject matter; they move—skip, hop, leapfrog, bob, buck, prance, shuffle, glide—all the while to the catchy, rap-like Hinglish chatter of the narrator-persona and the Karam Chand player:

O kinsmen of the Welfare State—behold your clerk!
Earns sixteen hundred a month of your *cash! A lark!*
His work? The Cycle Purchase Advance Part Settlements
Of nineteen point five rupees per month of other gents
Like him! Does the welfare of this—the cream, the fat,
Ever reach anyone other than the bureaucrat,
The Minister, the clerk, the peon? Thousands of files!
Stacks a metre higher than the clerk—who has piles
From roosting on some trivial matter for ages.
The more footling the subject, the many more the pages
Of comment and counter-comment—some clerks, of course,
Spend their office hours yelling themselves hoarse
Touting their wearunders all over the pavement
Of Junction Road. You object? Shouldn't they be sent
Back to work? And punished?—You say so, no doubt,
Because you'd like another eye or two gouged out.
May we add here?—that blind girl, poor thing—some kind soul
Took her to the Welfare hospital for that hole
In her face. The doctor—the usual Welfare quack,

Disinterested, on the bottle, with a bloody knack
For fuck-ups—patched her up. And then, examining
Her a week after, they saw sepsis, blossoming.
And Karam Chand?—Sick of his undies, he slithered
Away to buy a caste certificate from a bird
In the tehsildar's office. And from there, with strife
In his heart, he moved on, elsewhere, to a new life.

'Hmmm,' observed Commissioner Raghupati. In his later years as a civil servant, he had come to prefer 'Hmmm' to 'Interesting' and 'I see.'

Suroor leaned forward and added animatedly, 'In our sequent skit, we compare—juxtapose—our time and the Kautilyan—which, to my mind, is the archetypal Welfare State.'

One-eleven p.m. The Commissioner needed to return home for his bracing massage and his light lunch. He smiled at Suroor, scarcely disarranging the hard fat of his face, and pushed a paan into his mouth. He was a perennially hungry, carnal man. In his unending, unscientific tussle with obesity, he'd snacked for years on paans. Stocky, the hard fat enclosing cold eyes and a gap-toothed, brutish mouth, the sort of figure that, while erect, rocks all the time on the balls of its feet. 'The Collector told me that you and he enjoyed a long chat last evening.' Raghupati disregarded the minutiae of his work, but was on the ball, intuitively, about the stuff that cast long shadows. So to Suroor he added in a purr, 'I'll be delighted to attend the performance on Friday.'

Hot outdoors. A winter afternoon in Madna was usually thirty-five degrees plus. Raghupati namasted his way through the press of petitioners waiting for justice or some crumbs of largesse. As a civil servant, for twenty-three years, he'd seen crowds outside a good many offices of the Welfare State; the numbers had now grown, like the discontent and cynicism, and the clothes were different. Changing times, everyone looked less resigned, more sullen; in the air was less the whiff of those close to the land—who live by the patient rhythms of the earth—and more the reek of the sweat of suppliants who wait, fume and fret, and wait.

Two decades ago, when he'd been Assistant Collector at Koltanga and had all but sparked off a riot because he'd buggered his bungalow peon who hadn't liked it one bit, who'd caved in and squealed blubberingly to his parents, the crowd that had gathered around Raghupati then had, without altogether swallowing his protests, finally done nothing but complain to *his* Collector. It hadn't quite known how to touch—leave alone manhandle—him. In that golden time, he'd been a thousand rungs above the hoi polloi and their law that he administered. But with the years, that interspace had narrowed and warped considerably, and a few of them had even begun to dress like him—in tight safari suits of elaborate stitchery—and he simply couldn't risk buggering bungalow peons anymore, and could just about get them to massage him instead.

He rolled up his car window so that the driver could switch on the a.c. Officially, he wasn't meant to have air-conditioning in his car, as per a routinely silly economy-measure circular of Dr Harihara Kapila, the Principal BOOBZ Secretary, which had decreed, *inter alia*, that as per Cabinet Resolution No. CR.ES/4709/F-EM/69 dated etc., only Cabinet Ministers, Vice Ministers, Deputy Ministers, Chancellors and Additional Chancellors of the Supreme Council, Chairmen, Chairmen-Designate and First Speakers of the Summit Assembly, Master Judges and Commons Judges of the Capital Court, Presidents and Vice-Presidents of the Permanent Congress—in brief, the crème de la scum—were entitled to air-conditioning in their office suites, motorcades and those parts of their official bungalows that they used for office work. The rest of the officialdom of the Welfare State was advised to use in their office rooms water coolers, the sizes of which per area of room the circular specified. It—the circular—was silent on whether officialdom was meant to boil in its office cars and in those parts of its office flats that it at times used for office work. Four of the seventy-six registered employees' unions had moved various courts in the matter, alleging that the circular was offensive, discriminatory, even violative (of the Fundamental Rights Enshrined in the Consti) and unrealistic (since it discounted the prodigious humidity of most regions of the country that rendered all water coolers ineffective—and in fact, intolerable). The courts were still pondering.

The circular cost the taxpayers a little over forty million. The between-the-lines instructions of economy-measure circulars do tend to trigger off a flurry of economic activity; exhortations to be thrifty are generally understood to mean that one may buy whatever one wants, as long as it's the cheapest. Never bother about the best. It tends to be expensive and therefore brands you as wasteful and wicked. Remember that only crooks buy for more what they could've got for less, using the difference to accommodate their shares from each deal. Focus instead on the cheapest, the dirt-cheap, the sub-standard, and whenever possible, on secreting away for yourself a slice of that cheapest. All things must fall apart, therefore decree each office object to have a span of life, and periodically, routinely, replace whatever is not-new with the cheapest, no matter that it might not be necessary. Remember to treat the property of the Welfare State with an almost-manic brutality, much like a serial killer his victims.

Needless to add, the crème de la scum floats far above economy-measure circulars, which apply—with stolid severity—mainly to the submerged 96.4 per cent of the employees of the Welfare State—namely, the millions of peons and Assistants Grades I, II, III and IV, dafadars, Junior Clerks, drivers, book-keepers, Deputy Clerks, attendants, auditors, Senior Clerks, stenographers, cashiers, Principal Clerks, Auxiliary Diarists, storekeepers, Chief Clerks, typists, accountants, stenotypists, Head Clerks—for none of whom are the batteries in the wall clocks of their grey, grimy crowded halls replaced even once in ten years; their perks are the intact window pane, the not-yet-fused light bulb, the water jug that doesn't leak, the ceiling fan that rotates, the rexine of a table top that hasn't yet been shredded by some clerk crazed by inertia. In their halls—their boxed-in verandas and caged-off corridors—nobody provides them file racks for the knolls of files that rise all anyhow up to the ceiling, the snug burrow-lairs of ants, moths, termites, worms, beetles, cockroaches, mice, rats, moles, mongooses, pigeons. Some of that rot doubtless slithers into the quality of work of the inhabitants of these office warrens.

But the expenditure of a little over forty million. Opportunely, in good time, several original, attached, dependent and subordinate offices of the four hundred and eighty-seven Ministries and Departments of both the central and twenty-seven regional governments of the Welfare State bought over a thousand air-conditioners—and a good many fridges, freezers, chillers and ice buckets—for the offices, official motorcades and residential offices of their Cabinet Ministers and First Speakers, their Chairmen-Designate and Commons Judges. To that should be added proportionate portions of the costs and overheads of all the activities of all those involved in the issuing of the economy-measure circular—that frenzied dictating, noting, placing on record and compiling, photocopying, cyclostyling, ferrying to and fro, the drafting, minuting, typing, redacting, translating, the bullshitting, the time-wasting—plus bits of the scores of salaries, allowances and emoluments, of the expenditure on upkeep, services, electricity—on the four air-conditioners, for example, in the Treasury Minister's chambers that have to be switched on at least an hour before he turns up in the morning for the rooms to be chill enough to facilitate his brainwork, his ponderings.

Thus it was that the replaced air-conditioners tumbled down the ladder into the offices, Ambassador cars, bedrooms and puja-rooms at the homes of Raghupati and his several hundred colleagues strategically dispersed all over the Welfare State.

On cue, Sharada Prasad the driver switched on the cassette player along with the a.c. Raghupati preferred the fifties' and sixties' Hindi film songs of Mutesh. When Mutesh, in his doleful, reedy, atonal voice, sang of the aches of love, the perfidiousness of friendship, the ups and downs of survival—his range, in brief—he conjured up for Raghupati the image of a male rape victim singing under duress, while being buggered, or even—with Mutesh, as with Raghupati, anything was imaginable—fucked in the gullet. He played Mutesh almost always during his massages in his puja room.

Through the black-filmed car window, he noticed the sign painters on their scaffolding, flies on the giant billboard that dwarfed the Commissionerate gates. The black film itself—and all tinted glass, et cetera—had been the subject of another, more recent, circular of the Home Secretary. *To help the State in its effort against terrorists, gunrunners, smugglers, kidnappers and other anti-social elements, the police would henceforth regulate how tinted car windows could be. Welfare State-car windows could be darker than private-car windows, but should definitely not be opaque, i.e., a policeman should be able to see inside the car, easily, from a distance of seven feet (2.07 metres).* Or so Raghupati had deciphered the circular, which had been issued only in Hindi, the official language.

On the billboard that publicized only Welfare State

schemes and projects, Small Savings was making way for Family Welfare. Small Savings had been a smiling family watering a sapling. *SUSTAIN THE TREE OF LIFE*, had urged the branches of the sapling. Family Welfare was going to be the same trio—parents and one child of debatable gender—playing ringa-ringa roses around an inverted, crimson equilateral triangle, the heart of which would blazon the slogan: *ONE OFFSPRING, ONE HEIR*, an argument for birth control the inaptness of which for his quarrelsome, litigious fellow-citizens had struck Raghupati more than once. Time and time again in his career—as District Magistrate, as Joint Director of Land Records, as Charity Commissioner—he'd observed that his fellow human beings, on the whole, preferred the quarrel to the solution; that is to say, to them, the verdict of any court signified not the resolution of a dispute, but merely a temporary blockage of it. To satisfy their craving, tier after tier of tribunal and bench, council and board, ranged away to the horizons of the Welfare State, and each seat of justice resuscitated, infused new life into, a magical diversity of squabbles:

> *Me-laard, my neighbour has no right to enjoy gratis the shade of the mango tree that grows in* my *garden, on* my *side of our common boundary wall.*

And

> *Me-laard, North's four clubs, an unethical splinter bid expressing slam interest in spades with at most one club, was a studied attempt to mislead his opponents by underhand methods.*

To suggest to such litigants that they should restrict themselves to only one issue was in fact to ask them to sin against their progeny; heaven forbid, however could one not give one's heir someone to litigate against?

The two ad campaigns—Small Savings and Family Welfare—dated from the four months that Raghupati had been Deputy at the Directorate of Information, Public Relations and Visual Education (DIPRAVED). His boss of those days, Harihara Kapila—indefatigable, capricious, witty after a fashion—he'd thought up the acronym of the Directorate, for example—would ever so often declare, particularly in front of outsiders and women,

'After I take up a new assignment, for the first six months I maintain that I'm learning the ropes. For the next six, I blame my predecessor. Within one year, I begin to get the hang of things, i.e., I realize that the organization should be wound up.'

Later, when he'd scrambled up the ladder—advising his juniors en route to Suck Above, Kick Below—to become Regional Finance Secretary, he was credited with having successfully transformed ZBB—the Zero-Based Budgeting programme—into BOOBZ: Budget Organization on Base Zero. In the last decade of his unastonishing career, when he had less to suck and more to kick, and when he sucked better than ever before, he'd hang, behind every cushioned swivel chair that he'd rest his piles in, his favourite poster, framed in black. It parodied an ophthalmologist's eye chart:

I
DO
NOT
SUFFER
FROM I
DISEASE
DO YOU?

Raghupati coldly recalled that he'd all but broken his neck once, ages ago, under one such Family Welfare hoarding. Horrible, endless rain, he'd been in extremely slippery white keds (and goggles!—because of damned conjunctivitis), approaching a village in the middle of nowhere to take stock of a landslide, six dead, the ground like watery halwa, an office peon, turbaned and all, hopping and bobbing behind him with an umbrella for his head, the umbrella along with his dark glasses making him feel like an Aflatoon on a Let-me-meet-the-Great-Unwashed-for-their-votes tour, he concentrating on every step, but he must've been distracted by a body—a bum or torso, whether male or female he couldn't now remember—but when he, dazed from his tumble, had looked up at the muddle above him of outstretched hands and embarrassed faces, he'd first noticed, surrounding the askew turban of the peon, the maroon triangle of Family Welfare and alongside it, its neuter child. *My God, the State is everywhere; it grapples even with the vastness of a leaden monsoon sky.* In those few breaths, moreover, its obtuseness had humbled him anew; here, with no habitation in sight, a hoarding the size of a building, on it an inapt slogan, that too in English in a region wherein seventy-five per cent of the inhabitants were unlettered in their own tongue. Upright once more, while the diffident hands had spruced him down, he'd shoved the umbrella aside to gaze again at the distant trees and the immense, unending sky, to sense afresh the gooseflesh-caress of infinity, of the heavens belittling the concerns that move the earth. Later that week, to remind everybody that the earth simply couldn't get away with that sort of thing, he'd transferred the peon (the bobber, with turban) to an office two hundred kilometres away from his family.

To avoid the areas of Madna town that had been affected—if not by the plague itself, then certainly by the panic at the possibility of its presence—Raghupati's car swerved away from Junction Road to skirt the north boundary wall and railing of Aflatoon Maidan. Thousands had fled the town in the past week, claimed the more irresponsible newspapers. Certainly, the streets looked marginally emptier and there did seem to be less of a throng of pedestrians and hawkers on the pavements of the Maidan. But one could never tell. Perhaps the afternoon heat and the one-day cricket on TV had kept the citizens indoors. Besides, this was the Civil Lines part of town, spacious after a fashion, originally planned with a preference for trees and open air over buildings that simply wouldn't stop growing and their denizens who flooded the gutters.

Raghupati noticed, every now and then, at street corners and the occasional traffic light, an armed police constable. The rifle, he sneered to himself, was doubtless for protection in the event of the vector rats getting out of hand, not knowing their place and daring to abandon their nooks in the more fetid, filthier, more teeming parts of the old town. He could practically see Madna's wildcat Police Superintendent commanding a contingent or two to restrain the epidemic from touching the privileged, issuing orders to shoot at sight any subversive rodent that didn't comprehend curfew.

Ah no. The cops were visible because of the demonstration ahead that had already begun to snarl up traffic—more, that is, than was usual. 'U turn before we're sucked in,' Raghupati ordered the driver. It wasn't surprising that they hadn't spotted the protesters earlier, what with the swarm around them of bullock-carts, rickshaws, cycles, pushcarts, tongas, scooters, three-wheelers, tempos, Maruti cars and neanderthal public buses. The marchers moreover were themselves dwarfed by the twenty-foot high canvas-and-plywood hoarding that, mounted on a van, trundled, juggernaut-like, in their midst. While their car veered, backed, honked, turned, growled and slewed round, Raghupati abstractedly admired its artwork.

He noticed things, almost everything. Mobile billboards and sign painters on a scaffolding—yes, because they were out of the way and commanded one's attention—but also the workman in beige trousers on a balcony fiddling with a TV antenna, the whirr and cluck of pigeons atop the air-conditioner at his office window, an obscure clerk's haircut, his stenographer's new perfume. Being a top-notch civil servant (and only for the moment out of favour and in the cold), he'd over the years honed his survival instinct to a razor's-edge keenness. All the information that one's senses picked up had to be filed away for future use, for God alone knew what one would need when to surmount which flap. God would of course know because he was an A-one bureaucrat himself, absolutely top-drawer, wise, on the ball, amoral, utterly self-serving.

The hoarding on the van depicted the white-tiled walls of a Gents' Urinal and at the bottom the back of a man squatting to piss. Above him on either side rose the marble partitions of his stall. Before him, over his head, on the surface that would actually receive the piss, were painted a few horizontal lines. Way above, atop the flush tank, was the legend:

NEW CRITERIA LAID DOWN BY THE KANSAL COMMISSION FOR THE ANNUAL EXAMINATION OF THE NATIONAL CIVIL SERVICE COMMISSION FOR ADMISSION TO THE CENTRAL URINAL SERVICE AND THE FIRE BRIGADE.

Below, in the hoarding, beside the topmost horizontal line, was painted:

PISS THIS HIGH FOR FIFTEEN CONTINUOUS SECONDS IF YOU ARE AN ORDINARY, UNPRIVILEGED CANDIDATE FROM THE UPPER CASTES.

The other lines had been drawn considerably lower. Each had beside it similar instructions.

> *PISS THIS HIGH FOR FIVE SECONDS IF YOU BELONG TO ANY OF THE FOLLOWING BACKWARD CASTES*—followed by, in brackets, a list of names absurdly long.
>
> . . . *FOR THREE SECONDS, NOT NECESSARILY CONTINUOUS, IF YOU BELONG TO ANY OF THE FOLLOWING NOTIFIED CASTES* . . .
>
> . . . *FOR FIVE SECONDS ON ANY CANDIDATE FROM ANY OF THE UPPER CASTES IF YOU BELONG TO ANY OF THE FOLLOWING DEPRESSED CASTES* . . .

At the bottom of the hoarding, in large red letters, for all those who'd missed the point of the drawing, was the declaration:

> *WE WILL FIGHT TO THE FINISH THE RECOMMENDATIONS OF THE KANSAL COMMISSION. IF YOU VALUE JUSTICE, LIBERTY, EQUALITY, HONESTY AND TRUTH, JOIN OUR MASSIVE MARCH TO PARLIAMENT ON MARCH 24. FOR FURTHER DETAILS OF OUR RELAY HUNGER STRIKE THAT STARTS ON FEBRUARY 27, CONTACT AC RAICHUR* . . .

The bottom right-hand corner disclosed that the hoarding was the handiwork of the National Federation for the Human Rights of the Upper Castes.

Beneath the hoarding and atop the van, a fat man in off-white kurta-pyjama and a broom of a moustache periodically donned a surgeon's cloth mask—presumably against the miasma of the plague or the Kansal Commission or the state of the times—and doffed it to bay some doctrine into a mike in his hand. He was largely incomprehensible because of the din of the street, the ghastly quality of the public address system and the general woolliness of his thinking. Raghupati recognized him.

'Just call Raichur,' he told the driver.

Sharada Prasad leaned across to roll down the window and let the noise in. To summon Raichur over it, he simply switched on the car siren. When enough heads had turned, he beckoned regally through the window. He let the frightful wailing continue for a few seconds longer before switching it off.

'Sir good afternoon sir sir.' Raichur's voice boomed in the confines of the car. His moustache, fleshy cheeks and general air of sweat and sycophancy seemed to fill the window. 'Any instructions sir or orders?' Other faces began to crowd in around Raichur.

'I can't say whether I am more impressed or bewildered by your hoarding. Why has the man squatted to piss? All the qualifying marks are way above his head.'

'Sir, exactly.' Raichur nodded vigorously, exuding heat and sweat like steam. 'Kindly bear in mind the percentage of our citizenry that *stands* and makes water. Not more than seven, I'd say. Urine, sir, is a bodily fluid the touch of which we find particularly polluting.'

'More than the Kansal Commission? Or the plague?'

In response, Raichur snorted explosively, tricking a couple of the surrounding faces into cackling. The snort itself had been non-committal because Raichur hadn't been certain whether the Commissioner had been witty.

'What does the town think of the plague? Just because the government hasn't woken up to it doesn't mean that it isn't there.'

In her memorandum, Miss Natesan phrased the same concern quite differently.

> *I'm being packed off to Madna to battle the plague, but the question is: does the plague exist at all? I wish to draw your attention here to the headlines in*

various newspapers this month. The story first broke on the 24th of November and thereafter, every day till the 2nd of December, the plague was—naturally—big news:

'And now the plague.'
'DEMAND TO SEAL OFF MADNA REJECTED.'
'500,000 Flee Madna.'
'CENTRE CONFIRMS 24 PLAGUE DEATHS.'
'No Shortage of Tetracycline, Says State.'
'Multinationals Pulling Out of Madna.'
'State Denies Plague Deaths, Confirms Viral Pneumonia.'
'State Denies Multinationals Pulling Out of Madna.'
'State Working on Action Plan to Combat Epidemic.'
'UAE Bans Import of State Foodstuff.'
'Doctors Flee Madna.'
'PM's Directive to Health Ministry to Expedite Action Plan'
'Gulf Bans All Flights to and from State.'
'Remaining Madna Medical Staff in Militant Mood.'
'State Fighting Plague With Data of 1928!'
'Irate Mobs Attack Abandoned Madna Medical Clinics.'
'State Denies Use of DDT, Gamaxene Is Waste of Resources.'
'Red Alert in Capital.'
'Dacoities Increase in Abandoned Madna Houses.'
'Life Must Go On: Virbhim.'

and so on.
So far so good—if indeed I may use such an expression in connection with the plague. However, yesterday, on the 8th of December, something extraordinary happened; the plague disappeared altogether from the front pages of our national newspapers. Instead, our headlines were:

'Jayati Aflatoon Grants Appointment to Virbhim.'
'Bhanwar Meets Jayati.'
'Jayati and Fortune Smile on Virbhim.'
'JAYATI GIVES BHANWAR SAAB TEN-MINUTE HEARING.'
'VIRBHIM CALLS ON JAYATI; PROSPECTS IN PARTY SOAR.'

In brief, the scoop of the day was that the Prime Minister's sister-in-law—more strictly speaking, cousin-in-law—agreed to meet (in what is probably—by our standards—just a minor palace intrigue), at short notice, for ten minutes in the evening, a crafty, venal, lecherous, sixty-five-year-old Deccan politician who has for the last two years been trying to snuggle back into the lap—and nuzzle once more the bosom—of the Aflatoons. As a result of that meeting, Bhanwar Virbhim will probably be given a berth in the Cabinet and—Heaven help us in Aflatoon Bhavan!—very likely the portfolios of Culture, Heritage, Education and Welfare, because it, the post, is politically a graveyard.

Yesterday, the plague was on Page 3 and today, it's on Page 7. At this rate, by day after tomorrow, it'll be engaged in a tussle for space with the Crossword and the Thought for Today. My point is, does my presence in Madna serve the larger interest of the Welfare State more—and better—than my remaining here in Aflatoon Bhavan? I fear that the answer to that question is: Please reflect. How can we be sure of that when we aren't even sure of the plague?

Other questions arise at this juncture. Since I've been given no personal staff here in Aflatoon Bhavan, what is the guarantee that I'll find my staff awaiting me on my arrival at Madna? A Personal Assistant, a stenographer, a clerk, a peon? I have already sent a telegram in this regard to the Municipal Commissioner, Madna. Of course, he hasn't replied but that is only to be expected. Your good self must be fully aware that we in the Welfare State wake up only to the tenth reminder, much like a behemoth sluggishly stirring only at the tenth prod to its private parts.

Why need I travel to Madna when Madna has already showed up at Aflatoon Bhavan—in fact, has been here for quite some time? Placed at Annexures M and N are two recent photographs of the world we inhabit. One is of the grounds outside the Bhupati Aflatoon Memorial Hospital at Madna, the second is a view of Gate No. 17 of Aflatoon Bhavan, here in the capital. Your good self will notice that both photographs contain more or less the same details—namely, hillocks of rotting garbage, stray cattle, pigs and other animals, children answering the call of Nature, passersby with handkerchieves over their noses and mouths. How can one tell, in these two photographs, Madna from Aflatoon Bhavan? Of course, one can't. What obliges the Welfare State then to draft me to Madna when I can enjoy its air right here in my office by simply opening my window?

Your good self will no doubt point out to me that the difference between the capital and Madna is the plague. But the plague has struck in the capital as well! Today's newspaper mentions en passant on Page 7: 'Six Suspected Plague Cases in Capital.' It's here! And what is of even more interest to a cultural historian (like me, I might add) is that it's always been here!

A fact of which there exists compelling evidence. The newspapers themselves have published charts and data to indicate that the plague has been recorded in our country ever since 1500 B.C. I take the liberty of placing the relevant information on record here for your good self's perusal.

Chronology of the Plague in the Welfare State

1500-600 BC	The plague noted in the Bhagvata Purana
1031-32 AD	The plague reaches the northern plains from Central Asia following the invasion of Ghouse Mohammed (from Arab chronicles)
1325 AD	The plague in Barabar following the invasion of Talat Mahmud and again after Khalid
1403 AD	Badruddin's army destroyed by the plague in Ghatia

1617 AD	During Lehangir's reign, the plague reported from the northern plains, Ahmedab, Kudar and the Deccan; thus described by Edward Perry, the English Ambassador to the Khayalji Court
1707 AD	The plague in Avrampur
1812-38 AD	In Pathiawar, the eastern delta and Nanuch—said to have been imported from Persia
1836-38 AD	In Garwar and Tajputana—called the Pali plague
1895 AD	In Okalkata—diagnosed bacteriologically on April 17, 1898 by Dr Neild Cook—imported from Hong Kong (the disease, that is, not the doctor)
1896 AD	In Navi Chipra, first diagnosed on October 13, 1897. Spread rapidly—like the plague, as it were—to all parts of the country
1907 AD	A great year for the plague in all four corners of the land. A total of 1,315,892 deaths.
1926-27 AD	Severe epidemic in Mehboobabad and the Deccan
1947-52 AD	Temporary rise in the incidence of the plague in Okalkata
1954-58 AD	Reappeared in Gandhra and Shiasore and reported for the first time in Aflatoonabad.
1960-68 AD	Sporadic outbursts in Shiasore, Furas, Purachal and Tajasthan

We should be indebted to the Press Trust of the Welfare State for the above facts.
And to update the chart—the plague's also been around for the last two weeks in our national newspapers and for the last one year in Madna. I draw your good self's attention to the reports published in The State of the Times *on the 28th and 30th of November and on the 1st of this month relating to the proposed dramatic transfer of the very-recently-appointed Collector and District Magistrate of Madna, Mr Agastya Sen. The items went largely unnoticed in the general hubbub of the plague. It was intended to turf Mr Sen out to*

Gandhan (population: 42000) to be Deputy Chief Inspector of Steam Boilers and Smoke Nuisances. Before the orders were put into effect, he addressed a second press conference, at which he disclosed that he was being booted out for having addressed the first.
On November 27, the day after he joined his new post, Mr Sen had spoken to a handful of journalists for the first time on the subject of the plague in his district. He'd commented that he didn't know what the fuss was all about since his office, for the past year, in its quarterly statements to the regional government, had regularly reported Deaths Due to Plague in the District of Madna. The plague, he had elaborated, was endemic there, as much a feature of the region as famine, floods, cholera, typhoid, malaria and female infanticide.

'The plague, Collector Saab, is supposed to be extinct in our country—hence this colossal embarrassment over Madna—so are you sure?'
'How many Deaths Due to Plague, Collector Saab, have there been in the district in the last twelve months?'

Fifty-four, the Collector had replied, that is—your good self will note—more than double the total number notched up so far by the newspapers.

'Did Collector Saab know the difference between bubonic and pneumonic plague? That Madna had been hit by the pneumonic?'
'Fifty-Four. I rule out the possiblity of a mix-up between Deaths Due to Plague and any of the other figures that we periodically convey to Headquarters: Deaths in Police Custody, Suicides in Government Hospitals, Fatalities Due to Acts of God and Drowning Cases in Unlicensed Swimming Pools . . . Yes, the Municipal Corporation *has* shut down its swimming pool because of that unfortunate

accident last week—quite terrible, really, because I need to re-figure out the leg movement of the breast stroke. I intend to wheedle with them to keep it open just for me—the Steel Frame must work out and all that. However is one to manage a district if one can't first manage one's own goodly frame? . . . no, I didn't spot any dead rats in the pool—frogs, yes, but not rats. Well, eleven on last count but the official figure is nineteen and the buzz in the streets is that there isn't any plague at all. Instead, there is apparently a gang war on here, a fight to the finish amongst the diamond mafia, they say.'

Diamond Street Market after Junction Road and a right therefrom on to Diamond Change Bazaar. Raghupati's Ambassador car raced—in a manner of speaking—down routes along which, in everyday circumstances, it would have crawled, honking boorishly. Almost all the shop shutters were down—and not just because it was afternoon. Under their tarpaulin and plastic awnings on the pavements sat a mere handful of hawkers, half-hidden behind their suspended wearunders, handkerchieves, goggles and cloth masks, intrepid but subdued by the absence of custom. Garbage littered the streets—rags, broken bottles, plastic bags, reeking vegetable and animal refuse—and black pigs, stray dogs and vicious alley cats wandered amongst it, disturbed now and then only by the youth gangs, with their cloth masks resembling clusters of surgeons in some fancy dress pantomime, hunting—so Raghupati had heard—for vector rats. The contrast with the bustle around Aflatoon Maidan—a bare couple of kilometres away—was fearful. Here, in the older part of town, all was silent and bleak, as though time itself was wary.

Not wholly on account of the plague, though. Mere fleas and their carriers could never have compelled the diamond trade to down shutters. Raghupati believed the buzz that he had heard, that over the preceding months, Sukumaran

Govardhan had expanded operations, and from his half-mythical feats in the illegal timber trade, in skins, drugs and gunrunning, had stretched out a talon to touch diamonds and politics.

At airports, railway stations, bus terminuses, market places, cinema halls, university coffee houses and municipal toll tax collection centres, every now and then, whenever some new heinous exploit of his had come to light, the distinguished features of Sukumaran Govardhan had stared out at the world from the thousands of black-and-white Wanted-Dead-or-Alive posters that sprang up overnight on walls, doors and pillars. True, the posters did seem a little anachronistic at the end of the millennium, a bit desperate, even unbelievable—but on the other hand, they served to remind the citizens that the Welfare State in many ways *was* the Wild East and that in the matter of Govardhan, the police was at the end of its tether.

> *If You Have Seen This Man Somewhere, Don't Panic But Call 100 or 4763213 (6 lines) and Win Tax-Exempted Award of Your Dreams.*

On different occasions, the telephone numbers in the poster had changed but the photograph above the advice hadn't. It was blurred, magnified several times—a fleshy, clean-shaven, bespectacled, professorial face with a jungle of inch-long hair sprouting out of his ears and reaching out like black tendrils to the edges of the paper.

Raghupati's car turned in at the gates of his bungalow with a frightful honking and blaring to warn the Residence peons to switch off the TV and down their cups of tea. On the veranda, Murari, the oldest and laziest of the House staff, waited deferentially with a glass of chilled coconut water and what he considered the more important items of the morning's mail.

On his way to the puja room, Raghupati's penis twitched as he ripped open an envelope from the Civil Service Welfare Association. On his good days, his penis quivered even when he spotted a gecko on the wall, poised to pounce on some moth fluttering about in the wan blue of a tubelight.

His massage-boy, Chamundi, waited for him in the master bedroom on the first floor of the house. One of the boy's several duties was to smile, exhibiting his dimples all the time that he was with Raghupati. Whenever his smile slipped, which happened ever so often—when the Commissioner's cock swayed alarmingly close to his face, for example, or when he was huskily ordered to mix his, Raghupati's, spunk with the massage oil, usually mustard—the Commissioner'd lean forward and tweak his cheek rather hard.

Chamundi bolted the door to the veranda, Raghupati flopped down on the bed. The boy began to remove every item of the Commissioner's clothing. This took a while, since each piece—sandal, belt, hankie—had to be neatly put away before the next could be touched. 'Mai dream to make da seets run red,' faltered Chamundi, grinning from ear to ear in bashfulness at his pronunciation.

Naked, spanking his thigh with the buff envelope, liking the sound, arm flung around his masseur's shoulders, Raghupati strutted off to the adjoining puja room. Ten-by-six, windowless, red night light, incense, shivalings and Ganeshes all over the place, flowers from his front lawn, mattresses on the floor, freezing airconditioning, Mutesh's whine from the tape recorder. 'Here, before you start, just shave my armpits and my crotch.'

More than a month ago—at the last get-together of the Civil Service Welfare Association, a dinner convened in the capital to honour Dr B.B. Bhatnagar for having wangled, after two decades of undistinguished and venal self-service, a Ph.D degree out of the Bhupati Aflatoon International Open University—more than a month ago, Bhupen Raghupati had for the first time set eyes on Miss Lina Natesan Thomas. She'd been wearing a grass-green georgette sari that evening. It had slunk deep into the crevice of her meaty, rather attractive arse. On the preceding Sunday, *The State Today's* **Thank Your Stars** column had advised Raghupati that the dominant colours for Scorpios that fortnight would be red and green. His personal astrologer, Baba Mastram, who visited him thrice a week, rheumy-eyed and halitotic, had confirmed that very morning that green would be triumphant for him uptil Thursday. Thus it was that on the veranda of the Golf Club, when they, glasses in hand, were comparatively alone in a shapeless queue before the water cooler, Raghupati had plucked the sari out of the crack, in the process coming richly into his pants, which in turn he'd interpreted to mean that the gods were with him. He'd been about to ask Kumari Natesan whether she was virgo intacta, and if yes, whether she'd like to redden some bed linen with him, when up had bustled Chanakya Lala, a comparatively junior bureaucrat and Raghupati's erstwhile subordinate, the one whose after-shave could be sniffed twenty paces away.

'Shame on you, sir,' Kumari Natesan had hissed and stalked away, jiggling more than ever in her distress. For a moment, Raghupati'd thought that she'd meant the spreading wetness in his trousers. Then, calm of mind, all passion spent for at least half an hour, he'd sliced through the vapours and focussed on making polite conversation with a life-size, animate bottle of Fabergé.

While lathering Raghupati's crotch, Chamundi, as was his wont, began to prattle of office matters. 'After Saab left this morning, three advocates came, also one morcha to demand the transfer of the Keeper . . .' To speak thus of processions and petitions, of course, was to assert that one too was a respectable employee of the Welfare State, and not just a wastrel of the streets picked up for one's smile and one's tight brown skin. Officially, in different files, Chamundi was a Commissioner's-Residence-Telephone-Answerer, a Tribal-Quota-Daily-Wage-Gardener, an Eldest-Eligible-Male-Family-Member-Granted-Employment-on-Untimely-Death-of-Only-Wage-Earner-of-Selfsame-Family, a Reserved-Category-Class-IV-Transferee-from-the-Prime-Minister's-Grant-Project and a Hidden-Beneficiary-of-the-Integrated-Tribal-Development-Plan. '. . . And Makhmal Bagai Saab dropped in minutes before you arrived. Murari showed him into the camp office, from where he made a couple of phone calls, one even to Madam Saab in Navi Chipra . . .'

His camp office, regrettably, was not the room wherein Raghupati could officially indulge in camp, but instead, a specimen of a venerable colonial institution—simply the office away from office, set up at home or anywhere else, sometimes temporarily, but more often, like several other creations of the Welfare State, for a season that spanned for ever.

Triplespeak:

i) I, being such a senior officer, need a gang of lackeys at home to cook, wash up, wash the clothes, massage me, knead my wife's feet, look after the children, scrub the floors, scour the toilets, tend to the lawns and the grandparents, buy vegetables, drive the family around, switch on the television. However, I am too senior to be so foolish as to actually pay these lackeys out of my own (truly meagre) salary.

ii) The office, the Welfare State, should pay for them because, as per our Civil Service General Regulations (No. VI. 74. a.xiv. in conjunction with No. VII. 22.f.ix.), since I may be summoned for official work at any hour of the day or night, I am on duty every second of my life till I retire or die, whichever is earlier; every moment of my existence is therefore official, thus the State should cough up for every breath of it. Naturally, the more senior one is, the more indispensable one becomes—experience and all that; if the earth doesn't tremble when one walks, at least the downtrodden do.

iii) I am well aware that the welfare of its senior civil servants must not be seen as a priority item on the agenda of the Welfare State. It is therefore suggested that a) to justify the presence in one's official home of several office employees,

b) to pass off various kinds of domestic work as official and

c) to fork out official wages for the same, the simplest course would be to carry on a colonial tradition and open a camp office in the bungalow—a telephone with national and international dialling facilities, severe wooden chairs, a couple of photos of some Aflatoons, discoloured jute matting, a heap or two of grey files and casually-strewn, rough, off-white paper.

The Joint Secretary of the Civil Service Welfare Association had forwarded to Raghupati for comments and 'a preliminary reaction' a handwritten novella of complaint from Miss Lina Natesan. Her letter was addressed to the Union Cabinet Secretary and some half-a-dozen other senior bureaucrats. With an eye seasoned in scanning bilge, Raghupati riffled through the pages of near-hysterical prose. He'd have to try again to arrange for her transfer to a post under his thumb. His hooded eyes watched Chamundi thwack and pummel his left thigh. He shifted so that his tumescent penis could be bang under the boy's nose. The boy shifted too. Raghupati saw red. He reached out, grabbed Chamundi by the scruff of his neck and yanked his head down so that it bobbed inches above Tumescent, which, in welcome, began to perk up quite a bit. That restored Raghupati's good humour. He lifted his bum off the mattress and swayed his hips and his tool to the whines of Mutesh. Chamundi remembered to giggle nervously. He, however, knew that Raghupati wouldn't actually bugger or assault him in any other orifice without clearing it first with Baba Mastram.

'Babaji I've a lot of extra heat energy in me that I could—with benefit to both—transfer to the massage-boy. What do you advise? Today?'

'No, not yet, sir. Be patient. To fret under patience is to despair, but with calm to conserve, to augment one's sap, one's vital forces, is to overcome the world, and all in it.'

'Hmmm. And that new steno in my office, a very junior person—I'd want to share with her too, the instant the conditions are propitious.'

Raghupati did nothing important without consulting his astrologer. Had it been feasible, he would have checked with the stars even before buttoning up his shirt or scratching his elbow or breaking wind. A family tradition. Over the years, astrologers and palmists, yogis and fortune-tellers had advised him on whom to marry, what new first name to give his wife, when to copulate so as to beget only sons, when to officially drop his caste-revealing surname, what allonym to adopt, when to angle for a transfer, which posts were both lucrative and safe, whom to beware of, whom to trample on, whom to suck up to, when to separate from his wife, which functions to attend, what colours to wear on which occasions, what food to eat when, when to divorce—in brief, how, when and where to place every step of his life.

Baba Mastram had been his guiding light and troubleshooter for, off and on, two decades now, ever since the affair of the bungalow peon at Koltanga. In that time, whenever practicable, he'd arranged for the Baba to follow him wherever he'd been posted. He was now toying with the idea of buying him a mobile phone. He'd turned down two positions at the Centre because the Baba had counselled against both when he'd sensed that he wouldn't have been part of Raghupati's baggage on either occasion.

On most mornings, Baba Mastram's session with the Commissioner ended by eight-thirty. He then ambled around in the compound for a bit, drank a glass or two of coconut water, unravelled dire futures in a couple of sweaty palms, and at a quarter to ten, along with the domestics, hung about in a circle to watch the Commissioner leave for office. Afterwards, excitement over, they all got down to the day; they breakfasted for a second time. While readying lunch, they snacked, and throughout the day, quaffed litres of tea in front of the TV.

On Tuesday morning, Baba Mastram warned Chamundi to be particularly vigilant of his person in the next two weeks, and above all, not to wear green; nervously—and in gratitude—Chamundi massaged him with especial vigour.

On the quiet days, Raghupati's massage was followed by a bath, lunch and a nap. He generally returned to work at about four. Not that there was anything at that hour that couldn't wait till next week, but old habits die hard. By posting him to Madna and making him responsible for Land Revenue, Depressed Tribes and Forests Protection, the regional government had wished to teach—not the wildlife raiders and timber smugglers but Raghupati himself—a lesson. The Commissionerate had neither money nor manpower, none of those rungs and rungs of torpid employees ranging away to the horizon.

Just before he dozed off, he mentally composed a rejoinder to Miss Lina Natesan.

My magnificent Niss Natesan,

I was intensely moved that evening last month at the sight—or should I say, vision?—of a greyish-brown shadow in the crevice of your green-georgetted hips. I went mad trying to figure out what it could be. As you know, I do not put on my spectacles in front of ladies. At last, at 10.10 p.m., I realized that it was a stray wisp of your false ponytail, the rest of which tapers off at your sari-line. And then, at that very moment—a staggering coincidence!—I see God's hand here!—you scratched the crack of your arse, thereby pushing your sari deeper in. A less sharp-eyed man, admittedly, might not have noticed, but for me, sex is power is money, and I wonder how people can differentiate the three. I wanted to free your sari from your almighty, disdainful buttocks, and thence free your mind too, to haul you into the arms of power, because then you'll feel—and warm to—that power as well, and all the sex will overwhelm you in an indescribable rush.

Such were the anonymous letters that he'd never actually written, leave alone posted. What he had often mailed, however, to all sorts of acquaintances, were almost-blank sheets of Welfare State off-white foolscap onto which he'd ejaculated while lolling about in his office chair. At home, in his camp office, he typed out the addresses on a Devanagari manual machine: after all, as far as possible, all correspondence was to be in the official language. He'd been sending these billets doux out for some years now—rather generously, some four or five a week, to his office staff, colleagues, deputies, assistants and associates, to his ex-brothers-in-law and the office-bearers of the Madna Club, and further from home, to the Prime Minister's Office and the Governor's Secretariat, to the Resident and Executive Editors of *The State Today* and *Our Time*, the Chief Executive Officers of Chipra Zinc and Vindhyachal Oil, the Managing Directors of Airports

Authorities and Highway Transport Corporations, to the Cabinet Secretary and the Chairman of the Board of Industrial and Financial Reconstruction. On all sheets he—before fouling them up—typed in Devanagari, *Namaha Shivaya*. He thought it appropriate.

When he'd been jerking off, in a rather business-like manner, once, a couple of months ago, onto a letter addressed to Dr Harihara Kapila, his once-upon-a-time boss, he had been slowed down momentarily by the thought that forensic science could pretty easily trace his spunk back to him. Then he had recalled with a guffaw, *Hell, don't be silly, not our policemen*—and that very day, had posted off two more billets doux, one to one of the constables who was most often on night duty in the sentry-box at the gate of his Residence, the other to Madna's Police Superintendent.

For close to decades now, by and large, only sex-related statements had registered with Raghupati—that is to say, at official meetings and so on, he sat up in his seat, pricked up his ears, or blinked slowly, many times, only when a stray word or phrase, expression or idiom, hinted at, or suggested, the sexual. For example:

'Despite good rainfall, the production of rape in Pirtana this season has been poor, sir.'

'The trainees at our Industrial Institutes do not have even tools to get the hang of things with, sir.'

And,

'This is conduct unbecoming of a civil servant, sir.'

On his good days, when Raghupati was being bright as a button, it could be said that to him, everything sounded, looked, smelt, tasted and felt like sex. Experienced subordinates, when they wished him to focus on a topic, would use an appropriate idiom: 'VD's on the rise, sir, amongst the young of Ranamati, because of the improved irrigation in the area.' Button-bright Raghupati would correctly interpret this remark to mean: Better irrigation = richer sugarcane yield = more money = profligacy.

Aroused, keyed up, overheated, day in day out, round the clock, week upon week, like a mythic punishment that felt like a reward, a rut that had dominated him every second of his past two decades and had shattered, amongst many other things, his marriage, transforming each pore of his tingling skin—or so it seemed—into a hard-on. That is to say, twenty-three years in the service of the Welfare State had cracked him up. Its waste, inefficiency, sluggishness and futility had honed his sense of time running out at the speed of light and thereby sharpened as well his consequent excitation that was half-foreboding. Twice, sometimes three times, a day he would summon his PA Shobha just to paw her; at home, he'd rub against his dog or Chamundi—he'd always, with the approval of Baba Mastram, lined up someone, a sweeperess, a driver's daughter, a gardener. No backlash could sting him if he abused the right people. No backlash could sting him if he knew the right people—and indeed, himself remained one of them.

His sensualism was legend, of course, but officially, in all his years, he hadn't suffered any disciplinary action except for his frequent transfers—each to a post of substantial clout, patronage and personal gain, angled for with ferocious concentration and guile for months on end; from Deputy Director (Information and Public Relations), he'd moved to being Regional Joint Secretary (Home Affairs, Police Personnel); after four crucial years as Private Secretary to the Chief Minister (the eight-month-long wheedling for which had been so intense, so focused, as to be almost sexual), he'd arranged to become the Managing Director of the State Industrial Development Corporation; he'd spent two years as the Zonal Development Coordinator because he'd needed pretexts to officially wander up and down the West Coast states looking for nice tracts of land to invest in; when he'd learnt of these hectares south of Pirtana that were being developed as teak farms, he'd begun lobbying to become

Settlement Commissioner but just then, the government—his government—had fallen.

Totally befitting its waste and futility—Raghupati'd felt when he'd been Liaison Commissioner at the Centre—that the Welfare State, out of its contingency funds, had even forked out for the occasional prostitute that he'd slept with. They'd been organized by his Personal Assistant of those days, Satish Kalra, a Man Friday whose resourcefulness and amorality any Navi Chipra smuggler-builder would've been proud of. The expenditure on those encounters with the whores—a salesgirl from Mallika Arcade, a telephone operator from Aflatoon Bhavan, a part-time compounder from a private blood bank—had been passed off as having been incurred on liaison meetings with other state governments, on tea, Marie biscuits and so on.

Fondling himself, Raghupati coldly recollected that the part-time compounder had hinted—simperingly, with just a veneer of obsequiousness—that she'd be ready to forgo the fees for her visits of an entire year in return for permanent employment in any lowly capacity, in any of the several reserved categories of jobs, in any of the million warrens of the government.

'Don't be idiotic, I can't take a bribe from you.' Outraged, yet close to laughter, and at the same time obscurely aroused by the notion that he'd periodically possessed, squeezed and nibbled a body which'd all the while hidden a mind so plebeian, socially so inferior that the ultimate that it could aspire to were the drying-up dugs of the Welfare State.

She'd claimed that her name was Tina, and that she came from Mayong, in the North-East. She'd been short and cute, with wiry, shoulder-length, rather dirty hair. She'd always carried condoms in the zipped side pocket of her handbag, an indication of her preparedness that he'd liked. She'd looked sceptical about his outrage and had forthwith stopped scissoring his waist (his 'solid waste' is what DIPRAVED Kapila had always called it: 'learn to manage your solid waste, I say') with her shapely, hairy legs.

'Look, as per BOOBZ, there's a complete ban on all new recruitment, no matter which Department or Ministry, Centre or regional government.' He'd then rocked her a couple of times with his hips, to distract her from her silly conversation and get her back to work.

'No, not in all Departments—there isn't any ban on the police, or in the emergency services, hospitals, firefighting.'

The Welfare State hadn't been paying her either for her views or for the mulish determination that'd changed her face, and he hadn't cared for the ease with which she'd stopped calling him 'Sir' or 'Saab' in bed, so he'd rammed into her for another fifteen seconds, and then declared in farewell, 'You know, our country's not progressing because of people like you only.'

The following week, she'd sent him the first of her two anonymous letters on the subject of employment in the government. She'd signed both *Tina Munim*, but since that hadn't been her actual name, he'd considered the petitions to be simply two more in the endless list of unsigned letters received every week in numberless offices across the land.

The language of the letter had been the usual gibberish and the matter naive suggestions on how best she herself could fill up any of the vacancies in various posts reserved for candidates from the Scheduled Castes, Scheduled Tribes, Depressed Castes, Backward Clans, Suppressed Groups, Repressed Classes and Other Underprivileged Phratries. She'd attached her c.v., a page of preposterous lies.

He'd been stupefied. As always at such moments, blood had rushed not to his head, but to his crotch . The pages in his lap'd begun to dance in his twitching hands. Controlled by passions larger than himself, he'd unzipped his pants and tucked the sheets in between balls and tool. He'd come first over the c.v. During the second coming, God had hollered in his skull, 'Yes! This, this is what you've longed to do for years on every memo, note, receipt, reminder, report, paper, statement, return, application, minute, annexure and file! Yes, blobs of spunk on dust and cockroach shit! On an obsequious, hand-written, illegible, incoherent submission of a debatable claim, supported by a sheet of lies about the claimant's life! When someone grovels for your favour and you can jerk off on his entreaty—that is shakti! If there be Paradise on earth, it is this, it is this, it is this.'

Kumari Lina Natesan and her complaint remained on Raghupati's mind all day. 'Her conduct is unbecoming of a civil servant,' he grumbled to his PA Shobha. 'Please connect me to the Regional Principal Secretary, Personnel—and give me the line *before* his PA gives *him* the line, okay?'

Dr Harihara Kapila had recently taken over as the Regional Principal Secretary, Personnel. Raghupati had to endure his wit for the first five minutes before he could circuitously enquire what had become of his devious efforts to have Miss Natesan transferred, however temporarily, to Madna on plague duty. His question led only to a second explosion of KJs—'the conduct of a civil servant is unbecoming, I say, only when he can't rise to the occasion!'—(a KJ was the Civil Service epithet for the Kapila Joke. Rebel wits had even mooted once, at one of the quieter meetings of the Civil Service Association, that the State should frame a KJEA, an Endurance Allowance payable to those lionhearts who worked with Kapila).

On with the day. Raghupati summoned Moolar, one of his few Assistant Commissioners, to direct him to find out everything about mobile phones and to organize two for his official use. Moolar clacked his dentures in agreement and left. He was an efficient man.

Raghupati had known him for seventeen years, from his tenure as District Development Officer in Tekdigaon, the waters of which region had been reputed to be so full of harmful minerals that no native inhabitant had retained his teeth beyond the age of thirty-five. He believed that he'd never forget the vision of his first mammoth crop-cutting-training meeting there, during which, after lunch, dozens and dozens, row after row, of patwaris, Circle Inspectors, Block Development Officers and tehsildars (including Moolar), almost as one, had removed their dentures and rinsed them in the glasses of water in front of them.

'The mobile phone system hasn't yet reached Madna, sir,' Moolar reported half an hour later. His upper denture threatened to leap out and he paused to restrain it. 'At present, mobile phones can be used only at the Centre and some of the regional capitals, sir.'

Raghupati had always been alert to God's communications with him. Of course, you fool, you're being told to gift Baba Mastram not a phone, but a set of dentures. The present would also hopefully take care of the Baba's halitosis, usually a lethal deterrent to any sustained intercourse with him. Raghupati hoped that Mastram'd be pleased.

He was delighted. In return, on Thursday, just before he left for his second session with the dentist, he advised Raghupati that he could now go ahead with Chamundi.

'This week, sir, is propitious for the transfer of your heat energy to anyone with whom your skin is in physical contact. If you don't transfer, your surplus heat energy, finding no outlet, might attack your vitals.'

During lunch-hour, in his puja room, naked and elated, with his tool rising like a beast from sleep, Raghupati simpered at Chamundi, grasped the nape of his neck and dragged his head down towards his crotch. The boy, quick like an eel, jerked his head away. Blood swamped Raghupati's reason. He thwacked the boy's nose with the back of his hand. He was both inflamed by the jolted expression on Chamundi's face and moved by the blood that began to dribble out of his nostrils. A half-thought muddled him for a second—this was karma, whatever had this jewel of the sewers done to deserve this? An arousing pity made him fumble with the buttons of Chamundi's half-pants, and then with the worn elastic of his peculiar, mustard-coloured wearunder. The boy remained will-less, spellbound like a prey before its predator while Raghupati sat down on the edge of the pedestal of an idol of Ganesh and tugged Chamundi to him by his penis. A shaved pubes the colour of toffee and a black, fat tool. He tweaked back its foreskin and didn't notice the rich rings of crud beneath it before his tongue slithered out to tease the pink head.

Aaaaaarrgghhhhhhh. The pong of Chamundi's penis flung him back against Ganesh. Ggrrraaaaaaghhhhhhh. He wanted to vomit. His mouth, his nostrils, his tongue reeked of the accumulated smegma of weeks, months. He glanced up at the boy. Behind the blood on his face lurked a simper of nervous embarrassment. While getting up, almost mechanically, Raghupati picked up the brass incense stand and lashed out at Chamundi's nose. The boy staggered back, stumbled, cracked his skull against the wall and slumped to the floor, where he remained in a heap, still. Blood started to trickle out from his curly hair. Raghupati lurched out of the puja room.

In the bathroom, he gargled with Listerine for a minute or two. Bit by bit, as the smell of the mouthwash overpowered the stench of smegma and whatever-else-it'd-been, his rage shrivelled up and his sanity returned to him. While contemplating himself in the mirror, instinctively pulling in his tummy and puffing out his tits, he continued to mutter to himself, 'Cleanliness before godliness . . . These leeches of the Welfare State . . . Discharge your dues to your creator . . .' and other such disconnected phrases.

Exhausted, with the tang of Listerine now burning his tongue, he shambled across to his bedside table for paan masala. Abruptly, he remembered a vignette from the days when he'd been Assistant Collector at Koltanga. His neighbour in the Civil Lines Colony had been a doctor whose name he for the moment couldn't recall, a trainee at the local Primary Health Centre who had whiled many of their evenings away with tales of horror culled from his daily routine.

'The sarpanch swaggered into the Health Centre this morning without his goons. I was surprised to see him alone. He had two subjects to discuss with me, he said. One concerned the conduct of his cousin, a frightful drunkard who, the evening before last, had implored his wife, an Anganwadi worker and the family's single wage-earner, for some more cash for hooch and'd been refused; in a frenzy, he'd snatched up their two-year-old daughter and hurled her down on the ground. The child's skull'd split open like a pomegranate. The sarpanch wanted me to say in my post-mortem report that she'd died of Japanese encephalitis. He'd already taken care of the witnesses. They wished to stay on in their village, he said.

' "I'm sure that you can work out the details," he added graciously, "meanwhile, I've this other problem—" and he lifted up his kurta, tucked it under his chin, and hoisted up both his dhoti and his drawers to exhibit to me a penis the foreskin of which wouldn't retract.

'Raghupati Saab, the Welfare State must launch, on a war footing, the new IRHBTFP, Integrated Rural Hygiene Beneath the Foreskin Programme; as Assistant Collector, you must propose this revolutionary scheme to both the Departments of Health and of Rural Development. The logo for the project could be the rubber nipple of an infant's feeding bottle and the slogan, *Are YOU Sterilized Enough to Be Sucked?* Do you suppose that our Muslim brethren would protest against the programme on the grounds that it'd rather shrewdly route huge funds towards non-Muslims alone?' Dr Srinivas Chakki had then sighed. 'Development is a tricky business.'

Just then, the Mutesh cassette ran out. Raghupati welcomed the silence because it'd help him to think. He plodded back to the puja room. Chamundi hadn't stirred. The blood beneath his forehead, though, had clotted. The offending penis, Raghupati noted, was now dried up, black and sad. Chamundi was innocent and sleek in coma, unless he was dead, in which case he was innocent, sleek and problematic. Should he feel his pulse, Raghupati asked himself, or his bum? All at once, his bedside phone buzzed, loud and harsh; it never failed to make him jump.

He frowned, looking back through the doorway of the puja room at the phone. This was unbelievable. He'd instructed Murari and that lot a hundred times that he was *never* to be disturbed during his meditation. For them, never meant twice a week. The phone buzzed again. He strode across to it in a fury.

'Sorry to bother, sir, but Honourable Collector of Madna on the line, most urgent, sir.' Murari pushed the extension button down before Raghupati could start his abuse.

'Hello . . . hahn . . . Mr Raghupati? . . . Good afternoon, sir, this is Agastya Sen, how are you? . . . I'm sorry that I haven't yet been able to call on you, sir and I was wondering if I could later this afternoon . . . How kind of you, thank you . . . nothing that can't wait—except that it's driving me up the wall and preventing me from discharging my duties calmly and objectively . . . one can't, you know, from near the ceiling . . . I gather that you also handle Divisional Accounts, sir . . . it's a matter of the Travelling Advance that I took from my earlier office, of two thousand rupees for the train journey to Madna . . . the Accounts Officer here at the Collectorate tells me that I have to pay back to the government the bank interest that I might have earned on the Advance for the period that I didn't use it to buy my train ticket with . . . Yes, sir, only you can waive it . . . *waive* sir, as in—or rather, *not* as in wand, sea and hair . . . would four-thirty be fine, sir? I have some kind of inspection at the Madna International Hotel at five . . . Thank you, sir . . . Good-bye.'

THE MAGIC OF THE AFLATOONS

The Madna International is a decent-enough hotel and the only fully air-conditioned one in town. Winter—when its air-conditioning is likelier to be functional because the Electricity Board traditionally restricts its nine-hour power cuts to peak summer—is usually a popular season of the year with visitors who have work in the satellite factories, quarries and paper mills that dot the district. Usually, but not this year—perhaps because of the plague. For whatever reason, Rajani Suroor and the players of *Vyatha* found rooms at the International quite easily, even at a concession. Its proprietor, Dinkar Sathe, has always been accommodating, almost philanthropic, with all representatives of the government. Suroor was practically one—an agent, certainly, even if not an official representative—for more than one reason. The amount of money that *Vyatha* procured from various branches of the government, for instance, to diffuse through its street theatre diverse statements of official policy, and the ease with which it milked the State were both impressive. So was the facility, the rapidity with which doors in high places opened for Suroor. Government, of course, Sathe understood to mean power; whether legitimate or illicit didn't bother him. Its representatives therefore included any one who could wave the wand that—poof!—made obstacles disappear. Thus in his eyes, Sukumaran Govardhan, for example, the lord of the illegal traffic of the Madna jungles, could well be the Minister for Forests and Environment—though considerably more powerful.

Because of his faith in the wand of power, its wielders, whether permanently in office or temporarily in jail, were for Dinkar Sathe akin to magicians. Illusionists, tricksters, larger-than-life distracters, the best of them were on the ball, knew exactly what was going on—who could be milked for how much and for what in return—and enacted their roles with more gusto and skill than Suroor's roving players. Naturally, since they earned infinitely more for their pains.

All would agree that Madna's first magician is Bhanwar Virbhim, ex-Chief Minister of the region and soon-to-be Cabinet Minister at the Centre. Dinkar Sathe has known him for about two decades, has observed him climb with mounting deference, has liberally contributed to both his personal and party coffers on more than one occasion and has received in return, over the years, diverse significant concessions and favours—the first bar licence in the town, the permission to add two floors to his hotel despite the existence of stringently prohibitive Municipal laws, a plot of land, at a throwaway price, that had originally been reserved for a children's park, the suppressing of an unusually accurate and dreadfully embarrassing story in the local press about bonded labour on his teak farm, the protecting of his cartoonist brother from the fury of Virbhim's son over a series of devastating lampoons, and so on. Even though Virbhim has performed for the past few years increasingly at the Centre, he and Sathe keep in touch, naturally, because Madna is the Minister's patrimony.

His only son too, Makhmal Bagai, is well known to Sathe and is a frequent visitor at the International. Neither father nor son has retained his original caste-revealing surname for the obvious reason that for the legerdemain of politics, one travels light. En route, they have picked up, like a thousand others before them, whichever names they've liked the sounds of. It is standard practice in the Welfare State. Indeed, its best example would be the nation's extended first family, the Aflatoons.

They aren't one family at all, certainly not in the sense of being linked to one another by blood and genealogy. A couple of hundred years ago, a migrant family from the North-West—origins unknown—did settle down at Aflatoonabad and engage itself in one of the two professions traditional to that town—the confectioner's, the other being, of course, the conjuror's. Across the generations, some of its descendants did take to public life—the names Pashupati, Ghatotkach, Trimurti, Prabhakar, come readily to mind—but they would account for only a fraction of all the Aflatoons after whom have been named the thousands of buildings, monuments, institutions, gardens, shopping arcades, residential areas, stadiums, community toilets and other public places of the land.

The reason is quite simple—and rather peculiar to the Welfare State. At various significant moments in the history of the nation, both before and after its cataclysmic independence from colonial rule, in different regions of the country, any able aspirant to political power, quite early in his career—and overnight—simply became an Aflatoon. Documentation collectively being both the backbone and the memory of the Welfare State—it being altogether a different matter that individually considered, each one of those files, records, statements and accounts is as flimsy and fleeting, as fickle and provisional, as a used wrapper in a gale—documentation being paramount, each political hopeful produced at the right time, like a rabbit out of a hat, the required proof of identity—a hospital record, a school certificate, a Municipal extract, a court entry. Lo and behold, yet another Aflatoon! Except that at the moment of the manifestation of the new magician, there usually stood by no audience to witness the miracle because one doesn't come by audiences that cheaply, not even in an overcrowded country. However, by the time that the parvenu Aflatoon, of whichever political hue, came to be noticed in Municipal, district and regional circles, a decade or so would have passed and the assumed name would have become as snug as a second skin—peelable, of course, in moments of grave crises.

Bhanwar Virbhim, for instance, had once been an Aflatoon and it was rumoured of Sukumaran Govardhan too (not to forget Makhmal Bagai, who a couple of times had toyed with the notion as with a gun, but had been sternly rebuked on each occasion by his father for even thinking of tarnishing a fair name by adopting it). Compelling caste factors—votes, in brief, 'national emergencies', to use Virbhim's own compelling phrase—had guided him in his choice of various aliases. In general, he had picked wisely, having become Chief Minister of the regional government twice and between the two tenures, Deputy Minister for Information at the Centre.

However, ambitious and astute that he was, he did sometimes wonder whether in the long run, he'd played well his cards—and indeed, whether for him the game was over—because in the seven decades since Independence, the nation's sixteen Prime Ministers had all been Aflatoons.

These Aflatoons popping up, time after time, like boils all over the country—what did the original first family think of them? Not much, really. In the first place, it wasn't even certain of its own existence; however could it have the collective strength of purpose to reflect on and reject these obscure, small-town, provincial pretenders? It questioned itself but rarely; when it did, its examination was myopic. No two family members could agree on which line of descent constituted the main trunk of its tree—it couldn't possibly be Tirupati's, for instance, for his eldest had in the early twenties decamped with his Chinese masseuse and apparently died utterly content running his restaurant in Hong Kong. A trunk after all has to be rock-like, solidly respectable. We are a banyan tree, asserted those of the clan that could be bothered; with the years we spread and thrust down new trunks. In the vast area that we provide shade to (and in which in general we prevent any vegetation of worth from growing), it is quite possible that now and then some bastard sapling, resilient, doughty, survives to attain a respectable height and indeed, with time, comes to resemble one of our offshoots. Doubtless because it has imbibed some of our qualities, some—if you permit—of our magic.

Thursday evening. In the fifty-by-forty lobby of the Madna International Hotel, the players of *Vyatha*, some ten in all, led by their deputy, lounge about, awaiting Rajani Suroor's return from his round of the offices of some of the senior bureaucrats of the district. Headless, the players have spent the day roaming around the town, avoiding certain localities like the plague, searching for alternative sites for their shows. They now quaff tea before the TV, placed at a loose end by the day-and-night cricket match on it having been interrupted first by a duststorm and then, more permanently, by acts of arson in the stands.

Makhmal Bagai and Suroor arrive simultaneously at the hotel. Suroor is in the private taxi that he's hired for the duration of his stay in Madna, a sad, dusty, hot, noisy, off-white Ambassador, Bagai in his lorry-like Tata Safari, steel-grey, black-glassed, air-conditioned, monstrous. It augurs ill for Suroor that his Ambassador doesn't realize that it has to allow the Safari to precede it up the fifteen metres to the porch; Suroor moreover debouches and mounts the steps without so much as a backward glance. The third thing that puts Bagai off is that the single parking space available under the porch has been taken up by the one kind of vehicle that he cannot dislodge, an official car, again an off-white Ambassador but this one altogether from a different planet—gleaming, with wraparound sun glasses, an aerial, a siren and a large crimson light on its forehead.

The fourth thing that miffs Bagai is that Dinkar Sathe

doesn't receive him in the lobby. Indeed, no one does. In contrast, a large gang has abandoned the TV and is milling around that long-haired joker from that seedy car. 'See to things,' Bagai commands one of his cohorts who, smirking in anticipation, stalks off towards the reception counter. From where, a few minutes later, he returns, looking apprehensive.

'No one's available, Prince. The Collector of Madna dropped by on a surprise inspection and everyone's scurrying around after him.'

Bagai subsided into a sofa and glanced across at Suroor smiling intelligently at whatever his Deputy was telling him. On an impulse, he snapped his fingers at and beckoned to him. To his horror, Suroor, continuing to smile intelligently, snapped his fingers at and beckoned to him right back. Somewhat at a loss, Bagai then took out from his kurta pocket his father's gun, a .22, and aimed it at Suroor's face. 'Prince, no!' hissed a cohort in panic. Suroor, dramatic to the last, acted out being shot and with a moan and a hand over his heart, toppled back into the sofa behind him, perhaps to avoid further conversation with the Deputy.

'Find out who he is and whether he knows who I am.' Without enthusiasm, a cohort shuffled off in Suroor's direction.

Bagai weighed the gun in his hand. It was terribly unmanly to take it out, wave it about and finally not to use it, particularly when everybody was gaping at it. Both depressed and nervous, he placed it between his thighs on the sofa and covered it with the end of his kurta. To the female attendant who timorously tripped up to him to repeat that the entire hotel merely awaited the Collector's departure to focus all its attention on Bagai's wishes and to add that until then, whether there was anything in particular that he and his companions wanted, he calmly said, 'Ice cream.'

'Of course sir.' She was short, dark and pretty, in a sari of green and gold. 'Which flavours would you like?'

She was not servile enough. She spoke her few English phrases too facilely. She didn't look as though she was physically being attracted to him. She was about to spark off his notorious frightening temper. 'Who are you, Madam, to ask me questions? Why do you lie when you claim to know who I am? Has not the hotel been instructed time and again to phone my house every weekend to find out whether I'm free and likely to drop in with my friends for a drink, a snack or dinner? Yet nobody calls!' He had raised his voice and begun to glare at her but he would have preferred in the circumstances to deal with a male attendant. With a man—waiter, steward or porter-bouncer-concierge-lobby manager—he could in a matter of seconds begin his reviling, his pushing in the chest and cuffing about the head, his glancing over his shoulder to see if he was impressing any females in the vicinity with his manliness, his refusal to let an imagined insult slip by, his concern for, and support of the social order.

'Tutti-frutti-vanilla, sir?'

'And after the Collector leaves, whiskey,' suggested Suroor, beaming with confidence in his own endearing ways. He'd returned with the cohort and stood beside Bagai's sofa. He thrust out a hand. 'I had certainly been hoping to meet you during our stay in Madna.'

Makhmal was confused. Almost in reflex, he lifted up his kurta and retrieved his gun. He didn't like in the least the way things were unfolding. In a typical soiree at the International, within the first fifteen minutes, after the hotel staff had scampered about enough to appease him, the beers would've arrived and been rejected for not being chilled—and the pakodas for not being spicy—enough; a succession of hotel staff (in increasing order of importance) would've tried, as in a vignette out of myth, to pacify his anger. In the midst of the mess, sullenly munching, quaffing and eyeing a female receptionist or two, stone-deaf to the entreaties of, say, a

Chief Food and Beverages Manager, he, having learnt a trick or two from his father, would've played the caste card. It had never failed to thicken any plot. He'd've fixed his maroon eyes on the Manager of the moment and mumblingly accused some other hotel employee of having affronted his, Makhmal's, caste; how would never be made clear and in the circumstances wasn't required to be. It would've been in very bad taste to enquire—and moreover, not of much use, since over the years, the wide canvas of politics had compelled Bhanwar Virbhim and his family to own up to, and feel responsible for, a thousand castes. I am the voice of the downtrodden, I am the soul of *all* the depressed, backward, repressed, suppressed and unrecognized castes. Any imagined insult to *any* of those millions is an arrow in my heart. No matter *what* that poor innocent hotel employee might have thought behind his tits or expressed in his eyes, it insulted me. I *know* it, because caste is in the marrow of my bones, just as it is in his and in yours. You might want to shush it away and get on with it into the next millennium, but you won't go very far without having to return for it. It is integral to our lives and our state; however can you dream of welfare without understanding caste?

'Careful with your rod, prince,' warned a cohort. 'It's more potent than acid in their faces.'

Makhmal giggled. He loved filthy talk. He preferred it to sex. For him, in fact, filthy talk *was* sex. Ever since that genius Rani Chandra had thought up and launched her *Listen to Love* series of CDs and cassettes, and Bhupen Raghupati had gifted him a box set of them on his joining his father's political party, he, Makhmal, had lost interest in ogling, abducting and molesting the women on the streets of Madna. Instead, with a Walkman in his lap and headphones in place, he, calm of mind, all passion spent, had begun to beatifically wave, through the windows of the Tata Safari, at all the women that his motorcade had ploughed past. When the windows had been down, startled, puzzled, some of them had even waved back.

Makhmal was short, pale and soft. He had long, elaborately fluffed-up hair, hooded eyes and a thick moustache that half-hid pink lips and a gap-toothed mouth. At the age of thirteen, he'd failed his Fifth Standard school exams for the third time in a row and in passing, knifed his Social Studies teacher in the Teachers Only toilet. The Teachers Only had been the only toilet in the school with an intact mirror and young Makhmal had been in front of it, combing, inspecting and recombing his hair. For him, these moments of self-examination had always demanded extra concentration. Unfortunately—particularly for the teacher—Social Studies had peremptorily interrupted him—with a thwack on the back of his head—at the very moment when he'd been trying to get a lock to swing down over his forehead and flip back across his ear.

His conduct in general was one of the reasons why his father found it crucial to have as Madna's Police Superintendent an officer that he could trust. Over the years—first, when Bhanwar Virbhim had been an intelligent, ambitious, determined, ageing, frightful hoodlum, and later, when he'd risen, in stages, to become a Member of the Legislative Assembly, then Member of Parliament, Regional Minister, Guardian Minister, Principal Minister, Chief Minister and finally Central Deputy Minister—over the years, the outrageousness of Makhmal's offences against society and the law had kept pace with his father's increasing clout. It was almost as though the insecure son needed to continually test the range of the influence of the father.

It is one of the functions of the munificence, the kindness, of the Welfare State to allow within it the worst rogues to become utterly respectable. It is the macro view, the Hindu view. All is Maya, Salvation lies in Forgiveness, *Da, Dayadhvam, Damyata.* Thus a murderer like Bhanwar Virbhim could rise to be Central Cabinet Minister. Thus another killer, a depraved near-rapist like Makhmal could notify his candidature for a seat in the Regional Assembly from the constituency of Madna. Upon his announcement, the *Dainik* had asked him whether his criminal record would embarrass him in his political career.

'Not at all. Why? Look at our Parliament. One hundred and seventy-four Honourable Members have criminal records. I think that you want the State to discriminate against criminals exactly the way in which it discriminates against the lower castes. What is your caste by the way, may I know? We are innocent until proved guilty. Our Freedom Fighters went to jail, so you can say that they too have criminal records. Learn to give the downtrodden a chance to rise, to make good. Only then can the nation become great. May I have your card, please . . .?'

Near-rapist because Makhmal ejaculated too early. To prevent him from becoming depressed and therefore even more violent, wise Baba Mastram had pointed out to him that he was fortunate in that he could release his energy on all the women that he saw without being caught out by any subsequent silly medical examination of the victim. The idea elated him and kept him going for years on end. Not a thinking man. His modus operundee (a terrible, tasteless bilingual pun there, Bhupen Raghupati's, of course—*rundee* being Hindustani for whore) was to cruise the poorer quarters of Madna for flesh, snatch 'n grab off the streets, maul the mammaries of in the air-conditioned Tata Safari for half a minute or so (till he Miltoned, as it were), thrust between them a fifty- or a hundred-rupee note and shove out the possessor of a few kilometres down the road, shocked, in tears, but richer. Modus Operundee had stopped with Rani Chandra. Raghupati had suggested to Bhanwar Saab that the Ministry of Culture recommend Rani Chandra for the Revered Silver Lotus, the ninth-highest honour of the land, for her

Commitment to the Improvement of the Quality of Life. Bhanwar Virbhim hadn't responded. He never did. Silence was wisdom and energy conservation and took you places.

Uncertain about whom to shoot—Rajani Suroor or the female attendant in green and gold, and tense because uncertain, diffident about whether to fire at all, unsure whether everybody in the lobby was openly or secretly laughing at him, whether he'd impressed even one soul, and growing more peeved by the second, Makhmal Bagai lifted and aimed his .22 right between the faces of his two potential targets at a wall clock on a pillar some twenty feet away. He liked that Suroor had stopped smiling but nevertheless felt that that wasn't enough.

'Chocolate walnut chip, sir?'

'Stop flashing your rod, Prince. I think the Collector's on his way down.'

So was Makhmal's gun arm when in witless relief, Suroor's smirk reappeared. So Makhmal pulled the trigger. 'You rat,' he grunted beneath the bang; an epitaph of sorts for a strolling player in a small town unofficially beset by the plague.

Rodents and firearms feature as well in Miss Lina Natesan's memorandum, for they are equally prominent elements of the official life in Aflatoon Bhavan. We kick off at Page 7 of her novella.

Last Wednesday, when I entered my office chamber at 8.59 a.m., I smelt a rat.
In our chamber at that time, there were two. I do not believe that Shri Dastidar and I have any quarrel with each other. On the very first day of our professional relationship, I dispatched to him a note stating my

terms of reference: All communications with the undersigned, I represented to him, must of necessity be formal, official and recorded; there was neither scope nor need for informal exchanges in our chamber. I must add here that he understood my position immediately and admirably. We exchange memos infrequently but they are invariably terse and to the point. For example:

To
Junior Administrator (Under Training)

From
Under Secretary (Gajapati Aflatoon Centenary Celebrations, Our Endangered Tribal Heritage and Demotic and Indigenous Drama)

Good Afternoon. While you were out for five minutes or so before lunch, I received on my extension number an obscene phone call for you. The caller was keen to have *your* extension number, so I gave him Nilesh's. He snorted on hearing it—perhaps it was Nilesh himself. Otherwise, all is well, by the grace of Allah.

However, I should point out here that our exchanges are easier for him because he has personal staff. He just has to buzz for his peon and order him to summon his stenographer, to whom he dictates his memo. He was gracious enough in one of his very early notes to offer me the services of his personal staff, but naturally I had to refuse. The offices of the Welfare State do not run on charity. I have consistently maintained that there are limits to welfare.
In fairness to Shri Dastidar, he did formally seek my permission (in a beautifully-phrased note) before he started his tai-chi exercises in our room. I suspect that it was his tai-chi that spurred him to evict with such zeal the furniture of all our ex-colleagues from our

chamber. Since Stores did not help us in the least, Shri Dastidar and his peon, a crafty, middle-aged shirker called Dharam Chand, dumped those cupboards and racks in the adjacent Gents' Toilet.
The notes that we exchanged last Wednesday were, in brief, as follows:

I smell a rat. Any ideas?
I smell a rat all the time. It is the odour of corruption. Which particular file do you have in mind?

I should add here—parenthetically, as it were—that because Shri Dastidar firmly believes that every file and paper in the Welfare State stinks, he has levered out of Stores six rubber stamps to push all his official papers, memos, notes, minutes, reports, statements, documents and files around with. They are:

1) Please examine.
2) Please re-examine.
3) Please put up.
4) Please link up with previous papers.
5) Please process
6) Please forward with compliments to—

However, to continue with the events of last Wednesday. I set about whisking and rearranging the dust on my table. Pretty soon, I unearthed a dead rat the size of a small cat in the second drawer.

'A plague upon thee, Madam Junior Administrator!' *ran Shri Dastidar's note.*

For this crime and for several others, I suspect Shri Dastidar's peon, Shri Dharam Chand. The fellow has no manners and does not like women. I have requested Shri Dastidar a million times (in writing, of course) to instruct him to knock on the door before he enters but to no avail. Each time, he buffets the door open; it slams against the side wall and brings down some plaster while he dramatically pauses in the doorway to leer at me before sliding in like a fat snake. I surmise that Shri Dharam Chand disapproves of me because he stood to gain in the only file that I have received in my tenure here, the proposal of which I rejected because of its patent absurdity.

The Department had mooted that seven of its peons be paid an Overtime Allowance of twenty-four rupees a day for the months of August, September and October. For what? I had asked and sent the file back.

The file returned the same afternoon (Overtime files move like lightning) with some bilge-like explanation. Shri Dharam Chand, who was the file carrier, clarified to me that after office closed at 5.30 p.m., he always drifted over to the Minister's office to help with the work there.

I cross-examined him for close to an hour and learnt that he—along with the like-minded hopefuls that would've benefitted from the Overtime proposal had it slipped past Ms Argus the Undersigned—had been trying for the last six months for a transfer to the Minister's office. And how had they been trying? When the Minister, along with his Private Secretary, Officer on Special Duty, Personal Assistant, four Black Guard Commando Bodyguards, one daftary, one naik and three peons would debouch from his chambers to waddle the hundred feet to the lift, Shri Dharam Chand & Co., bowing and scraping to the Minister's heraldic peons in the first row of the cortège, would shoo stragglers out of its path even as the heralds were shooing them *out of theirs. Then, with heads bowed and buttocks projected at the right sycophantic angles, they—the Overtimers—would wait, grimacing with tension at the mere glimpse of power, beside the lifts until their doors shut. Then they would all careen down the stairs from the fourth to the ground floor to*

gape at the Minister and some of the riff-raff jam themselves into three white Ambassador cars. Car doors slamming shut one after the other like gunfire, sirens wailing, red lights flashing on car roofs, horns honking at the heavens to command them not to dare let their attention stray, hooray, they're off and away! Then, by degrees, a profound, welcome peace would descend on Aflatoon Bhavan. Shri Dharam Chand would blink, wake up and tot up his Overtime for that day.
I had asked Shri Dharam Chand on that occasion whether he had any idea how much the Minister's trips from his chambers to his cars alone cost the Welfare State every day and whether he, Shri Dharam Chand, felt no qualms at all about adding to that daily expenditure of over four hundred thousand rupees.

While on the subject, I should like to draw the attention of your good self to my representation at Annexure O wherein, inter alia, I have objected to the grave lapses in conduct of the Black Guard Commando bodyguards of our Minister. On more than one occasion, when I have either been striding to or coming away from the Ladies' Toilet on the fourth floor, which is two doors away from the Minister's rooms, I have had them brusquely waving their automatic weapons at me. I presume that that is not their customary way of saying Good Morning. On each occasion, I have ticked them off for conduct unbecoming with, and before, a Junior Administrator of the Welfare State, but they don't seem to understand any language. Instead, they vigorously prodded me aside with their guns. Undeterred, with my back against the wall, I continued to complain as the ministerial retinue approached me and then—wonder of wonders!—passed me by! However, I persisted in loudly pointing out to that group of processionally receding buttocks that if it permits a lady officer to be manhandled in the corridors of power in broad daylight, if it doesn't attend to the legitimate complaint of a Junior Administrator of the Welfare State, then—well—she is left with no recourse but to formally petition the higher authorities. My representation to the Prime Minister on the subject of the conduct of our Black Guard Commando bodyguards is at Annexure P.

Shri Dastidar frequently breakfasts in our room (He always invites me to join him but I usually decline). It is for this reason that large empty cartons of Kellogg's Breakfast Cereal (Wheatflakes. Whole Grain, Whole Nutrition) are freely available around his desk. Into one of these was stuffed the dead rat from the drawer. Shri Dharam Chand packed it quite professionally and we dispatched it to where it belonged, the office of the Municipal Commissioner, Madna. We feel that, for the time being, it can substitute for me.
We have sound precedents for our decision. The kind attention of your good self is drawn to a news item on the plague that appeared in The State of the Times *on December 3, a photocopy of which is placed at Annexure Q. The rats of Madna have not yet been tested because many of them, the newspaper reports, drowned in the recent floods. Many others have been, well, resettled along with the 1400 tonnes of garbage that is being lifted every day from the various quarters of the town. More to the point, since the hospitals, dispensaries and clinics in the district do not boast of all the medical facilities required to test for the plague and other similar epidemics, several other dead rats have been sent by post to Navi Chipra and New Killi for analysis. This interesting fact came to light at more than one post office in the country when, while sorting out mail, postmen began to complain of a breathtaking pong emanating from some of the packets. Several of*

the aggrieved postmen have gone on a lightning strike and till date, have refused to return to work until, to quote from their distributed memorandum, 'the State makes adequate provision for their welfare and safety from the plague.'

On the subject of their strike, the National Institute of Communicable Diseases has been approached by more than one newspaper to confirm whether the decision to remit by post dead rats all over the country has its approval. The Institute, however, has been silent on this and other issues for more than one week, perhaps because all its telephone lines are dead.

I would like to submit at this juncture that the dead telephone is emblematic of the quality and extent of communication between different Departments of the Welfare State. In this regard, the attention of your good self is drawn to the news item on Page 3 of yesterday's edition of The State of the Times *entitled:* Plague Patient on the Loose. *I quote:*

A 'definite' patient of pneumonic plague, according to the doctors of KLPD Hospital, is loose in the capital. He would have been in quarantine had the telephones of the Infectious Diseases Hospital at Swannsway Camp not been out of order.

A spokesman of KLPD stated last evening that a middle-aged man reported at the hospital on Saturday with all the 'classic symptoms' of the disease. He was diagnosed as having the plague by the doctors on duty but unfortunately, ran away while arrangements were being made to transfer him to Swannsway Camp.

Very little is known about the patient. His name is Chana Jor Garam Rai; he is a labourer from Bihar; he is now footloose in the city. He arrived from Madna on the Shatabdi Express on Saturday with a couple of friends. The train pulled in at about 7.30 p.m., that is, five hours late, so what's new. Shri Chana Jor Garam had been feverish for the past two days and was delirious for the entire train journey. A male Belgian tourist in the same compartment was galvanized into near-hysteria at the sight of the patient's delirium. Suspecting the worst, he immediately dusted himself and Shri Chana Jor with Gamaxene powder. He meant well.

Shri Chana Jor collapsed on the platform. His group had intended to carry on to their village in the Champaran district of Bihar and was infuriated because its plans had to be changed. The patient was taken to KLPD in a three-wheeler. The doctors there point out that all the hospitals in the capital have received instructions from the Ministry of Public Health not to take in any plague patient but instead to immediately dispatch them to the Infectious Diseases Hospital at Swannsway Camp. Therefore, they tried to contact the IDH to direct it to send its special vehicle meant for transporting plague patients. When they couldn't get through, the Medical Superintendent of KLPD, Dr L. Majnoo, decided to transfer Shri Chana Jor Garam to Swannsway Camp in one of their own hospital ambulances. However, while the vehicle was being lined up (repair the puncture, where's the damn driver?, try the self, push start the Neanderthal, go fill up some diesel), the patient and his friends slunk off in the three-wheeler that had all the while been waiting outside.

After his escape, KLPD Hospital officially decided to minimize its significance. Even though plainclothes men are on a twenty-four-hour lookout for Shri Chana Jor Garam at all the railway stations, no official red alert has yet been declared. 'But that is just a matter of time,' asserted one of the younger doctors of KLPD on the condition of anonymity, 'it cannot be otherwise; the patient had all the "classic symptoms" of the plague and had just arrived from Madna. What more proof does one need? I will burn my degrees in public if he doesn't have the disease.'

That will indeed be a small price to pay for the relief. That apart, it is needless to add here that the mood of the Emergencies Department at KLPD is feverish. With reason,

since Shri Chana Jor Garam was there for some time and might well have infected anything that he touched or exhaled upon. A sobering thought. Because of an acute, yet routine, shortage of the drug, the hospital staff has been dosed with tetracycline but not the patients.
In short, even though it is clear that the matter is being hushed up to avoid 'unnecessary panic,' get ready.

Tetracycline is difficult to come by in Madna as well. Overnight, its dealers and retailers have made it as rare a commodity as statesmanship and probity in public life. To distract himself from it, the Collector of Madna, Shri Agastya Sen, usually flits to any one of his several other insurmountable problems. They come in all sizes. Wishing to write a letter to his friend, Daya, in Navi Chipra, for instance, he asks Chidambaram, his Reader, 'Can I get some decent writing paper? Something I wouldn't be ashamed of?'

A late morning in winter beyond the enormous vaulted rooms of the office. From the stone corridor outside, from amongst the pigeons and the water coolers, drift in the rustle and shuffle, the occasional cough, of a hundred petitioners waiting to gnaw the Collector's ears with their diverse tales of tortuous, enervating injustice at the hands of a dozen different departments. The man-size windows are open and welcome in a variety of smells and the warm soporific air. They haven't had any electricity since the morning. Through the window on his right, Shri Sen can see, a hundred metres away, the compound wall of the Collectorate coming up. The premises had never had one and thus, every day for over a century, had welcomed, kept open house for, the cattle of the district. Generations of cows, bulls, calves, oxen and goats had come to love the grass and the off-white paper, the serenity and openness of the Collectorate compound. Pushing for the wall had been one of his predecessor's first acts on taking over the post some thirteen months ago. The wall was now two feet high, not likely to rise any further in that financial year and effective against everything but the urchins and the goats. The puzzled, disoriented cattle now wandered up and down Junction Road and into Aflatoon Maidan, holding up traffic and disturbing courting couples. The view from the window was silent and sunny, in spirit like a graveyard in an Ingmar Bergman film.

Shri Sen leans forward to note the comparison somewhere on his enormous desk for use in his letter to Daya. Meanwhile, a child, with his half-pants down to his knees, crosses his field of vision, hopping from spot to spot to look for paper to wipe his arse with. Madna faces an acute and chronic water shortage. The subject has been noted in Shri Sen's *To Do* list in his very first week in office.

The Collectorship of Madna is the seventh post that he has held in eight years. He is quite philosophic about the law that governs the transfer of civil servants; he sees it as a sort of corollary to the law of karma, namely, that the whole of life passes through innumerable and fundamentally mystifying changes, and these changes are sought to be determined by our conduct, our deeds (otherwise, we would quite simply lose our marbles); only thus can we even pretend to satisfactorily explain the mystery of suffering, which is a subject that has troubled thoughtful souls all over the world since time immemorial. It is also a hypothesis that justifies the manifest social inequalities of the Hindu community.

His *To Do* list is actually an enormous black diary full of cross-references and coded marginal scribbles. The cattle, for example, haven't been struck off yet; they've instead been relocated from April (that deals with problems pending within the Collectorate) to the September-to-December section (that is reserved for the police). The black diary is not the official diary of the Welfare State for that year. It was one of several gifted to Shri Sen in an eventful first week by various local businessmen, builders and industrialists. He chose it chiefly for its generosity of size and layout.

In the *official* diary of that year, he intends to maintain his dhobi account at home, which clothes sent, how many lost, how many torn, burnt, how much due, how much to deduct. The official diary was meant to have white pages and a chocolate-ish cover, but it looks more or less uniformly grey. It is carried about by the losers. Three million-plus copies are brought out every year by the Commissioner of Printing, Paper and Stationery for the Welfare State at a printing cost of a hundred rupees per copy. He employs three hundred thousand people and amongst other activities, supplies all the Departments of the State with, amongst other things, files, file covers, file boards, file boxes, notepads, envelopes and paper of dizzying sizes, sealing wax, pins, clips, tags, blotting paper and bottles of red, blue, green, black and blue-black ink. However, he cannot produce paper white and thick enough for Shri Sen when the latter wants to write to someone outside the Welfare State.

A pause in the day, in the never ending lurch from telephone call to unwelcome visitor to personal work to meeting to review to site inspection to social function to public puja to official inauguration to ghastly crisis to office files to telephone call. Just then, a goat looks in enquiringly at the window. It is a frequent visitor; it pops in sometimes to chew up some paper and crap between the almirahs. 'Fuck off, you,' orders the Collector. It does. This is power.

Every now and then in his career, once a week on the average, Shri Sen regrets his decision to join the topmost Civil Service of the country. On the other days, when he reflects, life outside the government appears tense-making, obsequious and fake. In contrast, within the Welfare State, he feels that he has at last begun to trip without acid—with his feet six inches above the ground, yet with an ear to it, walking tall, on a permanent high. There have been moments in the last eight years when he's caught himself thinking that he could quite easily have worked in the Welfare State for free. Of course, given his salary, he is doing almost just that.

Chidambaram sidles in at that point. Generally speaking, the more he sidles, the less welcome the news. 'Sir, milk-white paper not readily available in Stock, sir. I have sent the boy to Gaindamull's Stationery Mart on Junction Road, sir, to purchase . . . and there was a telephone call from the Circuit House, sir. Shri Bhootnath Gaitonde has left and is on his way here to meet you.'

All of a sudden, Shri Sen feels an urge to smoke a cigarette. He hasn't smoked even one in four years, but the desire still assails him every now and then. He manfully resists, remembering that he has the Welfare State to thank for helping him to kick the habit. For smoking and spitting paan all over the place have been banned by law in all the offices of the government. It is a regulation that Shri Sen has enforced with considerable enthusiasm and vigour, commanding the police to arrest and harass, in their own inimitable way, all offenders. The Welfare State has certainly helped the fascist in him to bloom.

As for dope, though governance couldn't wean him off it, it did manage to influence his mode of its intake. A Collector couldn't very well be seen rolling and puffing away at a joint, so he began to brew cannabis in his morning pot of tea and stuff pellets of hashish into his post-lunch paans. Paans were eminently Establishment—why, the Chief Revenue Divisional Commissioner had more than ten a day. He had a plastic wastebasket beneath his desk into which he periodically spat paan gob and residual cud (this disgusting habit was not an offence; if you kept your red paan spittle to yourself and your wastebasket, you were law-abiding).

Those in the know will corroborate that dope that enters one's bloodstream through one's stomach hits later, hits harder and stays longer than that through the lungs. Thus, in the course of his day, when Shri Sen wasn't on a permanent high, it could be presumed that he'd wandered further up—as it were, onto Cloud Nine. Moreover, during the past eight years, he'd discovered that cannabis and hashish, steadily imbibed, helped marvellously to lessen the pain and discomfort of his senselessly strenuous swimming and jogging sessions. Dope, he was convinced, was the antidote to much of the suffering of the civil servant. Thus, in his black diary, in the February section that was devoted to *Possible Ideas for Essays and Articles on the Welfare State*, he'd noted:

> *Cannabis and Piles: Didn't de Quincey and Sherlock Holmes have haemorrhoids? Please find out. Also, it is extraordinary how many civil servants have piles. In my eight years, I myself've met Kulmohan Singh, Killer Venkita, Shengupto, Singhvi and Tutreja. The Fellowship of the Rose. Surely sitting around on files can't be the cause. But how fascinating if there's a link.*

One of the challenges of his job that he'd particularly liked was acquiring dope simply and inconspicuously. The best dope in town was of course with the police, kilos and kilos of it seized in routine raids and swoops. The Superintendent of Police of Madna, Shri Pannalal Makkad, wise and wicked, had already sent the Collector a consignment of the best.

Though Shri Makkad, socially and culturally, came from a different planet, Agastyaji the Collector Saab got on well with him and considered him a friend. They had socialized twice in the first ten days—booze, reminiscences and a terribly late dinner. Shri Makkad's recollections of thirty-five years spent in the service of the Police State were what enthralled Agastya. For, as he joked all the time to whoever was listening, for the life of him, in his eight years of service, he hadn't been able to distinguish between the Police State and the Welfare State. There *wasn't* any difference between the two, was there?

The Welfare State, for example, was totally committed to Protecting The Planet, but who actually profited the most out of illegal tree felling and the criminal timber trade? The police, of course. The Welfare State had outlawed beggary, but just before the visit of Gorbachev or Nelson Mandela, when it actually wanted to keep the beggars out of sight, who did it turn to to round them up, stuff them into trucks and ferry them a hundred kilometres out of the city? The police, of course. 'We can never Eradicate Poverty,' Shri Makkad used to intone over his fourth whisky, 'but we can eradicate the poor. All we need is intelligent legislation.' When the intelligent legislation of the Welfare State backfired horribly, as when, on the basis of the recommendations of the Kansal Commission, it ratified the reservation of an awesome seventy-three per cent of all its jobs for different categories of Backward, Depressed, Repressed and Suppressed Classes and Castes, and thus triggered off nationwide riots that left officially eighty-four dead and unofficially 342, whom did it, the Welfare State, blubberingly beseech to stop the carnage? Its police force, of course, which later, frenziedly searching for a scapegoat, it blamed for provoking the riots in the first place. Agastya respected the police because it was everywhere and always there to create the shit, wallow in it, to take it. When his monthly Small Savings target, for instance, fell short by a few lakhs, he wouldn't bother to summon his slothful Assistant Directors of Small Savings to exhort them all afternoon to move their butts. No. Instead, he'd phone Makkad and ask him to send around his most persuasive Station House Officer to the more prominent traders and businessmen of Madna with an earnest appeal to participate in the State's laudable schemes. Again, when he wanted a train ticket in a couple of hours, or when he found that the garbage dump at the junction of the main road and his lane had mounted high enough for Moses, he'd turn—not to the Railways or the Municipality—but to the constables who hung around the gates of his house.

Madna is probably Makkad's last appointment before he retires. He'd been posted as Police Superintendent in that district once before. He is a widower. Rumour has it that he burnt his wife some twenty years ago in a fit of rage because she used to criticize his drinking. All of Madna can attest to his ill-temper.

During his first stint as Police Superintendent, at the Hemvati Aflatoon Welfare State Home for the Visually Disadvantaged, an infuriated attendant, with a hot ladle, had gouged out the right eye of a blind girl, just because at breakfast she had asked for a second helping of gruel. The incident, naturally, had stunned Madna and the entire region. Questions had been vociferously asked in the Legislative Assembly. The tabloids of the town, led by the yellowest of the lot, the *Dainik*, had plastered the face of the victim on their front pages and run interviews with the unrepentant attendant for days on end. Several protest marches and processions had been organized and the redoubtable Shri Bhootnath Gaitonde himself, on the morning of the District Planning and Development Council meeting, had led seventy blind students of the Home and about a hundred of their supporters in a dramatic silent march to the Council Hall. The—men of vision, shall we say? including Shri Gaitonde—had all worn dark glasses to—presumably—symbolically and visually underscore their support of the purpose of the march. The men of vision had thought the dark glasses a brilliant idea, but the Superintendent of Police hadn't. Makkad had been so incensed by what he considered tasteless and gimmicky exhibitionism that he'd verbally commanded the constables on duty at the Council Hall to swagger out and cosh the non-blind protesters about a bit. Unfortunately, the police coshed more than a bit and did not discriminate amongst the dark glasses.

Sixteen grievously injured and seventy-one with bumps on the head. Shri Gaitonde was rendered speechless with ecstasy at this heaven-sent opportunity to plague the Welfare State. And plague it he did, with elan and gusto, exploiting the mishap at every turn till the next elections, when he formed the New Vision Party and won the Madna seat of the Legislative Assembly. Of course, a high-level enquiry was ordered into the incident and the State appointed the then Managing Director of the State Industrial Development Corporation, Bhupen Raghupati, to conduct it. The Superintendent of Police, deposing before the Enquiry Officer, was aghast at the insinuation of the Inspector on duty at the Council Hall that he, the Superintendent, had ordered the lathi charge against the procession. When he learnt of the Superintendent's stupefaction, the Inspector, who knew what was what, in turn retracted his statement, instead owned up himself to having ordered the assault and on the advice of his well-wishers, pleaded temporary insanity on the morning of the march because of sunstroke and exhaustion. The Civil Surgeon of Madna, a pleasant sluggard called Alagh, certified that during the enquiry proceedings itself, the Inspector had suffered a relapse of the same whatever-it-had-been-that'd driven-him-round-the-bend and needed to be hospitalized immediately. After fifteen months of cogitation, the Enquiry Officer concluded that since the Inspector had acted when not in complete control of himself, he needed first to be issued a stern warning against such lapses of reason in the future and second, to be posted to a less strenuous job where he could be observed for a few months. Only thereafter could the extent of his guilt be accurately ascertained. In his recommendations, the Enquiry Officer himself suggested a transfer to either the Police Wives' Welfare Board or The

Police Sports Stadiums Authority.

In the February section of his diary, Shri Sen recorded this characteristic activity of the Welfare State as worthy of further scrutiny under the title *Withering the Buck*:

> *In his address to the nation on Independence Day next year, the Prime Minister would do well to exhort his countrymen to take to rugby. Perhaps one of the reasons that we pass so well is that there are so many of us around for the relay—and each time the buck passes, it's funny how it becomes vague, loses focus and direction, how its passing never ends—it just gets tired and disintegrates, withers, like a cripple paralysed on the grass verge of some monstrous highway, slowly crumbling into dust. A golden rule: When you're with your boss, always, always make sure that your subordinate is with you—someone to whom you can pass* on the spot. *In an emergency, even the driver'll do. If you're so inclined, you can even turn around and wave to the buck as it recedes, withers and disintegrates.*

'Chidambaram, phone the SP's office and tell them that Gaitonde is on his way . . . Do we have decent envelopes? . . . Probably not . . . Did you ask the boy to buy some envelopes as well? . . .' Chidambaram bows his head in shame. His bald dome gleams with the sweat of contrition. '. . . Never mind . . . Have our daftaris started remaking envelopes in their spare time? . . . I'm sure not, despite my recent circular . . . unofficially inform all our peons and daftaris—how many do we have? . . . forty-seven? . . . that if I don't see fifty remade envelopes from each one of them by the end of this week, I'll stop their pay.' This is power.

A sort of razor's-edge sanity as well. Agastya has always been a voracious reader of trash. Thus, he's taken to—and devoured—with enthusiasm the literature of the Welfare State—handbooks, manuals, statutes, reports, returns, gazettes, minutes, memorandums, documents, correspondence, affidavits, acts, and regulations; periodically, he distils what he reads into circulars for the edification of his office. He has sedulously maintained that though ignorance is bliss, knowledge is power, and the servants of the Welfare State need to know well the facets of their master.

His favourite bedtime reading is the *Revised Manual of Office Procedure.* It has often kept him up till the wee hours, marvelling at his master; it's been one of the richest sources for his exhortations to his subordinates.

> *To help you to use your time more efficiently in office and to ensure that you are economical in the use of the stationery and property of the Welfare State, your kind attention is drawn once more to Rule 17c (iv) of Section 28 of Chapter III. I quote ad verbatim from the Revised Manual. Please note that the Manual was last revised not in the last century, but in 1981.*
> *'i) Those note sheets that are blank on one side, do not contain confidential matter and have been retrieved from old files that have otherwise been marked for destruction should be used in new files for notes.*
> *'ii) Envelopes with communications inside them that are received from other offices should be carefully slit open (and not carelessly torn apart) and preserved. After a sufficient number has accumulated, they should be handed over to the peons and daftaries so that they can remake envelopes in their spare time. The correct procedure for remaking envelopes is to unstick the gummed portions, turn the envelopes inside out and regum the ends neatly. Pasting slips of paper on used envelopes is* not *the correct method of making them fit for use again. The last procedure, observed too often in our offices, smacks of laziness and lack of discipline. Also, its end product reflects rather badly on the financial resources of the Welfare State.*

'iii) All communications that have to be sent to the same address on the same day should, as far as possible, be collected together and sent in a single envelope or in the smallest number of envelopes that will with ease contain them all.'

As Collector and District Magistrate of, and the principal representative of the Welfare State in, Madna, I feel that it is one of my pivotal functions to encourage my colleagues and staff to continually reflect on the nature of their duties and responsibilities, and thereafter to suggest ways and means of improving our present system, for which—I am sure that my colleagues will agree—there exists ample scope. There is always room for improvement—even when one doesn't want it.

Though the circular was Agastya's, its inspiration could just as well have been Prime Minister Bhuvan Aflatoon or his Think Tank. They did that sort of thing all the time, though of course on a far grander scale. It was part of the magic of the new PM, of a government that was going places while breezing forward into the new millennium. In February of that year, for example, Agastya himself had attended a District Collectors' Conference summoned by Bhuvan himself, no less, at the Gajapati Aflatoon TFIN (The Future Is Now) Complex in the capital.

The Conference had been a pleasantly chaotic affair, with two hundred-odd cutthroat-keen delegates from all over the country, all spectacles and statistics, in an atmosphere of quiet turmoil, brimming with Black Guard Commandoes glaring menacingly at everyone else while bumping into one another, the sort of place to which one could ferry an old, insane or troublesome parent when one wanted to lose him forever.

The conference had puzzled everybody—quite naturally,

since it had been dreamed up by the Prime Minister's New Men as the best way of Getting to Know the Cutting Edge of Administration. The several rungs between the Prime Minister and the District Collectors—the Cabinet Ministers, Chief Ministers, Secretaries to the Centre, Chief Secretaries, Additional Secretaries, Principal Secretaries, Joint Secretaries, Commissioners, Directors, Deputy Secretaries, Joint Commissioners and Additional Directors—in all, about sixty thousand servants of the state—had felt left out, hurt, relieved and happy. The agenda had been freewheeling, that is, had followed whatever had brushed the tabula rasa of Bhuvan Aflatoon's mind. He himself had looked rather cute—fresh and starched in his white khadi churidaar-kurta set, his pink jowls and helipad nose glistening with the complacence born out of believing completely his white khadi-clad sycophant-advisors. 'Ever since I took over this hot seat,' he'd minced into the microphone with a beguiling simper, 'I've wanted to have a brainstorming session with you all, the scalpels—indeed, the scissors, knives, and pincers—and the hands, arms and legs, to boot—of my government . . .' Talk to me, tell me all, he'd declared in his otherwise-beautifully-phrased inaugural address, what's it really like out there.

The sixty thousand who hadn't been invited to the conference had been surprised that the Prime Minister was so foolish as to spend an entire day lending an ear to the hot air emanating from two hundred junior civil servants. True, all that blah did pull Bhuvan down a bit; he left at five looking more grey than pink.

Since, a year and a half later, Agastya proposed marriage for the first time to Daya in the main auditorium of the Gajapati Aflatoon TFIN Complex, it will not be amiss to devote a couple of lines to it at this stage.

It is an impressive, ten-storey structure. The original

building took eight years to construct and cost the earth. Over the years, to keep up with the times and the state of the art, it has—at impressive expense—been periodically renovated. It is the happening place of the Welfare State. It has a series of convention halls, the largest of which can seat two thousand, facilities for simultaneous translation into five international and fourteen national languages, central air-conditioning that works right through the most parlous summers, an enormous five-star cafeteria the weekly menu of which diplomatically does justice to the different regional cuisines of the country, an advanced closed-circuit television system, terrifically modern computer and communication gadgetry and—not the least—an unusually eco-friendly, open car-parking area, with bougainvillea, neem, gulmohar, jacaranda and unnoticed wild Congress grass separating the berths of tarmac.

Dominating the vast central lobby of TFIN Complex stands a not-bad-looking, two-storey-high, abstract sculpture in red sandstone that—obviously—is not meant to look like anything specific on earth, but sometimes resembles three mammoth, irregularly-concentric ovals, and at other times a huge stone female breast with an alarmingly large, inverted nipple ringed by a mysterious, presumably decorative, ovoid quoit of a lighter shade. The sculptor was the late Balwant Chhabra, dear friend of Pashupati Aflatoon. He took six years to create his gift to the Complex, christened it Om, was apoplectic when the press criticized it, married—almost in revenge—an ageing French yoga student and dope addict, and flew off with her to the west coast of France to shiver in the winds, complain of the cold and the food and feel sorry for himself before dying of a heart attack—of a broken heart, lamented his country after he'd gone.

Om is the primal sound of the universe, he'd explained to a mystified Pashupati Aflatoon, the-then Education and Heritage Minister, at the chaotic unveiling of the sculpture.

Om is the Beginning of Communication, of Connection and therefore of Existence, because it is the seminal Chord, the first vibration that shatters the vacuum. If The Future Is Now, then we're in tune with time and—here in this foyer of a Modern Temple of Discourse, Debate and Dialogue, how better to express the harmony of our intentions with the Beginning, the Now and the To Come, than by the concrete depiction of the Fundamental Sound?

'Bravo—yes, I now see what you mean,' Pashupati Aflatoon had pronounced with calm conviction, 'I think you should write it all down—exactly as you said—and give it to the Deputy Secretary, and we'll put it up on a black marble plaque right next to this thing. Very good. Thank you, Balli.'

'Payṇcho,' an aghast Balwant Chhabra is reported to have muttered in response. The entire event has been described in fair detail in the racy—but generally unreliable—memoirs of Balwant's half-mad half-sister, who was present at the unveiling because she never left his side, not even—it is said—at night. The work is in Punjabi-Hindustani. After Balwant took flight with his French dope addict, she plagued him with faxes and letters to move his arse to get European publishing houses to translate and publish the opus.

It *is* likely, however, that on that occasion, the sculptor did react to the Minister's suggestion with a Payṇcho because it was *his* primal sound—was—is—indeed, the fundamental expression of a whole culture, that of the north country. The actual Hindustani word of course is Bahenchod, that is, Sister-Fucker, but time, usage and a sluggish tongue have weathered the three syllables down to two and of them, honed the first and abbreviated and softened the second. More fragmented than Om, less solemn, more nasal, whining, less sure, less complete, nearer to the heart, more physical, Payṇcho more correctly expresses the Zeitgeist, the state of the times. In her memoirs, therefore, Balwant's half-sister continually alludes to his sculpture at the TFIN Complex as Payṇchom.

Of course, in her defence, it should be clarified here that the word doesn't simply mean Sister-Fucker anymore. The most respectable Punjabi and Hindustani speakers use it in everyday discourse as an exclamation, a succinct comment, en passant, on the human condition. 'This morning, payṇcho, it was raining payṇcho, so hard payṇcho, that I decided payṇcho not to bathe. Payṇcho the dog refused to payṇcho go out payṇcho for his morning potty payṇcho and he did it payṇcho on my wife's payṇcho office shoes.'

'Payṇcho! Free shoe polish! Payṇcho rush for a payṇcho patent!'

The above conversation takes place in Punjabi-Hindustani, in the dark, in the corridors of frequent powerlessness of Aflatoon Bhavan. The venue is typical, Punjabi Hindustani being the unofficial official language of the Welfare State. Available statistics indicate that seventy-eight per cent of the officers and staff of the national government speak it or have officially stated either Punjabi or Hindi to be his or her mother tongue. Further, ninety-six per cent prefer to curse and exclaim in it. Therefore, since the servants of the Welfare State generally are literate, middlish-class and respectable, *Payṇcho* becomes the most-often heard exclamation in Aflatoon Bhavan, a proposition easily proved by a stroll down its corridors, by candle-light, amongst the monkeys, inhaling the aromas of urine and tea. Balwant's half-sister's rechristening of his sculpture was thus, in more than one sense, inspired.

Pashupati Aflatoon did put up a black marble plaque beside Payṇchom. Engraved on it were a Deputy Secretary's version of the sculptor's explanation of the significance of his creation given to the Minister on the occasion of its unveiling. On the understandable artistic grounds that his work needed no written exegesis, Balwant Chhabra refused to have anything more to do with the plaque, the Complex or the Ministry. Hence, at the Deputy Secretary's suggestion that it would reinforce his cultural credentials, Pashupati Aflatoon agreed to have his own name engraved under the interpretation.

On the afternoon of the last day of the Getting-to-Know-the-Cutting-Edge-of-Administration conference, the father of all fires broke out in—and engulfed almost half of—TFIN Complex. Though the Enquiry Commission that was subsequently set up could not tell, after six months, precisely how and when the fire started, it was universally felt that the stars had been propitious in that it—the fire—had, as it were, warmed up, and got cracking, only well after office hours; thus, no lives had been lost, just some property worth a handful of crores. The engineers of the Public Works Department, in anticipation of the repair work to be distributed, were wined and dined for weeks on end by the contractors on the Approved Emergency Shortlist. Some of the engineers were even congratulated on their good fortune, as at the birth of a son.

A short-circuit in the wiring, guessed an onlooker. An electric heater left carelessly on long after the chapatis for lunch'd been warmed up, opined another. Sabotage, there are wheels within wheels, asserted a third, sagely. 'My God, can we do nothing right?' fumed Prime Minister Bhuvan Aflatoon, shocked, angry and depressed, 'has some ass thought of a second venue for tomorrow or do I have to think of everything?'

The happening slated for the following day was particularly dear to the PM because it was entirely his baby, conceived exclusively by him, without any inspiration or input from any member of the Coterie. 'Look, the New Industries Policy and peaceful nuclear bombs in mid-ocean and Revised Strategies for Increased Milk Production are all right—but what about the People? That's whom I want to meet. They've voted for me and they wave and smile and look so warm and welcoming despite the awful lives they lead. About five hundred million of them are illiterate, isn't that right? Well—how many of them have never seen a colour TV or a washing machine? Have never used a telephone? Leave alone understood the concept of a laptop? Do we have the figures? . . . I want to be in touch with them all the time, not once in five years, just to seduce them with my smile for their vote, from some open-air jeep, surrounded by AK-47s. I want them to see TFIN Complex—for which we'll have to think up a new name, at once, something Sanskritic and full of cultural resonance—you know, the latest in science merely carries on our rich, continuous cultural traditions, that science is in our rivers, our blood and our festivals—that kind of jazz. TFIN is a totally unacceptable acronym. It conjures up a tower of dented aluminium boxes—dal at the bottom, topped by, in order, greasy bhindi, raw onions, green chillies and cold, fat, spongelike parathas squeezed like the godforsaken into a train compartment en route to Auschwitz . . .' He waited, pleased, for the New Men—all his old school chums who had sucked up to him even then—to stop chuckling. '. . . Could we get some modern Sanskrit whizkid cracking on the new name? . . . But the People. I want to set up an exchange programme for them. They should all be brought here in trucks or something. They should see, understand, *feel* the new world in their own backyard—TFIN Complex, the National Information Coordination Plan, the Age of Science Pavilion, the Central Computer Institute, the Space Research Organization—I want those five hundred million illiterates to experience the wonders of technology and all that in their *own* country, behind which stand their *own* countrymen . . . and then, and *then*—we'll *reverse* the movement. All these Steel Frame fellows, for example, who focus all their energies on wangling for themselves junkets in the fleshpots of the world—let them all instead go and spend a week in one of our typical villages. Let them crap in the fields with stray dogs sniffing at their bums—and bathe at the well with some buffalo, dream of electricity and a radio, irrigation for their dining-table plots of land and cows as dowry for their sons. Let them get their heads blown off in some ancient, unending, mystifying, caste war—off-the-record, of course . . . What do you fellows think of the idea?'

The Old Chums had been enthusiastic. They loved spending the money of the Welfare State, issuing instructions, supervising the scurrying around of a city of officials, and holding leisurely brainstorming sessions to which they wore hand-woven, off-white kurtas and batik saris and at which they, to soothe their sensitive throats, sipped tepid boiled water in which floated a piece or two of lemon. After a couple of these sessions, a week later, Rajani Suroor returned to Bhuvan Aflatoon with the details of the OYE-OYE Happening.

Each of the five hundred-plus districts of the country would identify four sane, adult citizens—at least two of whom had to be women—who had never visited the capital city, had never ridden in a car and—mindful of the Prime Minister's befuddled outpouring—had never used a telephone or seen or touched a washing machine. The regional governments would ferry all the citizens selected to the capital where, for four days, they—the chosen—would experience some of the wonders of the modern world. The New Men adored this, this senseless mobilization of an enormous number of humans and a vast amount of resources and energy simply to satisfy the whim of the powerful. It was like being in the court of an emperor in the golden age. On all the evenings, Vyatha, Rajani Suroor's theatre group, would interface with the chosen to explore, through the medium of popular street entertaimnent—enacted by the communal fireside, as it were, with the more extrovert amongst the visitors in the key roles—their world, minds, their reactions to the whole trip, ideas on caste, gender equality, modernization, politics, the country. At the end of their sojourn, the chosen, as a climax, would meet, dine—and freely exchange views and ideas—with the Prime Minister. The entire programme could be officially called—if the PM permitted, of course—The Open Your Eyes, Open Your Eyes Happening. To which select representatives of the Steel Frame would certainly be invited.

The PM was ecstatic. He too like his coterie loved the ease with which the seed of an idea blossomed into a flower that could be touched and seen. When it grew unexpectedly into a monstrous weed, one needed solid chaps around one who'd continue to convincingly describe it, for example, as a stunningly beautiful, a perfect, orchid. One needed that sort of encouragement all the time, to get on with Progress, the happenings. He remembered perfectly that when his grand-uncle Trimurti Aflatoon had been Prime Minister and they had fought their fourth border war with their dear neighbours, they had celebrated their victory in a befitting manner, with holidays, awards, promotions, triumphal processions, glorious war memorials and an attitude of warm munificence towards the fresh demands of the armed forces, ignoring—naturally—at the same time, all the reports that described with some fervour how the unmentionables across the border too were celebrating *their* victory in similar style. This was the Information Age, dammit; one would drown if one didn't select what one wanted to hear—and one had to *arrange* for the right voices—it wasn't as straightforward as having a quick shower, you know—to pick and choose amongst those media barons and lords of industry with their salivating slippery tongues and tails that wagged like a battery-operated toy's.

'Rajani,' Bhuvan Aflatoon purred with affection, 'you might well be a visionary but for me, you also need to be a micro-level planner. Open your eyes yourself! Those wretched regional governments where we aren't in power would never pay for this show. Hunt around for some funds without dragging me into it. And where will those two thousand countrymen of ours stay? A camp somewhere, sanitation, transport, food and all that—alongside your campfires, of course. See if you can link it up with the Centenary.'

OFF-WHITE PAPER

Dr Srinivas Chakki didn't in the least like the ward of the Madna Civil hospital in a bed of which he lay. Mouldy walls, cobwebs, window panes opaque with grime, a dirt-encrusted floor, bedpans strewn all anyhow like a child's playthings, the electricity supply as wayward as a politician's ethics. His bed had no linen. Its mattress was stained and stank; its cotton had been dementedly gouged out in parts. His side-table was rusted and somehow furry with some kind of fungus.

The bed on his left was occupied by a young woman with tears in her eyes and dressing and plaster all over the right side of her face. She was a new neighbour in that he couldn't recall seeing her when he'd last been awake, though he couldn't remember either how long ago that had been. He was mentally awake enough to wonder why a victim of accidental or intentional violence had been dumped beside him.

'Aren't we in the Infectious Diseases Ward of this hospital?' demanded he of the hall. No one responded, perhaps because no one heard him save the woman in the next bed and she could make nothing out of his slurred mumble. Hazily, he puzzled over where Miss Shruti and Miss Snigdha could be. Perhaps the awesomely humid heat of the ward had metamorphosed them into a couple of the pigeons roosting on the dingy ventilators high up near the ceiling.

The forceful stink of the room—disinfectant, medicines, urine, rotting matter—reminded him that he wanted to piss but he didn't have the guts to confront the visualized filth of the toilet. Its yellow door, four beds down and opposite Dr Chakki, lay permanently ajar, perhaps because nobody wished to touch it. With reason, since in the few minutes that he spent gazing at it, three pissers shuffled up to—and not daring to cross its threshold, relieved themselves against—it.

The nurse on duty, whose duty it was to stride manfully through the ward and out the door that led to the canteen, doughtily ignoring the groans, whines and other types of summons from different beds, appeared at that point in his field of vision. She moved like a willowy dragon.

'Bedsheets, Sister Joseph!' bayed Dr Chakki valiantly, 'and a bedpan!' he added to her back. His vexation at her disregarding him suddenly spurred him into sitting up in bed. She had stopped to note something down on the chart at the foot of the second last bed from the door. 'Not having had, in my twenty years of public service,' he declared to her, but in a voice that didn't carry beyond his uncomprehending neighbour, 'the pleasure of being a guest of the Welfare State in any of its jails or asylums, I cannot comment on the cleanliness and hygienic conditions of those institutions—but my God, why don't we combine them with our State hospitals? How could anyone tell the difference?' He watched Sister Joseph disappear through the door and then turned to his female neighbour, who'd been observing him for the past few minutes with dryer eyes, 'Faecal matter, mouldy bandages, cockroaches, enormous spiders and rats. Rats at every step. Scurrying up your leg! Heavens—down which drain does the crores of rupees allocated to Public Health every year go? Does anybody here know what it takes to keep a hospital toilet clean?' He surveyed the ward. 'Some detergent. Some disinfectant. Water, a broom, a sweeper. How many sweepers does this hospital have? Seventeen. And what is its Maintenance budget for the year? Eleven lakh rupees. I am determined that the light of reason should pierce at least one skull in this place.' Exhausted, he flopped back onto his pillow and dropped off almost immediately.

He surfaced about an hour later to find Sister Joseph and the doctor on duty standing beside his bed, solemnly scanning his case history. 'Hello, Doctor Blue and Sister Moon, I presume.'

The doctor was bald and fleshy, with a stoop. Clearly a no-nonsense person, he, without glancing at his patient, shushed him—or tried to—with a commanding wave of his hand.

'I'm so glad that you've showed up because we in the ward had begun to think that we'd all been abandoned, like sinking ships.'

Without saying a word, the doctor thrust a hand out at Sister Joseph, who demurely slipped into it, from a sheaf that she carried, an X-ray, which he then examined with eagle eye.

'The patient is suffering from an advanced stage of pneumonic plague,' he announced.

'Thank you, but I ought to point out that that X-ray in your hand is that of a female. I'm a doctor myself, an entomologist. I can tell a woman's X-ray from a man's. You need to return to medical college, Eagle-eye.' To himself, Dr Chakki added, 'Time to go.'

Half an hour later, fatigued but free, he was in his own clothes and at the Qayamat Road gate of Aflatoon Maidan, mildly bewildered by the exertion of walking and the three-in-one hunger strike in progress before him.

Exiting from the hospital had not been easy. Two cops at Reception had barred his way and without saying anything, had simply looked as sceptical as boulders. He'd explained in English that he wasn't at all a plague case trying to cut loose but a patient of murine typhus which, as they no doubt knew, was not even remotely as lethal even though it exhibited similar symptoms. When their faces hadn't changed, he'd shown them a relevant newspaper clipping that he'd extracted from the clutter in his shirt pocket. The balder one had expressionlessly scanned it upside down while he, weak with excitement, had continued to gabble, 'Who indeed knows what's going on in the Welfare State? The news item in your hand is from the December 4 edition of *The State Express*.'

And Now Murine Typhus

Dr Sitaram Dhanuka, a Killi University academic who had predicted the outbreak of plague in a research paper published last January, now questions his own forecast. In a letter to this newspaper, he writes:

I note with serious concern the reports published in several newspapers that the hospitals and clinics of Madna and its environs, because of lack of trained medical staff and facilities and because of overcrowding, have released and continue to release into open society all those patients who test negative for the plague. I am amazed that the National Institute of Communicable Diseases (from which august political institution I resigned in protest in 1979) and hospitals all over the country need to be reminded of the existence of murine typhus, a flea-borne disease akin to the plague, with much the same symptoms and transmission route. It could even be argued—though I'm not for the moment doing so—that what Madna is battling at the moment is not the plague, but murine typhus.
The following symptoms are common to both diseases—high body temperature (102 to 105 degrees F), severe headache, a chill, body pain, a rash. I suspect that those patients at Madna who exhibited the above symptoms but still tested negative for the plague might well be afflicted with murine typhus, which is an airborne, rickettsial disease spread through the fleas of rats, dogs and cats. Its mortality rate is five per cent. I would strongly recommend to the hospitals of Madna that all suspected plague patients be tested for murine typhus as well. Otherwise, I fear that what we might have on our hands is not one epidemic, but two.

> Or even three. I read with bitter amusement on November 11 the news item on Page 4 of your paper that the National Institute of Communicable Diseases still refuses to recognize the existence in this country of a comparatively new, drug-resistant, potentially fatal strain of malaria, the perils of which I had spelt out in my paper on the subject as far back as 1978. Twelve cases and two deaths have been reported in the last three months from Sripura, Shagaland and Rassam. How many deaths will jolt the Welfare State out of its slumber? Yours, etc.'

The bald policeman had expressionlessly handed the clipping back to Dr Chakki and then with a wriggle of his eyebrows and a motion of his head indicated that he should retreat down the corridor from which he had slithered out.

'Of course,' conceded Dr Chakki graciously, 'but shouldn't you instead be more worried about the real threats?' and he pointed with his chin to the squad of Madna youth at the gates of the hospital. It had been a neck-and-neck decision, what to distract the guardians with—the gang at the entrance or any one of the other clusters in the compound, one munching peanuts and playing cards, a second enclosing a hoarse-voiced seller of aphrodisiacs, a third bickering with a different set of policemen.

Sedately, they'd strolled across to the gates. The youngsters, more well-meaning than wise, formed one of the many bands that scoured the choked drains and mountainous garbage dumps of their town for rats, which they trapped, stunned, performed—being a devout people—a little puja around, anointed with kerosene and ghee, set fire to and watched burn. In fact, one teenager—long-haired, large-eyed—did hold by the tail—at arm's length, it is true, and quakingly—a monstrous rat, grey-brown, furry, fat, about whose snout he clumsily waved a lit incense stick. A comrade waited beside him, bottle of kerosene in hand. Beneath the hubbub of the street could be heard from the group the hum of some religious chant.

'Heroic,' observed Dr Chakki, 'but one must add that while burning a knocked-out rat might possibly be a karmic experience, the zeal, the war fever of these juveniles might actually be helping the plague—or the murine typhus, as the case may be—to spread since the vector fleas are far more likely to flee from the corpse of a burning rat than the snug fur of a living one.'

He could have burst a firecracker in the constables' ears and still not distracted them from the rite. He waited till the kerosene and a spoonful of ghee had been sprinkled on the comatose rat, a lit match touched to its snout and the burning body flung down on the ground; he'd slid away to the enthralling squeals of the dying rodent and deftly sat down on the rear carrier of a passing, torpidly-moving bicycle. When the cyclist had turned around enquiringly, he'd pleaded in his pathetic Hindi, 'Just till the end of the road, sir. My head's spinning like a top.'

It did, just a bit, outside the Qayamat Road gate of Aflatoon Maidan, so Dr Chakki subsided onto the pavement and briefly shut his eyes. 'Hunger and thirst, sir,' declared he to himself, 'are to be fought with firefighting measures on a war footing.' So he determinedly entered the park and crossed over to the three-in-one hunger strike.

It was being enacted on a makeshift stage about three feet high, appropriately elevating the protesters a couple of steps closer to immortality. The awning had been fashioned with gaily-coloured bedsheets; beneath it, the organizers had arranged for mattresses, white sheets and some white bolsters, a couple of standing electric fans, some garlanded photographs of Gandhi, Ambedkar, a fistful of Aflatoons and a smiling, full-length one of the principal striker.

He is obese, twenty-six years old, unemployed, unemployable, with curly hair, melting eyes and a broom of a moustache. In the photograph, he is in a tight black shirt, tight white pants, white leather shoes and a white tie. On stage, he is in off-white kurta pyjama, supine against some pillows. Incense smoke wafts around him to underscore that the gods are with him in his struggle. A public-address system in the corner plays non-stop doleful shehnai music (switching to vigorous Punjabi rap only when he is propped up so that he can sip water).

Facing the stage are a couple of red rexine sofas for V∞IP visitors. They are crawling with children, so Dr Chakki steps right up to the platform, leans on it and informs the prostrate protester, 'I know you. You're A.C. Raichur. We've met before in Aflatoon Bhavan. You performed there.'

Indeed they have and he has.

Raichur had wanted to walk—to proceed on foot, to quote his application—all over the country for six years to spread the message of national integration and had believed that the Welfare State should sponsor him. The Department of Sports had opined that their Rules of Business didn't cover a six-year-long walk and that national integration was definitely more a Culture subject, *may therefore kindly see please.* The Joint Secretary of the Department of Culture was miffed at the very idea that a freeloader as unarty as A.C. Raichur could be palmed off on to him and sternly noted in the file: *We may please regret. The applicant doesn't at all fulfil the criteria of our Programme Number 6493 for the Promotion and Diffusion of Demotic and Indigenous Drama and Other Such Forms of Self-Expression. We may, if approved, forward to Home Affairs. National Integration, though they might not know, is* their *concern.* Eight months after his first application, an unctuous Raichur met and oiled the feet and calves of the MP—and by then, Deputy Information Minister—from Madna, Bhanwar Virbhim, for a good two hours, after which he implored him for justice from his government. Bhanwar requested his HUBRIS counterpart to sponsor Raichur's noble cause out of the Cabinet Minister's Discretionary Fund. After two months of frenetic paperwork, the Department granted him enough money to walk for four and a half days.

He was rather upset—but he didn't refuse the money. When he, wearing his black-and-white outfit, went to collect the cheque, he learnt that—well, even the Welfare State wasn't that soft a touch. He would have to spend the money first out of his own pocket and submit all kinds of documents as proof. If they satisfied the State, it would reimburse him. This was not strictly true. When he'd return to Aflatoon Bhavan with all his faked proofs of expenditure, the clerks of the Welfare State wouldn't give him his cheque right away, oh no. Instead, to quote from the February section of Shri Agastya Sen's diary, 'they'd inform him of the next passage of the labyrinth. Knowledge withheld is power. The clerks of the Welfare State wouldn't like to part with even an atom of information, either to the public or their superiors. When pressed, cornered, they will cede, piecemeal, incomplete info, bit by bit. If a procedure has seven stages and nine annexures, they will reveal this knowledge in a minimum of sixteen separate encounters, which will be routinely interspersed with occasions when they won't be available or will tell you nothing, or instead will hint at bribes.'

Raichur's outraged friends in the *Dainik* had suggested a hunger strike.

Galvanized, he sat up abruptly, his lips curled like a predator's. 'Dr Chakki, here! What a pleasure! Here, have a Coca Cola and some laddus!' He beckoned to one of the children on the sofas, who skipped off to the tables alongside the stage on which had been ranged baskets and baskets of food—parathas, alu chaat, idli vada, dal fry in bowls of banana leaves, samosas, condensed-milk burfis, podanpolis, omelettes. Raichur had objected to his sympathizers snacking while they were with him but had failed to dissuade them. They in turn had pointed out that the effect of a hunger strike would be far more sublime if enacted in the midst of Temptation. Ever mindful of advertisements for himself, he had decreed that the food was to be offered as well to any passer-by who stayed long enough and looked sufficiently impressed by the spectacle, and to the policemen on duty, of whom there were quite a few; the district administration—being a second target of the hunger strike for its arrest of Makhmal Bagai for having fired a gun in the presence of the Collector, no less, and for its refusal to release him on bail—had clearly felt that it should look as though it took Raichur's open disapproval of its firmness seriously.

'Two Coca Colas, please, without ice, and without a glass. I mean, I will drink straight from the bottle.'

'Not for me, though,' pointed out Raichur, 'I'm on—' and he gestured to the numerous banners in white, blue and red above his head and amongst the trees of the park, bright and pretty like the dreams of children, screaming injustice—but happily—against the Welfare State in general and its local representatives and the Kansal Commission in particular.

'Yes, very good, this three-in-one effort. An economy drive, in other words. Will you smoke? Will your principles allow you to?' With an effort, Dr Chakki hoisted himself onto the stage and sat down beside Raichur. He found his cigarettes, lit up and began to feel dizzy again. 'I'm interested in politics and governance. I study the subject. As a long-term beneficiary of the Welfare State, you'd be a suitable person to pose some of my questions to. Why, for example, do we continue to vote back to power such worthless specimens? . . . and while on the topic, I should add that I'm contemplating a white paper on the magic of the Aflatoons.'

In response, Raichur turned to the doctor and yawned

like a beast, slowly, throwing his head back and arching his back, generously allowing him to view his molars and tonsils. When he'd finished, he blinked a couple of times and said, 'I'm always ready to be interviewed. Please feel free to ask me whatever you want to know about me.'

'Whatever happened to your Walk for National Integration?'

For one thing, it had become a run. Rather than a long-term beneficiary of the Welfare State, it would be more accurate to call Raichur a long-term aspirant to the dugs of. When one had meant to walk for six years for a cause but had been constrained by lack of funds to four and a half days, it seemed more apt, to hasten the diffusion of the message, to run. His Nationwide Trot for Peace and Understanding had been flagged off from Madna by Bhanwar Virbhim himself. Unfortunately, three kilometres out, he'd been attacked by a mad dog and had had to be hospitalized; in his bed, he'd frothed at the mouth out of fear and had kept repeating that the dog had been very old, foolish, wilful, unpredictable and bad-tempered—a canine King Lear, in short.

Ironic, because far away in Aflatoon Bhavan, Under Secretary Shri Ghosh Dastidar, who had handled Raichur's Run, had in fact recommended that he be given more funds than he'd asked for on the grounds of the extra nutritional requirement. *It has been conclusively proved*, argued Shri Dastidar, *that the fitness level of one of our average national athletes equals that of the average, middle-aged, depressed, divorced, Scandinavian housewife, so what then of one of our average, out-of-shape citizens? It would be catastrophic to have him start his Run and, as it were, die on the hands of the government.*

Gradually, Raichur became a regular visitor at Aflatoon Bhavan. After he recovered from the dog bite, the Minister's office procured for him yet one more berth. They packed him off to some northern town to lead a public relay hunger strike against the recommendations of the Kansal Commission. On the second day, some passing terrorists shot at them, killing all the others and wounding him. Sitting ducks, one pro-Kansal newspaper called them. As for Raichur: ne'er-say-die-even-when-wounded, truly, because he came back—and with a new application.

Which is when Dr Chakki and some of his colleagues first heard him perform. He'd then wanted to make noises for a living, and a grant from Aflatoon Bhavan to start him off. He was simply terrific in his white shoes, white pants, black shirt and white tie. 'I'll begin with a sixties' James Bond trailer,' and he curled his lip. He would have liked to grin from ear to ear but his cheeks—dark brown footballs of frozen butter—prevented his mouth from stretching. Then his lips were sealed, and he began his impersonation. His cheeks ballooned even more, his eyes bulged, his nostrils seemed to blow scorching gas into his broom of a moustache. Above his tight black collar, his Adam's Apple bobbed up and down amongst all those chins like a ping pong ball trapped in a beaker of boiling water. His audience shut its eyes and was transported to a movie hall somewhere in 1967 . . . first the Theme Tune from James Bond for ten-to-fifteen seconds, then a riot of gun shots, followed by a deep, wry, very British voice speaking BBC—gibberish, of course, but it *sounded* like 'Care for a cup of tea? Shaken, not stirred?' . . . after which, a couple of atom bombs went off, and next a woman purred for ten seconds, a profoundly satisfying but well-mannered orgasm. Her soft groans ended with a couple of gasps that sounded like 'Oh James . . . James Bond' . . . and were suddenly overwhelmed by the most frightening sounds of a car chase. The roar of engines, tyres squealing, brakes screeching, sirens wailing, the blare of angry, scared car horns, the occasional rat-a-tat of gunfire, women screaming in the background . . . the whole climaxed in a ten-second, end-of-the-world explosion, succeeded by a moment or two of startling silence, and finally, just before a short reprise of the Theme Tune, in a deadpan, underplayed but effectively dramatic, stereophonic tone of voice, a few more stray sounds of gibberish-BBC: 'Silencers on Your Pussy,' 'Bad Sex with a Beretta'—a combination of the two, obviously the title of the imagined thriller. An outstanding performance indeed.

Raichur also had an interesting variation on the Bond. A takeoff on a Hollywood movie, though it is not at all certain that he himself considered them takeoffs. For him, they weren't funny, they were the real thing. The Hollywood one had the same sound effects and an excellent American twang. Its refrain, sometimes in a scream of rising panic and on occasions in a quiet and decisive drawl, sounded like: 'Let's get the helloutta here!' . . . He was building up an interesting repertoire, including the denouement of a Hindi film—the villain guffawing while he suspends the bleeding, blind mother of the hero over a vat of boiling oil—coconut or mustard, depending on the location—and a tour de force, the sounds of a group of protesters on a relay hunger strike against the Kansal Commission being gunned down by passing terrorists.

Shri Dastidar had tried to fit Raichur into Preservation of Vanishing Cultures, but savvy that he was, he knew that there was more money in Promotion of Indigenous Drama. More than one sage in Aflatoon Bhavan has predicted a rich haul and a fruitful future for him in the Department.

'We haven't seen you in the corridors of Aflatoon Bhavan for quite a while,' commented Dr Chakki after he had drained his second bottle of Coca Cola and had burped satisfactorily.

'I've been too busy here,' Raichur gestured once more—'answering the call of the nation—' at the pleasant chaos around him, 'but,'—reassuringly—'I will come.'

'Good. Thank you. I must now make a move. Where in

Madna do you think I could rest in peace for a couple of days? Where the crackpots from the hospital won't be able to find and harass me?'

'You come to my place. It's just five minutes from here. No no absolutely no problem no question of nothing doing. My wife and my family love my friends. Just five minutes from the Mall Road gate of Aflatoon Maidan. I always pop off in my vehicle for a quick snack with my kids. You come and stay and interview me all night no problem.'

Raichur's vehicle turned out to be a three-wheeler, a black and yellow commercial auto-rickshaw decorated with tinsel, streamers, coloured plumes, spangles and pompoms. Beneath the hole of its rear window had been tastefully painted what may well have been its owner's guiding principle: *I Will Never Say Die If You Forget Me Not.* Its driver was male, small, dark, unsmiling and eight-armed. While Dr Chakki examined his unusual waistcoat, Raichur elaborated, 'My wife made it. It was her idea, during the Puja season last year, to have our auto driven around by Mother Durga—with more arms than usual, of course—more dramatic. We charge a little extra for the privilege. Dambha—the driver here—loves it. It was so successful that we decided to have him—her—him as her—around all year.'

'He doesn't look as though he loves it,' observed Dr Chakki as he and Raichur settled down in the auto-rickshaw. For the passengers in the rear, the six stuffed, life-sized arms a foot ahead of their noses, jutting out of the driver's torso in all directions, severely restricted the view. Indeed, the bottom-most two protruded out of the vehicle on either side, looking from a distance quite lifelike, as though the driver was signalling an intention to turn both left and right at the same time.

'No, he's at the moment blue for family reasons. Given the size of his clan, it is surprising that he isn't miserable all the year round. A younger sister of his is in hospital. She had her cheek grazed by a bullet from Makhmal Bagai's gun, but we maintain that somebody else fired the weapon. It is shocking how much people will lie for money.'

The rickshaw shuddered and chugged through the bicycles, carts, cars and buses, missing not a single pothole as it skirted Aflatoon Maidan. Passersby and pedestrians gazed, grinned and waved at Durga. Dr Chakki, tired but upbeat, waved back, particularly at the policemen. Outside the Mall Road gate of the park, where the footpath broadened out into a sort of paved square, a crowd watching a play in progress had swamped the road. The rickshaw put-putted to a halt against a row of bums and tooted a couple of times to try and budge them before giving up.

To force their way to a ringside seat, Durga came in handy. From the tool box of the auto rickshaw, Raichur fished up a box of incense sticks, a tiny brass bell and a half-mask, the last of which he fitted over Dambha's head. It came down to his nose. Around the holes for the eyes—and stretching up to the ears—had been painted the long-lashed outlines of even larger eyes. To the mask was attached a wig of black, luxuriant, hip-length hair. With a lighter, Raichur lit an incense stick and wedged it between the fingers of one of the stuffed hands. The bell he slung over another padded pinkie. In his new avatar, the driver, listlessly chanting:

Mother, Mother,
Your mother's here.
Do not, Brother,
Quake in fear.
It's only my mask of a face
That makes me look a basket case.
Only the sinful and no other
Feel guilty before a mother

sliced a route through to the centre of the crowd.

The players of Vyatha all wore off-white shirts-and-trousers, or kurta pyjamas. Two of them, to form a door, stood erect three feet apart balancing a wooden slat on their heads. Before them on the pavement squatted an actor playing a peon. About him were strewn some used government envelopes. He was engaged in tearing open their gummed edges, turning them inside out and with a tube of glue, repasting their three sides. The hideous end-products he had stacked on his left. Now and then, rhythmically and without quite pausing in his labours, he would raise a hand to receive from a visitor his card or a slip of paper with his name and purpose of visit on it. Those chits accompanied by bribes he would pass on to one of the doorposts behind him, tucking into his own shirt pocket the currency notes. Those without he would simply slip into the oblivion of one of the remade envelopes.

Only the bribers, of course, crossed the threshold—after, that is, folding into the pockets of one of the doorposts a second currency note. The honest, stupid and persevering turned away, trudged a few steps, wheeled round, retraced their paces and rejoined the queue before the peon to hand him once more their name slips. As long as they didn't add the cash, they didn't step out of the circle, through the door and into the chamber. Where lolled a fat actor in a chair before a desk. His callers addressed him as 'Respected Private Secretary, sir.' When Dr Chakki and Raichur tuned in, he was on the phone swinging a deal, that is to say, the stretched thumb of his left hand was at his left ear, he was delivering his dialogue into the mouthpiece formed by his pinkie, and the intervening three fingers were fisted.

Tuning in to the play was not easy. The hubbub of the street and the laughter and comments of the spectators blocked out most lines; they in turn were totally drowned out by the stentorian, off-and-on, rapidfire commentary of the narrator-persona—tubby, with the hooded eyelids and flared nostrils of a dragon—and the thunderous drumrolls that preceded and followed each of his proclamations. Hence—and because of the inadequacy of his Hindi as well—it took Dr Chakki a while to grasp that the Private Secretary, on behalf of his unnamed Minister, was chatting to a foreign supplier of paper while the suppliant before his desk was a native manufacturer of the same commodity.

Suppliant (briefcase in hand): I beg to remind you, sir, that I offer you the same quantity and quality at fifty crores—virtually half the price, esteemed sir.
Private Secretary (into the phone): Minister would be rather taken aback at anything less than two point five per cent.
Peon (without stopping either his assault on used envelopes or his pocketing of cash): The same crappy paper at the top end of the ladder too—so why bother to climb?
Suppliant (to Private Secretary): Our percentages too, sir, are more attractive. As an added incentive, there's a percentage of the percentage exclusively for you. Consider it akin to a festival bonus.
Private Secretary (chuckling suavely into the phone): Come come—in dollars US of course. Minister has always been very pro the open society and human rights. He would feel like a traitor with any other currency.
Peon (musingly): Honourable Minister's cut alone could buy us several billion envelopes—but of a quality far superior to our needs. Who'd use a sack of silk to throw his garbage out in?

Dr Chakki was distracted from the play at that point by the sudden appearance at Durga's elbow (at one of his eight, more accurately speaking) of a long-haired, bespectacled, groovy-looking man. 'What an interesting idea,' murmured

Rajani Suroor half to himself, as he examined Dambha's getup with intense curiosity, 'Look, Mother Durga, dear,' he cooed as, gripping the young man's shoulder, he began gently to propel him towards the actors, 'Why don't you join the queue that wants to meet the Minister?'

Dambha smiled beneath his mask. 'Yes, why not? I could ask him to save my sister's face.'

Durga in single file triggered off more than one appreciative laugh amongst the audience. The sentinel peon added his share by demanding from the goddess a considerably larger entry fee. 'You've so many more hands, revered Mother, with which to give.'

'Or take.' Dambha swayed and writhed so that the fingers of one of his padded arms could graze and try to fish for the money in the peon's shirt pocket.

Rajani Suroor was in near-ecstasy. 'I've picked a natural.' Almost all the spectators were in agreement with him. A handful who weren't had just arrived in a white Ambassador. They carried bicycle chains, bamboo lathis and hockey sticks. Beginning with the fringe of the crowd, they started, with a shove and a curse here, a lunge and a threatening gesture there, to encourage the audience to disperse. After they had thus cleaved a passage through to the performance, they attacked the players with their weapons.

Exclaiming incredulously, Rajani Suroor had moved forward towards the hoodlums. Two of them pitched into him. The thwack of a hockey stick on his skull was sharp like a rifle shot. A second blow as he toppled altogether stilled him.

Dr Chakki watched them scramble into the car and it squeal away. Its number plate read: Something Something JB 007.

THE PRIME MINISTER VISITS

The December of the plague scare, continued. Agastya Sen believed that one of the many important duties of the Collector of Madna was to swamp his subordinates with paper. Typical of his correspondence with his staff would be his demi-official letter of December 12 asking the tehsildars and Sub-Divisional Officers of the district to pay more attention to his demi-official letters. They didn't.

So in his memo of December 17, he beseeched them to ensure only one thing when they submitted any information to him, that it should not absurdly contradict the information that they'd given him on the *same* subject the week before. To his mind, his request was simple and reasonable. He failed to understand, therefore, why they all found it so difficult to comply with.

Of course, there had been times when he hadn't had to refer to the previous week's report to feel totally foxed. One could take as an instance the last statement of the Resident Tehsildar:

> *There are no cases pending for regularization under Section 31AA of the BP of FC on H Act, 1947. Hence the information called for by the Department for the quarter ending June 30 may be treated as Nil.*

He had sent the file back with a question for the tehsildar. *What does the BP of FC, etc., stand for?* As he had suspected, the tehsildar did not know. The Collector had suggested to him that it might well be the Beastly Practice of Effing Criminals on Housetops Act, 1947, and that the tehsildar could consider writing thus to the Department. He did.

More to the point was the last report of the Leave Reserve Deputy Collector on the position of borewells in the district on July 31:

Total Number of Borewells in the District as on June 30	:	854
Number of Borewells Constructed in July	:	8
Total Number of Borewells in the District as on July 31	:	858
Total Number of Functioning Borewells in the District as on July 31	:	72
Number of Functioning Borewells Constructed in July	:	6
Total Number of Borewells repaired in the District in July	:	84
Total Number of Borewells Yet to be Repaired	:	Figures not available

The statement went every month to the Commissioner, the Departments of Rural Development, Water Supply, Agriculture, Planning, Revenue, Relief and Rehabilitation, and to the Geological Survey. At least they had stopped sending—or rather, it'd be more correct to say that Agastya had stopped signing—totally illegible copies of such statements. Some of his subordinates would recall that that—the incredible nonchalance with which illegible junk was being put up for his signature—had been the subject of his circular of December 15. Very early in his tenure, he had sent dozens of files back with the following note, in place of his signature, on each one of the letters or statements placed for issue in them: *I will not sign something that I cannot read.* None of those files had ever returned to him. When he had enquired, he'd learnt that—why, those letters and statements have been dispatched, sir.

How, he'd asked.

You'd signed them all.

I wrote a little note of protest, you fool, I signed nothing. Can't you read?

Many Departments have replied, sir.

On that occasion, the Class III Employees' Union and the *Dainik* raised a big fuss against the Collector's having used unparliamentary language against a clerk. To make amends, he had agreed thenceforth to call the concerned clerk a spade.

The stenographers and typists of the Collectorate excused their idleness and lack of typing skills by squarely blaming the poor quality of carbon paper that was supplied to them by the Commissioner of Printing. It was a poor pretext and did not hold water with Agastya. For, he felt, even the most vocal of its detractors would not deny that the Office of the Commissioner of Printing and Paper was—and had always been—consistent. Its carbon paper was much like its other paper—grey and smudged, the tint of the sky at twilight over a soot-belching power station.

Bhootnath Gaitonde was imposing in a Mujibur Rehman kind of way. He strode into the office with a handful of his vaguos. Public life had made him taller and fairer since his days in Bhayankar, had deepened his voice and added resonance to his chuckle. As per Department of Personnel and General Administration Office Memorandum No. 25/19/64—Ests (A), dated 8.10.1974, on the subject of Proper Procedure to Be Observed in Official Dealings With MPs/MLAs, Agastya rose from his chair to receive the Member of Parliament. The circular specifically mentions that 'an officer should rise in his seat to receive the member', which to Agastya had always sounded a bit pornographic. He loved it, this whole thing.

The Madna seat had fallen vacant when Bhanwar Virbhim, with an eye on that wider canvas, had decided to become a Member of Parliament. Naturally, the Legislative Assembly seat was his patrimony for his son, to be nurtured by the family well into the next millennium. Bhootnath Gaitonde, then a potential rival, had been simply bought off and encouraged instead to try for Parliament from neighbouring Jompanna South.

Pleasantries for a few minutes before the sparring; tea, coffee or cola? . . . Shri Sen politely pointed out to one vaguo that for the hoi polloi, chewing paan was not allowed on office premises, so would he go out pretty far away please . . . Eventually, Bhootnath Gaitonde got down to taking guard . . . there are so many issues that we need to clarify, Collector Saab . . . how do we begin? . . .

Item Number One was the hunger strike of A.C. Raichur, except that it had now transformed itself into a threat of self-immolation. 'Ah!' beamed Shri Sen, happiest when refusing with reason on his side, 'that's out of our hands. We've forwarded his representation to Home Affairs, copy to the Kansal Commission. Our people have met him to try and dissuade him—the press has been totally irresponsible. He isn't really an emergency, not like Rajani Suroor. Raichur isn't going to cop it for a few months yet—in fact, I'm told that he's put on weight because of the amounts that he eats at night . . . what exactly are you after in his case? . . . ahhh, human interest! . . . why don't you raise the subject in Parliament? . . .'

A.C. Raichur had been forced to heighten the level of his protest because of the utterly unexpected way in which, during the past week, Rajani Suroor had hogged all the spotlight. Not merely the local press, but the national dailies too—and radio and TV as well. Why, even the devious means by which Makhmal Bagai had managed to get bail had gone almost unnoticed in the papers. Raichur had been enviously impressed by the importance of being a friend of the PM.

In a specially constructed, air-conditioned cabin in the Madna Civil Hospital, the friend lay in coma and was thus several laps ahead of Raichur in the race for immortality, an aspect of his hunger strike that had irked the latter not a little. It seemed to him that Rajani Suroor had received—and continued to receive—far too much attention. He'd even been on the front page of *The State of the Times* for the first couple of days. With him had been catapulted into the spotlight the unlikeliest and least deserving of this unfair world—slugs like Alagh the Civil Surgeon, for example, wrenched out of pre-retirement torpor by the pin-prick questioning of hard-boiled, big-city, English-speaking journalists.

'In reply to an earlier question, Dr Alagh, you'd stated that Suroor's condition was "mysterious, not serious." We'd be glad if you could elaborate.'

'Between you and me, that comment was off the record, you know, made just within these four walls and for their ears only.'

'Well, for the ears only of this press conference, Dr Alagh, did you mean that Suroor's unconscious state has confounded some of the finest medical minds of the country—mainly because *they* can't explain it away? That all we need to do is to call in some even finer?'

'Yes, contusion worse confounded, so to speak—off the record, of course.' Not many chuckled, most being unsure whether Dr Alagh had been inopportunely witty or was just plain nervous. Alagh himself would have been at a loss to understand his own remarks, so unsettled had he felt ever since the Thursday of the attack on Suroor. Not an hour's respite had he enjoyed since that afternoon—first the flustered junior doctor on duty to him at home, and after that youngster, at the hospital, the deluge: the Police Superintendent, the Commissioner, the Collector baying on the phone from Rameri, the Surgeon-General from Navi Chipra, the Deputy Secretary (Health), the Joint Secretary (Home Affairs), the Resident Under Secretary to the Chief Secretary, and the morning after, three experts in person from the capital, tense, taciturn and balding, a team organized and packed off to Madna at the behest of the Prime Minister, and instructed by him personally and simply to save Suroor.

Which had been achieved, felt the experts dissatisfiedly, by the local Civil Surgeon himself. He seemed all right—a bit lazy, but fortunately no fool. His report of Thursday afternoon clearly showed that he had taken the crucial first few steps in the right direction, thank Heavens.

> *. . . Patient's pupils, pulse, blood pressure, reflexes and breathing checked and found to be normal. No signs of vomiting. External wounds on scalp, not skull. Bruises on body but no broken bones. All indications of severe concussion but no deep internal haemorrhage. Cerebral angiography was called for and done. Confirmed the absence of internal bleeding. Patient definitely unconscious and definitely alive. By this time, anxious enquiries from very senior district officials made clear the V∞IP status of Patient, so Undersigned telephoned the Surgeon-General before* he *could phone him. Thereafter, through the night, Undersigned was more on the telephone than with Patient. He, Undersigned, was instructed to await the team of experts rushing down from the capital and till then to do the essentials and not anything silly. Accordingly, he readied the operation theatre and ordered his staff to check Patient's pulse and blood pressure every fifteen minutes. To prevent bedsores, Patient was to be shifted about every*

six hours. Needless to add, Patient's head has been shaved and his superficial wounds treated. A catheter has been inserted for his urine. He has been changed into regulation hospital clothes, that is, our standard off-white pyjama and top.

Over Friday and Saturday, the experts suggested the expected: that two tubes be pushed down through Suroor's nose, one to his stomach for food, the other to his lungs for extra oxygen (an oxygen cylinder on a trolley took up a fair amount of room beside the bed); that he should be immediately attached to a cardioscope and a drip, and that the nearest water bed ought to be procured at the earliest. Naturally, enemas would have to be administered as and when required. If his condition continued to be stable, shifting Suroor by helicopter to a—well, better-equipped—hospital or medical centre could be considered after three or four days. Meanwhile, it was the wish of the Highest Level that the patient be provided with an air-conditioned cabin. Since they didn't exist in the Madna Civil Hospital, perhaps the simplest would be to construct one around Suroor. On a war footing, please.

It was obvious to Agastya that Bhootnath Gaitonde hoped to use the crisis of A.C. Raichur to embarrass Bhanwar Virbhim but, unfortunately for him—Gaitonde—the crisis, by Welfare State standards, just wasn't critical enough. When faced with a crisis, what all civil servants longed for was a bigger crisis. In the bureaucratic mind, the tensions of a demonstration, for example, were easily resolved by an outbreak of the plague, which in turn could be totally wiped out by the worst calamity of all, the visit of a Prime Minister. It was a bit like the ancient law of *Matsyanyaya*, of the Big Fish gobbling up the Little Fish, and of being gobbled up in turn by even Bigger Fish. What with the assault on Rajani Suroor and the subsequent decision of the PM to drop in to see his friend at the Madna Civil Hospital, poor Raichur had lost the race within metres from the start.

Exasperatingly small crises like Raichur, or the persistent telephone calls of the District Minister for a favour disguised as an order, Shri Sen defused by simply going away on a tour. The district of Madna covered 17,000 square kilometres and one could always find a hundred reasons—cases, inspections, enquiries—for driving out into it. Out there in the landscape, time moved like a bullock-cart. It didn't matter that the telephone didn't work and everyone seemed to wait in the shade all day only for the sun to set. Routinely, he returned to headquarters calmed, refreshed to the point of being zonked, because he'd forgotten the crisis that had sent him away, so had the office. Or it—the office—had been overwhelmed by a graver emergency and had therefore abandoned the preceding crisis, that is to say, considered it resolved.

And Commissioner Raghupati, too sated by cynicism to be upset at the legitimate absence of a key official from the scene of a flap of the magnitude of the Suroor incident, yet perennially alert to the possibilities of exploiting any turn of events to unexpected advantage, found time, even in that first confusing week after the attack, to direct a series of letters both to the central and regional governments on the subject of impressing upon National Telecom the urgent need of arranging for the mobile phone network to fan out across the length and breadth of the country, and of providing official portable sets to key district officials for better governance in general and more effective disaster management in particular.

Agastya had a longish note on *Matsyanyaya* in the February section of his black diary, except that he called it *Nutsyanyaya*. He could find an example of lunacy wherever he looked in the Welfare State, but no one else seemed to bother, most found it funny or pleasantly incomprehensible. He was compelled to believe that everyone recognized the madness but accepted it as law—Item Number Two on the agenda of Bhootnath Gaitonde, for instance, the visit of the Prime Minister to Madna a week later, would certainly qualify as an example of Nutsyanyaya. Why was he coming? Did he know that his forty-five-minute-long visit would cost the government over six crores of rupees? Of course, he couldn't very well declare to the world that he was flying down fourteen hundred kilometres from the capital at state expense only to look in on a friend, so his party and the regional government, to justify his appearance, had organized a public meeting for him in Aflatoon Maidan and, to quote from the official Top Secret Circular, 'a personal inspection of the supposedly-plague-stricken areas'. When he zipped to the capital's airport from wherever he was to board his plane, eight other steel-grey, bullet-proof, opaque-glassed, souped-up Hindustan Contessa cars, wailing and squealing, would zip with him. Someone was paying for all that zipping about. All along the route that the Prime Minister would take to the airport, and all along a decoy route that he wouldn't take, constables would be posted fifty metres apart for two hours before the zipping and for half-an-hour after. That was seven hundred man-hours of the police force. Along those two routes, traffic would be stopped by stressed-out policemen for seventy-five minutes before and fifteen minutes after the Contessas. One could thus add to the costs of the Prime Ministerial visit the value of one hour in each of the lives of at least five thousand people. Agastya firmly believed that a survey ought to be undertaken of the opinions of those citizens fretting away in one of the traffic jams created by the Prime Minister. He'd quite willingly have passed the questionnaires around himself. He could in fact *see* himself in the role—miraculously a boy again, in white shorts, red tee-shirt and red-n-white baseball cap, teeth gleaming white against a skin blackened by the sun, thrusting sheaves through open car windows, madly happy at being on the move with a purpose and at being paid for it, enjoying the sweating, unhappy enervated faces within and outside the cars, flinging into the confusion these questions that had so much topspin in them.

i) Do you vote?
ii) The Welfare State has used **your** *money to lead you up to this jam. Does that bother you?*
iii) Would you be very upset if the Prime Minister is blown up at this moment? Of course, that would lead, among other things, to the mother of all traffic jams.
iv) Do you care for the official view that the Prime Minister's journey is more important than yours? His time too?
v) At such moments in your life, are you reminded of the New Vision Party's assessment of our Prime Minister? To quote from their last election pamphlet: 'By temperament, looks, bearing, demeanour, intelligence, wit and character, Bhuvan Aflatoon is well-suited to be Lobby Manager of Claridge's Hotel in the capital.'
vi) Why have we allowed our present statesmen and bureaucrats to mess things up completely?

That they had Agastya did not doubt in the least. It seemed to him that he could cite without pause a million examples. On the 7th, 14th and 26th of the previous month, for instance, Dr Onorari Kansal, the Chairman of the eponymous Commission, was summoned to the Centre for talks, i.e., to discuss routine palace intrigues. On each occasion, he travelled from the regional capital to the Centre by the State Government helicopter. Being a man with many things on his mind, on each occasion, he forgot back home his favourite sleeping suit, an off-white kurta-pyjama set that had been gifted to him by his astrologer, erstwhile Chief Secretary (and present Cabinet Secretary) Shri Manorath Shukl. He sent the helicopter back each time. Thus at least one State Government made, at the common expense, at least three extra return trips in the preceding month from one regional capital to the Centre to ferry a favourite sleeping suit.

In contrast, in the district of Madna, Agastya himself had found concrete evidence of at least eighteen cases in which poverty had forced families in the block of Jompanna to sell themselves, literally body and soul, as bonded labourers for seventy-five rupees per year, that is, for the price of three litres of petrol for a car idling in a traffic jam, *per year*, year after year after year. Every day, in other words, those families woke up and, in return for some scraps of food and water, worked in the fields and homes of their masters till they died, after which their heirs inherited their burden. At the end of the year, that seventy-five rupees of course wasn't made over to them. Their masters paid themselves back—that is, wrote off for the amount a part of some mythic, ancestral debt.

Now, felt Agastya, were the Prime Minister to announce that he was rushing down to Madna to meet face to face the bottom of the pile—the families that starved to death, the parents who sold their daughters to pay off their debts, the villagers who trudged four hours a day to ferry five litres of muddy water, the poor who, tortured and beaten, lost their lives because of some incomprehensible caste offence, the godforsaken who were burnt and mutilated so that they could beg at the traffic intersections of the cities—were the Prime Minister to decide to encounter, face to face, without a single, interfering intermediary of the Welfare State, some of the millions who were truly in need of welfare, *that* would be an occasion worth commemorating, the event of the millennium.

vii) Why don't you—sweating, overweight, bespectacled, fretting, moustached—get out of your car and take over from our present statesmen and bureaucrats?
viii) Why do you want the Welfare State to leave you alone?

Because all its representatives that one encountered spelt trouble, that's why. The bribe-gobbling cop and telephone linesman, the venal Corporation clerk and electricity-metre reader.

ix) Or is the cause within you—the frightening, limitless greed of the middle classes? You've fattened monstrously in the last fifty years, but you'd like to be left alone, wouldn't you, to get on with your gormandizing and navel-gazing?

And so the questions had run on in Agastya's head for weeks, months and years. With a craftsman's skill and a cop's doggedness, he'd returned to them a dozen times a day, to chisel, polish and hone them in the hope that their subject would at last catch the light.

(x) Do you want the most capable men and women of your country to
a) sell wearunders, bags of cement and sunflower cooking oil,
b) run a newspaper,
c) or a hotel,
d) or a Market Research Bureau,
e) or the country?

To him, the issues and solutions seemed eternally important; yet, Nutsyanyaya reigned all around him—an office of the Commissioner of Stationery the size of a city, for example, that couldn't produce simple white paper, or a Deputy Secretary, Administrative Reform, for instance, who, as part of some Renewed Economy Drive, was being paid a salary to circulate instructions to peons to make new envelopes out of used ones.

xi) What scares you most about government? Is it Nutsyanyaya?

xii) Would you then say that it's more frightening to be outside the Welfare State than within it?

Agastya himself didn't think so. Nutsyanyaya was truly everywhere and nobody could escape it. He hadn't, for example, that February afternoon after the Collectors' Conference summoned by the Prime Minister at the TFIN Complex had got over.

For a variety of reasons, Agastya'd cycled down to the Aflatoon Tiffin Box from his uncle's house, a bare ten minutes away: a) Lutyens's City was one of the few places left in the country where one could still cycle; b) An office car from the Liaison Commissioner's office required enormous amounts of wheedling with the lower orders; c) No civil servant ever travelled in a taxi—that would be like asking him to clean an office toilet or to carry his own files.

Of course, no civil servant ever travelled on a bike either. So must have thought the cop who had come upon Agastya unlocking his cycle from the fence of the canteen lawns of the Tiffin Box. Hey, you, etc. He couldn't have liked very much Agastya's face or his manner of answering back, because he actually roughed him up quite a bit in the few seconds that he had before some others turned up. Of course, as a consequence, the policeman landed himself in temporary but deep shit.

So did Agastya. As a fallout of the constable's assault, but without the necessary permissions from the intervening rungs, he wrote a letter to none other than the Prime Minister on the subject of Nutsyanyaya.

... Sir, may I officially be allowed to keep a gun to protect myself from the police? As the District Magistrate, I may be relied on to use it judiciously.

Certainly, necessary training in the use of firearms would have to be imparted to us during office hours. I have made unofficial enquiries with the extremely cooperative Superintendent of Police of Madna and he has assured me that procuring a firearm, even a rocket launcher if need be, would pose no problem . . .

. . . The question that begs to be asked, sir, is: why are we whittling down the generalist administrator's executive control over our police force? In one's youth, one used to naively believe that one should join the service of the State because once within, one was safer from our police force than when one was without. What a dangerously foolish notion! I am reminded in this connection of what a dear colleague and an old friend of mine, Mr Dhrubo Jyoti Ghosh Dastidar, tells me that he told the Selection Board of Eminent Bureaucrats at his job interview. The Magi asked him:

> *Mr Dastidar, why do you want to join the Civil Service?*
>
> *Mr Dastidar: Because within the Civil Service, one is likelier to have a peon, a Personal Assistant, and an Ambassador car as buffers between one's good self and the rest of the government.*

Mr Dastidar still holds the record for the lowest marks ever scored by any civil servant at his entrance interview. I have already written to him describing in detail my misadventure at the Aflatoon TFIN Complex and underscoring my conclusion: No One Is Safe from Them Anywhere, Boy! *He naturally sympathized with me body and soul and suggested to me what in fact is my next proposal to you.* Sir, Give Us Uniforms. *Exactly like the cops have, threatening to explode around the belly and bum like terrycot covers stretched beyond endurance over bags of cement and twin ghatams, the navel visible like a hairy Peeping Tom's eye at a keyhole. However, our uniforms, though of the same colour as those of the policemen, should be a couple of shades lighter to make it clear to all that we are above them and their dealings. Mr Dastidar disagrees with me on this point. He would prefer that our uniforms be a couple of shades darker to indicate that we can be more menacing when we want to be. The image that he has, he tells me, is that of the thundercloud.*

May I share with you my thoughts of those dreadful moments when the cop was beating me up on the perfect lawns of the Tiffin Box?

i) However could this be happening to me? To me! I can recite almost all of J. Alfred Prufrock from memory! I sang back-up vocals on Knockin on Heaven's Door on Yuva Vani in my college days! I've bought the poems of Rilke and that too with plastic! I've holidayed in Majorca, Madrid and L'ile Maurice! You can't touch me! I speak English at home, all the time! I have white American friends! I am to have dinner this evening, in three hours' time, with the Prime Minister, where Jayati Aflatoon and Rani Chandra, people like that, will be present!

ii) How to explain all this to this frightful ape with these fists of stone?

iii) This is the stuff of counter-revolutions. Just you wait, you fucker of the lower orders, and I'll show you how the Steel Frame snaps back.

I have taken the liberty, sir, of retaining the original swear-word to give you a sense of the extent of my outrage. 'We are truly lucky that we are so far above the classes whose welfare is our headache,' opined my colleague Mr Dastidar, when I tried to explain to him on the phone my feelings about the cop who beat me up. 'Imagine—had we been like them, we'd have been envying people like us. Ugh. And then again I think, since we ourselves aren't so hot, our disgust and fear of the Great Unwashed are the only proof we have that we aren't *like them. It's time now for our revolution, as usual two hundred years behind Europe.'*

This surely, sir, is the heart of the matter, the core of the problem. How many thousand rungs beneath the cop in question does one have to descend to be able to see at last, face to face, the—if you permit—etiolated worms beneath the pavements, the most squashed of the downtrodden, the starvelings who inhabit the other side of the Welfare Line? Surely the Kansal Commission could've reached out to them, *could've declared its goal to be to locate and uplift the millions who have no clout whatsoever, who are the wretched of the earth who've never sucked at the mammae of the Welfare State.*

Instead, mused Shri Sen in wonder, they didn't mind spending over six crores of rupees on the Prime Minister's forty-five-minute-long visit to Madna. Didn't anyone have any sense of priorities, of right and wrong? I mean, dash it, this wasn't the Army—vast, secretive about the unimportant, tyrannical and insane. This was the open society where thousands claimed to know what was going on. Yet, every time the Prime Minister left the capital, his entire Cabinet zoomed off to the airport to see him off. That was forty-two Ministers, one hundred and sixty-eight Black Guard Commando bodyguards, forty-two Private Secretaries, forty-two Officers on Special Duty, eighty-four Personal Assistants and eighty-four peons, give or take a few dozen, away from the parking lots, the corridors and the desks of power for four hours each.

How nonplussed, how rudderless, the whole jingbang, the entire white Ambassadocracy, had felt, like chicks being abandoned by the mother hen, when the upwardly-mobile Prime Minister had switched, all of a sudden, to steel-grey Contessas for his motorcade. The twenty-first-century men in his Cabinet, after a few weeks of chin-stroking indecision, had followed suit, but the shrewd nationalists—Bhanwar Virbhim, for example—had retained their white

Ambassadors—with, however, 1800 c.c. Contessa engines under their bonnets.

The overriding virtue of the Ambassador is that, though it's descended from the British Morris Oxford, it's nevertheless a tremendously indigenous car. Lots of character. When one travels about in it, one can never be accused of not having the nation's interest foremost in one's heart. For forty years, the Welfare State has bought mainly Ambassadors for itself, some thousands a year, and has thus kept them in the forefront of the industry. The Prime Minister's infidelity is therefore cataclysmic; it is also the first step towards God knows where. The Maruti Suzuki Esteem? The PAL Peugeot 309? The Ford Escort? The Daewoo Cielo? The Mitsubishi Lancer? The Tata Mercedes? It was all quite upsetting, Agastya concluded, and truly made one feel that one was losing one's identity. However could one remain a servant of the Welfare State while sitting in a car that actually effectively chilled one's brow, that glided and purred, that while moving didn't sound like a body-repair wing of an automobile workshop?

'Our agenda for the Prime Minister's visit, Collector Saab,' pronounced Bhootnath Gaitonde, leaning back in his chair and eyeing Agastya with grave doubt, 'will include A.C. Raichur setting fire to himself in public, in protest against the conclusions of the Kansal Commission. The event will be quite dramatic because we hope to synchronize it with the precise moment when the PM's motorcade enters Aflatoon Maidan. Raichur will rise from his hunger strike only to douse himself with kerosene and light up. My party has of course formally written to you and the police on this subject, giving sufficient advance notice and so on. It is incredible that the government has accepted the recommendations of the Commission without examining the implications for the institutionalization of the inequalities of caste.' Bhootnath Gaitonde waited for Shri Sen to react; he in turn waited for his visitor to continue.

'My party will also raise two issues of finance with the Prime Minister. One: that since the district of Madna didn't have a helipad, one had to be built just for his visit. Does that bother him or not? Two: Twenty lakhs has been given to the Madna Civil Hospital to clean itself up for his visit. Our Civil Surgeon is mentally not equipped to handle such a vast sum of money. Cynics at the hospital have suggested to him that on that day, he should issue himself a certificate of illness. I've been told that you've officially disclaimed all responsibility for the PM's visit to the hospital.'

'No, no, not at all,' laughed Agastya with innocent joy, 'I merely wrote to the Department of Public Health that our Civil Hospital was one of the filthiest places that I've ever seen in my life and that a sight of it might upset the Prime Minister no end. Which is why I'd suggested that Rajani Suroor be moved out of there while the going is good. I don't give him any chance if he floats up out of his coma while he's with Dr Alagh and actually sees what he's been lying in now for almost two weeks. If you ask me, he comes to every morning, struggles up into consciousness, eyes his surroundings and shocked, relapses into a deeper swoon. Then the nurse on her rounds notes that he's slipping.'

'And Chamundi?'

'What's that? A new goddess?'

Bhootnath Gaitonde chuckled politely for a nanosecond and elaborated, '. . . The boy has simply disappeared from the Commissioner's house. About a fortnight ago, the Commissioner was interrupted during his afternoon massage by a telephone call from you. When, after a couple of minutes, the Commissioner returned to the massage room, Chamundi had vanished without a trace. Odd, but due to the pressure of office work, Commissioner Raghupati had absolutely no time to think of it then. Nobody has seen Chamundi since. This is his brother here, Dambha.' Gaitonde indicated one of the vaguos, more red-eyed than the rest.

Like a well-rehearsed exit in a play, at that point, the others rose and quietly left the room. '. . . Chamundi's relations tell me that the Commissioner was—is—greatly attached to the boy. They want to register an FIR with the police but have been unable to so far. They then of course came to me. The police and the Commissioner believe that the boy simply went home into the forests of Jompanna. He succumbed to a typical tribal instinct, they maintain, that all of a sudden revolts against order, routine, discipline, work and all the other indicators of our notions of the civilized life. He was fed up, in short, and needed a break.'

'It is not improbable.'

'Chamundi's family thinks differently.'

Agastya waited for Bhootnath Gaitonde to get to the point. He was curious to hear exactly how the other would phrase it. Some beating about the bush, then finally in English, 'homosexual assault', like a Latin legalistic term, 'in situ', or 'pro rata'.

'Oh dear. Sodomy and suspected murder. In the circumstances, it isn't surprising that the police want to wait for a body to turn up, dead or alive. So should you, at least till the Prime Minister departs. Think of how much you'll hurt the Commissioner with your accusations.'

'We will of course link it up with the other sexual assault case, that of the civil servant, Kumari Lina Natesan Thomas. She's accused Raghupati of sexually attacking her at an official dinner and he's apparently going to receive a court summons. You're no doubt aware of that?'

'Ah yes—Kumari Lina . . . already the stuff of legend, Gaitonde-ji, and utterly admirable. A great pity, that I haven't yet had the honour of meeting her. Yes, it does seem that the Commissioner'd offended her in some way or the other at their first meeting, and on a matter of principle, she refused to let the matter rest . . . a useful thing, principle. One wishes one had more of it oneself. No meetings, files, paperwork, inspections, reviews . . . one can focus all one's energies on representations and written complaints instead, addressed to all one's bosses from the PM down to Shri Raghupati. You of course know that he's due to move now, any day. He'll be going to the Centre as Joint Secretary. Minister Virbhim can't wait to surround himself with his henchmen, naturally. Meanwhile, the pressure is on us to prepare a backgrounder for a White Paper for the Department on this whole Rajani Suroor business. I told them that it'd be easier to draw up an off-white paper.'

Bhootnath Gaitonde's manner seemed to suggest that Shri Sen shouldn't be chuckling in office all the time. 'For us, the class implications of the mysterious disappearance of Chamundi are clear. We intend to give this resonantly symbolic act the widest publicity. It is what in essence all your Welfare State programmes do to all your beneficiaries—what else is buggery but base exploitation, tell me? . . . Vyatha, Suroor's drama group, is very enthusiastic about the theme that I've proposed to them. I met its second-in-command at the Madna International a couple of days ago. An absolute tiger in his enthusiasm, though in appearance, more a dragon—a Bengali too, perhaps you know him?—I've suggested a full-length street play that will revolve around Chamundi, how the innocent boy has been ensnared by the web of the Welfare State . . . the entire family frankly rues the day when the grandfather became one of the first beneficiaries of the Integrated Tribal Development Plan . . .'

Well, not perhaps the *entire* family, since it is more accurately an enormous tribal clan that stretches up to the horizon and beyond. Beyond because Chamundi's agnate uncle, for example, a one-legged father of two nubile daughters and half-a-dozen younger siblings, has for some years been residing far away in the capital—more precisely, beneath the new Trimurti Aflatoon Centenary Celebrations Flyover. As for his more immediate kin, his sister has been discharged from the

Madna Civil Hospital with a livid scar on her cheek and a numbness in all her faculties. She returns to the International Hotel to learn that they don't want her back with her new face. She is thus poised to sink back to her roots in the jungles of Jompanna. Chamundi's elder brother, Dambha, is fed up of riding an auto-rickshaw in Madna rigged out as Durga and is on the lookout for starting off anew elsewhere. He would have quit the district months ago had he not been dissuaded by his wife, who is blind and was last in the news eight years ago when she had been attacked with a hot ladle by an attendant at the Hemvati Aflatoon Welfare State Home. A truly unfortunate—but representative—clan, dispersed in an enormous diaspora and up against it everywhere, its members individually and haphazardly thrashing their limbs about to stay afloat and above the Poverty Line, dimly aware that unless they seized and moulded their futures themselves, the single miracle that could officially deliver them would be the arbitrary decision of some state planners to improve the economic health of the nation by simply lowering that crucial line.

Up against the plague too, even though it was one of the few misfortunes that hadn't touched them yet. For Commissioner Bhupen Raghupati had decided—and suggested to the Police Superintendent—that the AWOL Chamundi could profitably be considered a victim of the epidemic and should anyone enquire about him anywhere, he was to be told so. Inspired by the idea, Makhmal Bagai, fresh from jail but unrepentant, had proposed the same diagnosis—or else—for both the scar on the face of Chamundi's sister and the long trance of Rajani Suroor. The Civil Surgeon had taken three days' Casual Leave to mull the theories over.

'Hmmm'-ing, and 'I see'-ing intelligently at regular intervals, Shri Sen switched off while Bhootnath Gaitonde ran on. His conscience reminded him that he was being paid, inter alia, to listen to whoever sat in front of him. In turn, he pointed out to his conscience that he was sure that his concentration was commensurate with his pay.

In his years in the Civil Service, time and time again, usually when he'd been plumb in the middle of something, Agastya had stepped outside himself, observed for a while whatever he'd been doing, and then asked himself whether it—his activity of that moment—would in any way, directly or indirectly, immediately or eventually, actually help the absolutely poor, the real have-nots, the truly unprivileged, the utterly godforsaken—in brief, the supposed primary beneficiaries of the Welfare State. His answer had always been no.

For one thing, development, to be successful, had to be achieved by stealth. No one must know. If the word spread, everybody would move in and walk all over one.

For another—well, how *did* his day pass? 1) Listening, off and on, to Bhootnath Gaitonde, a middle-aged, dark star of an unimportant, Leftist-ish political party. That was certainly not going to help anybody. What else?

2) Pushing files on different subjects. Signing a clerk's General Provident Fund Loan Advance. Grabbing hectares of some hapless soul's land for a thermal power project that would take off two decades after. Answering tedious Parliament and Legislative Assembly questions. Allowing agricultural land to be used for generally illegal, non-agricultural purposes. Enquiring into the misdeeds of a Municipal Officer who retired four years ago. Replying to lengthy audit objections. Sanctioning special holidays in the district. Permitting the Electricity Board to build a substation beside the Primary School. Sending two hundred different kinds of statements to fifty different offices. Writing stinkers to subordinates, drawing their attention to earlier stinkers. Ordering other offices to depute their staff for special drives.

Disallowing a peon's Medical Reimbursement Claim. Gearing up for a V∞IP visit that would always start three hours behind schedule. Unwinding thereafter. Tearing down encroachments and slums. Watching from his car their inhabitants attack the police. Inspecting the records of a district treasury or subordinate office. And so on. None of that even remotely touched the lives of those at the bottom of the pile. What else during the day?

3) A seven-hour-long District Planning and Development Council Meeting, the miasma of which was interrupted only by a stultifying lunch. At such gatherings—Members of Parliament and of the Legislative Assembly, local politicians, prominent citizens, chums of the party in power—all harangued the government in general and the bureaucracy in particular for their misdeeds. Their revelations and accusations were on the whole accurate and had the sting, the fury, of those done out of a deal. Not even one such allegation or denunciation, in Agastya's experience, had been prompted by any sense of justice, propriety, fairplay, ethics, decency or right. However, being fundamentally clearsighted—or innocent—he still believed that these concepts existed and had meaning in the Welfare State. As far as possible, for example, and without cracking up, he wanted to ferret out and help the neediest of the needy, the sort who actually died every now and then of hunger; he wished to work out a system, a method, by which these millions could be precisely located, to cleave through the mountains of off-white paper to arrive at the heart of the matter, the essence of the Welfare State. Of course, working out that system would require more off-white paper. Fortunately, there'd never be a shortage.

Sure enough, he'd ruminated in his black diary:

Out of all these schemes, plans, projects and programmes of ours that look so snazzy on paper, who benefits in the end? After every bugger down the line, that is, has wolfed down his cut? It's almost always

> *someone familiar with the system, isn't it? He's benefitted before from some other programme, so he knows how those dreadful forms are to be filled up, which twenty-three documents are required, whom to bribe to get what faked. If he himself can't apply the second time round under his own name, then his mother, father, wife, sister, sons, uncle or cousin can, or he himself can under an assumed name. Not that he doesn't need the peanuts that we dole out, but surely, in this monstrously populous, economically haywire country, there exist millions who need them* more. *Of course, one column of the dreadful form will routinely ask the beggar whether he or his near and dear ones have ever sucked before at these dugs, or at other dugs, of the State. We might run out of milk for them, but not for ourselves, and never will we run out of paper. If only we'd all been cows.*

Bhootnath Gaitonde left after decades, with an assurance, however, that they would see each other again within the hour at the special meeting convened by the Commissioner to discuss the minute-to-minute programme of the Prime Minister's visit.

The special meeting was actually two. To the second meeting had been invited the Army, the Air Force, the police, Public Works, National Highways, the Municipality, Public Health, the District Council, the Intelligence Bureau, the Security Branch, the District Education Officer, the press and media staff, General Administration and of course Protocol. All of them had to attend the first meeting too, formal invitations to which had only gone out to the elected, political and other heavyweights of the district. The two meetings would naturally discuss the minute-to-minute programmes of the Governor and the Chief Minister as well, since they were the principal among the many dignitaries expected in Madna before and for the PM. The second meeting would actually chalk and iron things out—who would garland whom, when the Army would salute and where the schoolkids with their paper flags and patriotic songs would be lined up. The first meeting had been organized mainly to ensure that no one felt offended at being left out of the Top—but open—Secret deliberations of the second—which of course the invitees to the first wouldn't attend, it being hush hush and restricted only to about a hundred officials.

To be honest, the second meeting—which would be the first of a series of many, held with increasing frequency and panic and decreasing method—would map everything out but the nitty gritty. How many in the helicopter? Who were the others? The exact time of arrival? Was Bhanwar Virbhim part of the entourage or was he now officially in some other camp? Would the PM's food taster be on the flight? Where was lunch? Was the helipad to be sanitized twenty-four or forty-eight hours before the landing? Could they presume for heavens' sake that the police would not insist on photographs on the temporary identity cards that would be issued to the privileged who would be allowed into the V∞IP enclosure at the helipad? No V∞IP enclosure at all? Did they know what they were saying? Would his route to Aflatoon Maidan skirt the plague or pierce through it? Was it really necessary to have armed gunmen on the rooftops all along the route? Provide them packed lunches and bottled mineral water? Really? Why don't we set up Committees for each macro event and sub-committees for the micro events? Well, micro as in bottled mineral water for armed gunmen en route? Who would clear, from the Security angle, private video cameras? Not you? You only do TV channels? Then who? Will we need separate passes to have access to the twenty-four-hour control room? Is the visit to Rajani Suroor in the hospital official? Oh, a private diversion? At the Maidan, a maximum of how many chairs on the dais? Chairs with armrests? Are sandalwood-scented garlands acceptable to the PM? You know, because of sandalwood and Sukumaran Govardhan?

The list of questions was never-ending; further, they

changed with every meeting. Those answered and settled beyond doubt on Monday became irrelevant on Wednesday. Is the Prime Minister's Private Secretary a vegetarian? was Monday's question. He isn't coming, was Wednesday's information, but his Principal Personal Assistant is. Well, what's his name? Not much is known of this one but he keeps a vow of silence on Thursdays.

Different sections of the vast police network of the Welfare State—Intelligence, Security, Anti-terrorism, Vigilance, the regional police—knew some of the answers to some of the questions but they weren't telling. For one, they couldn't—no one could—be absolutely certain of their information. For another, to reveal it was an unnecessary security risk, that is to say, knowledge is power. I do my job, if others had done theirs, the country wouldn't have gone to the dogs.

When they did communicate what they knew, it was either because the news was stale and safe or it had already been passed on by somebody else. The transmission was almost always oral—by wireless or telephone; firstly, because writing stuff down took time; secondly, because notes and faxes became records, the undeniable, ineradicable evidence of an event, and therefore avoidable. The receivers sometimes wrote the information down and telegrammed or faxed it back for confirmation, which hardly ever arrived, usually because by then the facts had changed. On the rare occasions when minute-to-minute programmes weren't turned around at the last minute and Headquarters could boast of a responsible and dutiful set of officers, the written confirmations trickled in, in twos and threes, a week or so after the event.

Between Bhootnath Gaitonde and the two-in-one meeting, the Collector of Madna tried to meet all his hundred waiting petitioners in under half-an-hour. His best timing till then had been twenty-eight minutes for one hundred and thirteen of them. He was however tripped up completely by the forty-third, a spirited eighty-year-old woman who claimed to be a Veteran Freedom Fighter. Her bewildered rage didn't look as though it could be assuaged by thirty undivided seconds of the Collector's time. Sighing, Agastya settled down to focus on her complaint. The letter to Daya would have to wait a while. Chidambaram glided in with some sheets of whitish paper and the local newspapers. Without interrupting his 'Oh dear'-ing and 'Let me see'-ing, Agastya ran his eye over the headlines. He was comically outraged by one leading news item. He summoned Chidambaram.

'The *Dainik* has this time confused leptospirosis and the plague. I mean, where do these people live? I want you to ask the PRO to arrange to send an intelligible rejoinder . . . perhaps even organize a press conference . . . the subject can be . . . The Rats of Madna: A Comparative Survey . . . that should cover just about everybody . . .'

Places weren't marked for the officials in the meeting hall of the Commissionerate but nevertheless, they all sat in strict pecking order to the left of the Commissioner around an enormous round table, facing the members of Parliament and Legislative Assembly and other worthies. On Agastya's right sat Madna's Superintendent of Police, Panna Lal Makkad. Atop the files that Agastya had carted along for psychological support lay the sheets of whitish paper that he hoped by the end of the meeting would become his letter to Daya.

Makkad was gruff and glum, with hooded eyes, and a toothpick and fist in his mouth. Post-lunch was clearly not his time of day for special meetings. While the Chairman of the District Council declaimed on the need to have the Prime Minister commemorate his historical visit by inaugurating the unfinished new premises of the Madna Janata College, the necessity therefore of completing construction in six days and the general criminal laziness of the district civil engineering staff, Makkad belched and yawned at regular intervals before falling into a light doze with his eyes wide open. At four-thirty, after the non-official special invitees had taken a quarter of an hour to physically quit the hall, and the Collector had jotted down a few points with which to reassure—if not lull—the assembly into believing that all for the PM's visit was well, Makkad leaned across and breathed into Agastya's ear, 'He isn't coming, you know. Don't tell anyone because you aren't supposed to know officially till next Monday.'

The Collector controlled an urge to clamber on to the table and do a striptease. He instead observed the armed forces, clearly miffed at the civilian notion of their place in the hierarchy, gather up their things and reposition themselves in correct descending order alongside the Commissioner's right elbow.

'His piles acting up?'

'Sort of, what with all the drama that's going on. His advisors fear his being upstaged by Sukumaran Govardhan. Who, it is true, *has* sent out feelers for a trade-off. An unconditional surrender for a general pardon; then run for Parliament, and with his crores, back the right horse for PM.'

Fact tarted up as fiction, garnished as fantasy, but nonetheless fundamentally fact. Agastya began to love the meeting. He valued them in particular when they—almost officially—became pointless. 'Has he decided whom to surrender to?'

'He naturally wants it to be the PM. Live TV coverage while he ceremonially hands over a couple of flame throwers. The PM's Secretariat has snapped its fingers at the idea. A criminal can't simply start from the top. He must wait a bit to get there.'

'So the buzz is true—he and Bhanwar Virbhim and the rest of Jayati Aflatoon's caucus to orchestrate a palace coup, following proper democratic procedure, of course.'

The Superintendent merely smiled in reply and while continuing to gaze beatifically at the armed forces, settled down to snatch a quick supplementary nap.

A PEST IN THE CORRIDORS OF POWER

To rendezvous with Daya at the earliest, and at the expense of the Welfare State, far away in anonymity, peace and quiet, the Collector of Madna suggested on the phone to the Under Secretary for Demotic Drama at Aflatoon Bhavan that he be summoned to the capital fourteen hundred kilometres away to report, in person, to the Centre on exactly what happened in broad daylight to Rajani Suroor.

'Sure, good idea', agreed Dhrubo. 'Bring that pest from the hospital, Alagh, along. Make it a delegation.'

He looked less like a pest and more like the dragon of the comic-strips, Dr Alagh the Civil Surgeon of Madna did. He had hooded, sleepy eyes and a long nose, almost as wide as his mouth, with inordinately-flared nostrils. His lips were pale and thin, but his mouth enormous; when he smiled, his face became quite pear-like. The gaps in his teeth could comfortably allow the exhalation of fire; perhaps they—the gaps—had been created by his breathing under stress. Certainly, both his moustache and goatee had an uncertain, wispy, singed look. Appropriately, his remaining teeth were dark brown from smoking.

Except for a patch of forest above his left ear, he was bald. He wore that patch long, oiled it, dragged it up and across his dome down to his right ear where, mission accomplished, he abandoned it; tendrils of hair wandered all over his scalp, determinedly searching, like vines, for support.

He was short and podgy, perennially shabby, generally in sandals and off-white trousers and bush-shirt. For the meeting at the Centre, he carried a leather briefcase with his wallet, a small towel, his cigarettes, some Nivea cream for his chapped lips and a few books in it. They made him feel intellectual and creative, like a college student with a future.

They weren't of much help, though, in the jungle of Aflatoon Bhavan. A cop stopped him and Agastya at the doors and asked them in Haryanvi-Punjabi, in a lazy, friendly way, 'And you, Hero Masters, where d'you think you're off to?'

Alagh Saab (as he liked to be called) began to stutter in Hindi, 'We wanted to—Culture ... a report ... Under Secretary ... appointment ...' He glanced at Agastya for guidance but the latter didn't much wish to converse with a cop. Besides, he—Agastya—was comfortable only in Bengali, Hindi and English. Haryanvi frightened, and Punjabi appalled, him. He was also depressed at being one of the only pair to be stopped in the leisurely after-lunch influx into the building.

The cop wriggled his eyebrows at them. 'What's in that bag? A bomb? An AK-47?' He commandingly stretched his hand out for the briefcase. Mesmerised both by the power of the law and the Haryanviness of the policeman's personality, Dr Alagh numbly handed it over. A Surd breezed by with a cheerful invitation for the cop. 'Coming up to the Coffee House? For something piping hot before we fuck your mother?' A large group of folk singers that had just been cleared by Reception guffawed.

The cop's paw emerged from the briefcase with T.S. Eliot's *Notes Towards the Definition of Culture* and the Nivea cream. 'What's this for?' he demanded, pushing the Nivea under Dr Alagh's nose, but he didn't really want an answer. He was about to rummage deeper when he—'Aha!'—caught sight of the leather strap of a simple automatic camera around Agastya's neck. He looked sternly from one to the other. 'Spies, perhaps! Photography is strictly banned in Aflatoon Bhavan—you'll of course tell me that you didn't know that.'

'It isn't a bomb, for Heaven's sake. It's silly to ban

photography in the office when you have at least five hundred photocopying machines in each Department.'

'Deposit this camera at Reception and get a pass from them for whoever you want to meet.'

'Look—we *have* been to Reception! We have an appointment at 2.30 with the Under Secretary for Demotic and Indigenous Drama. We *tried* his intercom from Reception but there wasn't any reply because he *never* answers his internal phones. There's nobody in Aflatoon Bhavan, he's often declared, whom he'd care to receive a call from. The man at Reception understood but couldn't issue us a pass because as per rule, he has to first confirm the appointment on the intercom with the officer to be visited. He suggested that we should explain the background to you and that you'd be sure to follow and let us through . . . are you wondering whether the Under Secretary for Demotic Drama answers his *external* phone? *He* doesn't, but mercifully his PA does—that's how—'

'HUBRIS DESCENDING!' All of a sudden, from the speaker above the cop's head, a deafening, panicky whisper, as though from an archangel under stress. 'Attention, Main Gate, Reception and Parking . . . HUBRIS descending . . . Attention . . .' The electrified cop straightened his beret, pulled his stomach in and roaring his intimidation at the throng around him, began to march towards the elevators twenty paces away, vigorously shoving to left and right all the potential assassins who awaited the Minister's descent. Agastya and Dr Alagh, who happened to be on the right, with one shove were propelled considerably closer to the stairs. Returning the camera to its case, Agastya watched for a couple of seconds the faces of the others gaping at the elevator while they waited for it to open to debouch Bhanwar Virbhim and his cortege; then he and Dr Alagh began to mount.

To restore his nerves, he needed to piss, smoke and drink

some tea. In the corridor on the fourth floor, to locate the loo, he followed the overpowering stink of urine. En route, he was distracted by a sign that read in both Hindi and English, *Toilets This Way*, but which pointed the way he'd come. In two minds, he about-turned and hesitantly retraced his steps till the stairs, where he stopped. The pong of urine to him now was as confusing as the Toilets signs because every now and then, in his bewildered passage down the corridor, it had mingled with the smell of hot, thick, sweet, milky tea.

The corridors of Aflatoon Bhavan had once been a handsome five metres in width, but over the years, the cupboards, desks, chairs, electric fans, coolers, shelves, sofas, stools, teapoys, clocks, folders and files had edged out of the twelve-hundred-plus rooms and sidled along down the passages in search of *lebensraum*. Virtually every inch of common zone in the building—foyer, corridor, lobby—was now piled high with junk; only those spaces declared by the Black Guard commandoes to be sensitive from a security angle—that is to say, those areas that would catch the Minister's eye in his shuttling from motorcade to elevator to office, escaped the rubbish, the lumber. That still left quite a few kilometres of corridor. The fire-escapes, storerooms, garages and the dead-ends of passages all resembled the aftermath of an earthquake, a riot or a bombing—discarded, broken furniture and mountains of files, documents, booklets, official publications, piled all anyhow, one atop another, restrained from blocking off the heavens only by the ceiling. At regular intervals in the corridors, painted signs on the walls exhorted denizens and visitors, in two languages, to Keep Quiet, Refrain From Spitting and Smoking and to Maintain—separately—Peace and Communal Harmony, Cleanliness, Dignity of Office and Due Decorum. Paan stains, that covered the discarded furniture and files like enormous drops of red rain, had on occasion soared up to splotch some of the signs.

'Where'd you think the toilet can be, Sen saab?'

'Westward ho. Can't you smell it?'

Shrill giggle. 'Yes and no. At times, it smells like tea.'

Same thing, though, pondered Agastya the thinker. On each floor, the Gents was two doors away from a Department Canteen. The two stinks were in one sense Welfare measures, generated so that even the blind could find their way to both refresh and relieve themselves. The not-so-blind too, perhaps, because those *Toilets This Way* signs had been quite misleading, hadn't they? They'd've staggered on and on down these corridors in the wrong direction till their bladders would've burst. Of course, they could always have squirmed into any of those crevices between desk and almirah. One could think of them as resthouses for travellers on the Road of Life. The Toilets signs therefore were reminders of All That Misguide. They were also subtle and potent advertisements of the Department of Education—seventh-to-eleventh floor—for its Literacy Commission. The workers who actually measured, hammered and put these signs up—how many of them, d'you think, asked Agastya of himself, could read them?

Uh . . ., he replied.

Exactly. They—and their brothers—also erect our road signs. That is why, if you want to go, for example, from Aflatoon Bhavan to, say, the Pashupati Aflatoon Public Gardens—to restrict the example to the family, as it were—and you scrupulously follow the signs that you can decipher from your driving seat, it should take you about a year, plus-minus two months. We won't make it, you know, as a nation until—to take only one instance—the people who put up our road signs and the people who need to use them, to decipher them from their cars, are the same.

How interesting . . . why doesn't someone get rid of all this junk? One could sell it for lakhs of rupees to the kabadiwala. Surely the Welfare State would welcome the revenue.

No, too dangerous. Too many decisions. Which kabadiwala was one going to call? The man on the bicycle ringing his bell beneath one's bathroom window while one shaves in the morning—'Hello, come over to my office tomorrow morning at eleven with all your friends and buy off me three hundred truckloads of junk'? How would one prove to Audit that he didn't bribe one for being so kind? Even a one-per cent cut on the sale of all the clutter of Aflatoon Bhavan would be more than a salary for the whole year. No. One would follow procedure. There exist rules even for the proper disposal of office junk. One calls for a minimum of three quotations from interested parties. If the value of the rubbish is estimated to be above a certain amount, one advertises in the newspapers. Which newspapers? *All* the major newspapers of all the SAARC countries? Perhaps, since the kabadiwala is quite a SAARC institution. Then, mindful of the Official Language Policy, one routes the Junk Disposal File through the Director, Official Languages. The quotations then are examined and processed at the appropriate level.

Further, what is junk? Speaking of levels, which one would best define it? There, on Agastya's left, those lemon-green booklets dispersed all over those desks and sprouting out of that cupboard—three thousand of them were published some four years ago. Two thousand seven hundred remain. They are the Minister's Welcome Address on the Occasion of the Inauguration of the Plenary Session of the Trimurti Aflatoon Birth Centenary Celebrations Committee. What was one to think—were those booklets junk?

Under Secretary (Ways and Means and Administrative Reform) had certainly thought so and—to use officialese—Initiated A File on the subject. *Permission is sought to call for quotations from interested dealers in scrap*. Oh dear—one would've imagined that the nation'd gone to war. But Ways and Means had fought back like a hero—Kit Carson, absolutely.

The proposal is not meant in any way to insult the august office of the Minister. It is only intended to allow Aflatoon Bhavan to breathe a bit. Improvement of the Work Environment. It is alternatively submitted that the booklets be circulated amongst our Higher Secondary Central Schools as proposed models of English prose for those students of Standard Eleven who offer English as their Optional Third Language. Of course, if approved, more copies would have to be printed. The views of Director, Official Languages may kindly be solicited in this regard. However, it should be pointed out here that copies of the official Hindi translation of the Welcome Address, regrettably, are not immediately traceable in Aflatoon Bhavan. If required, a second official Hindi translation may be commissioned after a decision has been taken at the Highest Level. Naturally, a parallel enquiry would have to be initiated into the absence or disappearance of the Hindi texts.

Not surprisingly, the file was still drifting about in one of the abysses of Education—after all, what was four years in the life of a Welfare State file? Not even a heartbeat. Meanwhile, there mouldered those masterpieces of oratory. Passersby had often been offered copies. Of course, before one actually disposed off all those booklets and files, one'd have to consider the invaluable insulation that they provided to the entire building in winter. An indisputable fact, when one recalled how many clerks had snugly slept for months ensconced among them.

The Gents' Toilet was large, greyish, brightly-lit, wet and crowded. Dr Alagh stepped up, gritted his teeth, fumbled with his fly, managed to undo its buttons in time and as he let go, sighed with relief and shut his eyes. A couple of seconds later—in midstream, as it were—he squeaked in disgust as he felt something warm and—well, urine-like—spray his left foot. He opened his eyes. In a nanosecond, he yelped in horror as he realized that the piss wasn't his. He jerked his leg away, glared at the profile of the pisser on his left and hoped that the dirty look would suffice because he didn't quite know what to say. What *could* he say? Mind your spray? Look before you spatter? Yet, equally clearly, his glare had no effect because his neighbour—small, moustached, with a lined, desiccated face—was pissing with his eyes closed, leaning against the marble partition that separated him from Dr Alagh. Who hurriedly stepped down to avoid being further irrigated.

But who continued, however, while rebuttoning himself and rolling up till the knee his left trouser leg, to glower at the bum and back of the off-target pisser. Which is when he noticed that the pisser's right arm tailed off at the elbow. He held the edge of his kurta in his mouth and the strings of both his pyjamas and his undies in his left hand, thus leaving himself no means by which he could catch his penis to guide its stream. Dr Alagh stopped glowering.

Revolted, confused, abashed and curious, he watched the pisser skilfully knot up with one hand and amble off towards the sinks. Where he stopped to shake hands with a friend. Who had to let go of his crutch to extend his hand. They chatted. At that moment, the cleaner who was swabbing the floor neared them and—in warning, perhaps—clicked his tongue a couple of times. The pisser leaned sideways, shook hands with the cleaner and said something. The cleaner responded in sign language. One of the doors of the WCs creaked open and out stepped a man in sun glasses, with a walking stick. He tapped his way towards the door. Two places away from Dr Alagh's at the urinal, a short, podgy man with the lost, open face of a victim of Down's Syndrome, half-turned to holler a greeting at the blind man, who responded cheerfully. Near the window, a teenager with a left leg badly deformed by polio, was feeding what looked like chapatis to a large monkey that squatted on the sill on what appeared to be a bundle of files.

The flash of Agastya's camera disturbed most of them. For a few seconds, it had been quite challenging. He hadn't been able to decide whether to centre on the one-armed handshaker or the monkey.

'Photography is strictly forbidden in all Welfare State premises, sir.'

'Yes, not to worry.' From his wallet, Agastya took out his temporary laminated photo pass of the Bhayankar Middle Income Group Swimming and Recreation Club and flashed it under the one-armed peon's nose. 'That's all right. PM's Secretariat. Administrative Reform Division.' He clicked the monkey, the files, the grimy window, the scummy sink. 'We've received more than one complaint about this monkey menace in these corridors. That they're keeping the officers and staff away from work.'

'They are divine, sir, hardly a pest,' warmly protested the one-armed pisser. 'Attendance is particularly thin today for a different reason. By the way, I am Dharam Chand, Personal peon at the Minister's Residence and Joint Secretary of the Aflatoon Bhavan Class IV Employees' Union. I have—' he phallically raised the stump of his right arm—'applied for exemption from plague duty. Meanwhile, three hundred and forty-four Under Secretaries of the Central Ministries, mainly of the Departments of Official Languages, Food and Rationing, Civil Defence, Physical Education, Prohibition and Excise, Town Planning, Vocational Training, Sales Tax, Dairy Development, Rural Broadcasting, State Lotteries, Water Resources, Land Records, Books and Publications, Employment Insurance, Ayurvedic Sciences and Malpractices and Village Industries have trooped off to the Supreme Court with a petition that: one, accuses the Welfare State of wilfully playing with the lives of its public servants and two, suggests to it that if it still insists on playing God, it should draft to Madna, given the subject matter of the mission, only the officials of the Department of Public Health.'

'Oh dear. Madna is from where he has come—' Agastya jerked his head at Dr Alagh '—and specifically to meet two Under Secretaries. Have they been sent off there or have they marched off to the Supreme Court instead? Under Secretary for Demotic Drama Shri Dastidar and Under Secretary for Freedom Fighters (Pre-Independence) Dr Jain? Though the latter of course we wish to consult in his personal capacity as a homoeopath.'

Dharam Chand's eyes became smaller and craftier. 'Madna? And are you a bounty hunter? A grant stuck somewhere?' He strutted across to the monkey on the window sill to deposit beside it a paper packet of yellowish, greasy sweets that he had pulled out of his kurta pocket. It was a daily routine for him, one of his ways of appeasing the gods for his thousand crimes.

Some of which he had, once upon a time, under the name of Karam Chand, committed in Madna, a place which, despite its insignificance and general ghastliness, is central to this story. Madna is representative of ten thousand other small towns and five hundred other districts in a land of a billion people. The events that occur and the characters who exist there could quite easily be located in any of the other dots on the landscape. Indeed, it would be more useful to say that many of the incidents—the outcry over the plague, the disappearance of Chamundi, the attack on Suroor, the ping-ponging of Agastya Sen—take place in Madna principally because they have Madna-like qualities.

Ditto for the characters. It is not therefore an extraordinary coincidence that three of them from Madna—the Honourable

Collector, the Honourable Civil Surgeon and Dharam Karam Chand—should be found at the same moment in the Gents' Toilet of a government building fourteen hundred kilometres away in the country's capital city. For at any given time (during office hours, it must be clarified), Aflatoon Bhavan is crawling with Madna types from all over the land. The building's size, after all, must not be forgotten. Fourteen storeys, six wings, twelve hundred rooms for thirty-four departments of the government, nearly twenty kilometres of corridor—how could all that space not be temporarily occupied by at least a minuscule percentage of the billion hopefuls of the country?

Like Dharam Chand, for example, whose—it must be remembered—tortuous, eight-year-long journey from Madna to Aflatoon Bhavan had been instructive and illustrative enough to have become the plot of a quintet of street plays that Rajani Suroor had crafted for Vyatha.

Retribution atop a local train
awaited this marginally insane
ex-attendant of the School for the Blind,
Madna. Upper-class travel of a kind,
on the roof, ticketless, with friends, a breeze
of a journey on most days, relaxed, at ease—
one always had to grip something stable,
of course, in case the slow train, unable
to keep steady, jerked over points, or lurched
around curves without warning. That day, perched
on the third bogie from the rear, waiting
for the train to start, Karam Chand, hating
the delay, had both his hands in the air,
running a filthy comb through his sparse hair.
A sudden twitch, like a start, beneath him,
just the engine's spasm, but to the rim

of the roof slipped he and scrambling about
for a hold (pink comb still in hand, no doubt
because he wished to complete his toilet
before descending), went over. And yet
witnesses claim that it could have been more
hideous, for he did manage, before
the train began to glide forward, to roll
his torso off the track. Of course, the whole
thing took a second. His forearm remained.
River of blood. Squeals. Rags of shirt-sleeve, stained.

Rajani Suroor had found the biography of Dharam Chand intensely emblematic. They had met on another local train seven years later during one of Vyatha's performances in a second-class compartment.

'Here, let me treat you to samosas, bread pakoras, chutney and tea while in return you tell me the story of your life.'

Within those seven years, Dharam Chand had come to own a few hectares of sugarcane land somewhere in the north and two modest houses—one regularized, the other about to be—in one of the oldest slums—practically National Heritage quality—in the heart of Lutyens's City.

He had also fallen into the habit of attending office in Aflatoon Bhavan just twice a week.

Why? Shri Dhrubo Jyoti Ghosh Dastidar, till recently one of his three bosses, had asked him.

Because I've lost my mind, he'd explained, and continually forget that I've a job in Aflatoon Bhavan. When Shri Dastidar had raised his eyebrows, he'd elaborated that he felt terribly depressed and guilty at having tricked, and been ungrateful to, the Welfare State.

Six years ago, the government'd decided to clean up the stretch of slum at Gadarpur that fronted the Airport Road because the Lieutenant Governor'd complained that it looked unspeakably ghastly when he drove past it with foreign

V∞IPs—Fidel Castro, Olaf Palme, people like that. However, the Urban Development Secretary had written back to the Secretary to the Lieutenant Governor that the government had no money for the project. No problem, asserted the Lieutenant Governor, clearly a statesman with zip and vigour. I shall ask my industrialist friends to chip in.

No problem, sir, declared they, and many thanks for the advertising opportunity. So the government had relocated Dharam Chand and a few thousand of his neighbours on fifteen-by-fifteen plots of marshy government land in the middle of nowhere twenty-five kilometres north of the city. Dharam Chand and Co were encouraged to move with soft—feather-touch, interest-free—loans of a few thousand rupees each. Which none of them has yet paid back, of course. For one, the period of repayment is thirty years. For another, they just stopped trudging to the bank with their instalments. Too much of a bother. Besides, no one's pressing them very hard.

From the point of view of Dharam Chand, the dislocation had been brutal. The middle of nowhere was christened Senapati Aflatoon Nagar. It had no schools, no markets, post office, hospitals, doctors, bus services, parks, service roads, cinema halls, nothing. All of that bobbed up, certainly, practically overnight, cancerously, with the speed and quality of growth of the boom satellite town. At first, with the money that the government'd given him, on his fifteen-by-fifteen plot, he built only one room. With plywood and cloth, he partitioned it. He, his wife, his keep and his four daughters stayed in one half; he leased out the other. In a couple of years, with the rent, along with a House Building Advance and a Loan Against his Provident Fund from the Department, he built overhead a second room and a loo. Thus, in easy stages, the bare plots of Senapati Aflatoon Nagar became proper, Municipality-approved, two- and three-storey houses.

In a few years, therefore, when their ghetto-in-the-wilderness had become almost respectable, with the unassuming, settled air of a fifty-year-old slum, Dharam Chand and his neighbours sold their houses for several lakhs each and returned to invest in their old haunts in Lutyens's City. Not exactly the same stretch alongside the Airport Road that they'd originally occupied, of course, because that was now the fourteen-storey Kamalavati Aflatoon Office-cum-Shopping Complex—but to all the pavements, parks, open spaces, road shoulders and disputed plots in the vicinity. Where the Municipal Corporation wouldn't let them rest—and thrive—in peace. They were continually being menaced by demolition drives, bulldozers and the police. Their days were a blur of bribes, threats, stay orders from the courts, petitions, demonstrations and minor riots.

His attitude to the Welfare State was therefore schizophrenic. In the first place, he hated it for having dislocated him simply to make crores of rupees out of the sale of land that he'd come to believe was his own—his patrimony, as it were. After all, many of those dispossessed had been the original squatters beside the Airport Road a good thirty years ago, long before either the airport or the road. However, at the same time, he hated himself for feeling grateful to the Welfare State for the free plot, the soft loan, the chance to legitimize his existence, to become a property owner, the landlord of a two-storey structure. After he'd sold what he'd built, even though the money'd been welcome, and had helped him towards buying his hectares of surgarcane land and his modest slum tenements, he had still felt foolish and naked, empty-handed, as though he'd wronged both his family and his future. He'd then blamed the State, as a grieving child his parent, for having allowed him to sink again into the mire.

'That's truly sad,' Dhrubo'd opined, 'and touching, but how

is it linked to your showing up in office only on Tuesdays and Thursdays?'

'Very well, sir. I'll bring you fresh sugarcane juice from my fields.'

The offer of which'd placed Dhrubo amongst the chosen—the select few officers whom Dharam Chand thought worth his while to butter up—right alongside, for example, the newly-promoted Deputy Financial Advisor and Dhrubo's part-time adversary, Mrs Minu Tutreja. She was attractive, venal and artistic, and therefore ideal for the Department of Heritage. She came from a small town not far from Dharam Chand's fields of sugarcane, a fact that'd pleased, flattered and excited him no end and made her even more worthy of the gifts of the flasks of juice twice a week.

They were a familiar sight—Mrs Tutreja and Dharam Chand in the corridors of Aflatoon Bhavan. After her promotion, she'd been allotted Room 4609 in Wing N of the building. The car park for the Department of Heritage vehicles was outside Gate 13. Even after two months at the job, she had very little idea of how to get to her room from the gate and was terrified that she'd permanently lose her way in the maze of corridors and floors and languish for months—shrivelled, starving, unwashed, unheeded—in Atomic Energy, Jails and Urban Land Ceiling, Rural Development, Revenue and Forests, Public Relations and Protocol, Cooperation and Transport, Rehabilitation and Labour, Horticulture and Command Area Management, Dairy Development, Fisheries and Tourism, Law and Judiciary, or Industry and Company Affairs. She therefore had to be led—practically by the nose—to and from her room. In her first week after her promotion, while she'd been traipsing along in the corridor behind Dharam Chand en route to the loo, simpering back at everyone who'd beamed sycophantically at her, cutely crinkling up her nose at the better-looking males, revelling in her combination of official power and personal helplessness—sure enough, the lights had gone out. She'd shrieked softly a couple of times, invoked a handful of gods and for support and succour till illumination returned, clutched on to the soft, lifeless stump of Dharam Chand's right arm. Thereafter, all her guides had received instructions from her office staff to have on their persons official candles and matches or flashlights that worked. All phallic symbols, please note, Dhrubo had pointed out to Dharam Chand, including your right arm. Dharam Chand's eyes had widened and shone with respect.

She was quite easy to work with. She brought to her job a welcome single-mindedness. In her twenty-three years of service, the one country in the world that she hadn't yet visited officially was Mongolia. Thus, while governments toppled all around her, she got down to business.

'How is our Heritage Exchange Programme with Mongolia? Dead or alive?'

'It's one of our very best. Madam.'

'Good. Please put up a draft of a letter from me to our Ambassador in Ulan Bator . . . strengthen bilateral relations . . . mid-term review . . . Ministerial delegation . . . an exhibition of Buddhist relics . . .'

The third officer to whom Shri Dharam Chand had been assigned at that point in his career had been Shri Dastidar's colleague and room-mate, Miss Lina Natesan Thomas. His official relations with her have been described in some detail in her memorandum on the general administrative difficulties faced by her in the functioning of the department.

> *I have in passing mentioned above the peon Shri Dharam Chand's several crimes against me. To justify the use of the plural, I will engage the attention of your good self with just two more examples. On October 29 last, when I arrived in office at 8.59 a.m., I found, while settling down, an unmistakable teaspoonful of*

semen next to the official water glass on the bottom left hand corner of my desk. I was surprised, to say the least. I shot off a memo to Shri Dastidar. Since he doesn't get in before ten on most days, I had to wait for quite a while for his rejoinder. Meanwhile, Shri Dharam Chand banged open the door more than once to look in on me—in itself most unusual, since he generally doesn't show up until an hour or so after his superiors. On each occasion, he smirked at the teaspoon, next at me and then slammed the door shut. Suspicious, to say the least.

In his memo, Shri Dastidar was most incisive: Preserve it in an envelope for subsequent DNA analysis. We will catch the blackguard yet.

The off-white On Welfare State Service envelope still reposes beside my personal copy of the Civil Service Leave Encashment Rules, 1972 in the bottom-most drawer of my desk.

I am given to understand (from Shri Dastidar's speculative memo on the subject, placed at Annexure R) that amongst the members of Shri Dharam Chand's caste, to offer a teaspoonful of one's semen to someone is to threaten him, to warn him to lay off, much as the symbolic presentation of a betel nut in certain other primitive Indian communities denotes that the recipients' testicles are to be replaced. I should record here that I myself am a staunch Roman Catholic.

Whenever I visit the Ladies' Toilet, namely about four times during office hours, I am unfailingly trailed by Shri Dharam Chand whistling and singing two Hindi film songs: 1) Ganga Tera Pani Amrit *and* 2) Ram Teri Maili. *(I make so bold as to enquire at this stage whether the knowledge of our official language of your good self is good enough for you to understand the above two phrases. I take the liberty of translating them in any case. The first means,* Ganga, Your Water Is Ambrosial *and the second,* Ram, Yours Is Dirty.*)* *Shri Dharam Chand sings rather well.*

He, however, dresses inappropriately for office. Middle-aged men of the lower classes ought not to wear tight blue jeans to work, even occasionally. How is one to distinguish our college-educated, dope-smoking, English-speaking, unemployed idler from a representative of the submerged nine-tenths if both are going to wear jeans? Moreover, your good self is surely aware that all Class IV employees of the Welfare State—and they number over seven million—get a Uniform Allowance of Rs 44/- each per month and a separate Uniform Washing Allowance of Rs 27.50 per month. Where does all that money go? To buy jeans. Because in my two months here, I haven't spotted even one peon, naik, dafadar, jamadar, orderly, sweeper, bearer, watchman, chowkidaar, mali or night watchman in uniform. They have all at one time or the other worn jeans.

Shri Dharam Chand's argument against wearing his uniform is that it is made of khadi and that khadi is shabby, ethnic, indigenous and dull. Khadi makes its wearer feel crumpled, grey, poor, deprived, backward, depressed and dispossessed. The Welfare State's policy to enforce khadi only on its Class IV employees clearly indicates its desire that they forever remain Class IV in spirit.

Rubbish, Shri Dharam Chand. Our politicians wear khadi. The Prime Minister wears it. The clip of his Cartier gold fountain pen looks splendid against it.

Ah, but that's khadi from another planet. Whereas ours is Welfare State khadi. I know, Class IV types like me in the Khadi Board spin hundreds of thousands of metres every year—and then the Board sells all of it back to the State to be distributed to the likes of me, and we use most of it to shroud our corpses before burning. Khadi burns well. Sound Welfare State economics, khadi. Spend an enormous amount of time, money, infrastructure and manpower fundamentally to transfer funds from one Department to another and incidentally, in passing, create a product that no one wants, but stuff that z-grade product down the throats of your Class IV employees and then pay them peanuts to swallow it.

Moreover, the Prime Minister, continued Shri Dharam Chand, wears starched white khadi. Our Washing Allowance doesn't cover starch. Our Employees' Union has sent at least twenty memorandums to the Welfare Secretary to initiate an Additional Uniform Starching Allowance but no one listens to anyone here.

It was pointed out to Shri Dharam Chand that Mahatma Gandhi wore khadi too.

Well, when I return from South Africa and England and after I've become famous and can roam around leaning on women for support, what I wear won't matter, will it.

I gather that Shri Dharam Chand follows me to the toilet because he has been directed to do so. This is a secret administrative fallout of my representation at Annexure P, that is, he has to verify the general conduct of our Black Guard Commandoes and apparently protect me from them. While I am in the toilet, they chortle and guffaw outside and, from the shrieks that filter through to me, prod one another's private parts with their AK-47s.

A dear friend of Shri Dharam Chand, a short young male with thick lips and curly hair, is a permanent inhabitant of the Ladies' Toilet on the fourth floor, that is to say, I have seen him in there, three-to-four times a day, every day, for the last two months. He is always half-naked, in large white-leather boots with splashes of paint on them and mustard-coloured boxer-type underwear. Shri Dharam Chand for some reason calls them wearunders. I have asked him why his friend couldn't dress and have been informed that the half-naked one is a painter. It is true that whenever I enter the toilet, he makes a pretence of washing a paintbrush

at the sink. The pretence is truly bizarre because there hasn't been any water in that toilet in the time that I have used it and on seventy-four occasions, no water taps and on twenty three occasions, no sink.
A glance at my representation at Annexure S will reveal my strong suspicion that Shri Dharam Chand and his young friend, in league with the Section Officer, Stores, have been merrily trafficking in taps, toilet sinks, flush tanks and other sanitation and plumbing articles. Their modus operandi is simple and effective. One accomplice is permanently installed inside the Ladies' Toilet, busy all day long with hammer and wrench. The mastermind, using a foolproof pretext, pops in four times a day to check on progress. The stolen stuff goes out of the window and down the scaffolding that is permanently up in Aflatoon Bhavan because of its size and the lethargy and venality of the painters contracted by the Welfare State.

At the sink, apprehensive of the monkey munching away a bare two feet above and to the left of his head, Dr Alagh, standing on one leg, rinsed his left calf and foot. He almost lost his balance out of fright when, suddenly, from behind the animal and out of the blue beyond the window, bobbed up a human head, curly-haired, thick-lipped. It didn't startle the monkey, however; the latter merely turned and perfunctorily bared its teeth at the painter who in turn aped it.

Just then, the lights went off, but only in the toilet and a section of the adjoining corridor. It could have been a routine power failure, terrorist sabotage, a routine economy drive, a snafu due to overloading or routine illegal electricity tapping. Agastya felt that they would do better to get on with their appointments than to hang around in the dark in a weird loo.

To their discomfort, as they left the Gents', the monkey abandoned its food, hopped off the sill and began to trail them. Nobody else seemed to notice or be perturbed by it. Its small restless eyes squinted ceaselessly about as it followed them into the Departmental Canteen. It paused momentarily as they settled down at a plastic table near one of the windows, then, red bum held high, stalked regally off to perch on another window sill. Agastya relaxed just a bit.

The monkeys of Aflatoon Bhavan weren't hostile, they were simply unfriendly. There were at least three thousand of them. They'd been there longer than anyone could recall, since the Word, practically. Administration had summoned Pest Control once, but he'd said that they didn't do monkeys. Under Secretary (General Maintenance) had also written a couple of times to the Ministry of Environment and Forests to prod the zoo to come and round them up. (During the first week of the plague scare, incidentally, a rustle from their building *had* been heard but it'd later turned out to be only a woman clerk shifting in her seat while knitting during the morning session.)

Three thousand monkeys. Agastya wondered where on earth they stayed. Perhaps they had addresses with pin codes or some of that www stuff. It was funny—uncanny, really—how they—the monkeys—had a problem only with Personal files. Just once in the history of Aflatoon Bhavan had one of them actually pounced on a civil servant and made off with his file. The victim had been Chhote Lal Nilesh, then Section Officer, Departmental Enquiries. The monkey didn't even scratch him, unfortunately—it was repelled, so the story goes, by Shri Nilesh's general sliminess. It simply landed on Nilesh's shoulder, coiled its tail around his neck—not out of love, one would imagine—reached down for the file, kissed Nilesh twice, once on either cheek, in the French manner, in gratitude and farewell, and then lazily loped off with its booty. Personal files tend to be a bit exhibitionistic, after all. All bound in red parchment, with those flags in huge letters simply screaming for attention—CONFIDENTIAL, FOR

RESTRICTED CIRCULATION, TOP SECRET, FOR SECRETARY'S EYES ONLY. Civil servants should rather blame themselves for arousing in the first place the curiosity of their resident apes, who became quite popular after the attack on Nilesh. Missing files still continue to be attributed to them. It's much simpler, everyone agrees—though less permanent—than arranging, in somebody else's room, for an accidental bonfire.

Waiters continued to careen past them, bent sideways at alarming angles to counterbalance the weight of five-to-six trays, one atop another, poised equably on left shoulder and upturned, backward-pointing left palm. On each tray, Agastya could see rows and rows of identical, tiny steel bowls; those on the top tray were full of some mud-coloured gravy. The waiters wore crumpled, off-white khadi uniforms and extraordinary, foot-high, maroon turbans all brocaded in gold; they looked like the proud crests of a flock of some rare, gigantic birds bobbing, bouncing and nipping about against the grey-and-brown shabbiness of the canteen. To each waiter who shot past them, Agastya serenely and pleasantly repeated their order for tea. Some of the waiters'd grunted, but one couldn't be certain that it'd been in response.

The tea finally arrived, tepid, sweet, mild dishwater in a cracked cup. Well, what else could he expect for fifty paise, demanded Agastya of himself, Darjeeling Flowery Orange Pekoe from Fortnum and Mason? A fundamental law of economics in the Welfare State, Sir—subsidy breeds substandard. You're in a Departmental Canteen, remember, a welfare measure for the *employees* of the government, not to be confused with any of the welfare measures for the *citizens* under that government. The canteen buys its raw stuff—rice-dust, oil-and-used-engine-oil, flour-dust, potatoes-and-worms, curry-powder-and-the-good-earth, cockroach-and-lizard-shit—from the Department of Raw Materials and Civil Supplies—

pretty cheap, special rates and so on. It's a tortuous, instructive journey for the bags of sugar and the cans of kerosene, from one warehouse to another godown, from a depot to a storehouse to a truck to Aflatoon Bhavan. *Everyone* steals en route—it is Clause 28(iv) of the Public Distribution of Essential Commodities Act. *Notwithstanding any law or regulation to the contrary and for the time being in force, all dealers, purveyors, transporters, merchants, middlemen, tradesmen, caterers, canteen managers and the suchlike, of food, raw materials, provisions, foodstuff, provender, rations, groceries and the suchlike, meant for the eventual consumption of the employees of the Welfare State, may, whenever deemed fit, adjust to their convenience, the quality and quantity of the edibles and consumables under their charge.* It is the reason why there'll always be rats in government warehouses, their ground excreta in government wheat, monkeys in Aflatoon Bhavan and gods in Heaven—somebody has to be around to take the shit, to foist the blame on, scapegoats for human misdeeds. If he analysed the ingredients of his cup of tea, he'd find that it *wasn't* worth more than fifty paise. It was completely off the point to argue that outside the sphere of the Welfare State, far far away from that indescribable Departmental Canteen, in a normal, decent, ordinary cafe or restaurant, a cup of tea cost about twenty times more. That was only natural because it was twenty times closer to what a cup of tea should be. The Department's Class IV Employees' Union had till then strenuously resisted all attempts by the Canteen Management to raise the prices on the menu. The proposed hike for tea was to one rupee—a hundred percent increase. Criminal! Would people never understand? In the Welfare State, everything was free or as close to free as cheap could get. Give us this day our daily crud.

They temporarily parted ways after tea, Dr Alagh to try and find the two Under Secretaries whom they'd come to meet, Agastya a quiet corner where he could smoke a joint.

Eventually, the Civil Surgeon located at least the room of one.

Not many more signs could be put up on his door. Beneath his bilingual nameplate hung a board that took up half the door. It described his designation in full, in both Hindi and English: *Under Secretary: Gajapati Aflatoon Centenary Celebrations, Our Endangered Tribal Heritage, Promotion and Diffusion of Demotic and Indigenous Drama and Other Such Forms of Self-Expression.* The third sign read: *No Visitors Without Prior Appointment,* underneath which was the suggestion: *Please See My PA In Room 3872, D Wing, Desk IV.* The fifth board reminded all passers-by that *Visitors Without Prior Appointment* (were) *Not Encouraged.* The sixth stated quite simply: *Please Do Not Spit Here.*

The seventh and last plate read: *This Area Meant for Parking of Official Cars Only. Any Car Unauthorizedly Parked Will Have Its Tyres Deflated. By Order of the Under Secretary Administration. Thank You.* It had been stolen about a year ago by the Under Secretary from the car park downstairs because he'd liked it and had wanted to see how many passers-by would actually read it on his door and find it odd. In one year, no one had complained.

Dr Alagh knocked. No response. He knocked again, then bravely opened the door. A tall, plumpish man concentrated on his tai-chi exercises in the centre of the room. At the second desk, a solemn, bespectacled attractive woman paused in her writing to glance up forbriddingly at Dr Alagh.

'Oh hello! . . . I was looking for the Under Secretary for Demotic Drama. I've an appointment with him.'

Without quickening or disturbing the slow, flowing rhythm of his arm movements, the exerciser pointed to the vacant chair behind the first desk and remarked in soft, measured tones, in harmony with the undulations of his body, 'There is no response from the incumbent's seat. Please try after some time.' Then the exerciser pointedly—but fluidly—turned his back on Dr Alagh.

Who, nonplussed, shut the door and read the boards and nameplate on it one more time. Had he just encountered one Under Secretary and her gigolo or two Under Secretaries, of whom one, for reasons of state, was nameplate-less? Mr Tai-Chi had been more poised than unfriendly. How many minutes was after some time? Perhaps he should go off somewhere to unearth the Collector of Madna. Or he could ferret out in one of these warrens the Under Secretary for Freedom Fighers (Pre-Independence). He ambled off, nervous.

Meanwhile, to avoid passing under a monkey that squatted atop a steel almirah and bared its teeth at everyone that tramped past, the Collector of Madna had purposefully turned into the first open door. A huge room that looked small because of the usual chaos of tables, chairs, almirahs, shelves and hillocks of files. There was just one man in the room, hunched in a chair by a window. Agastya threaded his way across. The man wore a brown suit and sparkling-white, new tennis shoes. He had yellowed, sad eyes. Beside him, on the table, lay his opened lunch box. At his feet glowed the room's single electric heater, on the wire frame of which were being reheated, in twos, the chapatis from the lunch box. On one of the cleaner files beside the heater lay the chapatis that'd already been done. The silence was companionable.

'How will you reheat the vegetables and the dal?'

The man pointed to the flat metal pen-tray. 'That fits very well on the heater. We stir with the stencil pen. Have you had lunch?' asked he courteously.

'Yes, thank you, but please do go ahead . . . It's way past lunch hour, isn't it? . . . Actually, I came in in search of a light for my cigarette.'

'Smoking is forbidden in all Welfare State offices,' said the man sadly, dextrously replacing the chapatis on the heater with the last two from his lunch box. 'I tend to have my lunch late because of my arthritis and my piles. I have to complete my special joints-and-neck-exercises every morning, so I can't reach office before eleven. Where's the time for lunch at one? . . . during lunch hour, everybody saunters off outside to soak in the sun and eat peanuts and oranges . . . in our Department, only Under Secretaries and above are entitled to electric heaters in their rooms. Presumably only they need to keep warm in winter. I represented, arguing that I ought to be issued one on account of my arthritis. General Administration ordered me to face the Medical Board. I represented, arguing that the members of the Board committee belonged to castes traditionally hostile to mine. A final decision is still awaited. Meanwhile, I befriended the Section Officer, Stores, at our Lunch Club.' He picked up the pen tray from the table, tipped its contents—ballpoints, pins, clips, erasers, markers—into a drawer, wiped it with a duster, then paused to glance shyly at Agastya, 'Are you sure you won't join me for a late lunch? . . . If you really want to smoke, you may light your cigarette from the heater. Here, use this paper'—handing him part of a blank sheet that he'd torn out of the nearest file—'but please smoke at the window and try and exhale with your head *out* of the window, if you don't mind.'

'With pleasure. You wouldn't mind, of course, if my cigarette is crumpled, hand-rolled and smells a little eco-friendly?'

'Not at all.'

The phone rang, a muted but insistent, urgent, brr-brr. The man in the white tennis shoes ignored it, perhaps because he'd started lunch, at all times a sacred business. It wasn't easy to discern which phone to pick up, since each of the eight desks in the room had an instrument, and they all seemed to be ringing.

Agastya made himself comfortable on some files on the window ledge. It was a good place to finish his joint; then he'd get back to locating Dhrubo. Sighing richly, he exhaled dragon-like through where the pane was meant to be. Before him, not a hundred feet away, were the rows of windows of some other wing of Aflatoon Bhavan. From his seat, he could see nothing else, no sky, no ground, just the occasional pipal sapling tenaciously finding life in the damp walls, the black waste pipes and the trash of fifty years thrown out of a thousand windows. Where they weren't slimy-green with damp, the walls of Aflatoon Bhavan were a dusty grey. One in two window-panes was broken, two in three windows wouldn't shut. Pigeons roosted on the occasional air-conditioner. Families of monkeys went about their business on diverse floors, under different ledges, much as though his seat was a vantage point from which to view a cross-section of some simian apartment block. He couldn't see much, though, of the interiors of any of the rooms that faced him. Those windows that hadn't been sealed off by air-conditioners had been stoppered by brown files, by mountain ranges of off-white paper, chunks of which, in landslides, had joined, on the overhangs below, the plastic bags, the newspaper wrappers of lunches, the dry ink stamp pads. Nothing, no record (the mountain ranges seemed to say) is ever thrown away. Naturally not. After all, government is based, and acts, on its records. Records are its history and the ground for its planning, are vital for Audit and Parliament, for continuity in governance, for the protection of the taxpayer's interests. In 1950, the Hakim Tara Chand Committee, in its report on *Documentation and Codification in the Welfare State*, had pointed out that to house the permanent records of the Central Ministries and Departments alone, the National Archives, against its 1949-capacity of twenty linear kilometres of shelves, would need four hundred-plus linear kilometres.

> *It may be noted here* (to quote from the Foreword of the report) *that the requirement of shelf space of ALL the Departments of the nineteen REGIONAL governments of the Federal State was felt to be beyond the purview of this Committee; also, that it focussed*

> *only on the Centre's PERMANENT records, assuming—optimistically, it must be admitted—that it, the Centre, had organized well its system of weeding out its Himalayan quantities of paper, of separating its permanent files from its ephemeral transactions, its land records from its applications for Casual Leave.*

The record is silent on precisely what the Welfare State did with the Hakim Tara Chand Committee Report. In the Bhanwar Virbhim regime, however, a proposal under consideration moots the setting up of the Taj Babbar Committee to study anew the vexed question of the updating of the recommendations of the 1950 Committee. Professor Taj Babbar, as is well known, is a prominent educationist and the ex-Principal of Madna's Janata College.

Nothing, therefore, is intentionally jettisoned—one never knows when one will need what, and later, one doesn't want to be blamed, as they say, for acts of omission and commission. *But* it's *altogether* a different matter—and it can't be helped, you know—if some of that record simply slides, wilts, gives up, falls by the wayside, drops dead.

As for the living, Agastya couldn't spot very many human figures; it was that uncertain, somnolent time of the afternoon. Occasionally, a head leaned out to spit paan into the air; at another window, a figure gargled and washed up after yet another late lunch.

'Should I answer the phone?'

With his mouth full, the man raised his eyebrows and his shoulders, and even curled his lips a fraction.

'Which phone is it?'

'All of them. They're all extensions.'

'Why don't *you* pick it up? It might be important, or even for you.'

'I've said hello to you already,' said the man coldly, 'it's enough for the afternoon.'

Agastya descended from his seat, walked over to a desk

nearer the door and lifted the receiver. Just then, the man advised him, 'If whoever it is first wants to know, without preamble or introduction, where *you're* speaking from, you must retort, "From my mouth. Where are *you* speaking from?" That'll teach them. I always do that. It hasn't taught them anything, but it does give the conversation a flavour.'

'Hello . . . from my mouth. Where're *you* speaking from? . . . no, nothing, nothing at all, I said, whom d'you wish to speak to? . . . yes, this is Aflatoon Bhavan, Department of Culture, Heri—'

'This is Atomic Energy, not Culture,' objected the man politely, clearing up after lunch, sweeping crumbs and leftovers directly onto the heater, from which merrily flew the sparks, like Tinker Bell, onto the floor and the occasional, vicinal mound of files.

'Really? . . . But how odd that Under Secretary, Vanishing Musical Traditions should be just about three doors away . . . the man on the phone wants to know whether the office is open on Monday.'

'A good question, tell him that.' The man now stood at attention, ramrod straight beside the desk, chin up, shoulders back, chest out, stomach in, knees locked, gazing into the middle distance. He inhaled deeply and as he spoke, began to swivel his neck, with agonizing slowness, from extreme left to extreme right and back. 'We're all tense this afternoon. You see, including the weekend, there are six official holidays next week. Monday's the only working day. Tuesday is a new holiday—the Bajendrabadkar Centenary as a sop to the Marxists. Wednesday of course is Christmas, Thursday is the martyrdom of Guru Shankar Shambhu, therefore a Restricted Holiday—the twenty-third of the year—very tricky that, what in government circles is referred to as the RH factor, and Friday's the Declared General Strike, the Viraat Bandh of the opposition—so nobody'll waste time trying to reach office. It's interesting that we've never had week-long official breaks in December before. April, August and October have traditionally been the better months from that point of view. It's a development that I'm sure all of us will welcome.

'But we learnt this morning that Mother Almeida's more ill than ever before—which is saying quite a lot, considering that her heart stopped beating last month and her lungs gave up pumping last Saturday. She's ninety-five or thereabouts. When she departs, that's a holiday, for sure—maybe even two, who knows?—but we're all pretty tense, you see, because if she'd said, Good Night, World, this morning, then Home Affairs would have declared the holiday today itself, which would have disappointed us acutely, because we'd all have been in office anyway—after eleven, at any rate. I've never taken a single day's leave in my twenty-nine years of service. One doesn't need to, I say. Once I finish my exercises and reach office, it isn't so bad . . . some of my women colleagues went out to the lawns with their knitting and everything earlier than usual this afternoon. While in the sun, before they start their peanuts and oranges, they intend to hold a Special Prayer Meeting for the health of Mother Almeida. All are cordially invited. Ideally, they'd like her to leave us on Sunday afternoon. Otherwise, please, please, God, let the gentle soul live all of next week . . . tell him not to be so lazy and to phone Home Affairs if he's so keen to find out about Monday.'

'He wants to know whom he's speaking to.'

'Well, give him your name.'

Nervous, in two minds, without saying anything, Agastya put the phone down. It immediately began ringing again. Ignoring it, he watched his host carry a plastic water bottle to the window, rinse his hands, gargle and spit out into the void three mouthfuls of water, return to the desk, pack up his lunch box in a plastic bag, in passing drop a cupful of water to douse a spark atop a mound of files that had been smouldering menacingly, flick invisible specks of dust off his suit, and with a last, sad glance at Agastya, toting the plastic bag and the water bottle, make his way to the door.

It unnerved Agastya to realize that he was going to be left alone in the room. 'Oh, I ought to be leaving too. Many thanks for the light for the cigarette . . . Aren't you going to switch off your heater?'

'It isn't mine, you know. I always leave things the way I found them. It is a sound principle in government. Doesn't ruffle any feathers. You rise faster.'

'Yes. Should *I* switch it off then?'

'*After* I leave, please, if you don't mind. If you receive a shock or something, I don't wish to be late at my desk, you follow.'

'Naturally.'

'We usually wait for the power cuts to effect our economies in consumption . . . I should get back to my desk before the lights go off. I've quite a way to go, you know. Irrigation, A Wing, eighth floor . . . Water Resources Management . . . Wastelands Development Corporation . . . leave the heater on, actually. If the power doesn't fail us, my wife'll be pleased to return to a warm seat. Okay, goodbye.'

In the corridor, the mewl of a siren, terrifyingly loud, almost made Agastya forget where he had to go. As usual, nobody around him seemed to be affected by—or indeed, even hear—the din. Its hideousness—the wail of a thousand police cars—drew him forward like a magnet to its source, one of the two elevators in the west lobby. *Out of Order*, flashed the red sign above its doors, on-and-off, on-and-off, perfectly synchronous with the modulations of the siren.

'It sounds like a fire alarm,' muttered Agastya to himself.

'Payṇcho, it *is* a fire alarm,' declared—almost shouted—a voice at his shoulder.

He was surprised to see Dhrubo. 'But it is attached to the elevators and has been primed to go off only when they malfunction. It is the first mystifying principle of firefighting on a war footing.'

'Yes,' hissed Agastya. The ear-splitting noise had sent his blood pressure spiralling and his heart off pit-a-pat, pit-a-pat, like a long ping-pong rally. 'Do you know where I can find Dr Jain, Under Secretary, Freedom Fighters (Pre-Independence)?'

'Of course. I'm going to him myself. We enjoy a special relationship because his present PA is my ex.' They began to climb the stairs.

Dr Jain's present PA and Dhrubo's ex, coincidentally also a Jain, was in Dhrubo's opinion, a first-rate PA. He understood things in a flash. Early in their acquaintance, Dhrubo had asked him one of his fundamental questions: *Are you being paid by the Welfare State to reach office on time in the mornings or not?* Ever after, they had vied with each other to be more or less punctual. Office started at nine, they were both in, every other day, by half-past, thanks to Dhrubo's bicycle and Shri P.A. Jain's Chartered Bus. He disapproved of Dhrubo's bike, incidentally, and felt that his boss should drive a car, or better still, wangle an official car like some of the other Under Secretaries did. He'd been particularly outraged by Dhrubo's asking for a loan from the Department to buy his bicycle—it reflected badly on his PA, Jain'd muttered.

From nine thirty to ten thirty—till the peon came—free and undisturbed, they planned their day. 1) Send the peon with the bicycle to the repairwala at the gate of Aflatoon Bhavan to pump air into its tyres and check for hidden leaks, 2) phone and phone till one's fingers become stubs and till one gets on the line the Secretary to the Principal of the Hiralal Aflatoon High School and Centre for Non-Formal Literacy and beg her to reveal whether they've admitted one's niece, 3) send the peon to the Department's Welfare store to buy hairoil, washing powder, dried mango, mosquito repellent cream, two kilos of rice and three cakes of Lifebuoy soap, 4) contact Sodhi in the Commissionerate of Estates to find out whether he knows somebody in the Municipal Corporation who can fix one's property tax, 5) ask the peon to cover with brown paper one's niece's new school textbooks, 6) try and extract from the Film Festival Secretariat two extra free passes for the forthcoming Latin American Cinema Retrospective, 7) send the peon on the bicycle to the office of the Principal of the Hiralal Aflatoon High School with the letter of recommendation from the Minister's office that one has faked . . . and thus the day of the civil servant passes. By the time one has finished with one's PA, one is quite exhausted.

The other Jain, the doctor who looks after freedom fighters, is the Department's homoeopath—very experienced and wise, by all accounts. Staff and officers come from far and near, from all over the building, to consult him. He's extremely reasonable and freely prescribes by proxy. For example, his own PA would accost him at his desk with:

'Jain saab, my neighbour's son suddenly became deaf this morning.'

'I see. Algebra exam?'

'We don't think so. TV hasn't attracted him all morning.'

'How old is he?'

'I don't know. He looks twelve.'

'Any family history of any irregularity?'

'I don't know. His mother has the hots for me, but perhaps that isn't related.'

'Difficult to say. Give him these two powders . . .'

Dr Jain liked looking after freedom fighers because they gave him lots of free time for his homoeopathy. He was a good soul—he was quite upset when Dhrubo's second promotion was withheld. It reflected badly on the service, he muttered. And sharp—and mindful of his colleague's good name; it was he who had suggested that in winter Shri Dastidar could bring two jackets to office, one for his goodly frame and the other to be draped for the day on the back of his chair, to reassure all those who came calling for a response from his seat. It was the easiest way to slip into Aflatoon Bhavan, incidentally. The next time the cop at the gate stopped one, one could just point heavenwards and mumble, 'Consult Jain Saab.' He practised his homoeopathy gratis, of course, for the love of the craft.

'What's with the camera around your neck?' asked Dhrubo of Agastya between the eighth and ninth floors.

'Ah. I plan a photo-exhibition on the Innards of the Welfare State, for which I was hoping to touch you for a grant.'

'Any time for old time's sake, save during my tai-chi. We are at the moment tied up with the celebrations of the thirtieth anniversary of the nation's Finest Hour in Athletics—you know, when Silkha Singh came in fifth in the heats at the Rome Olympics. Perhaps next week?' On the landing of the tenth floor, Dhrubo continued, 'May I ask why you need to consult Dr Jain? Or is it a delicate matter?'

'Well—for Dr Alagh's piles. You see, in the last harrowing fortnight in Madna, miraculously, his haemorrhoids have improved—virtually disappeared, actually. Somebody in Vyatha, that theatre troupe, told him that one little-known symptom of the plague is its beneficial—but temporary—effect on piles.'

'I'm not sure,' responded Shri Ghosh Dastidar the tai-chi performer, breathing easily as he took the stairs two at a time, 'whether my office-chair isn't a piles giver. You're familiar with the principle?' He waited on the eleventh floor for Agastya to catch up. 'I've submitted a proposal to the Anthropological Survey for funds to study the alarming phenomenon of the sizable number of civil servants who have piles. Piles and piles—if you'll permit—of clerks, Section Officers and above, sitting in the same chairs for seven hours a day, munching plates of pakodas and gulping down twenty cups of tea in the course of their labours. Surely the force of gravity—I argue in my proposal—will find it easier to tug down a colon when it can focus for such a considerable length of time on its target. In an Appendix to my project outline,

I've set down an interesting corollary to my main argument, namely, the fascinating relationship between a senior civil servant's piles and his Personal Assistant.

'I've cited the example of the Liaison Commissioner Dr Bhatnagar and his PA Satish Kalra. Do you know Dr Bhatnagar? Know of him? A legend of a man, a gem, one of our very best. Destined for the UN, absolutely. The longer Dr Bhatnagar is held back from what he feels is his forte, i.e., a key posting in one of our Economic Ministries, the worse his piles becomes, naturally. Equally naturally, being so senior, he can't possibly speak directly to his doctor, who is after all merely a General Practitioner attached to the office, and therefore a sort of freelancer on the payroll of the Welfare State, a part-time junior of his, in effect. Loss of caste, absolutely, to speak to him face to face, or even on the phone. A Doctor of Ideas cannot stoop to listen to the counsel of a Doctor of Medicine, even when it's for the pain in his own arse. So he waits for his PA to phone him in the morning and whimpers and moans to him the intimate physical details of his agony. The PA then phones the Doctor of Medicine and summarizes those details for him—to wit—"The pain in my arse has a pain in his arse." He next listens to the doctor's prescription, then phones Bhatnagar Saab and relays to him a careless precis of it—for example—"You've to apply Trusted Hadensa, sir, to the affected part, rest in bed all day, no disturbance, no phones, and call him—I mean, I've to call him—in the morning, sir"—and immediately after switches off while the Doctor of Ideas bawls out both the PA and the GP for failing to sympathize with and understand his arsehole. To improve that understanding, Kalra the PA spends the entire day alternately phoning the two doctors ... In passing, I've suggested to the Anthropological Survey to grant me funds to study the economics of that day of the PA, and of his relationship with his boss's bum. You really ought to meet it, and feature it in your photo-exhibition.'

'A legend, you say?'

'A lion of the civil services, a model for all seasons.'

BOOBZ

For his first meeting with the Liaison Commissioner, Agastya Sen had worn a tie and carried a briefcase in which he'd put his tiffin box, a bottle of boiled water and the day's snipped-out crossword from *The State of the Times*. He'd been on leave for close to six months before that and had put on weight. When he'd take off his shirt and tie, he'd feel as free as toothpaste emerging.

After eight and a half years in the Civil Service, his professional career had fallen into the rhythm of a few months of work followed by as many months of leave as his bank balance and the Welfare State would allow. The government was usually quite generous with Leave Without Pay.

On his return from Aflatoon Bhavan in December, he—apparently due to Makhmal Bagai's lobbying—had been booted out of the Collectorship of Madna in the last week of the year and been made Deputy Chairman of the Coastal Regions Manure Supply and Marketing Structures Authority. Within a fortnight of his taking over his new assignment, the recommendations of the Central Ninth Pay Commission had finally been accepted and given effect to by the State. As a result, civil servants all over the land had received: 1) numerous cyclostyled circulars in the regional language full of inferences and reasoning, percentages, months, years and the sign @, and 2) at last, long after the circulars, a bonus the equivalent of about two months' pay. It hadn't been called either bonus or pay, but Agastya couldn't be bothered. It had seemed ridiculous to him to waste time, energy and paper differentiating between emoluments, arrears, defrayments, acquittances, settlements, remittances, disbursements and payments when all that was being discussed was a couple of thousand rupees. When he'd seen the State Order distributing the chickenfeed, he'd counselled himself, 'Time to take wing, my dear. Set the wheels in motion.' So he'd written to his boss, the Coastal Region Zonal Commissioner, 'I beg to take whatever leave is due to me because I need to visit my native place urgently since my mother is serious.' His command of officialese was excellent and one was hardly ever refused leave when one's parents were serious.

Once every fortnight, from a hole in the Prajapati Aflatoon Welfare State Public Servants' Housing Complex Transit Hostel in the capital, he'd sent a telegram to the Zonal Commissioner: *Mother still serious.*

He waited in the waiting room of the Liaison Commissioner's office from ten-thirty onwards. The Commissioner's PA, one Shri Satish Kalra, periodically looked in on him, first to usher in a peon who'd brought him sweet, milky, rather nice coffee, then to silently thrust into his hands, at intervals of half an hour, *The India Magazine*, *Business Today*, *India Abroad*, *What Business of Yours?*, *India Today* and *Inside Outside*. Shri Kalra was an averagely tall man with a huge head, a young expression, grey hair and a stoop. His facial skin sagged. He dressed impeccably. Later, Agastya learnt from the others in the office that Kalra had once been immensely fat, out of some book of Don'ts, but had, some five years ago, mysteriously and rapidly lost weight.

From ten-thirty till two, one by one, different heads popped in around the door to briefly stare at him—just checking the new Deputy out—he in his tight cream shirt and tie, all tits and tummy, inhaling and feeling slightly sick at his day's nth cigarette. Just after two, Kalra came in once more to escort Agastya to his own room. On the way, he told him that the Liaison Commissioner would be a little late that day in reaching office.

Agastya finally met him the next morning. Dr B.B. Bhatnagar was in the midst of dictating to his PA. He liked being called Doctor Saab. He had a Ph.D on Third World Economic Initiatives from the Bhupati Aflatoon International Open University. The Ph.D had of course been attained on office time. For two full years, he'd made various subordinates of the Liaison Commissioner copy down for his thesis different paragraphs from a dozen other Ph.Ds. Then, with his contacts in the government, he'd sent his Ph.D supervisor and others on his jury panel off on one official junket after another—a seminar in Bangkok, a symposium in Hawaii, a conference in Rio, three nights and two days in Hong Kong, four nights in Sydney. After his Ph.D, he preferred to refer to himself as an Economics man, Commerce and all that.

Dr Bhatnagar had four receding chins, soft, dimpled, demure folds of skin shying away in layers from his bird nose, his Hitler moustache and his gold spectacles. He had pink lips and eyes. Behind his thick glasses, the edges of both his upper and lower eyelids were turned outward, thus lining his eyes pink and giving his expressionless pupils a rosy tinge.

Behind his enormous desk, he sat balanced on a chair that rested precariously on just its rear legs. With a pencil in his left hand, he explored the jungle in his left ear for crud and animal life. His right hand clutched the desk for support. Periodically, to simulate the Thinker, he would raise his right hand to his chin, lose balance, flay his arms about for equilibrium, and finally lunge forward to land the chair with a thump on all four legs.

'Good morning, sir. I'm Agastya Sen.'

'Good morning. Don't disturb my chain of thought just now. I'm feeling very creative. Kalra will tell you that I'm usually at my most creative in the mornings. You may sit down. You couldn't call on me yesterday because I'm too senior, that's all right. I joined the Service twenty years before you did, while you were wetting your short pants probably. We won't meet very often because of your juniority. I will leave notes for you with Kalra, and you may phone me at 8.30 every morning to receive your instructions for the day because, as I pointed out just now, I'm at my most creative in the mornings. If I'm in the middle of my puja at that time, you may phone me again at 8.45 and—I'll be frank—if need be, again at 9 a.m. You may now listen carefully to—and try to understand—this first draft of a White Paper on BOOBZ, that is to say, Budget Organization On Base Zero. Yes, Kalra, where was I?'

Agastya quietly collapsed into the chair next to Kalra. On the edge of the seat on his left perched the office's Public Relations Officer, a small, fat, wicked-looking man with eyes radiant with anxiety, eyebrows that wouldn't stop wriggling, and a goatee. He'd taken off his shoes and socks and was vigorously rubbing the spaces between his toes. He'd overwhelmed the large room with a prodigious foot stench. Agastya wanted to leave the room and the job at once. Dr Bhatnagar, however, dictated right through the foot stench, so senior an officer was he.

'Hahn, Kalra . . . please take down . . . on the other hand, as a resultant implication of my feedback comma which is based on integral considerations comma—no, Kalra—make that integral subsystem considerations comma there is bound to be a sharp interface in coordination stroke communication stop. The specific criteria for the regulated flow of effectual information will have to be worked out per se comma but it is imperative that there is an initiation of critical paradigmal development comma and a crucial tertiary feedback on the functional interrelationship of hardware comma fourth generation technologies and the system rationale stop Regards stop Read it back to me.'

Kalra read it out loud, dispiritedly, in silence and

footstench. After he'd finished, Doctor Saab pushed his pink lips out in a thick, dissatisfied moue and after a long, contemplative minute, suddenly landed his chair with a decisive thump, startling them all and snapped out, 'Okay, fax it immediately, send a telex too, crash, and in the post copy, highlight the thrust area.' They all watched Kalra get up heavily from his chair, lumber to the door and leave the room. Doctor Saab seemed to wait for him to reach his seat, then he picked up the intercom and brayed, 'Hahn, Kalra, Doctor Saab here . . . come in, please, I want to add one more line to the fax.' While they waited for him, Doctor Saab looked at the PRO while informing Agastya, 'It's terrible, I'll be frank, but I can't leave these policy statements to anybody . . . Hahn Kalra—' Dr Bhatnagar rocked back to an impossible angle to observe his PA through his nostrils. 'Take a line before Regards. Quote In any case comma I'm having examined the commensurate set-off that the PO stroke HA may like to give in a costing exercise to such an eventuality Unquote.'

Doctor Saab called Agastya by his first name because it was a sound Management technique. He'd picked it up when he'd been 'in Commerce . . . later, I'll be frank, Business Administration at Harvard and all that. They asked me to stay on for my Ph.D but I said no, my government needs me—which is not quite true, because only a section of government needs me, the forward-looking, dynamic, creative section . . . Why were you on long leave before you joined us? Family problems? I understand from Personnel that you've availed of long leave quite often, in fact, virtually twice a year in the last eight years.'

The entry just then of a small, sexy, North-Eastern woman mercifully prevented Agastya from replying. Doctor Saab's face became the colour of his lips and he began to trill incoherently. To make the room worthy of her, he sent Footstench out at once. Babe and Agastya exchanged Looks.

'Ah ... come, come ... Madam Tina is our Office Superintendent ... this is Shri Agastya Sen, the new Deputy Liaison Commissioner ... he's been posted here to assess the new BOOBZ programme ... you may go now, Agastya ... Kalra will help you familiarize yourself with the office ...'

The Liaison Commissioner liaised between two governments, the regional government several hundred kilometres away, and the Centre. He was a sort of ambassador of a particular province to the government in the capital city of the same country. Hundreds of cases of the regional government, in any one week, would be pending with Big Brother at the Centre—a Ways and Means Advance with Finance, a Drought Relief Sanction with Agriculture, Political Clearance for the Chief Minister to travel abroad with External Affairs, a proposal to take over a sick cloth mill with Textiles, Industries, Commerce, Economic Affairs and Labour, a scheme to mutilate the coastline beyond recognition with Environment, and so on. The Liaison Commissioner was meant to chase up whatever was important. He was Mr Fixit. His entire office had been created and existed only to doggedly prod the Welfare State into moving, shall we say, different portions of its mammoth, immensely sluggish arse. In him, the government thus officially acknowledged that—God damn the citizenry!—even for its own OFFICIAL work, nothing moved in the Welfare State unless it was prodded. The Office of the Liaison Commissioner cost the country about one crore per year. There were thirty-four of them in the capital. Plans were afoot to have each province similarly represented in each of the thirty-three other provinces in the land.

Quite often, the government posted a jerk as Liaison Commissioner. After all, it had to post its jerks somewhere. They loved it, the perks, the absence of stress, the hundreds of kilometres between them and their boss. Dr Bhatnagar had three phones on his desk that never rang. They occasionally buzzed, Kalra asking him whether he wished to speak to whoever was on the line. Dr Bhatnagar never did, because the people that he would've loved to speak to—the Secretary-General of the United Nations, for example, or the President of the World Bank—never called, and their organizations never even acknowledged his letters. Kalra routinely transferred all of Dr Bhatnagar's calls to Agastya.

Accepting them was pretty unpleasant. They were almost always from Headquarters, i.e., the Secretariat hundreds of kilometres away, and almost always accusatory, sarcastic, recriminatory. The entire office had been tutored to say that Dr Bhatnagar was away at a meeting in the Ministry and when pressed, to add, the Home Ministry. Presumably, Agastya had concluded, since it was the vastest, the size of a bloody city, and also because it was sort of true, wasn't it, since the bugger was always at home, scheming with, and being pushed around by, his wife, a pale, fat, unpleasant woman with fish-eyes and shoulder-length hair. Agastya was quite nonplussed to discover that Dr Bhatnagar too, and quite seriously, meant home whenever he said Home Ministry. 'I'll be tied up all morning in the Home Ministry.' From him, such a statement could not be a witticism, and certainly to a subordinate twenty years his junior, unthinkable—unless it was a literal truth. Perhaps, long long ago, it had been a joke between husband and master, so rare that it had been cherished, and therefore oft repeated, and thus had become so familiar that to the ears of the bureaucrat, it'd begun to sound just right, not a witty euphemism, but the thing itself.

'I run my office from the Home Ministry.' Dr Bhatnagar's boast simply meant a costlier telephone bill for the office. Every one hour, both Kalra and Agastya were to telephone him at home to report the significant events since the last call. On the fourth day after he'd joined, Kalra advised

Agastya to concoct a bit, since the statement that 'Nothing's happening, sir,' particularly when sleepily delivered, would exasperate Dr Bhatnagar no end. Fabrication came quite easily to Agastya, but the passing years had also taught him the virtues of moderation. Buddha-like, he chose the Middle Way. Doctor Saab was never to be told either that 1) anybody more senior than him had phoned him, or that 2) somebody from an Economic ministry had called the office. Such cooked-up reports would fluster him and Sherni Auntie (Tigress Auntie, Kalra and Co's affectionate name for Mrs Bhatnagar) beyond measure. They'd go into a huddle from which they'd emerge after half an hour with the decision that Dr Bhatnagar should hare off to work to harass everyone there till well past closing time with nervous, mindless crap of a quality of which only he was capable. 'Kalra, take a fax to the Commerce Secretary . . . Agastya, speak to the Additional Private Secretary to the Industries Secretary and ask him whether he wants me to phone his chief now or later . . . Tell the PRO to deliver personally this evening a bouquet of fifty yellow roses to Mrs Khullar, you know, the Chairman of the Public Service Commission . . . he should first take the flowers home and have Mrs Bhatnagar okay them . . . Kalra, take a fax to the Finance Secretary . . .'

Thus Agastya, following the Middle Way, every hour, to Dr Bhatnagar's house, in Hindi:

'May I speak to the Liaison Commissioner, please?'

Kamat, the Residence peon—he and the Bhatnagars have been made for each other, a match in Heaven—in Hinglish: 'Who shall I say is calling?'

Agastya, in Hindi: 'It's me, you undie, U Thant.'

Ages later, Kamat: 'The Liaison Commissioner wishes to know what the subject of your call is.'

'If he doesn't want to get up, tell him not to bother. We merely received a telephone call from—' Agastya routinely disconnected at that point and immediately left his room in search of Madam Tina, marvelling at how much they relied on the inefficiency of their telephones to help them in their work. He was safe now from Bakra Uncle (Uncle Goat) for at least one hour, which was when he'd repeat the same farce. For Dr Bhatnagar to phone him back was not an easy task. He couldn't of course, because of his seniority, simply pick up the receiver and dial Agastya's number. He had to order Kamat to phone the office exchange and ask the operator to tell Agastya to phone Dr Bhatnagar. Fortunately for Agastya, all the telephone operators at the office hated Kamat only fractionally less than they hated Dr Bhatnagar; none of *them* was likely to interrupt his card game to deliver any of Kamat's messages.

When they next spoke, Agastya would not refer to his last interrupted phone conversation with Kamat until Dr Bhatnagar broached the subject, and then he'd state, airily, 'Oh, that! Yes sir, Deputy Secretary, Pensions and Administrative Reforms phoned . . . I think he knows you and wants you to put in a word for him for some post that he's angling for . . . yes sir, terrible, these fellows, sir, no shame . . .'

The first new marriage proposal was a postcard from Dadar, Bombay, from one Vishnu Bhatt, Professor Emeritus of Numerology, typewritten, stark in his Office Post File, all stamped and recorded in the Inward Register of the Dispatch Section.

'Dear Doctor Agastya Sen,
I learn that you are still available. I have for you a very interesting combination in my second daughter, Kumari Lavanya, an accomplished sitar player and a Bachelor of Dental Surgery from Baroda . . . If you show interest, I will dispatch you post-haste her photograph and her bio-data. I saw your date of birth in the Union Civil List, calculated from it and concluded that Lavanya

> *and you are superbly matched. Never in my thirty-four years of numerology have I come across such a perfect pair of numbers . . .'*

Agastya wrote on the postcard, *'I'd prefer a perfect pair of knockers. Dictation please, Steno,'* and flung it in the Out tray. If his stenographer ever turned up with it, he'd reply politely recommending somebody else, Dhrubo perhaps, or the steno.

The second marriage proposal was from Kalra on the intercom. 'Good morning, sir. Doctor Saab wants to know why you haven't married yet.'

Doctor Saab himself had two almost-nubile children, Bitiya and Baby. Baby was a twenty-year-old bespectacled male, a washed-out student of Physics somewhere. Bitiya the daughter, also bespectacled, was older by a year or two, chubby, wan, smug, plague-like by reason of her parentage. Agastya had met them because the entire office spent most of its day ferrying the office cars to different parts of the city to drop and pick them up. For which it, the office, couldn't of course touch Doctor Saab's office car, an off-white Ambassador with black windows that squatted like a toad at the office entrance, blocking the way, ready to scud off at a moment's notice to answer the Call, from the Cabinet Secretariat or the Department of Economic Affairs or, what was most likely, the Home Ministry. Thus in the course of the day, Bitiya and Baby popped into office quite often, between extra Physics tuitions and clumsy tennis at the Gymkhana Club, to fax and phone friends and relatives in Ahmedabad, Jaipur and Bombay.

'Kalra, does Bakra Uncle want me to interface with Bitiya?' 'Interface' was one of Dr Bhatnagar's favourite words. Agastya had explained to Kalra that it was Management language for sixty-nine. Kalra had been rather grateful for the idea. It had thenceforth enlivened a little his gruelling dictation sessions.

'No sir, may your tongue be cut off,' said Kalra in Punjabi, 'for even imagining an event so gross. Sherni Auntie is on the lookout for a kayastha from the cow-belt for Bitiya, definitely from one of the two top civil services, preferably from the diplomatic service. She ordered Doctor Saab to ask me to find out from you whether you'd like her to find you a match. Which is to say that she's already begun hunting.'

'How much does she make out of each successful transaction? I just want to know for my General Knowledge. To remain young, one must learn something new every day.'

'Yes sir. Lots, I'd imagine. A significant percentage of the dowry finally decided on. She'd certainly make about ten times the amount that Doctor Saab picks up from his faked Medical Claims and Travelling Allowance bills. Small minds win small sums. Slow and steady always finishes the race, but comes in second last.'

'Thank you for your observations, Kalra. Your wisdom encourages me to seek your counsel. In my youth, I would have fobbed Sherni Auntie off by admitting that I was already married to a Norwegian Muslim who was at present dying of breast cancer in England. Doctor Saab, though, might use that as a pretext to wangle an official trip to Europe. What do you think?'

At which wangling Dr Bhatnagar is simply wonderful. His expertise forms one of the objectives of growing up within the Civil Service. When one joins it at about the tender age of twenty-two, one is packed off to one of the dots in the vastness of the land to learn about and function in the wiles of district administration. One usually grows up rapidly in those two years, sporadically dreaming of a post in Paradise, namely, the regional capital—to which, eventually, over the years, one makes one's way. Once in the regional capital, one sets one's sights on the Centre, where all the action is, where the foreign trips are. When one arrives at the Centre, one proceeds to scheme for a slot in an international agency—

FAO, UNICEF, ILO, UNDP, WB, UNO, IMF, UNHCR—by Jove, the wide world at one's feet, and in one's pocket!—and a salary in dollars US to be spent in Kuala Lumpur, Bangkok, Geneva, New York and Paris.

Agastya's explanation for the civil servant's lust to travel abroad at official expense is the by-his-standards-princely daily allowance that he is paid for his trip. That allowance, depending upon one's seniority, varies from dollars US seventy-five to one hundred. Abroad, wherever he goes, the civil servant, thanks to the great Indian diaspora, always finds an accommodating countryman to shack up with—and a McDonald's to eat hamburgers in. He thus manages to save, in a trip of one week, out of his daily allowance, the equivalent of two months of his pay (from which saving, before returning to his native shores, at the last truly international airport, he buys girlie magazines like crazy). Everything, reasons Agastya, is economics—that is, when it isn't politics. His first official trip abroad is to the civil servant what the Fall was to Adam; nothing is ever quite the same again. Someone like him from the Embassy to ease him through the cold discomfort of Immigration and Customs, those spacious, silent cars, everyone in what to him look like snazzy suits, those women in skirts, the endless clack-clack of their heels on clean pavements, that frenzied wining and dining, the whirl of one official meeting after another, all handshakes and smiles, in which nothing is ever decisively discussed, the insane sightseeing, the frenzied, high-risk whoring in Djakarta, Bangkok, Amsterdam—having experienced all that *and* having gained two months' pay in the process, the civil servant returns home to find his job rather shabby and dull, without any fizz. He begins to dream of more foreign jaunts, to befriend Joint Secretaries in Commerce and Personnel, to speak the lingo of External Affairs, to invite the chaps from Banking and Finance over for slap-up dinners, to snoop around for the off chance in Agriculture and Fisheries; Dr Bhatnagar had even started to correspond *regularly* with an incredible number of Ambassadors and High Commissioners. For him, any occasion could trigger off a fax.

'Kalra, take a fax to our Ambassador in Mauritius . . . My dear Katju comma Yesterday was Gudi Padwa here—Gudi Padwa in italics, Kalra—comma a holiday comma you know comma the New Year in many parts of the country and I thought of you . . . you will recall that last year comma on exactly this day comma you and I met in transit at Frankfurt airport . . . you were dashing off to your new assignment in Port Louis whereas I was whizzing off to Honolulu to interface with our chaps there about a few Personnel Administration tricks that I'd picked up at Manila . . . when do we see you next? . . . I could always pop down to Port Louis were it not for this enormous comma absolutely wretched pressure of work over here . . . it's sad comma but true comma that in our system comma those who work comma get more work and those who shirk comma get the promotions exclamation mark . . . My dear wife sends her warmest regards to Lekha and you dash perhaps warmest—warmest in quotation marks, Kalra—is the most appropriate adjective for this unusually stifling March-April this year exclamation mark . . .'

Every morning, with a snowballing sense of O-brave-new-world-that-has-such-people-in't, Agastya would read the office copies of the faxes, telexes and letters that Dr Bhatnagar had dispatched, over the past few months, to the four corners of the world. 'Kalra, why don't I send copies of these faxes and telexes to Headquarters as part of my BOOBZ study? This is what we do, have a look and swoon.'

Kalra was surprised. 'But we *do* send them copies of each and every one of our communications.'

BOOBZ could equally aptly have been called SFS—like an obscene hiss from a lout on the road at something passing that had caught his fancy—*sfs*, that is to say, Start From Scratch. Like many other Management ideas, BOOBZ was simply plain common sense whisked up with jargon. Underneath that froth, it merely suggested to an organization to plan its budget with no presumptions, to examine each of its activities anew for its utility, to start from scratch every time. Is your organization fulfilling the functions that it was created for? Is the salary of this particular employee justified? What has been your growth in the previous year?—twenty pages of questions completely irrelevant to the functioning of government. BOOBZ in the Welfare State, though the brainchild of an earlier Regional Finance Secretary, was given extra impetus by the present incumbent, Dr Harihara Kapila, who was to Dr Bhatnagar what a five-hundred-rupee note is to the currency of Monopoly. He was a genuine Economics whizkid and he truly wanted, with all the naivete and zeal of the whizkid, to run the nation like a private sector corporation, to see the Ministerial Cabinet function like a boardroom. Fortunately for him, the new Chief Minister had given him a free hand because they both belonged to the same sub-caste.

Caste is truly everywhere, even in space: so Dr Kapila rationalized subsequently. It isn't a coincidence, for example, that our first—and only—astronaut was a Brahmin . . . other things being equal, send a Brahmin into the heavens. He'll be more appropriate for the gods. Caste is a much more reliable factor than merit, you know . . . because merit? Every Tom, Dick and Harry has merit, but how many have the right temperament, the right ethos, genes, lineage, morality, attitude, biases, hangups—in short, the right caste—for a job? By allowing me to do what I want with BOOBZ—which is a much easier, more memorable term, by the way, than the original, rather vacuous ZBB—all that is what the Chief Minister is saying. I've got to where I am because of my—and his—caste. We should be proud of his vision.

Under BOOBZ, Dr Kapila froze all recruitment to the government. 'Our offices are all overstaffed,' said he. He's crazy, said everyone else.

'If you don't give me men,' thundered the Director-General of Police, 'I will *not* line two alternative routes for kilometres on end with constables fifty metres apart from the airport to Raj Bhavan for two hours before he lands each time the Prime Minister comes visiting!'

However was one to reason with the top brass of the Police State?

In that infernally crowded city, they didn't *have* an alternative route from anywhere to anywhere else. Dr Kapila suggested that the DGP deploy his constables from elsewhere in the police force. After all, over fifteen thousand of his men guarded the V$^{\infty}$IPs who stayed in the Central Municipal Area of about forty square kilometres, that is, fifteen thousand of his Special Task Force, not counting his staff in the various police stations, anti-crime bureaus, on traffic duty and all that. The State spent over three hundred crores every year on V$^{\infty}$IP security alone. The DGP knew better than anybody else what frenzied lobbying went on amongst their men of state to get on the Intelligence Bureau Endangered List. One had truly arrived when one was declared a Z-category security risk. One was officially allotted five bullet-proof Ambassador cars with souped-up Isuzu engines, a posse of Black Guard commandoes and a colonial bungalow in the Sanitized Central Municipal Area. The Security budget paid for the doing-up of those cars: velvet seats, synthetic-tiger-skin dashboards, a bottle of scent beneath the rear-view mirror, a stereo—security requirements, of course. The Security budget also provided for raised boundary walls topped by barbed wire for all those colonial bungalows—and fifteen thousand men of the Special Task Force watered those vast lawns and hung about at the gates to keep the rest of the gawking nation out. All those men doubled up, didn't they, as gardeners, cooks, nannies and housekeepers. They rushed off to the store when Madam ran short of curry masala or spring onions. Dr Kapila suggested that the DGP pluck them out of V∞IP security duty and use them to line his streets for the Prime Minister.

Outraged, the DGP dictated a stinker of a note to the Home Secretary, warning the nation, inter alia, of an apocalypse were recruitment to be stopped to the police forces. Following the usual route—Director-General to Home Secretary to Chief Secretary to Minister of State for Home Affairs to Home Minister to Secretary to the Chief Minister to Chief Minister—the note flitted about in the Secretariat for three days. The Chief Minister had no time for the apocalypse, so his Secretary wrote on the note: *Seen by CM. The views of Finance may be solicited.* Off shot the note again on its billiard-ball route.

Dr Kapila loved this sort of thing the most—the impressive advocacy to a superior, through the use of cold, clear reasoning, of doctrinaire ways and means of effecting logical economies in the Welfare State. On notes such as the one from the Director-General of Police, he could dictate for months without pause.

> *If intelligently implemented, BOOBZ could change the face of the government, that is, if sensible economizing is at all one of our objectives. It ought to be one, since we are closer to bankruptcy than we've ever been before.*

It was only natural, Dr Kapila felt, that the DGP had expressed the anxieties characteristic of those feudal lords who fear most the diminishing of their fiefdoms. That BOOBZ concerned itself not with the balance of power between

Departments but with planning would never enter his head. The police forces, he would assert, have always welcomed organizational innovation and new man management techniques (as long as they didn't touch either manpower or budget). Under the mantle of V$^{\infty}$IP security, Dr Kapila knew that the government protected scores of vague persons whom nobody even knew the existence of and whom only the nation's taxpayers might want to get rid of once they found out how their money was being wasted. At the same time, two of the country's last four Prime Ministers and three regional Chief Ministers had been, in the preceding decade, either mowed down or blown up. Thus, *one*, notched up Dr Kapila, they spent more and more on Security every year. They were at 303 crores that year from the previous budget's 292. *Two*: Their Endangered List continued to grow even more steadily than their population. Recent additions included the Minister of State for Handlooms, Women and Child Development and the Chairman of the Committee to Celebrate the Completion of Forty-Four Years of the Nation's Federal Polity. *Three*: They could not protect the very few that they needed to.

Dr Kapila sighed and looked out of his ninth-floor Secretariat window at the world's largest slum and the grey sea beyond. The air above Bhayankar still looked smoky from the fires of the hellish election riots of the preceding week. They hadn't yet finished identifying the dead. He was abruptly reminded of his last trip to the northern states.

He'd been sent there as a Central observer for the previous elections some months ago. On the road somewhere just outside Yugandhar City, eleven-ish in the morning it had been, a straight, unremarkable stretch of State Highway with wheat fields on either side, their white Ambassador had been merrily staggering along when, all of a sudden, the skies'd been overwhelmed by a squeal of sirens that had frighteningly grown louder every second. Shuddering with dread, their car had pulled up on the shoulder of the road and breathless, they'd all gaped at a hillock of dust rushing up the road towards them, like the elements signalling the approach of Robur the Conqueror in one of his futuristic, amphibious vehicles. In a second, it had resolved itself into a convoy—an open jeep, two off-white Ambassadors, a closed jeep. Lights flashing, sirens now earsplitting, it—the convoy—had shot past them with the roar and whoosh of a jet plane. The two jeeps and the second Ambassador had been stuffed with—had oozed, as it were—Black Guard commandoes and policemen in various coloured uniforms. With some kind of small cannon, a sort of Rambo erect beside the driver in the first jeep, rigged out in regulation khaki beret, sunglasses and moustache, had waved pedestrians and terrified cyclists away from the convoy. Whatever from? Dr Kapila had wondered. From karate-chopping the vehicles as they passed? Or kicking the tyres? Perhaps from piddling on the ferociously winking lights on the roofs of the cars? The first Ambassador had been black-glassed, secretive and ludicrously menacing, like a rapist/blackguard in an F-grade cheap-thrills film. The windows of the second had been down perforce, or else the dozen or so commandoes in it would've asphyxiated. It—the second car—looked as though it'd just careened out of a farcically violent comic strip—Asterix, perhaps; a dozen determinedly baleful mugs under black berets hanging out of the windows, an occasional hand clutching a reputedly ammunition-less automatic weapon (ammunition-less because of one of the routine Economy Drives. Bullets were expensive and of course the police knew that not everybody on the Endangered List needed all the paraphernalia—five cars, fine, but bullets in the guns of their guards? Oh no no. *Reputedly* ammunition-less because bullets was a Security subject, and Security had always been hidden in billowing clouds of unknowing, like a masked rioter behind the exploding smoke bomb, exploiting the camouflage to do his own thing).

What could be the purpose of such a convoy? To irritate and scare traffic and the citizenry? To amuse and depress the inmates of other vehicles? 'That must be two dying Prime Ministers being rushed to Intensive Care,' Dr Kapila had murmured.

'Ha ha sir.' His driver, a local, had then explained in Punjabi, 'But that isn't so. That was the Superintendent of Police of the district, sir, going to office.'

Dr Kapila sighed and returned to his dictation charged with an obscure missionary zeal. He must stop the rot, guide the drifters, stem the tide; he had all the ideas, but how to convince the people who called the shots? Should he buy time on Zee TV? Because nobody read any more—even electronically-typed, double-spaced English notes. Perhaps he could seat the Cabinet in front of the TV for half-an-hour of prime time and have a toothy, nubile thing emcee a show called The Boobz of the Welfare State. Some good citizens to sing Hindi film songs before a studio audience, a few film clips, a couple of risqué jokes, a fistful of social issues and every now and then, a Hindi film personage, preferably female, to chat about the benefits of the Boobz programme. Perhaps then the Cabinet would listen.

Ah well, until then, the show must go on. 'Please continue . . . *BOOBZ is one method by which we can halt the enormous wastage of financial and manpower resources that has become a fundamental characteristic of all our activities . . . Since this is a Secret note, it will not be out of place to describe in some detail here a typical example of how the Welfare State allocates its resources . . .*' With a bitter half-smile, Dr Kapila at this point balked. How to choose from a million? Without losing objectivity, without becoming near-hysterical, how to lead up to the instance of Bhanwar Virbhim at the golf club?

Golf was a social thing for Dr Kapila, Manila and all that, the right people. He'd been rudely surprised one Sunday morning to spy on the course a handful of Black Guard commandoes scanning the surroundings with eagle eye while bumping into one another, hideously conspicuous against the green, an invasion of aliens. When he'd spotted in their midst the golf-ball-like figure of his ex-Chief Minister and present Central Minister, Bhanwar Virbhim, he'd felt as unsettled as a schoolboy catching sight of his formidable class teacher meekly standing in a long line to buy kerosene at the local market—however could he be here? With the Minister, teaching him the rudiments of the game, had been his loyal sidekick, the reputed sharer of his mistress, squat, safari-suited Bhupen Raghupati.

The sight had needled all of Dr Kapila's caste and class prejudices. The Golf Club was for the select—for speakers of grammatically-correct, correctly-accented English, for those who occasionally holidayed in Europe, for that sort; so how come this local from some horrendously obscure small town, who still wore (Dr Kapila was certain) string drawers instead of (the damn uncomfortable) VIP Frenchie undies, and who still didn't know that one didn't burp in public, how come he now loved his game of golf? Had *we* come a long way, baby, sir. Bhanwar Virbhim on the green had indeed looked like the Revolution. Dr Kapila had disapproved. Where would one be if people began to rise in society at the speed with which they rose in politics?

Ranga the Club Secretary, an ex-Finance Service man who favoured checked trousers and who had a bald dome and grey, shoulder-length hair, had not approved either. 'You see, these fellows—' stabbing with his pencil in the direction of the commandoes, '—wear studded boots the size of suitcases. We might as well simply dig up the turf. I'll have to speak to the DGP.'

He did. The Director General of Police then sent a secret note to the Private Secretary to Bhanwar Virbhim pointing out that in the opinion of Security, for a sniper, an Endangered Listee waddling about in the vast open spaces of a golf course was a dream come true. 'The Minister is strongly advised to give up learning the game till such time that he remains on the E list.'

Bhanwar Virbhim would not have risen thus far had he ever wilted under a routine caste-and-class offensive of this kind. He asked his Private Secretary to write a Secret Note to the Private Secretary to the Home Minister to suggest that the Black Guard Commandoes ordered to protect him, Bhanwar Virbhim, should be instructed to walk barefoot as and when the occasion demanded.

The note billiard-balled its way down to the DGP, who wrote on it that he found the proposal of the Private Secretary *unrealistic. Are the Black Guards supposed to protect the Target every second of the period that they are on duty, or not? That is the question. What if—Heaven forbid—something were to happen to the Target at the very moment when the heads of the Commandoes are down and their hands and minds are busy with their shoelaces? Whose head will then roll in the fallout to compensate for the Target's?*

The note arrived on Dr Kapila's desk as a fat file full of comment and counter-comment. Bhupen Raghupati had mooted that on Bhanwar Saab's golf days, his contingent of commandoes could be doubled and that the second lot could be barefoot. The DGP had approved of the doubling because it increased his fiefdom, but not of the bootlessness. *Security cannot compromise on quality, on anything that will affect performance. What if—Heaven forbid—something were to happen to the Target just when a thorn or sharp object pricked the bare feet* *of the commandoes, and their hands and minds were occupied with the distraction? Who would then be held responsible for the tragedy? Please find out what kind of footwear is acceptable on the golf course and how much it will cost us to shod ALL our commandoes. For it is my duty to point out here that other V^{∞}IPs on the E List might well want to emulate Bhanwar Virbhim. Please solicit the approval of Finance for the extra expenditure.*

The more time Dr Kapila had spent in Finance, the more he had come to believe that very few citizens—normal people—would understand the Welfare State economy. After years of sporadic focusing on the subject, he'd honed the tumult in his head down to a few basic ideas.

For one, the amount of money that the typical civil servant in Finance could visualize, conceptualize or mentally handle at one time usually depended on the file that he was dealing with but in general, did not exceed fifty thousand rupees, that is to say, his average official monthly earnings multiplied by as far as his fingers could take the figure.

Even though this first conclusion of his sounded like one of his own poor jokes, Dr Kapila had seen it borne out time and time again by the facts. If one asked a Finance man for clearance for any sum *less* than fifty thousand rupees as a loan, for example, against one's *own* Provident Fund account to i) buy a car, ii) marry off one's son or iii) cardinal sin!—zip off to Mauritius on a holiday, it was a fact that, quoting his own last Economy Drive circular, he would turn one down.

Yet, when one returned to Finance with yet another harebrained proposal to spend five hundred crore rupees on a new rural water supply scheme—which was merely the fifteenth cosmetically-doctored version of the system that'd been in existence for the last forty years—Finance okayed it, principally because five hundred crore rupees was way, way beyond the comprehension of its men; about one hundred thousand times more than what they could visualize.

Dr Kapila had once believed that the civil servants of his Department would approve the new rural water supply scheme and turn down the request for a loan to buy a car with because:

i) they were wicked, loved power and adored harassing their colleagues,

ii) rural was far away from them, fortunately remote and incomprehensible. They felt sorry for it, and

iii) they felt noble okaying noble schemes.

Time had however forced him to change his opinion. Why, only two weeks ago, Public Health had sent them a proposal for an extra expenditure of forty-four thousand rupees on Additional Tetracycline for Madna District. His Deputy Secretary'd promptly shot it down, pitilessly scrawling beneath the initial note: *Bad planning. PH should've provided a minor cushion for such eventualities in its original Firefighting Against Acts of God Subhead.*

Dr Kapila's first conclusion was his second as well. Fifty thousand rupees, he believed, was also the largest sum that the average, corrupt civil servant could look forward to as his share, and both mentally and physically handle as a bribe, per transaction per person, that is, after all the palms'd been greased in proper hierarchical order and the dust'd settled right down the line. Venality, however, was not a subject that Dr Kapila was comfortable with. Even after almost thirty years of service, it continued to shock and at times nauseate him.

When he'd been young—or rather, younger—he could swear that they hadn't taken any bribes. Almost swear. Well, *he'd* never taken any. What he meant was—the lower orders, twenty years ago, might've taken a hundred—or a maximum of five hundred—rupees to push or lose a file, or a peon might've taken ten rupees off a petitioner to allow him in to meet the officer, or a constable—and there Dr Kapila'd always pause. The less said about the police, engineers and Welfare State doctors, the better. Some fixtures of life, like the Milky Way, have been there in the space around us since time immemorial.

But nowadays! The ethics—and the stakes—stagger the mind! And People Like Me, shrieked Dr Kapila silently, with My Background! It is *horrifying* that they too are merrily milking away! Not some lower-caste fellow—some incompetent, barely literate Kansal Commission appointee, the holder of a sad undergraduate degree from some obscure regional college that functions out of a ghastly Public Works building that has broken windows and no electricity—one wouldn't've been surprised, you know, to hear that *they're* still raking it in. But members of the Golf Club, for instance! Who read Alvin Toffler and buy Music Today CDs—civil servants like that slithery Chanakya Lala who, after a decade of dedicated service, reputedly owns a couple of hills in some North Indian resort town—my God, he went to my school and my college—though, fortunately, twenty years after me—but crookedness that close to one's skin is deeply unsettling.

And the figures that one hears are truly mindboggling! A lakh of rupees for each No Objection Certificate to pull down and rebuild a one-thousand-square-foot apartment! The rates have apparently been quite mathematically worked out and—some say—are indeed quite reasonable.

Chanakya Lala often reminds Dr Kapila of Kaa the snake in his daughter's old Walt Disney video of *The Jungle Book*. Lala is tall, slim, bespectacled, with a womanish sway to his hips in his walk. He stinks of perfume; in fact, in a drawer in his office, he keeps a bottle from which he regularly bathes himself. It is his way of preparing for meetings. That scent of his—airy, pine-forest-like—Dr Kapila has come to consider one of the odours of corruption. Lala wears his gold watch on his right wrist, which Dr Kapila finds truly disgusting. He is unfailingly well-dressed and well-mannered, Suck Above, Suck Below. He invariably shares his booty with the dacoits who are his political masters and with whichever of his official superiors is willing. He has enterprise and has managed over the years to milk the most diverse Departments—Urban Housing, Rural Rationing, Education, Food and Drugs, Excise, Animal Husbandry. You see, no matter where you are, there always will be a law which you'll interpret, one way or the other, in favour of one party. Why do it for free? Especially when your own salary's so ridiculous that you *are* practically working for free. After all, don't you owe a decent life to your children?

The above specious arguments would never've occurred to me, is what Dr Kapila tells himself. However did they occur to Slither? When Dr Kapila'd been Lala's age, every morning, he'd—in a manner of speaking—get off his mother's lap, touch her feet, seek her blessings, grab his tiffin box from his wife's hand and go off to sweat in the car on his way to work. Was Lala then a sign of the changing times? How did he get rid of his mother and replace her with a wily dealer in foreign exchange? Or could the changing times themselves be attributed to the moral decline of the Aflatoons? The rot starts at the top? The apocalypse round the corner, time's running out for the nation—and just look at the Joneses!

Lala of course was in the big league; the amounts that he supposedly gobbled up in bribes were hardly the norm. Of course, Dr Kapila had steadfastly held that those who could prove his deductions wrong were most welcome to step forward. In fact, by doing so, they would solve some of the riddles and dispel a little the fog that envelopes the economics of the Welfare State. Were he to be interrogated on the subject, he'd confess that soon after taking over as Regional Finance Secretary, he'd been so intrigued by the economics of white-collar venality that he'd felt that he must pose some questions to the experts in the field. He'd thus sent anonymous questionnaires on scented paper both to Chanakya Lala and to Bhupen Raghupati. He'd been partly inspired by some curious sheets of off-white paper that he'd received now and then in his office post, unsigned—indeed, blank, save for some large, yellowish stains on them, thick, like dried cream. Though he hadn't signed the covering letter, he'd made it clear that the filled-in questionnaires should be posted to the office of the Regional Finance Secretary and that the information disclosed therein would of course remain totally confidential. He was disappointed that neither ever replied. He found that typically self-centred and cowardly of them. They needn't have *signed* the filled-in sheets. Surreptitiously, they squeeze and suck at the dugs like crazy, but scurry away like rats when they feel the mammoth, sluggish body stir.

Dr Kapila'd been quite pleased with the acuity of his questions. Though unanswered, they summed up the disquiet of any thinking Economics man in the country.

i) Apparently, the total amount that the State loses a year in bribes is a little over ten thousand crore rupees. However did the statisticians arrive at such a figure? Have you answered such questionnaires before? If so, how come I don't know? Who'd sent them? Have you kept a copy?
ii) When did you start being corrupt? Was your father corrupt? Your mother? Was she a Customs official, by any chance? Did you ever steal money from your servant?
iii) Do you prefer bribes in cash or in kind? Diwali gifts of laser-disc videos? Johnnie Walker Blue? Paid holidays in Goa? With pussy?
iv) Is it true that Mrs Raghupati began life as a profitable foreign exchange racketeer? Capital gains tax, securities, trade cartels, import/export regulations,

over-invoicing, duty evasion, bank charges, gold smuggling, tax havens, chronic balance of payments crisis—that she understands and freely uses such phrases daily? Is it a fact that she abandoned her Economics degree in her second year in college to try her luck at the Miss India Beauty Contest?
v) Don't you find it morally baffling that criminals like you are nowadays—sort of, well—admired?

Dr Kapila himself did. At the Golf Club, twenty years ago, he imagined that someone like Lala'd've been shunned—like the pariah in the play school who's done potty in his pants—but in the present Dark Age, it depressed him to see that when a Lala type stepped out of his after-office-hours, chauffeur-driven, personal Cielo, and womanishly swayed into the foyer of the Club, cootchie-cooing to his kids on his mobile phone because he'd simply no time for them in the evenings at home, heads of other Lala types turned; they waved from across the hall and loudly, in Hinglish, invited him over for a drink.

Changing times, no doubt—and hence morally baffling. One couldn't easily distinguish anymore between the Club type and the Lala type. They both wore Arrow shirts and perfumed themselves as though their deodorizers were extinguishers for their armpits on fire.

vi) Please confirm that what follows is your modus operandi. In any given set-up, you will first identify the principal source of power. Once identified, you'll push, with single-minded sycophantic intensity, to get close. When within sucking distance, you'll genuflect. Then, your relationship having stabilized, you'll magnanimously share your booty and your soul with him.

Dr Kapila knew of bureaucrats who, whenever they met the present Head of the political party in power—which was about twice a week—in greeting, touched his feet with their hands, and on holidays and festivals, with their foreheads—and when they feared his displeasure, with their lips. When Dr Kapila sat across from such colleagues at meetings or stood beside them in the Officers' Only urinal gazing pointedly ahead at the tiles before their noses, he'd often wanted to ask them how it actually felt, physically, to kiss someone else's feet. The owner of which—the Soul of the Masses, the Beacon of the Downtrodden, the Great Light himself—had reputedly told his inner circle about the more sycophantic civil servant: 'If I ask them to eat my shit, they'll gobble it up with salt, pepper, chilli powder and gratitude.'

> *vii) However can you* do *it? How can you face an applicant across your office table and how can your lips and tongue frame words like: 'Perhaps we can meet in the evening to discuss your case'—or whichever words wicked people use in such circumstances. How come* my *middle-classness makes me uncomfortable and suspicious in front of any applicant in a safari suit and mobile phone and your middle-classness makes you want to befriend him?*
> *viii) It has been suggested that you accept bribes only from persons officially richer than you. Given your salary, that means a lot of people, doesn't it? Do you therefore consider yourself a socialist? Do you dread the forthcoming Pay Commission Recommendations because they'll upset your calculations?*
> *ix) May I include here an anecdote for you to mull over? It concerns a certain Agastya Sen who, three years ago, was an Under Secretary—and my subordinate's subordinate—in the Department of Labour.*

He dealt with Gulf Traffic—namely, he processed the papers of the thousands of skilled and semi-skilled workers—electricians, plumbers, carpenters, masons, fitters, welders, tailors, gardeners, barbers, garage mechanics, undertakers—who were lured by crafty middlemen every month to the Persian Gulf with the promise of a better—if not life, then at least pay. His task was Herculean—to eliminate, as far as possible, the craftiness of each deal, to establish its bona fides, to try and ensure that the worker, in each of thousands of cases, wasn't being ensnared, for example, into a kind of slavery, or some flesh racket, or into becoming a courier for the drug trade. The pressures of the job, as Sen discovered on Day One, were enormously harrowing—an unending stream of oily, bright-eyed visitors whose every syllable seemed to insinuate at a bribe, phone calls from the most unexpected higher-ups about how to decide certain cases; from three in the afternoon onwards, another endless line of bouquets, boxes of sweets, baskets of dry fruit—as though he'd just got married or promoted, or the country'd won a crucial one-day cricket match. Upset, feeling as though he was about to drown, he began to refuse all the gifts, even the flowers. His obstinacy made his visitors look at him sadly and long.

By the end of Week One, honest, upright, upper-middle-class Sen learnt that he simply couldn't trust his superiors and Dr Kapila's immediate subordinates; by the middle of Week Two, his personal staff either. Close to cracking up, he nipped off to Personnel to ask to be transferred. Oh no, hang in there, admonished Personnel, after its usual fashion and because it couldn't be bothered. You've been sent there to clean up the muck. You're doing a great job, we hear. Keep it up.

Sen stayed those days in one of the holes in the Prajapati Aflatoon Welfare State Public Servants' Housing Complex Transit Hostel near the Pashupati Aflatoon Public Gardens. Those familiar with the Transit Hostel and its ghastly layout know that outside each flat, alongside the doorbell, is a handy letter box in which the residents receive their daily milk, newspapers and their occasional mail. Three Sundays after

Sen had joined the Department of Labour, at eight-thirty in the morning, along with two packets of full-cream milk, *The Statesman* and *The State of the Times*, he found in the letter box of his flat a blue plastic packet that contained twenty one-hundred-rupee notes.

He was infuriated at having his Sunday morning disturbed by a petty feeler of a bribe. With its presence, the money clouded his morning tea and his 5BX exercise session. He needed to get rid of it before it ruined his entire day. At eleven, cursing his potential bribers, he put on his crash helmet and with the plastic packet in his knapsack, rode off on his bicycle.

Beneath the new Trimurti Aflatoon Centenary Celebrations Flyover lived Sen's favourite beggar family, a one-legged father, two nubile daughters and half-a-dozen younger siblings. He thrust the packet into the hands of one of the daughters and, overcome with emotion, sped off without waiting to see her reaction.

He hadn't travelled more than thirty metres from the spot when a sudden, frenzied and sustained yelling made him brake, stop and look back. A motorcycle—with two men on it, both in dark glasses, and with the pillion rider tucking something into his shirt front—flashed past him. The entire beggar family was out on the street, bawling, waving their arms, bringing traffic to a screeching halt, gesticulating frantically in the direction of the motorcycle, shouting at one another and at startled pedestrians, darting forward for a couple of steps, then stopping short as though they'd changed their minds, then springing forward again.

With a shrill ring of protest from his bell, Sen took off after the villains. He hated motorcycles because they thought that they were sexy. He much preferred the knee-pumping openness of his Atlas bicycle. The booty-snatchers were nowhere in sight. At the first traffic light, he barked at the auto-rickshaw driver idling beside him, 'Which way did they go!'

'Who?' asked the auto-wala, not unreasonably. Offended by Sen's urgency, he dug deep into his nose and emerged with a comet—to wit, a hard head of snot with a long, liquidy tail—which he examined for a moment before flicking at Sen for his inspection. But in God's scheme, all acts have a purpose, because in jerking his head away from the comet, Sen spotted the duo on the motorcycle on the other side of the street, shooting away from him, back the way he'd come and up the flyover. 'Stop the thieves!' he snapped at a neighbouring cyclist and jumping the red light, U-turned and zipped off after them, with a policeman's enraged whistle screeching in his wake.

Sen was an instinctive economist—one of the nation's finest, was Dr Kapila's firm opinion. Even on that bicycle, darting crazily through that indisciplined Sunday-morning traffic, he was breaking down and docketing away for further analysis some of the less obvious but nevertheless fascinating aspects of the activities of the past few hours—the Welfare State subsidies on petrol, for instance. Of what use were they? Why was the taxpayer paying for the energy source of the motorcycles of the hoodlums of the land? And unemployment, a knotted, vexed question. Had his quarry of the moment, those damned robbers of the poor, ever enrolled at an Employment Exchange or answered the advertisements of the Staff Selection Commission? Had they ever joined the service of the Welfare State, for example, in the Department of Rural Development and had they been clerks disbursing the funds of the Consolidated Agricultural Regeneration Programme, would they have robbed the poor more, or less? On the motorcycle, moreover, the scoundrels had—strictly speaking—merely snatched back their *own* money—or rather, their boss's—and had in fact been hard at work, carrying out instructions for which they'd be paid a fee, or even a monthly salary; as delivery boys or Courier Supervisors, they probably had legitimate roles in some illegitimate organization, in the books of which their wages were all properly accounted for.

Their zipping about on a motorcycle therefore was licit economic activity, whereas as clerks, while siphoning off funds in Rural Development, they'd actually be converting white legal money into black, thereby adding their bit to rock the touch-n-tumble balance of the State economy. To say nothing of their dubious contribution in their paperwork towards achieving the objectives of the Consolidated Agricultural Regeneration Programme. All in all, therefore, as an economist, a thinking man, keeping the welfare of the state in mind, *ought* he to chase the motorcyclists?

A road block and a diversion at the bottom of the flyover. Just a board in the fast lane, propped up on a flower pot. It read: ROAD CLOSED. USE—↑, the arrow pointing at the heavens. Sen braked before an awesome Ganesh belly and demanded peremptorily, 'Who is it? PM? Real route or decoy?'

But he'd lost the chase, he knew it. He must learn for the future, though, how to dig deep for, emerge with and flick a comet, all in one smooth movement.

It would be a useful counter-missile against the flying nosey of other cyclists which, he'd concluded after a few weeks' pedalling in the capital, was the third most dangerous thing on the roads after public buses and the white Ambassador cars of the government. One couldn't of course fight the flying nosey of others with one's own because when one, without pausing in one's cycling, swivelled one's head to blow one's nose in the air, one's nosey unfortunately flew *backwards* to bespatter the cyclists behind one.

He returned to his flat, defeated. He felt weird and foolish all day, tense, jittery, expecting the police to come and harass him any minute. In the evening, he dropped in unannounced—as was the custom in the Transit Hostel, it being as informal as a slum—on one of his neighbours, Dr Srinivas Chakki, an entomologist in the Ministry of Public Health. Over many cups of tea, Sen described and analysed the events of the day and life in general in the Department of Labour.

'What was most significant, Dada, was that I, in person, even though it was only for less than a minute, could actually hand over what to them is a substantial sum of money, to some of the poorest of our poor—though of course, statistics and reports indicate that our urban poor are quite well-off when compared to their rural cousins. My beggar family actually has to pay some kind of rent, for instance, to some subterranean creature to be allowed to exist under the flyover. But nevertheless, it seems to me that I committed today a perfect, pure act of welfare that lasted all of forty seconds—that is to say, I pounced on the ill-earned money of some wicked man and handed it over—the well-thumbed, greasy, germ-packed cash, the naked notes themselves—to a bunch that needed it more than me. Could welfare be clearer, cleaner? None of that junk about helping the needy to stand on their own two feet. Because you don't know either who the really needy are or what they truly want! Because your Village Information System functions not on fact, but on caste and clout! No fourteen-page forms to be filled in triplicate by an illiterate and submitted along with six annexures and a bribe at the Block office forty kilometres away after waiting in a queue for six hours—for all of which the applicant'll get sixty rupees a month. No insanely complicated bank loan to buy a dried-up, malnourished cow when what the bugger really needs is water for his three square feet of plot. No, none of that. Just plain, hard, filthy cash passed on in a second to the female adults of the family for them to do what they like with. No imposing on the good citizenry that breathes at the bottom of the heap your own doctrinaire theories on what constitutes the good life. Only give them the means to define for themselves, by a process of trial and error, what the good life is.'

'I wish you wouldn't call me Dada. Just because we're Bengali, you think that I can and want to be called Dada. Well, as the Bengalis love to say, we should change the system. I've a theory or two up my sleeve that however need some honing before I can roll my sleeves up and make them public.'

The next morning, Sen made it a point to reach his office before everyone else. As soon as his PA showed up, he asked him to call the police, declaring that within the span of one hour that morning, there had been both an attempt to bribe him and a subsequent theft. His PA had looked doubtful, had raised his eyebrows, pursed his lips and gone away. He'd returned a while later to inform Sen that they hadn't reckoned with the Police State. The Station House Officer of the local police station had apparently told the PA that he wasn't going to move his arse all the way to Aflatoon Bhavan for an official as lowly as an Under Secretary and for crimes as mundane as bribery and theft.

The Steel Frame in Sen had then swung into action. 'Did you speak to him in Punjabi, English or Hindi? . . . Put him on the line, I'll suck his balls dry in Punjabi.'

By cop standards, the SHO was tall, slim, even good-looking. Sen's PA later explained that their particular police station tended to have slimmer and better-looking men because the entire force collectively made a—well, minor—killing—just enough for their tea and cigarettes—out of seducing, terrorizing, beating up, sodomizing and blackmailing the closet homosexuals who cruised after dark in the Pashupati Aflatoon Public Gardens.

'Well, you ought to've told me all that before. Was that why the meeting was such a cock-up? I mean, was I supposed to turn him on or he me or what?'

The SHO had entered and saluted Sen with elaborate, stylized insolence, boots detonating on the floor, et cetera. While Sen'd wondered when to ask him to sit, then or a bit later, the SHO had sat down, sighed, asked him in turn whether he could smoke and lit up while Sen had begun to point out to him that smoking was forbidden on Welfare State premises.

'Ahhh . . . too late . . . perhaps next time,' the SHO had

lamented in Punjabi, examining his cigarette and exhaling richly at the table top. 'Why do we issue regulations that we can't implement? It gives governance a bad name. Makes the public conclude that we aren't serious—I'm so sorry, would *you* like to smoke?'

They'd got down to business. Sen had worked most of it out. 'I usually turn up in office pretty early . . . before everybody else, before the day starts. I go through my files, plan my day, prepare for my meetings. My desk is usually spotless, from the way I'd left it the evening before. I've instructed my peon not to dust it. I dust it myself. He didn't look hurt that I'd further lessened his workload. I keep the duster in the bottom drawer on the right-hand side of my desk. This morning, when I opened the drawer for the duster, I noticed on top of it a blue plastic packet. That drawer, I must make it clear, has never contained anything other than two dusters, a sheet or two of blotting paper, some pieces of chalk, and a fair amount of rat shit, both dry and fresh. My skin began to tingle, gooseflesh and all that, as I opened the packet. It contained hundred-rupee notes. I counted them. My fingers were clumsy. Twenty in all. I folded the packet neatly—neater than it was, in fact, put it back in the drawer, picked up the duster and began reorganizing the dust on my table—my mind, as they say, in a whirl. I distinctly remember that I shut the drawer before beginning to dust. To cut a long story short, while dusting, I felt an urge to visit the toilet, so I went, leaving the duster on the table beside the phone, to the Officers' Toilet, which is in the East Wing, next to the canteen of the Department of Mines. I was away from this room for about nine minutes—not more, I'd imagine. We can time it, if you like. I returned, finished dusting and opened the bottom drawer to put the duster back. The packet had disappeared. I searched the other drawers of the desk, the cupboard, those shelves . . . it wasn't anywhere . . . I spent some time wondering whether I should simply forget the incident or report it as a case of attempted-bribery-cum-theft. I finally decided on being straightforward.'

By spinning this yarn and lodging a complaint with the police, Sen'd actually hoped, in a schoolboyish, Enid Blyton-ish, Five-Go-Off-and-Bugger-George-on-Smuggler's-Hill kind of way, to confound his adversaries, to show them that they were dealing not with a cretin, but with a major player, who knew the ropes and could call the shots. The meeting with the SHO therefore could be considered a turning point in his official life.

For lazily, through the cigarette smoke, after hearing him out, the SHO drawled in Punjabi, 'I've a constable waiting outside with your PA. We'll call him in, you dictate your complaint, he'll read it back to you, you both can sign it, we'll give you a copy. But tell me, when you submit an FIR like that to your Tax Officer, saying that you've lost, say, ten thousand rupees—that's simpler, and more respectable, than adding all those confusing details about the blue plastic packet and the Officers' Toilet—does he grant you tax exemption or what?'

The upshot of the encounter—and indeed, of the whole episode—on the oblique economic implications of which Dr Kapila solicited the views of the addressees of his secret questionnaire—was that Sen decided that till his retirement from the service of the Welfare State, he would not, to use officialese, take a decision on any official matter unless and until he was sure that it did not stink. His decision considerably eased his workload. After his retirement, he looked forward to a career in revolutionary politics. At least politicians, he'd point out to himself, without any sense of being funny, were comparatively straightforward in their crookedness.

On the note from the Director General of Police on the subject of doubling the number of Black Guard Commandoes on golf duty and buying all of them shoes acceptable on the golf course, Dr Kapila saw that predictably, his Department had cocked up, missed the point, not seen the wood for the trees and for the nth time, had substantiated his, Dr Kapila's, axiom that very few civil servants understood Welfare State finance. For, to a man, all his subordinates—Desk Officer, Assistant Secretary, Deputy Secretary, Joint Secretary—had turned down the two hundred thousand rupees on the golf shoes as wasteful expenditure and en passant approved—as though a trifling matter—the proposed six crore rupees on the doubling of the Black Guards. Dr Kapila sighed and dictated a fourteen-page memo on the subject, thereby fattening the file a bit more. He included in his outpourings all his foreboding about the nation, his horror at the endless, snowballing waste, at the body politic completely out of joint, his conviction that the need of the hour, as always, was an intelligent review of the economics of the state, was the immediate and serious implementation of programmes like BOOBZ.

It was not wise, he knew, to send a *fourteen*-page note to the Chief Minister, but he couldn't help himself. Sure enough, the file returned with his views clearly not read with the love and care that they required. '*Seen by Chief Minister. We may allow the number of Black Guards to be doubled. Security cannot be compromised. They may be allowed to buy appropriate footwear for the golf course. The police force is the backbone of the Welfare State. Chief Minister is impressed and intrigued by BOOBZ. Finance Secretary is therefore directed to consider appointing Special Boobz Officers to examine and analyse the economic viability of certain organizations of the government the reason for the existence of which has for quite some time puzzled more than one mind. Examples abound—the office of the Liaison Commissioner, the Director of the Official Languages Cell, the Commanding Officer of the State Mobile Civil Engineering Column, the Director of Tabulation and Punching in the Regional Sample Survey Organization, the Deputy Examiner of Books and Publications . . . the list is almost endless. Finance Secretary may also kindly examine in the first place the economics of appointing Special Boobz Officers in these bodies.*'

HUBRIS ASCENDING

K~~U~~M K~~U~~M ~~BA~~LA M~~A~~L~~I~~ Adore
___
~~B~~H~~U~~PEN R~~A~~GH~~U~~P~~A~~T~~I~~ Love

Kum Kum Bala Mali adores Bhupen Raghupati. Bhupen Raghupati loves Kum Kum Bala Mali. Adore and Loathe, Love and Hate, Sweet and Sour, S and M—the Minister's Secretary in the Ministry of Heritage, Upbringing and Resource Investment was pleased with the outcome of his computations. With his wang ascending, leaking, licking its lips, struggling for *Lebensraum*, as it were, in the trousers of his safari suit, he looked up from his desk at the object of his desire for that day.

She'd written earlier for an appointment with the Minister because she had a housing problem that she wished to discuss. Her letter, on fancy handmade paper—along with the compellingly negative notes of the Department—lay before the Minister's Secretary. Her perfume suffused the room—indeed, made him breathless.

He had for long held a theory about perfumes. All human aromas—everybody knew—were an invitation to sex. They emanated from the body's erogenous zones. The more potent the perfume, the more erogenous the zone. Bad body smells indicated a desire to be mastered, to be down below, an I-have-the-mind-and-body-of-the-Great-Unwashed-so-please-defile-me signal. Good aromas showed a desire to allure, to be approved of, to sniff and be sniffed, sadomasochistic psychological insecurity. So sensitive was the Minister's Secretary to odours that on his acute days, he could virtually *see* the sexual organ—whether pussy or prick—on which he'd focused all his shakti, oozing, sweating out its welcoming scented fluids through constricting cottons and into the air. He himself unfailingly daubed his armpits and crotch every morning with Yardley's Aftershave Lotion.

While Kum Kum Bala Mali droned on, smiling at him, fluttering her impossible eyelashes, creasing her make-up, he doodled on his note pad, beside his last round of Love-Like-Hate-Adore, a Cubistic sketch of a fecund thatch, beneath it a curious apple-shaped form, from which a pair of thighs split wide apart and beckoning ripples of aroma exuded in sets of four wavy lines each. This was Raghupati's favourite doodle. When time permitted, he'd usually add a symbolic worm emerging from—or boring its way into—the apple. It was one angle on the world.

The letter was quite another.

9, Ganapati Aflatoon Marg
8 January

Respected Bhanwarji Virbhim Sahebji,

Do I need to introduce myself? By using up a few lines to describe myself, do I not insult your intelligence and your knowledge of the world? I'd certainly have thought so, but much to my surprise, the civil servants in your ministry hold different views. I must say that I was astonished to receive, in response to my preceding letter on the same subject, a standard cyclostyled reply from the Under Secretary (Housing For Cultural Luminaries), enclosing a form that asked for my bio-data.

I did not send it. Instead, in my rejoinder to the luminary, I declared that if he needed to read my bio-data to know who I was, then he was not qualified to be an Under Secretary in the Department of Culture. His latest cyclostyled salvo orders me to vacate my bungalow by the end of February.

It's now or never, observed Raghupati to himself; remember that time's running out at the speed of light. 'Madam Mali, may I ask of you a favour?'

'Why—of course.' Smile, flutter flutter.

'Will you have dinner with me, one evening this week? Just you and me? For me, it'll be a dream come true.'

'Oh, I'm very—I don't know what to say!'

'Then say nothing! And I'll take your demure silence to mean a bashful yes! You don't know—you *CAN'T* know what you mean to me! You're the raging beacon of my adolescence—ohh, those Sixties films! *Ishq Mein Doob Jaa*, *Lachhmanjhoola*, *Aag Ki Rekha*, *Ek Gaon Mein Pardesi*, *Bumbai Kahan Hum Kahan*, *Jhuk Gayi Sita*, *Guftagu Chalti Rahe*, *Naa Mat Kehna*, *Aakash Mein Teen Badal*, *Subah Ki Aasha Mein*—I could recite the names of your Golden Jubilee films forever, truly! When you announced after *Do Raaste Mein Teen Kutte*—my God, more than fifteen years ago!—that you were going to quit films, you caused as much heartache in the nation as Partition . . . there were a handful of suicides reported in the papers, I remember . . . so what d'you say, Madam? Dinner on Thursday?'

'Yes, I suppose so—may I phone you? . . . I'll have to check my diary which, unfortunately, I've left at home—but you do think that you can solve my bungalow problem?'

'Shall we discuss that over dinner? A dinner and a long evening alone with you, Madam, is all that I ask in return. A favour for a favour. Tit for tat. The entire edifice of the government, Madam, is based on a quite feudal system of favours. It's even been drafted into our rules and regulations in the form of the powers of discretion granted to our public servants to interpret the law . . . think of the joy that you can give me and I you. The people that you must've seen in the waiting room all, all have favours to seek and to grant, like barter in a primitive society.'

Raghupati saw the ageing actress to her car. It gave him a chance to brush against her, touch her shoulder, her upper arm. Rocking on the balls of his feet, he watched her car, a steel-blue Maruti Esteem, crunch its way up the gravel to the gates of the splendid colonial bungalow, plumb in the heart of Lutyens's City, that he'd chosen for Bhanwar Virbhim upon the MP's joining the Central Cabinet as Minister. An exquisite villa, magnificently proportioned; on its lawns, one felt munificent oneself. Would Kum Kum Bala succumb to his ardour? Would the aroma of the sap gushing about in his veins make her swoon and wilt? Ahh, life was wonderful. Perhaps she wants it bad, and at this very moment, in the cold comfort of her car, listening to the latest Rani Chandra CD and dreaming of his, Raghupati's, squat tight body—much like a thickening phallus with its foreskin pulled back—she was wetting her wearunder and regretting not having torn them off in the camp office. Ahh, hold on to your longing till Thursday, Janum! Later, when her file had inched its way up to Bhanwar Saheb, she'd of course have to contend with his advances as well. She might even—who knows?—be partial to his kind of attractiveness—successful, fat, powerful, black, amoral, lumpen, treacherous, taciturn, risen-from-the-depths-and-still-rising. One could never account for human tastes. Ohh, the wonder of it.

Raghupati strolled across the lawns to inspect the progress on the putting green that he'd suggested to the Minister could be developed on the West Garden. Having selected the bungalow for Bhanwar Saheb after an exhausting fortnight search, he justifiably felt quite proprietorial about the place.

It ought to be said in defence of the Welfare State that it is by and large democratic. Irrespective of class and status, it gives everybody—high and low—a bad time. The higher-up you are, though, the more clout you have to fight and exploit it.

Which is why, about a month ago, after Bhanwar Virbhim had rested on Jayati Aflatoon's feet his forehead, and the plague epidemic in Madna had sidled off the front pages of the national newspapers, and she, pleased and tickled, had suggested to her doting cousin-by-marriage the Prime Minister that Bhanwar be accommodated at the Centre, Virbhim, even though acutely disappointed at having been allotted Heritage, Upbringing and Resource Investment, had decided to accept the portfolio with the correct facade of gratitude and joy, and to bide his time, because while waiting, he would be paid, housed and chauffeured about, and through a judicious granting of favours and an intelligent manipulation of the law, he'd use the months to augment his vote bank, consolidate his power base and expand his camp following.

As a first step, he'd summoned to the capital his loyals—Bhupen Raghupati and Baba Mastram among them—to help him organize himself. The Baba was to decide on an auspicious date and time for the Minister's entry into Aflatoon Bhavan. Raghupati was to set up the Minister's personal offices—one for each of the Departments of Culture, Heritage, Education and Welfare, a fifth for coordinating among the other four and a large sixth one in the camp office at home. That involved, among other things, the selection of a hundred and seventy two staff members, including Personal Assistants, stenographers, clerks, typists, peons, chowkidaars, gardeners and daily wage labourers who could cook, sweep, scavenge, and massage Madame Bhanwar Sahiba's elephantine legs, and the choosing of curtains, carpets, tables, chairs, air-conditioners, cupboards, idols, cars and smaller idols for the cars. Setting up the Minister set back the Welfare State by the usual one crore.

'Make hay while the sun shines' was a principle that had

generally guided the actions of both Bhanwar Virbhim and Bhupen Raghupati for many a year. By instinct, children of the tropics that they were, they'd made money whenever they could, for who knew what the morrow would bring? With the years, however—naturally—they'd become sophisticated, the stakes had shot up to the moon—inflation and all that, it even upsets the calculations of avarice. Yet, at the same time, old habits die hard, and they were citizens of a poor country, and thus it was that Raghupati had first of all recruited Shri Dharam Chand, the one-armed peon in the Ministry of Heritage, Upbringing and Resource Investment and a valued henchman of the Minister from his Madna days, to oversee the takings from the other recruitments—at an average of twenty thousand rupees per selected candidate. The hopefuls had turned up in droves from the various other Departments and Ministries of the government, and from the employment exchanges and surplus cells of the staff selection commissions.

Of course, one could also make hay in inclement weather. Truly the land of opportunity, the Welfare State could boast of thousands of officials, great and small, who hadn't let a single chance to rake it in slip by—the accountants who charged a percentage for each salary, increment, allowance and emolument that they paid out to their colleagues, the section officers who picked up fifty rupees for each day of unauthorized leave that they permitted their clerks, the drivers who siphoned off petrol and diesel from their official cars for sale—at bargain rates, of course—to their buddies, the peons who made thousands of rupees extra from faked overtime bills, their superiors who took cuts from them for passing those same bills—the list is long, varied and intricately interwoven, and the corruption terribly insidious. There have been times when completely honest—and comparatively honest—officers—Agastya Sen, for example, and Dhrubo Jyoti Ghosh Dastidar, Kumari Lina Natesan and Harihara

Kapila—have wondered whether they are in fact as honest as they've always thought themselves to be—the idea of honesty having become more and more slippery with the years—and secondly, what good being honest has done them.

One was honest when one didn't ask an applicant for fifty thousand rupees before one issued him a telephone connection, and one was not honest when one suggested to another applicant that she could pick up that grant from one's Department for her song and-dance routine if she slept with one—that difference had always been clear. But not much else. In the mornings, on one's way to office, one dropped the kids off at school in the office car because the school fell en route. That wasn't dishonest, surely. But if the school was madly out of the way and started two hours before office, and one still used the office car and driver for the kids? And to pay the driver for the extra hours, allowed him to fake some more overtime? No, that wasn't dishonest either, that was merely a reasonable extension of the personal use of a legitimate office perk. As a civil servant, one was dishonest when one used one's official position to hurt, exploit and abuse the citizens, applicants and beneficiaries of the Welfare State. But when the civil servant or the politician did the same things to the State itself? No, that didn't sound very heinous either. What the hell, that was almost a perk too—one needed merely to stretch a bit the notion of a perk. Why, everyone did it all the time—faking his income tax returns, fudging the values of his immovable properties to reduce stamp duty, avoiding capital gains, wealth and municipal taxes, concealing assets in insolvency proceedings. These weren't truly violations of the law, because the law became an ass when it was applied to its creators. It wasn't seriously meant to be, it was mainly intended to impress on its citizens that the Welfare State meant business. Particularly when it didn't, naturally, because one needed to keep up appearances. And it didn't really, the State hardly ever meant business. It was too slow, lethargic, large, will-less, smug. Smug because its directive principles were noble, will-less because having framed them, it seemed to've drained itself of the power to see them through. And its mandarins weren't helping it any because they needed to help themselves first and thus move up a rung or two on the social ladder. They liked the government because milking it was both easy and respectable, anything but a disgusting crime. Stealing from it made them rich, of course, pushed them way up above the Poverty Line, as it were, but it also made them cats, lions—dragons, if you wish—major players, dynamic achievers. When one has the right background and belongs to the right class, an infringement of the legal code does not necessarily violate the moral norm, especially when, in the process, one becomes far richer without actually stealing from any one individual.

Naturally, one's idea of one's own honesty was continually being teased by what was going on all about one—everybody else seemed to be raking it in and quite enjoying the process. One kept one's mouth shut and turned a blind eye because it was none of one's business and one wasn't being paid to wade into deep shit, particularly somebody else's—but that was being dishonest, wasn't it, no two ways about that. One couldn't countenance dishonesty and remain comfortable in one's skin. Which thickened, fortunately, with the years, so that, like Raghupati, for example, after twenty-three years of distinguished service, one really had the hide of a rhino: one could've skinned oneself and not noticed.

Raghupati and the Baba were also to select, together, a suitable bungalow—or rather, two suitable bungalows, one for the Minister, the other for Raghupati himself. The Commissioner of Lands, Estates and Built-Up Properties sent them the standard list of vacant, suitable accommodation in Lutyens's City that would be commensurate with the

Minister's status, may kindly see please. Raghupati did, and not very kindly. His practised eye scanned the list and saw through it in seconds.

'Those rascals have sent us the official list of bungalows meant for those Ministers who haven't served at the Centre before and therefore don't yet know what's what. Come, Babaji, we've to hunt at night.'

For the civil servants who are transferred to the Centre from outside the capital, it is standard practice to search for suitable official accommodation at night. After sundown, in their official cars with the official list of vacant, suitable accommodation commensurate with their status in their hands, they cruise the wide, dead, tree-lined streets of Lutyens's City, looking for—and stopping to inspect—houses and flats that are dark and that otherwise show no signs of habitation. Then they routinely check to see if the nicer ones are listed in the sheets in their hands. They never are. That too is standard practice.

The difficulties of their search are compounded by the frequent official and unofficial power breakdowns that have become as much a part of capital life as the monstrous traffic jams created by the Prime Ministerial convoy's actual and decoy road routes. When they wish to explore further the surroundings of a house or a flat that appears uninhabited and thus promising, they, equipped with torches and a walking stick or iron rod—to protect themselves from the assault of some ill-tempered stray or pet dog—begin to bang on gate or door till somebody responds. Conversing with shadowy strangers in the dark, they feel dislocated, disoriented like the citizens of a nation at war, and wonder whether the members of any other profession, after so many years of distinguished service, househunt in similar fashion.

'Stop breaking the door down. Yes, who is it?'

'Uh . . . do you stay here?'

'What do you think?'

'No—I mean, do you stay here officially or are you a trespasser?'

'You need help, brother.'

In many cases, it is a neighbour who responds to the banging on the gate or door. He too is equipped with a torch and a weapon. If they wish, they can duel in the dark.

'Yes? May I help you?'

'I'm looking for a house.'

'Yes? Which number?'

'Uh . . . any number . . . any vacant house . . . is this one occupied?'

'If you're senior enough to move in on the sly, you shouldn't be making such a racket.'

After a couple of nights of house-hunting, the civil servants return to the Commissioner of Lands, Estates and Built-Up Properties with the addresses of three or four houses that they've liked, any one of which they wish allotted to them. The Assistant Commissioner scans the addresses, purses his lips and forwards the list to the Private Secretary to the Minister of Urban Affairs. Urban Affairs was once called the Ministry of Works, Housing, Roads and Edifices. As Prime Minister, Bhuvan Aflatoon officially rechristened it because he felt that Urban Affairs sounded more compact, honed, polished and directed. It could not, moreover, be abbreviated to an absurd acronym. The Prime Minister's Office suggested to the Department of Constitutional Languages to pay Softsell, the ad agency that thought up the phrase Urban Affairs, a fee of fourteen lakh rupees. The ministerial change of name cost the taxpayers of the Welfare State twenty-seven lakh rupees in stationery and nameplates alone.

Traditionally, in the Office of the Private Secretary to the Minister for Urban Affairs, the bribe rates for the allotment of official accommodation to civil servants are fixed according to location and carpet area. Changes in the rates are okay only up to a point, beyond which the overly avaricious Private

Secretaries and Personal Assistants would be guilty of conduct unbecoming of a civil servant. Those stuffy, old-fashioned bureaucrats who refuse to cough up the bribe—and who sometimes are silly enough to complain—wait for about a year for accommodation, and are then allotted a flat on the sixth floor in the suburbs somewhere, in a grey building without a lift, or on the ground floor right next to an illegal abattoir.

The air in the Private Secretary's rooms was very fragrant, almost overpowering. Every hour, a daily-wage labourer padded about the luxuriously-carpeted floors, spraying room-freshener everywhere. Closer to the person of the Private Secretary, the more refined bouquet of his aftershave—airy, pine-forest-like—mingled with the rather vulgar scent of the room-freshener. With Raghupati's entry, moreover, a blend of Yardley's and sweat was added to the heady mix.

Pleasantries . . . 'It's good to see you in this key post . . . your eyes are gleaming more than ever before . . .' Then down to business . . . 'My Minister has finally decided on two bungalows to house himself and his immediate staff. Both are on Ganapati Aflatoon Marg, Numbers 21 and 9. Neither of course features on the list that the Estates Commissioner sent us . . . a Security requirement, apparently . . . Number 21 is vacant and is meant for the Minister himself. The number is auspicious and the few changes required are fortunately quite minor . . . the kitchen at the moment faces east, that of course will have to be shifted to face north-west—at the very least . . . the Master Bedroom will also have to be moved to the east side. Then the number of stairs to the first floor are six short—our Baba is quite definite that the required figure shouldn't be less than twenty-one . . . one wall of the camp office will have to be knocked down for windows—so that we can benefit from the favourable four o'clock light. The swimming pool needs to be filled up and made into an exclusive Visitors' Hall—anyway, these are minor details, the main issue being that the Baba has vetted and cleared both the bungalows as auspicious. Number 9 unfortunately is at the moment occupied by the One and Only, Fair and Lovely Kum Kum Bala Mali—so the lurid posters of *Baap Ko Jala Kar Raakh Kar Doonga* called her. Can your Ministry issue her an order directing her to allow me to move in with her? . . .' Stag chortling. '. . . The location, conjunction and combination of Numbers 9 and 21 are exceedingly favourable—this type of positioning of houses is extremely rare and therefore doubly propitious, so Baba Mastramji has confirmed. I suggest that your Ministry write to Kum Kumji to prod her pussy a bit, come come, Madam-ji, your time's up, pack your bags. I've found out that she was given official accommodation as a Nominated Cultural Luminary—extraordinary, some of the categories that our people come up with. Your letter could inform her that her Discretionary Allotment's being cancelled because there hasn't been any Significant Contribution to Culture from her in the last sixteen years—certainly none since the cabaret-in-the-rain, song-and-dance milestone in *Moochhon Ki Kasam*—do you remember it? Wet clothes, mammaries the size of Asia, jiggle jiggle, nipples like the heads of street urchins at your car window, some Bharatnatyam steps, crooning into her armpit, then all of a sudden, soaking see-through wet, she was at a temple before Kali, praying and warbling: *Hey Ma, Aap Ke Paas Main Chhoti Si Aas Le Kar Aayi Hoon*, that is to say, Hey Ma, I've Come to You with a Small Arse . . . Our censors didn't ban it! A truly broadminded culture, ours . . . and by any standards, an extraordinary admission before a divinity, apart from being an outrageous lie. I can tell you right away that when you ask Kum Kum to vacate, she'll defend herself with the argument that as a Culture Luminary, from her present address, she's interfaced with so many other Culture Luminaries, both national and global, that the bungalow is now no longer mere Welfare State accommodation, but a Seat of Culture. Send her reply to me. I'll take care of it—Security Reasons, I think, should suffice. Then we make her an offer she can't refuse.'

Raghupati's progress across the lawns was feudal. Peons, attendants, gardeners, sweepers, washermen, housekeepers, drivers, masseurs, cooks, milkmen, constables, chowkidaars, watchmen, bearers, jamadars, dafadars, orderlies, daily wagers and indefinable lackeys all stopped idling, straightened up, cringed, beamed and saluted him. Each of their appointments had been either a favour granted—whenever possible, at a price, and to be redeemed in good time—or a debt repaid; whenever possible, the debts repaid too had been construed as favours granted. Dozens of associates, comrades and cronies of Bhanwar Virbhim, of his Begum and their redoubtable scion and Honourable-Member-of-the-Legislative-Assembly-to-be, Shri Makhmal Bagai, of Raghupati and Shri Dharam Chand the peon—dozens of their acquaintances had sons, nephews, brothers-in-law and protéges who were either jobless or underemployed and who needed the aegis of Welfare. Raghupati had signed up as many as he could, age, education, experience, knowledge, competence no bar. Like countless others, he liked being munificent at the expense of the Welfare State. The BOOBZ ban on recruitment applied only halfheartedly to the personal staff of Central Cabinet Ministers, that is to say, like many other policies, it had to be sternly fought, with clout, from within. Minister desires—such a clause should supersede the law in practice; such was Raghupati's belief—why else would one wish to serve the State? Minister desires, for example, the seat of the occupant of the Seat of Culture at 9, Ganapati Aflatoon Marg as a token of gratitude for a favour rendered.

Raghupati desired just as much the seat of the prospective

lackey who approached him at that moment from the bungalow, bearing on a tray a glass of milk. He was Dambha, the elder brother of the still-AWOL Chamundi.

Almost a month after his brother's disappearance from Raghupati's house in Madna, Dambha had suddenly showed up in Lutyens's City with a hope of employment on compassionate grounds and letters of recommendation from two local, powerful timber smugglers. Bhanwar Virbhim's son, who wasn't very good at letters or indeed in general at anything written, had even spoken to Raghupati on the young man's behalf. Whom Raghupati had found rather fetching and from whose sullen, morose professed ignorance of his brother's whereabouts had jumped to the unnerving conclusion that Chamundi was safe and lying low, vengeful and plotting, flat out on a bed in a hut in his tribal village somewhere in the ravaged, discontented forests of Jompanna, plumb in the heartland of Sukumaran Govardhan country.

Raghupati hadn't been lying when he'd stated that on that December afternoon of the day before the attack on Suroor, after he'd spoken to the District Collector on the phone from his bedroom, he'd strutted back to the adjoining puja room and found that his massage boy—who till a minute before had been unconscious and bleeding from the head—had disappeared, merged into the blue.

Officially, no one had seen him since. The blood stains on the floor Raghupati sponged off before descending. He didn't even mention Chamundi till eight-thirty the morning after.

'Where *is* he? I can't be bothered with this irresponsibility. Do we have anybody else with hands supple enough for a massage?'

Out of sight, gradually out of mind. Besides, in the ensuing weeks, everything else had gone Raghupati's way so splendidly—Minister Virbhim's return to the lap of the Aflatoons, his own consequent new post, the presence of

Baba Mastram in the capital, the silly Natesan court case—that with time, he had begun to feel quite confident of managing any fallout from the Chamundi business.

In Lutyens's City, at 21, Ganapati Aflatoon Marg, therefore, he asked Dharam Chand to accommodate Dambha suitably. In turn, Dharam Chand attached the newcomer to the milkman to whom he, Dharam Chand, had rented out one of the servants' quarters of the bungalow. Part of the rent was paid in milk. Mrs Milkman also did the house, ironed the clothes and washed Begum Virbhim's wearunders, it being terribly *lèse majesté* that male hands should ever touch them. Milkman Junior, socially more upwardly mobile than his father'd been, grew orchids, broccoli and artichokes in the back lawns; they were sold to the capital's fancier hotels. On every left-over square metre of kitchen garden, he'd squeezed in potatoes, tomatoes, papayas, pumpkin and coriander. Some of that was sold by handcart in the back lanes of Lutyens's City. Father and son had also opened up a dhaba in the courtyard of the servants' quarter—entry from the service lane, of course. It provided tea, rusks, biscuits and *plat du jour* lunches and dinners to the vast population of underlings and factotums in the area. Of course, cups of tea and plates of food—lumpy islands of congealed rice rock steady in a lake of reddish gravy, on the surface of which floated an oil slick—were also sent up, as and when required, to the bungalow. Officially, the dhaba didn't exist because it was a Security risk. When not on duty, however, the Black Guard Commandoes guzzled there for free. Milkman paid Dharam Chand four thousand rupees a month as rent, of which three thousand reached Raghupati, of which fifteen hundred reached Begum Virbhim. From the minister's salary, the Welfare State deducted five hundred rupees every month as rent for the entire bungalow.

Raghupati asked Dambha to wait while he downed his glass of milk. Hot frothy milk at four o'clock sharp, straight from the udder, as it were, was his way of cutting down on tea and coffee. It made him feel full and ill all evening. His fingers brushed the other's as he picked up the glass. 'So how are things with you? . . . How are the cows? Is the bull fucking them well or does he need goading? You look well-hung, you could teach him a trick or two. Now that you've almost joined the Welfare State, you'd better watch your organ, oil it, take care of it, or else it'll shrink. The State's been known to have that effect under its Integrated Small Tools Programme . . . Are you any good at massage? . . . You are? Excellent! Why then, you're overqualified for us! You milk cows—squeeze, squeeze?—grow and sell broccoli, run errands for a dhaba *and* massage bodies—and yet you hope to join the Welfare State as a lackey on daily wages . . . yes, job security and all that—there's none, incidentally, while you remain a daily wager. There's only the promise of permanent employment dangling before you while you're pushed around and exploited. The good life starts when you become a *permanent* servant of the government . . . and gets better and better as you climb the ladder—take the case of your present demi-god Dharam Chand, in whose presence I dare say that your organ begins to leak out of nervousness . . . some years ago—so the story goes—the *moment* he was made permanent—he was then called Karam Chand, but that's *another* story—he stopped going to office and instead began selling wearunders, in earnest, all day—near the railway station of his native town. He was at that time an attendant in some State-run blind school. After some weeks, his boss the Superintendent asked him to return to work. Dharam Karam Chand was so offended by the order—an insult to his status of a permanent employee—that is to say, it's temporaries like you who've to fetch, carry and obey without question, the permanents have an option—so Dharam Karam, deeply disturbed as a consequence of the felt insult, in the course of his official duties, gouged out the right eye of a blind girl—and nothing permanent happened to him as a result. He became a fat file, of course, part of the collective memory of the Welfare State—it's the natural outcome of the buck-withering process. And that's why you'd like to join us, isn't it? . . . Well, I too like being close to and part of our fat files—those Himalayan ranges built out of thick, brown, depressing, faded-even-when-new covers and millions of pages of thin, cheap, off-white paper produced at astounding cost—surrounded by all that, you feel snug, as though you belong and your identity fits, like a tiny screw somewhere under the bonnet of a car. You're doing your bit, you feel, to run the country even when you're ferrying the kids of a Controller of Rationing to school. Did you know that Dharam Chand feels that it's time to change his name, now that he's moved up and is with the Minister? A new lifestyle, a new identity, a smooth snake shedding its skin. He's toying with Naram Chand . . . good boy, thanks for the milk. Come over to my camp room for a trial massage after dinner tonight. About ten-thirty, after Shri Bagai leaves, okay dear? . . .'

A submissive Assistant Engineer from the Electricity Board waited a few paces away, head down, file in hand, the correct junior courtier. The false ceiling in the camp office was in place and the third air-conditioner had just been fitted; would Minister's Secretary Saab care to see?

'Yes, after I inspect the West Garden. Have those silly electricity bills been sorted out yet?'

The Assistant Engineer shuffled about and giggled in nervous excitement. 'Yes sir. No sir. I understand that the Honourable Minister has written to the Honourable Power Minister, sir. I'm sure that it'll all be settled soon.'

'I'd even advised that the Divisional Manager be

transferred because of his attitude. Has that happened?'

'Yes sir. No sir. Not yet. In fact (nervous giggle), he's appealed to the Power Minister against what he calls Unnecessary Interference in the Smooth Functioning of the Government.'

'How smooth does he want it to be? Like the shaved cheeks of his arse?' Shrieks of nervous laughter.

The previous inhabitant of 21, Ganapati Aflatoon Marg, had been a Hindi film actor—a matinee idol—and an ex-Member of Parliament, a Nominated Culture Luminary to the Upper House. In his time, he was reputed to have earned fifty thousand rupees a day, year after year. He owned a flat in Bombay City, a villa in the suburbs, a sort of castle by the beach and two office complexes. He had air-conditioned—at official expense, of course—the outhouses of his official bungalow to house his Siamese cats. He had surrendered the bungalow to the Commissioner of Estates after a titanic, two-year struggle (it had even been mooted that the Army should be sent in to evict him). His argument—spread over a dozen letters addressed, among others, to the President of the Union, the Vice-President and the Prime Minister—had been, more or less: 1) However can a petty bureaucrat ask the idol of the masses to move his bloomin' arse? 2) And yet people continue to wonder what is wrong with this country! 3) Why doesn't the Army move in first to evict its own hundred Generals from the bungalows that they've overstayed in for years?

Matinee Idol left behind at 21, Ganapati Aflatoon Marg, among other things, an outstanding electricity bill of some eight lakh rupees. Raghupati found it outrageous that the Electricity Board should bother Bhanwar Virbhim, the new occupant of the bungalow, with the sins of the previous one. Not that Raghupati considered it a sin—indeed, it was standard practice. One fitted a bungalow of that size with fourteen air-conditioners and six geysers and one used them as befitted one's status, but to pay one's electricity bill emitted terribly wrong signals; it clearly meant that one was slipping down the ladder. Only people without clout paid their electricity bills. Those with, never received any. They instead asked for—and got—official air-conditioners in their loos.

By serving the representatives of the people, one serves the people. Were the Electricity Board ever to ask Raghupati why on earth it should forego its dues outstanding against the occupant of 21, Ganapati Aflatoon Marg, he would've reasoned such. Or, since every second of the official life is official, the office should bear all expenses incurred. Then again, the bounty of welfare extends in all directions and knows no bounds; only the niggardly and the shortsighted think of economies. In a large country, you have to think big.

'The macro view,' explained Raghupati expansively to Makhmal Bagai, in Hinglish, long after office hours, in his camp study, over glasses of Johnnie Walker Blue, 'has always been the need of the hour. Sit on the moon, and in the cold blue light, gaze down on the remote, quiet, sombre, beautiful and tranquil earth. Distance provides perspective and objectivity. All our squabbles and tensions will be seen for what they are—fundamentally petty, trivial. What, for example, is a roadside brawl, a disruption of some piffling street play, in the grand scheme of things? Nothing, merely a ripple, just frolic.'

The whisky was a gift from Makhmal, who'd flown in that evening from Navi Chipra. Raghupati loved the richness of its fumes. For years now, whenever he'd had a cold or a sore throat, he'd inhaled from, and then sipped, a peg or two of neat good Scotch. In a sensationalist article on espionage in the *Illustrated Weekly*, he'd read once that Indian spies could be bought over by just one bottle of Scotch. He hadn't found the notion particularly absurd or objectionable. Of course, it depended on the whisky. A bottle of Johnnie Walker Blue, for example, golden, limpid, perfect, seemed a reasonable wager for one's soul.

The stronger the bouquet, naturally, the worse the stink that one is trying to subdue. By that standard, Makhmal Bagai was a two-week-old, putrefying, maggot-ridden cadaver. He routinely doused different parts of his body with scented hairoil, talcum powder, aftershave lotion, eau de Cologne and deodorant. The charm that he always carried with him was a tiny sandalwood Ganesh, the powers of which were periodically revived, as it were, by dips in sandalwood oil. To neutralize his foul mouth, he ate over a dozen perfumed paans a day (he and Raghupati shared, among other things, the same taste in paans). He liked incense to be lit in the rooms that he occupied, however temporarily. His attendant of the day carried, beside his paan box and mobile phone, a box of incense sticks; his manifold duties included lighting one of them up before Makhmal could notice its absence.

'Whenever the case of Miss Natesan surfaces in court, that will be my argument—me-laard, the macro view. A point of order. The sight of her sari squeezed into the crevice of her bum upset my love of order, so I plucked it out. With my thumb and forefinger. I could've used my teeth. Why should my love of order so convulse the harmony of the world? Me-laard, reflect instead on the larger issues—bonded labour, corruption in high places, freedom of speech, the suppression of immoral traffic, crimes against women, caste reservations, violence in politics, the Police- or the Welfare State. Leave that fat, charming and pig-headed Lina Natesan to her memos and reminders.'

'I could arrange for some acid for her face. Take her mind off her bum.'

'That won't be necessary. Her face is nice, don't spoil it. In fact, after that cock-up with Rajani Suroor last month, your father and I both feel that for a while, we could do without your help, thank you.'

Makhmal didn't feel secure without a weapon. It was usually a switchblade. Were he to reflect on the subject, he'd've been both puzzled and relieved that unlike him, the wide world didn't believe in the perfect simplicity of the efficacy of violence. My God—how much people talked, and wrote, and argued! Use a gun, boss, or a hockey stick, because time's running out, look, gurgling down an unplugged drain.

When he'd dropped out of school, his father had packed him off to the North because he'd wanted Makhmal to broaden his horizons, get out of Madna, out of his hair, see the country, maybe find a vocation. At his uncle's sweets shop in Dundimandir, Makhmal had sat behind the cash counter for six months, acquired a taste for the scent of rose water, improved his Hinglish, broken a bottle of Limca on the jaws of an ill-tempered customer who couldn't wait for his change, and from his associates picked up a Punjabi manner of pronouncing English words. The accent had waned with the years but could still, every now and then, particularly in moments of stress, bob up in his delivery. 'Jealous' became 'jaluss' as in 'jalopy', for example, 'shock' was 'shokk-uh' and 'memories' 'mammaries.' He didn't have very pleasant mammaries.

'Miss Natesan's case shouldn't pose a problem. I've discovered that the judge is likely to be S.H. Sohan, who in his after-hours is a Punjabi poet. I've spoken to him on the phone—in Punjabi, of course—and I've an appointment with him early next week. Would me-laard like to be, I asked, our Official Delegate to the World Poetry Conference in Honolulu? Return air ticket, six free days in a deluxe hotel, per diem at par with international standards, facilities for simultaneous translation into five international languages while me-laard recites his immortal verse in Punjabi before Nobel laureates, literary agents from London, publishers from New York—would me-laard do me the honour of deigning to accept? In reply, he fellated me on the phone. If the case comes up, who knows, he might send Miss Natesan to jail for conduct unbecoming of a civil servant . . . Just press the bell—I need some milk to make a new, great cocktail.'

Incompetent and dangerous, Makhmal had had no choice but to enter politics. In his late teens, he'd been quite an asset to his father during both the Parliamentary and the Assembly elections—dropping in at polling booths with jeeps full of gunmen to terrorize voters and steal ballot boxes, bribing policemen with petty cash, food and cheap whisky to look the other way, whisking away and beating up members of rival gangs, shooting rounds off into the air when things looked too quiet—ahhh, politics was the good life. After the third elections, Bhanwar Virbhim had appointed him one of the General Secretaries of the State Political Party. He'd wanted his dunderhead son to learn some of the facts of life, to revere wealth, not to remain forever retarded, to grasp that money was infinitely more powerful than the gun, that nothing was socially more respectable than power, that to be on the right side of the law, one simply needed to be above it. Expectedly, Makhmal's record of violence earned him Z-category Black Guard Commando protection. All those guns, that screaming motorcade, the awed, frightened faces of bystanders, went to his head. Fast cars began to attract him almost as much as weapons.

In the one week that he'd spent in Madna jail, his father once again had become a Central Minister. Virbhim had let his son stew a bit behind bars because he'd correctly gauged that it would look great on his own cv. Finally, before using his clout to extract Makhmal, he'd conveyed down the line that that would be the last time that he'd be interceding on his son's behalf. One more misdemeanour and Makhmal would be quietly tossed out into the cold.

Being a fool, the son didn't see—or didn't care—with what agility his father's ambition, his arrogance, was ascending. Not his father's alone, for it was in the air. The stars, no doubt. Jayati Aflatoon, Sukumaran himself—already half-legend and now aiming for the heavens—Dharam Karam Chand, Baba Mastram, Bhupen Raghupati—their fortunes were all sap-filled and on the rise.

Raghupati in particular considered himself quite lucky over the Lina Natesan mess. Time and again, he'd plagued Baba Mastram for an angle on her.

'She has a knack of attracting calamities,' the Baba had divined after a couple of days of thought. 'Perhaps she irritates her stars too, who knows?'

'When they fail, mortals can but hope to try to help. I feel that I should repay the love that she doubtless feels for me but which—messed-up introvert that she is—she can never reveal even to herself in this life. So I've decided to recommend her name for one of our long-term, government-to-government, foreign training courses. I'm glad to learn that she will be accepted at L'Institut Europeen D'Administration Publique at Strasbourg. She'll soon dazzle Europe with her reports. Once there, Paris and all that, who knows, she might even find true, requited love. So, after Judge Sohan, that's my second safeguard against the siren.'

Things that didn't concern him didn't register with Makhmal. He was on his first visit to his parents after his stint in jail but had no wish to meet either of them face to face. He would have liked Raghupati's counsel on how to plan his future in politics but felt that he already knew too well—and would be utterly bored with—what he would hear. He wished to be Minister of State for Coal and Mines for he'd heard that bribes for the lease of a mine could touch a crore of rupees. Think big, think quick, that was his style. Change it, is what Raghupati'd been advising for ages.

'Coal and Mines is Big, Big, child. Remember that just to get Heritage and Time Pass, Bhanwar-ji brushed Jayati Aflatoon's feet with his forehead. Wait a while—the hierarchy needs patience and cunning. In the meantime—I've told you before—stop carrying guns. Stop slapping the Opposition with your slippers in the Well of the House, particularly when the indefatigable governor is in the midst of his inaugural address of the Budget Session. Stop lifting up your kurta to display your pyjama-strings to female members of another party. So what if the TV camera's on you? Some of your viewers might actually wish for better returns for the one lakh rupees per second of taxpayers' money being spent on running the Assembly. A new leaf, therefore, for the new age, Makhmal. Learn to give speeches on weighty subjects. Learn to read. Clamber on to one respectable bandwagon or the other—three or four, if possible. Make a start somewhere. Let me see . . . When you learn to read, my dear gem of the Deccan, I'll give you a comic-strip called Asterix. Our Assemblies remind me of his life and times.'

Half in alarm, Raghupati watched Makhmal's face crumple up with the strain of expressing an idea. 'I must have a reason to discipline myself. In the last three years, I've attended as a special visitor nine sessions of the Assembly. The anti-aircraft gun scandal, the sugar deal, the securities cover-up, the bank fraud, the telecom fiddle, the fodder swindle, the urea scam, the insurance racket, the export licence rip-off, that's what we discussed. And side by side, the desecration of places of worship, the bomb blasts, two nuclear explosions, one official and one unacknowledged border war and the riots after riots after riots. Not a whisper, in three years, about welfare, about the good of the common man, whoever he might be. Why should I discipline myself?'

'Hey Ram! . . . For a long time, your father and I've believed that the inside of your skull must resemble the stuffing of an old, old mattress, the sort that is periodically redone by those wandering mattress-makers . . . don't you wish to follow your father's footsteps? Distance yourself as much as you can from your past. Change it whenever necessary, it's as natural to human beings as blushing. Look at him, it's the silly season here, so he's swished off to Madagascar to sign a Cultural Agreement. It wouldn't be necessary for me, he said, to accompany him because the text of the Agreement was straightforward—just the Director (Cultural Agreements) would do. She's forty-two, with fat chewable lips and watermelons on her thorax. Your father's been complimenting her on her saris for some weeks now. Ahhh, the call of the flesh.'

Amongst his wearunders, safari suits and bottles of anti-flatulence pills, Bhanwar Virbhim carried with him to Madagascar an impressive array of cassette tapes on both Northern and Southern classical music. Some were gifts for his host Ministers in Antananarivo, the others were for his own listening pleasure. As Culture and Heritage Minister, he needed to know at least something about the musical traditions of his country. Ditto for literature, painting, the fine arts, the works. Thus within a week of his taking over the post, Bhupen Raghupati had suggested to him that his, the Minister's, day should begin, be filled, and end, with appropriate music. CD players, tape recorders, discs and cassettes were bought. Peons crept into Bhanwar Saab's bedroom on tiptoe at five in the morning to switch on an apt bhajan. They were transferred to places far far away if the tapes had been incorrectly cued and if, as a result, the

Minister had to suffer some notes of music inappropriate to—and therefore inauspicious for—the hour and day of the week. What good, Raghupati would thunder at his staff, is the Ministry of Culture, Heritage, Education and Welfare if it can't even provide its Minister the music of his choice at the hour of his choice? Remember that he doesn't have time for music and yet he needs to hear it, to imbibe it—therefore the right kind of music, and always in the background.

While in the foreground? Politics, need one ask? The politics, for example, of an appropriate past, both personal and public. An example of the new personal past, from the opening paragraph of Virbhim's speech at the annual convocation of the National Academy for the Performing Arts—Bhanwar Virbhim as created by Bhupen Raghupati: '*In my college days, my father would give me a certain amount of money every week for my bus fare. I saved that money by walking to and from college. With the money saved, twice a month, I'd buy tickets to local Kathak concerts and ghazal evenings . . . Once* (chuckle chuckle) . . .' Such fictions are perfectly natural and harmless, and come even more easily when no records exist of the persona of the reminiscences having ever set foot inside any college anywhere in the country, unless it be in some police file for harassing a female student, smashing chairs and windowpanes, and making bonfires out of the property of others.

And the new public past. As Heritage, Upbringing and Resource Investment Minister, alive to the sense of history, in the very first month of his tenure, Bhanwar Virbhim commissioned a set of social scientists to write, in phases, the—as it were—memoirs of the nation. The standard texts were outdated (he minuted in Hindi in the file on the subject) and completely colonial in their approach. They didn't do justice to—in fact, didn't even mention—the pivotal roles played by certain subaltern political movements, social classes and most significantly, less prominent castes—for example, Bhanwarji's own—in any of the significant developments in the country in the last two hundred years. The best way to inform our fellow citizens, surely, was to provide them some A-one reading matter. The work of the new social scientists would be supervised by a Committee of Experts comprising, in the main, retired bureaucrats with just-published, flatulent memoirs. The books would be written in English and, after the texts were approved, translated into the eighteen official languages recognized by the Constitution. In all, there were to be twelve tomes that would cover the history, geography, sociology, anthropology, geology, biophysics, environment, botany, zoology, religion, language and culture of the country and its peoples. The entire project was to cost the Welfare State seventy crores over a period of five years. Out of the panel of names of suitable savants submitted to him, Bhanwar Virbhim rejected seven and added eleven new characters out of his own pocket. Those recommended by him were all either from his part of the country or his caste or both.

The intelligentsia of the Ministry of Heritage, Upbringing and Resource Investment was quite appalled and too spineless and devious to fight back directly. In its routine manner, it diffused the word. Thus two Sundays later, for instance, the *Weekend Today*, that claimed a readership of over two million, ran an eight-page article, an extract from a longer work entitled *The Magic of the Aflatoons*. It was written by a Dr Srinivas Chakki, an entomologist by profession and a Thinker on the side.

> ... *How does one enter the record books? One way is to act so as to be worthy of them, so that history, as it were, will remember one. Another, far easier, way is simply to rewrite the record book and include oneself in it. Do not merely devote all the space of the book to the also rans, but also analyse the motives and*

performances of the never-rans. History as determined by the would've-liked-to-runs . . .'

After a couple of paragraphs of this style of attack, Dr Chakki hadn't been able to resist broadening his target to include—indeed, aiming way off the original mark at—*all* Members of Parliament and of the Legislative Assemblies.

It had been hoped when we became independent that in pursuit of an ideal of the trusteeship of the national wealth, the leaders of the State would set examples in austerity and take no more than five hundred rupees each per month as salary. It is noteworthy that several decades on, our legislators have not belied that hope in the letter, but as for its spirit, as the French would exclaim, oo la la! Our guiding lights, forty years after Freedom, still vote themselves a monthly pay of five hundred rupees (that is to say, roughly the equivalent of a few packets of Rothmans Twenties), but over the years, have invented a wide variety of devices for augmenting that income on the sly. They of course routinely give themselves free housing—four-bedroom-villas plumb in the heart of Lutyens's City—free cooking gas and water, free telephones and transport, and a multitude of other benefits. They also take care that at all times, their basic salary of five hundred—which is all that they reveal to the taxman—remains below the taxable income. One notes of course in contrast that their perks, when received by you and me, are madly taxable, thanks to them. After all, they make the laws. That's what they're being paid those Rothmans for. Yet they decided—in passing, as it were—that they needed an incentive to attend office, to come to work. So they provided themselves a daily allowance—non-taxable, of course—for being present in the House. Attentive readers of this paper will recall that several years ago, it'd been the first to point out that our guiding lights, like errant college students, were in the habit both of cutting the House after roll call and of noting their attendance even for the days on which they were absent. Ah, the power of the pen! For, after a spate of such articles had held them up to ridicule, and accused them of continuing in Parliament the fine traditions of their college days, the signatures were dropped but alas, the per diem remained. They still earn it for the entire duration of the session and, for good measure, for the three days preceding and succeeding each of their sittings. Acknowledging their own need to form a little capital on the side, they allow themselves to sanction cooking gas connections and allot ten telephones per annum to their nominees, no questions asked.

It has been calculated that were our guiding lights to be regarded as ordinary mortal citizens liable to taxes, their current emoluments, for each one of them, on the average would work out to about twenty lakh rupees per annum (not counting their guns, of course). Other things being equal, as our economists say, how many of them would command such a figure in the open market is not a question that need detain us here.

What we could however pause to discuss is their credibility. Leadership in general involves setting an example. It is only the captain of our national cricket team who leads with the bum. The question is: is a leader expected to do anything after he's emitted all the right noises? 'Roll up your sleeves . . . tighten your belts . . . remove poverty (better still, remove the poor) . . . pull up your socks . . . and shed a tear for the downtrodden . . .'

To help you to shed that tear at the right time, at the right place—here, have a car! Do my readers know that in the next couple of weeks, a proposal will be voted through in the Daanganga Assembly to provide interest-free car loans of three lakh rupees to each of its four-hundred-plus Members? In their speechifying, the legislators to a man have lauded the 'gracious, humanitarian, forward-looking, development-oriented, poverty-alleviating' proposal. Apparently, they find it difficult to cover their constituencies on their own. Since they don't own cars, to reach the people quickly and effectively they are forced to accept the proferred help of various contractors, businessmen and industrialists. This they'd rather avoid. So would the Regional Finance Department this proposal. It will cost the state more than twelve crore rupees and of course, it will be impossible to recover any of the loans, particularly from those legislators who lose their next elections or, unfortunately, die. The section of the Motor Car Advance Rules 1949 that deals with elected Members of Parliament and of the Legislative Assemblies—they significantly having excluded themselves from the definition of 'public servant'—is notably silent on this point of recoupment. No proposal has been mooted so far to amend these Rules. Various former ministers of Daanganga, it should be recalled here, already owe the state more than four crore rupees.

Please also do consider where these legislators will drive their cars to! Daanganga's 70,464 villages have an average ten kilometres of road length for every fifteen hundred square kilometres of area. I am indebted for this confusing statistic to the National Bureau of Information, Demography and Official Data. Translated, that means for the region a total of about two thousand six hundred kilometres of road, at least a third of which would lie in some of the world's most inhospitable terrain, namely, the Gayaladh plateau. What is quite marvellous is that even when they have their cars, the Special Allowance that they give themselves at present for not having cars will stay—

inflation, rising prices and so on, runs the argument. That is, say, Rs 2000 per month as constituency allowance—presumably to cover the costs of travel between Legislative House and Constituency, you'd think—but wait! Because, at the same time, they enjoy unlimited free first-class train- and deluxe, air-conditioned bus-travel for three persons within the federal region per legislator, the three persons being his good self, his personal secretary and his bodyguard. Nobody wants to kill them, *you'd argue. You'd be surprised.*

There is only one argument in favour of giving our legislators soft loans for cars. They'll all be plied as long-distance private taxis, of course—the New Markand-Daanganga Lake run being particularly profitable, as has been proved over the years by all our civil servants who've so far used—or availed of, as they'd say—the Motor Car Advance Rules 1949 to buy private cabs. Some of them've cogently argued that it's the simplest way of solving the problem of public transport for the hill resort at Daanganga Lake during the peak tourist season.

Not to forget, in the midst of these meanderings, that each of our guiding lights also gets a crore of rupees for the development of his constituency. They want more—to speed up the process of improvement, they say, because time's running out. Well, so will the money—fortunately—leaving us with nothing but the question: has socialism been a very good thing for anybody other than the socialists?

There had been times when Dr Chakki had thought that he would never ever finish *The Magic of the Aflatoons.* Every time—whether in Madna or back home at the Prajapati Aflatoon Transit Hostel—that he'd believed that he had the essay wrapped up, some incident had bobbed up in his memory or in the newspapers and simply screamed to be included. The first draft had been fourteen pages long; the latest stood, vacant, incomplete, at page forty-seven. He'd even toyed with the idea of converting it into a periodical journal that would be a beacon, an icon for their troubled times, wise, statesmanly, therefore with a circulation of forty-three and steadily dwindling because too respectable, too much Nuclear Disarmament and not enough mammaries. In it, he would run a column, quite simply called *Sleight of Hand* and discuss threadbare therein the marvels of the week.

Of the previous Thursday, for instance, when HUBRIS Minister Bhanwar Virbhim in the Senate, while replying to a Starred Question, had likened the tumult in the House to the chaos of Chor Bazaar, the market for the resale of stolen goods. Dr Chakki had not found the comparison funny. Instead, he'd thought it deeply insulting to the tradesfolk of Chor Bazaar because they, unlike politicians, shriek purposefully, dispose of whatever they take up and do not cheat unreasonably, dealing in amounts befitting the poverty of their State. *Sleight of Hand* would then suggest that the Minister, in a formal statement, apologize in the House to all the shopkeepers of all the Chor Bazaars of the country. Think of their six million votes, it'd say.

The evening before, Bhanwar Virbhim had had to fly out to Navi Chipra for some urgent political skullduggery. The Welfare State paid for the three tickets, of course, on the reasoning that every second and every act in the lives of Ministers and officials is official. As is usual with our oligarchs, felt Dr Chakki in a fever of outrage, when it comes to their personal work, they truly behave as though they lead a nation on the move and going places. Thus at 5.30 p.m., the staff of the Minister ordered the booking office of National Airlines to reserve two Executive Class seats for master and mistress-sharer—Minister and Secretary—and a third Lumpen Class seat for some unidentified bag-and-golf-clubs-carrier on the seven o'clock flight that same evening. Some lionheart, some unsung war hero at the booking office, pointed out that people had already begun checking-in for the flight, that it was jam-packed, but that through some sleight of hand, he could just about accommodate the Minister in Executive and unfortunately nobody else. Then the parleying began and lasted for a couple of hours. The flight was delayed till the Minister, Raghupati and the caddie boarded, sighed and sat back in the seats that they'd wanted, content. Almost. Of course, on Friday, it was learnt that the lionheart in the booking office would receive his orders of suspension from service that day.

Had that been all, it wouldn't have interested Dr Chakki in the least. What intrigued him, in fact, was that Bhanwar Virbhim always sat in the front left window seat of any plane (or car or bus or bullock-cart, it may safely be imagined). He had been advised so by Baba Mastram. It had probably something to do with staying ahead of the competition, though while up front, he'd be well-advised to watch out for his back. On that Wednesday's flight, however, he couldn't get the seat of his choice. Apparently, the boarding card for it had already been issued to the wife of the Domestic Aviation Minister. Physically lifting the aircraft and carrying it off the runway would have caused less of a stir than trying to convince her to change her seat. In any case, why on earth should she?—one could have asked, most reasonably—once allotted, allotted.

Bhanwar Virbhim hadn't thought so. After beaming a greeting at Madam Minister, all through the flight, he had sulked and unseeingly flipped through the pages of some glossy. Behind that enormous chocolate-brown dome of a forehead, however, the great brain had been ticking away. Two days later, he formally petitioned the Privileges Committee of the House.

Like many other citizens, Dr Chakki was a bit foggy

about the Privileges and other Committees of the House, but he surmised that their work had very little to do with the welfare of the people. Bhanwar Virbhim's argument before it, he imagined, would be that as a Principal Minister, he was entitled to certain privileges, one of which was the seat of his choice in the Executive Class section of an aeroplane whenever he flew. When he can't sit exactly where he wants to during a flight, he must argue, somebody or some institution has breached his privilege and thereby insulted him—and through him, the State that he represents at all times. Not granting Bhanwar Virbhim the front left window seat on *all* flights that he cares to take, therefore, would be like making wearunders out of the national flag.

Over the weekend, Dr Chakki had asked around. Apparently, the privileges of the privileged hadn't been either defined or codified. Naturally, he concluded. The vaguer the law, the larger its ambit. The more the privileges, the more refined the caste. In his ideal republic, the welfare of Bhanwar Virbhim was not a subject that the State would want to spend much time and money on.

He had been piqued even more by the Starred Question that the Minister had parried and deflected in the House. It had been asked by a witless Independent, the usual front for some disgruntled backbencher.

> *Has the government finally decided on the proposed surrender of Sukumaran Govardhan? Why on earth is it taking so long to fix a date? Astrological clearance? Or haven't the national parties finished squabbling yet over which of them he will join?*

Insidiously, over the past few weeks, the transfiguration, the apotheosis, of the fabled dacoit-smuggler had begun. A newspaper report in the *Dainik* of Madna had stated that Govardhan had donated, incognito, several lakhs of rupees to start a primary school in his mother's name in a predominantly tribal area of the coastal region. *He waits for permission to bow down in contrition before the people*, trumpeted a full-page advertisement in *The State Today*, without specifying the *he*. A second news item claimed that he had sent by envoy a blank cheque for the Plague Relief Fund to the Regional Principal Minister. Philanthropist, humanitarian, champion of the poor—the phrases had started to appear—even statesman. In some of his posters, after the phrase *Wanted Dead or Alive* had been neatly stencilled, *For Parliament*.

In one of his speeches at a public function in Madna, Bhanwar Virbhim had gone even further and suggested that Govardhan was blessed in that he had at last seen the light. The occasion for the speech had been a routine three-in-one: Virbhim's first visit to his constituency after signing up as central Minister, his dropping in as sitting Member of Parliament on the unconscious Rajani Suroor in hospital, and thereafter his benediction of A.C. Raichur's never-ending hunger strike, to mark the forty-fifth day of which, the Minister had, from a dais rigged up under the trees in Aflatoon Maidan, held forth in his typical, slow, deep, soporific way on the similarities amongst Govardhan's desire to be restored to life, Suroor comatose in Madna, and Raichur's self-denial for a better world.

In the sparse audience that afternoon could have been spotted two players of Vyatha, in town on an emergency, namely, an infection of Suroor's urinary tract. At Vyatha, they all took turns to visit Madna once a fortnight, not that they were of any help at the hospital. All that they ended up doing was squandering their tight budget on second-class rail fare. Had Suroor, to a man felt they, been shifted out of that town and taken to the capital, at least the troupe would have saved its finances.

He wasn't—so the players learnt that afternoon from the horse's mouth while listening to the Minister—because Madna was considered to be as good a damned spot as any in the world for miracles. Suroor must rise from where he has fallen in time to be part of the committee that would welcome and accept Govardhan's surrender. One must always give the godforsaken—whether small-town, gross man or distinguished villain—the chance to make good. If they goof up, why, it simply means that one has underestimated their underprivilegedness.

In his reply to the Starred Question in the House, Bhanwar Virbhim had impressed even that jaded audience with his disingenuousness and his double tongue. He skirted all the facts that even the children of the alleys knew. Sukumaran Govardhan after all was to sandalwood smuggling what Kellogg's is to breakfast cereals. For over two decades, his gang of murderers had razed hundreds of acres of sandalwood plantation, hanged by the same trees forest officers, shot dead police officials, terrorized and exploited entire villages, and God alone knows stolen how many hundreds of crores of rupees of the national wealth. His surrender would only marginally be less of an event than the nation's achievement of independence. It—the surrender—was to be televised live for over two hours on the National Channel. His life had already inspired eight violently romantic Bombay films, in all of which he'd been depicted as a modern Robin Hood. Hood he certainly was. After over two decades of brutal criminality, he had nowhere to go but into politics. It was being bruited about that he intended to officially and legally change his name to Sukumaran Aflatoon and contest the Parliamentary elections from Baltod, where he'd already bought up his entire caste vote. He had once over two hundred criminal cases registered against him. Of course, before the law, one is innocent until proved guilty—and so he was free to fight the elections, but in the last ten years, the two hundred cases had been as effectively forgotten as the sandalwood, for their witnesses had quietly retracted their statements and been encouraged to crawl back into the woodwork.

In the discussions in the House, the Minister eulogized Govardhan's philanthropy but omitted to mention that behind the setting up of almost all the smuggler's charitable trusts could be seen terrifically well-planned moves to either evade tax or grab land. Always a sound investment, land. Well, felt Dr Chakki, if the record of the House was going to comprise Virbhim's fictions, there would be no harm in adding the half-truths, the rumours, the whispers. It could include, for example, the one from last March, namely, that to escape unscathed from the urea scam, Sukumaran paid the Minister in the PM's Secretariat two crore rupees just to have forty-five seconds alone with the Prime Minister, on the red carpet, on the tarmac, before the Great Man boarded his plane. Or the old one from his past, that he'd arranged for the deaths of his father and an uncle when he'd sensed that they were going to sell him out to the police. Or the near-certainty that he had abandoned ivory only because he found the cocaine traffic as lucrative and less cumbersome. Or Dr Chakki's favourite Sukumaran myth, that no matter how late the hour, at the end of the day, after his bath and his prayers and before nodding off, he needed to deflower a virgin every night—perhaps again on a red carpet.

In the future, Dr Chakki fancied that he himself would be appearing quite often before the Privileges and other Committees for both his incendiary journalism and his reformist thinking. Well, he was quite ready. Once he had broken through the avarice of the self-serving classes and prodded them to see that the welfare of all was in their own interest, he could with an airy heart explain to the Bhanwar Virbhims that he wished to be judged not by those legislators for whom he had scant respect, but by the people. The Committees, nonplussed, would half-heartedly threaten him with jail. He would welcome the idea, for it had for a long time been one of his intentions to expose prison conditions in the Welfare State. To save face, as it were, they might even sentence him to four days' imprisonment in the Apnalal Aflatoon Marg jail, but grant him A-one status in it; to wit, a Brahmin among the inmates. He would be provided a cot with a special mattress and bedsheets and be entitled to the luxuries of newspapers and food from home. He would take along with him an amulet of a tiny sandalwood Ganesh—to remind himself, with its perfume, of why he was there—and he'd write about those four days for the next four weeks.

Bhupen Raghupati did not notice that the Dambha who brought in the jug of milk and an ice bucket had changed since the afternoon. At five o'clock, he had received in the servants' quarters-cum-milkman's dhaba an expected, long telephone call from Madna. He'd spoken guardedly, in dialect; in any case, nobody around him could have followed the coded talk of money, accomplices, hits, dry runs, his Durga suit and weapons. After the talk, he had looked happier, more confident. With his ambition rising, he'd felt on top of the world, quite the emissary of the gods.

It took Makhmal a couple of seconds to place the vaguely familiar face. 'Ah—it's you.' He'd of course forgotten the name. 'Settling down here?' Dambha blushed, pleased at being recognized. Makhmal stretched out a regal hand. Dambha touched it, then abashed, dropped to his knees and touched his feet. He hesitated for a moment, then got down on all fours and brushed Makhmal's toes with his forehead. Makhmal grunted in appeasement, reached forward and proprietorially squeezed the youth's anus and all of a sudden, guffawed, 'I hope Jayati Aflatoon responds the same way with my father!'

Red-eyed and abruptly pensive, he gazed searchingly at Dambha's face, at the adult, knowing mien that had emerged from behind the artlessness.

EFFICIENCY BAR

The following October. Early in his career, while examining the junk in the official pen tray on one of the desks, Agastya had come across an ear-cleaning pen. Steely-grey in colour, it was made of some aluminium-like metal. Its nib, about an inch long and made from the same material as the body of the pen, was like the end of a ball-point refill, only more rounded, considerate, more moulded to the intricate inner spaces of the ear. When he'd realized what it was for, Agastya had been touched by the wisdom and the courtesy of the Welfare State. Instinctively, in each new office, he'd looked for it first thing on his desk and had never been disappointed. Tickling one's earwax with it was a wonderful way to unwind when the tensions of office became insupportable.

It was in his left ear and he in the midst of his pre-lunch office crash (that is to say, with eyes wide open, body behind his desk swaying in sleep, mind at home, files open before him, hand jotting and signing away) when the door opened to admit a man who looked as though he expected Agastya to spring out of his chair to receive him. He was tall, fiftyish, slim, with gold-rimmed spectacles, a trim jet-black wig, well-fitting dentures and bottle-green safari suit and no moustache. While Agastya struggled to wake up, he, not a man to waste words, strode up to the desk and introduced himself. 'Mr Sen? Good afternoon, I'm Dr Harihara Kapila, the Regional Finance Secretary. You'll recall that we were in Labour together three years ago. I'm in the city for a dozen meetings with the Centre, but I thought that perhaps we could lunch together, that is, if you're free?'

'Yes sir . . . no sir . . . of course sir, what an honour . . . if you'll just give me a minute to . . .' He rushed to Kalra's room. 'What gives?'

Kalra too was surprised, a rare occurrence. 'Maybe he's heard of how well you work. Would you like a drink to buck you up?'

'Yes . . . What of Doctor Bhatnagar's post-lunch trauma-meeting? You'll tell him, of course. I can *see* the envy and curiosity pushing his colon up, up and out of his mouth . . . You know, he caught me with the stencil-pen in my ear.'

Dr Kapila had naturally been given one of the office's newer Ambassadors, air-conditioned, black-glassed, fitted with a stereo and a bottle of scent on the velvet-coloured dashboard. 'Where would you like to lunch, Mr Sen?'

'The Bageecha, sir.' Mr Sen was feeling happy after two large, quick rums. 'It's new, sir, an air-conditioned greenhouse, very interesting, tropical lush stuff, enormous potted plants, practically sky-high, all fake plastic, and sometimes a live band that specializes, according to the crooner, in rarities—which means terrible songs that no one in the restaurant has ever heard before. He's clever, thinks the crooner, because if you send in a request for one of your favourites, an oldie goldie, what in my youth I would have called An All Time Classic—*Now Or Never*, for example . . . did you too, when you were young, sir, categorize books, movies and songs into All Time Classic, Classic, All Time Great, Great, All Time Time Pass and Time Pass? . . . Agonising, these decisions of one's nonage . . . But the fuc—crooner. He'll read your request, blowjob the microphone, crack a joke into it about your request—very personal, in bad taste—and then sing something else, which'll sound as though he composed it that morning in the bus, squeezed in the crush of peak hour, with his nose jammed into a couple of armpits.'

'Twenty-five years ago, when I was Assistant Collector at

Pinchpaguda, your father was my Commissioner. How is he now?'

'In fine fettle, to use one of his phrases. Strong enough to break a camel's back. Not that he'd want to, of course.'

'Please give him my warmest regards when you next communicate with him.'

'Certainly sir. Raj Bhavan has a fax now, for sure. Do you want to fax him yourself, directly? When your regards arrive just like that, out of the blue, I'm sure that he'll be very—well, warmed.'

'I have the Raj Bhavan fax number somewhere already, thank you.'

Their waiter was moustached and in the black and white of a penguin. Dr Kapila waved the booze menu away. Agastya recalled it to order a Scotch and soda. 'I'm nervous, sir, if you don't mind, to be frank. Alcohol, I've noticed, sharpens my wits. In office, at least. And this is a working lunch, certainly. Finance Secretary and all that.'

'When I chose you for your present BOOBZ post, I'd remembered what you were like. You must be a chip off the old block, I'd reminded myself. Menon in Personnel told me that you'd whizzed off on long leave because from your Manure Supply post, you wanted to avoid going back to Madna as Collector for a second time—and that you returned from leave for the BOOBZ post only because you ran out of money.'

'Ah, but Menon the triple agent didn't tell you *why* I ran out of money. Because I had neither a PA nor a peon while I was on leave, that's why. Meaning that to collect my monthly pay cheque from the Treasury, I had no lackey to send, so I'd to go myself. The Treasury of course is part of your empire, isn't it, sir? The clerk wanted three hundred rupees before he released me my salary. Don't be silly, you fool, I retorted, I belong to the Steel Frame, you can't expect me to bribe you, harass somebody else.

'My reaction must have offended him because as a result, he packed me off on a sort of treasure hunt in the Treasury. Here, get an authorization from the Treasury Officer, the Drawing and Disbursing Officer's clearance, the signature of the Accounts Officer, the counter-signature of your Controlling Officer and a copy of the sanction order, duly certified by at least the Assistant Financial Controller. Toughski-shitski, marathon man, chip off the old block, absolutely, that I am, I plodded off on the first round of the hunt. I joined a queue of forty-odd losers, all lumpen, waiting to meet some bugger who wasn't, as we say, in his seat. The peon at the door, crafty and smelly like some creature out of a fairy tale, officially had no idea when the bugger would return but for a bribe could ensure that I slipped in to meet him first of all, way before the lumpen. Class consciousness, I dare say.

'Look here, I thundered, Steel Frame and all that, the lawful Descendant of the Child of Empire. The peon retorted that he'd summon the police and turn me in for impersonating an Honourable Member of the Civil Service. Shattered by the encounter with the real world, unable to control my trembling calves and chattering teeth, and with my blood at sub-zero, I prepared to wobble off to borrow some money from my uncle to last out the month. Man, what a fucking jungle. At the next table pleaded a doddering old bird whose pension they had suddenly stopped. It had taken him *six* devastating visits to find out that the cause was the Proof-of-Life Certificate that he needed to submit once every five years, that he obviously hadn't deposited in time and—silly man—that was not to be confused with the attested receipts of payment that were required every month. It simply wasn't enough proof of life that he had showed up in person before the clerk.

'Who was being admirably logical, patient and unhelpful. He was a nobody, a mere clerk, a file-pusher and -preserver, certainly not a taker of—ugh!—decisions. Go and meet my boss, he'd suggested helpfully—after taking pity on the old man, as it were. The boss of course hadn't been available on any of those six visits. The clerk had even mooted that it was time for a revolution.

'It boggles the mind, sir, that *millions* of similar cases of harassment occur *every day*. I'd even propose that as an economy measure, we substitute for life imprisonment for our criminals a series of such encounters with the Welfare State at what Dr Bhatnagar—our Ace of Spades—would call the operative level. It would surely finish the criminal off within weeks and we wouldn't moreover have to suffer any of that tiresome rubbish about Human Rights in our jails. I've thought most of it out. The thugs can choose from the electricity, telephones and municipal offices. The complaints that'll be thrust on them will be some of the standard ones—the phone's been dead, for example, ever since it's been installed and just because one's written in in rather strong terms, one's received a bill of two lakh rupees, that sort of thing. One can pick and choose from the Grievances columns of any of the daily newspapers.

'Two: I've decided that the rapists and murderers will be dispatched to our State hospitals to be treated for tuberculosis. That wouldn't be—if you'll pardon the expression, sir—a criminal wastage of resources because apparently we all have either active or dormant TB. If not, it can be quite easily picked up from the OPD itself. Rest assured, sir, that the hospital will take care of them all. They'll cut them open, insert—and abandon—a rusted pair of scissors in the folds of the small intestine, stitch them up again right as rain and send them off with a pat on their backs for being so cooperative on the operating table. Each time the rapist returns with a complaint of high fever, pus in his belly button and an agonizing tummy ache, they'll slice him open and slip in another rusted instrument. No wonder that our hospitals whine all the time about shortfalls in surgical appliances.

'Three: Should women criminals be packed off to the labour room? Need more be said? Your kind attention is invited to one of the State hospitals in the north somewhere, where, just before lunch, an intern found himself alone with a woman in labour in the delivery room. Alone because, according to the muddled newspaper report, everybody else had downed tools—a vulgar expression, I've always felt—in a lightning strike. The intern must therefore, before anything else, be applauded for his heroism.

'The foetus was in breech. The intern, having no idea what to do, panicked. He rushed up and down the corridors for a while, blubbering for help, but found nobody else on duty, apparently, except a second heroic intern who was going nuts trying to patch up some fat puling hunger-striker who'd been shot at by passing terrorists while he'd been protesting against something completely different—the Kansal Commission, I think. The first heroic intern returned to his responsibility, steeled himself, groped, found a leg of the foetus and yanked. He must have heaved pretty hard because, according to the box item, he stopped only when he realized that he'd left the head and shoulders behind. The report added that it was then that he zipped off to participate in the lightning strike.

'From your expression, sir, I gather that you didn't think that to be an appropriate yarn to accompany an apéritif, and that you wouldn't wish such an adventure even on a criminal. But why do these horror stories happen only to the poor, the wretched, the fucked of the earth? Why not to our serial killers or to Dr Bhatnagar? The Welfare State exists—has been created—for them, hasn't it, for the economically, socially, culturally damned. So we build them a hospital to which they walk fifteen kilometres to have their babies delivered. When we satisfactorily face these questions, we'll be on our way into the next millennium with BOOBZ. *God Deliver Us from Our Interns*, by the way, was the title of the news item.

'One of the biggest fears, sir, of the old block, incidentally, is that he'll have his heart attack while in harness, that unconscious, he'll be limousined off to the Intensive Care Unit of a Welfare State hospital—from which, naturally, he'll never return because he'll be at the mercy of the behemoth. After so many distinguished years in the civil service, what is *my* daily prayer? Heaven help me, O Lord, from any encounters with the State as a private citizen. Against the cop, the telephone linesman, the property tax assessor and Dr Bhatnagar, I must have my PA, my peon and my white Ambassador car. How many civil servants do you know, sir, who zip off on long leave just for the heck of it? A handful, I bet. They're too scared.

'Calves still trembling, I'd phoned Dhrubo for counsel. Dhrubo Jyoti Ghosh-Dastidar. Do you know him? He's a couple of years my junior in the cadre, but we've been friends since KG. He's here in Aflatoon Bhavan and is my mole at the Centre. He knows people in Personnel. Last week, he managed, for example, to avoid being posted as Deputy Chief Assessor of Confiscated Contraband. He tells me that the villains are unhappy with me and want me out of the way. A monstrously unjust world.

'Dhrubo it was who had suggested that I immediately return from leave, join an office somewhere and send a cop off to the Treasury for my salary arrears. We aren't a Police State yet, I'd reminded him loftily. Once installed here, I requested our top agent, a genius at liaison, the backbone of this dungheap, Madam Tina, to do the needful. She returned with the bank. Arrears that I hadn't dreamed of existed, lots of Regularization of Pre-Revised Pay Scales Emoluments, and Advance Interim Reliefs. Spirit soaring with visions of freedom, sick to death of Dr Bhatnagar, I applied for leave on the grounds that my mother's become serious once more.'

'Doesn't he know that she's dead?'

'He's God's bad joke on Asia. Nothing that doesn't

concern him moves a bloody centimetre. So he hasn't yet recommended my leave application. Fed up with him, I then sent in last week a letter of resignation from the civil service. Those are the only two pieces of paper on his desk. He can't handle either.'

A second waiter drifted over with the real menu. Agastya ordered a third Scotch, chicken tikkas, prawn fried rice, mutton curry and pork vindaloo. In pointed contrast, Dr Kapila asked for some light vegetarian crap, an eggless salad, a raita, mineral water, that sort of thing. Agastya gazed at him both happily and warily, that is, he'd half-guessed what the lunch was for, he didn't care, he liked the impression of his companion that he'd received of a shy, gentle, well-bred and slightly boring nature, and he still wanted to see how he, Dr Kapila, would play his cards. It was good to be drunk. Sober, such a lunch with a teetotaller, vegetarian, Brahmin, senior civil servant who had, moreover, a genuine Ph.D in Economics, for him would have been inconceivable.

He'd been reluctant to speak of their work in the office and had tried to hide his unwillingness by babbling of other things. He couldn't see how he'd be able to convincingly explain to an outsider the pointlessness, the horrifyingly comic futility and irrelevance of the daily acts of their official lives. Dr Kapila wouldn't believe him and would probably mentally dismiss him as juvenile, silly and unnecessarily mean. He couldn't have believed himself.

Not when he described, just as an example, the routine crisis that all of last week had convulsed the office, truly a place of no illusions. A fine morning, the sun had promised to be clean and warm, it had looked as though the West Indies would lose the cricket, so one-half simply hadn't turned up at office and another quarter had melted away after attendance. Dr Bhatnagar had been tied up—literally, Agastya liked to imagine—in the Home Ministry. Kalra and Agastya therefore had settled down on the sofa before the telly in Dr Bhatnagar's office room. Agastya had been feeling particularly good all morning because the office car had picked him up from home on time—well, almost, give or take an hour.

Those were his principal moments of office-related tension during the day. Would the bugger show up or not, or would he have to phone Footstench only to learn that none of the cars were free because Sherni Auntie and Bitiya had commandeered one each? Three times a week on the average, when the car failed to turn up, he, cursing the life that he led, would drive to office in his uncle's falling-to-pieces Ambassador. Apart from the moments when the traffic frightened him to death, the twenty minutes that he spent behind the wheel tended to be self-harrowing. Just why are you, in your fucking middle-age, wasting your life away, driving a kerosene tin that's going to break down on you right now, in the next five minutes, even though you spend five thousand rupees every month on it and a further five thousand on petrol? And just where's all that money coming from? Why aren't you outside this car, begging on the streets, on crutches at a traffic light, importuning the windows of cars that contain suckers like you? However, when you think of where you're heading to, of the smog-like, grey blankness of the day to come, can you will yourself to change gears, steer this wheel, pump these brakes? Quite often, in a routine traffic jam, he'd got out of the car, lifted the bonnet, feigned a breakdown and pretended to fiddle with what he thought were called spark plugs simply because sitting behind the wheel had become unbearable, because he needed to have something to do, even if it was only to add to the chaos by accidentally, in passing, touching and disturbing a wire or tube that would actually lead to the car not starting up when the snarl at last showed signs of letting up; it seemed as good a way of passing the day as hanging around in office. So low had his self-esteem been on such occasions that he'd distinctly heard disembodied voices snickering to one another: *Aha—the arsehole's on his way to office* and *The monkey's prick is down and out and blue.* The voices had made him feel like Joan of Arc till he'd realized that they'd snickered in Hinglish, the language of tomorrow.

In office, they hadn't expected Dr Bhatnagar to show up at all. Not only because of the West Indies, but also because of the successful official dinner that he'd hosted three evenings before, to which he'd invited, inter-alia, to be frank, the key Additional Secretary in External Affairs who dealt with UN postings, along with some of the chaps in Commerce. At the dinner, he'd drunk one Scotch rather quickly under the cold fish-eyes of Sherni Auntie, got high more on nervousness than alcohol and wolfed down the food with both hands because it'd been both sumptuous and free. All evening, Sherni Auntie had as usual supervised with eagle eye the loading of the tiffin-carriers that had been dispatched home at regular intervals of half-an-hour to satisfy the nutritional needs of her expanding children. The office mini-van, dubbed the Gravy Train by Agastya and the Dining Car by the cooks, had been specifically assigned to the kitchen for ferrying the food. Overseeing the stewards during the filling up of the tiffin carriers was essential, so Sherni Auntie had learnt through bitter experience. For on the occasions that she hadn't been around, the poor things at home had received what she indignantly called stepmotherly treatment—to wit, two compartments of curry but no pieces of mutton, dal but no fried fish, boiled rice but no chicken biryani, potato chops but no paneer tikka, potato fingers but no devilled eggs, chapatis but no methi parathas, a couple of tins of condensed milk but no carrot halwa. 'It's the greed and vulgarity of these lower fellows,' Dr Bhatnagar had clarified, sucking gravy off the fingers of his left hand. 'You see, they're simply not used to good food and all that.'

At these dinners, the duties of Agastya, Kalra and

Footstench were to wear ill-fitting suits and hang around. Periodically, they'd fade into one of the anterooms of the Liaison Suite and sort of bathe in Glenfiddich and Royal Salute. After each Patiala peg, they'd munch mouthfuls of cardamom and walk out slowly and carefully to check on things, particularly Sherni Auntie, short, white, snub-nosed, not especially fat elsewhere but with the fattest, jelly-like arse that the Liaison Suite had ever seen, complete with a subcutaneous life of its own. Time and again, Agastya watched the faces of the guests when it traversed them; there was not one head that did not swivel to observe its gelatinous passage. It petrified the entire office, her husband most of all. In front of it, he behaved as nervously as, to use Kalra's carefully-chosen simile, a child before its stepmother. 'He's an orphan, didn't you know?' The omniscient PA had revealed. 'Which goes to show, doesn't it, that even orphans can be bastards.'

The Liaison Suite of course was the set of rooms on the second floor of the office building where the Commissioner threw his official parties when they, the rooms, were not occupied by some V$^{\infty}$IP from the regional government. Kalra had explained that during the Golden Age, the Liaison Suite had been built and christened by the-then Commissioner Bhupen Raghupati. A rare combination of vision and drive, he'd needed a place where he could fuck in peace the whores that were procured for him. Since he paid for them out of the office contingency fund, it was only fitting that the State pay for the place too.

At these official dinners, alcohol greatly increased Agastya's appreciation of Dr Bhatnagar's qualities, prominent amongst which was his skill at name-and-designation-dropping. 'It is with pride, sir,' Agastya had declared after a few weeks under his tutelage, 'that I wish to report that I'm learning to pick up your droppings.' Thus, through the evening, whenever he felt Dr Bhatnagar's pink eyes on him, he bent his head and stuck his bum out at the correct sycophantic angle and began to nod his agreement with whatever bilge Doctor Saab was trilling out at that moment.

'Yes, it was Geneva—Captain Chandra was rather keen on the post, but you know, to be frank, he's an ex-airlines pilot, so low IQ and all that, and to quote Ambassador Saleykhan—he has too much ego-sheego. In fact, Ambassador Saleykhan'd proposed my name—Ambassador Saleykhan—' it was clear that Dr Bhatnagar liked to pronounce the word 'ambassador'. He lolled it around on his tongue like a dildo and his mouth remained open in an O for a second after each emission—'I speak of '85, when I was learning the ropes in Geneva and Ambassador Saleykhan was being tipped for Brussels—for which I'd been sounded out, of course—it's no secret that Ambassador Saleykhan was rather grateful that I'd refused—declined, I should say—my sabbatical, you know, at Harvard—so Ambassador Saleykhan and I've been together for donkey's years—brothers-in-arms, partners-in-crime and what have you . . .'

Usually, for close to a week after each official dinner, Dr Bhatnagar would withdraw into the Home Ministry to confer with Sherni Auntie, to analyse and dissect each move and utterance of the evening and thus to tot up his chances of a rosy future. Periodically, of course, in those days of retreat, he'd order Kamat the Residence peon to phone and harass the office.

'Bakra Saab's on his way over. An emergency, Kamat said. Must've run out of food.' Gupt the Hindi stenographer thus interrupted Agastya's and Kalra's session before the telly. Gupt's post was an Official Language Requirement. He doubled up as Kalra's PA because he had absolutely no work. 'Bakra Saab wants an in-house meeting immediately.'

In-house meant Agastya, Footstench, Madam Tina, Kalra and a couple of others. A disgusted Kalra refused to go downstairs to receive Dr Bhatnagar—a policy requirement—and dispatched Gupt instead, certain that the sight of the

PA's PA beside the car door would infuriate the Doctor no end, but he was past caring.

If there was a point to Dr Bhatnagar's meetings, it was usually well-hidden. They tended to be long, incomprehensible, soporific pep talks centred around his cherished Management themes: the Modernization of Administration, the Techniques of Negotiation, the Human Factor: Means Or End? The Will to Change, Strategies for Objectives and the Bottom Line. Someone, usually Kalra, took notes at each of these sessions. They generally stopped all of a sudden, most often when Dr Bhatnagar began to feel hungry. Each of them ended in a flurry of telexes and faxes, aimed at whoever it was that week that Dr Bhatnagar wished to seduce by the power of his positive thinking.

Just a handful of comatose subordinates around his battlefield of a desk, but one could actually nod off under his nose if one wished to, he being too senior to stoop to officially notice such insubordination. He didn't much like any interruptions of his flow and all questions had to be reserved for the end. Not that his inferiors had worked out any tactics beforehand, but skill and experience alone had devolved upon Footstench the responsibility of encouraging Dr Bhatnagar to meander on for the duration of the session without disturbing the peace. At every third or fourth phrase therefore, Footstench's goatee would bob up and down in agreement, or his black eyes would gleam in admiration, and even when, during the post-lunch sittings, they threatened to close and his rhythmic rumbles of approval began to sound like snores, he'd still continue to emit his steady murmurs of appreciation: '. . . absolutely . . . we've to keep an ear out for their demandments . . . yes, to come to the nuts and bolts of your grassroots . . . get down, of course, on the brass staff . . .'

The Wednesday of the near-debacle of the West Indies, Dr Bhatnagar surprised his in-house team with his black wig, his soft contact lenses and his new go-getting manner. 'If four baskets of the very best mangoes have to be picked up from the West Coast and personally deposited in Hyderabad for a marriage positively by Sunday, what's the best way to do it?' The new Dr Bhatnagar had come straight to the point of the meeting, except that his in-house team took half an hour to realize it. Finally, Agastya suggested that they fly Sarwate the Dispatch Clerk out for the mission because in any case, he'd be disappearing a week later, on leave, to get married in Hyderabad itself. If they packed him off by plane—at the State's cost—*and* a few days earlier, it'd be the ideal wedding present from the office. Everyone applauded the idea. Dr Bhatnagar actually said, 'Bravo' and shot off a fax to the Additional Secretary, External Affairs, repeated to about six other people: *Apropos our emergency telecon this morning at my residence re Operation Hyderabad Mango, am completely in control and charge of the situation. Consider mission accomplished. Any other fruitful interface desirable, please convey the needful. Regards.*

The very next day, the new Dr Bhatnagar sent Footstench off on the first flight after the mangoes. Kalra later explained that the Doctor—that is to say, Sherni Auntie—had had an afterthought. Apparently, the Additional Secretary had been so pleased with Dr Bhatnagar's promptness that, at the latter's suggestion, he'd upped the baskets of mangoes to five, the fifth being a gift for the Doctor himself. However, on Wednesday afternoon, while reviewing his plan of action, Dr Bhatnagar had suddenly realized that the last basket would take a long time to reach its destination since Sarwate the Dispatch Clerk would be away for a month. In a panic, he'd phoned the Home Ministry on the hotline, the red phone on his desk that Kalra had been instructed to use only to contact Sherni Auntie.

From the official dinner to the wig and contact lenses, Operation Hyderabad Mango, all in all, cost the Office of the Liaison Commissioner about eighty thousand rupees. Money well spent, since Dr Bhatnagar got his UN assignment shortly after. It made Agastya curious to see the UN, where the civil servants of the world congregated; the scope would be breathtaking.

The costs of the wig and contact lenses were borne by the Welfare State under Medical Expenses. They should not, strictly speaking, be computed along with the expenditure on Operation Hyderabad Mango since they belong to a larger strategy. They were in fact the fallout of a policy decision of the Home Ministry, taken keeping in mind the highest level, namely, Prime Minister Bhuvan Aflatoon, at that point about twenty months old in office, and his coterie, youngish, full of ideas, forward-looking. Whatever would their expectations be from the few successful, go-getting, experienced, yet mentally alert members of the Steel Frame? No spectacles, certainly, just sleek reading glasses. A decent-looking pate. What else?

No black Ambassador cars, because it'd been rumoured that during his autumn break on one of the Nicobar islands, Bhuvan Aflatoon had referred to his motorcade as a group of fat black dung beetles too stuffed with shit to more than crawl. There must've been some truth to the rumour because it will be recalled that not long after Dussehra, the motorcades of the V$^{\infty}$IPs of the Welfare State switched from black Ambassadors to steel-grey Contessas.

What else was in? Signing files, looking at papers, like the PM only on Thursdays so that decisions could be announced on Fridays and effected—things could get cracking, in Dr Bhatnagar's words—on Mondays. On Thursday afternoon, therefore, Kalra on the intercom to Agastya:

'Good afternoon, sir. About the resignation letter that you handed in, Bakra Saab wants to know whether you're serious or whether you're fed up.'

'I'm fed up. It's my mother who's serious.'

'Well, he's finally decided not to do anything about it, except that he isn't yet sure whether he should tell you. You see, he and Sherni Auntie have been advised not to rock the boat until the UN assignment comes through. Thus, in the past few days, on top of that enormous burden of the affairs of state that rests on his wide, steady shoulders, has come to perch—and rock—in his words, a new Beast of Anxiety. Am I rocking the boat when I send a fax to our High Commissioner in Australia congratulating her—inter-alia—on her fifty-fifth birthday? When I allow Sherni Auntie to have a second office car for the day since my revered mother-in-law is visiting? When I sign the letter forwarding, three weeks late, our Performance Budget, to the government? And when I decide to attend in person the General Body Meeting of the Gajapati Aflatoon Centenary Celebrations Committee—with Shri Agastya in tow, of course, in case I need someone to glare at when somebody more senior glares at me—which of my decisions can rock the boat? . . . To quote him again, in any decently-managed organization, one is paid, as the years pass, for the width and steadiness of one's shoulders.'

To resolve the uncertainty of his resignation, Kalra then advised Agastya to seek an appointment with the capital's happening astrologer, Baba Mastram, though he also warned him that getting five minutes could well take six weeks. The Bhatnagars had tried for a month and had succeeded only when Doctor Saab had accepted Kalra's suggestion that he himself speak to the Baba's PA, because the latter had made it clear to Kalra each time that they had chatted, that he didn't much care to speak to suppliants' PAs. It was the Baba who'd advised the Bhatnagars in sonorous Sanskrit, in a three-minute session that had cost them a donation of twenty thousand rupees—not to rock the boat, to allow Luck, as it were, to clamber aboard.

The office, to a man, prayed for Dr Bhatnagar's departure. It had prayed the previous summer too, when the UN had let it down. 'The rains won't come,' Footstench, a minor oracle in his own right, had proclaimed, 'until he goes.' Sure enough, last year's monsoon had been catastrophic for the agriculture forecast.

Agastya wondered whether, as a sort of surrogate offering to the gods, to egg them on, as it were, into egging on the UN, he should gift Baby Bhatnagar a couple of his sweaters. The original idea, of course, of presents to the Bhatnagar family on appropriate occasions had sprouted from the good Doctor himself. Its expression varied from the subtle—'Agastya, don't phone me tomorrow before nine forty-five. It's my birthday, you see, and we've organized a rather long, early morning puja'—to the circuitously direct, as in Kalra to Agastya:

'Good afternoon, sir. D'you remember the reddish-brown turtle-neck sweater that you wore to work on Monday? . . . Doctor Saab admires your taste in clothes and thinks that it would be a gracious gesture if you were to gift that sweater to Baby this week—dry-cleaned, of course. It's a good week for Baby to receive, so the stars foretell Sherni Auntie. If you do, he might even consider forwarding your letter of resignation with his recommendation . . . no, just trying his luck, I think, seeing what he can grab before he departs. In return for the sweater, he also offers his counsel: "Don't quit, don't be silly. You haven't married yet, your worth on the market'll vanish without a trace, like hot samosas and chutney on a cold, rainy day. With your useless English Literature-civil service background, you're unemployable. Out there in the jungle, your upbringing itself will be an insurmountable Efficiency Bar." '

Dr Kapila finished his lunch quite early and while patiently watching Agastya gorge his, chatted of BOOBZ, how essential it was in theory and how impossible in practice. After they had ordered dessert, easily and smoothly, like a knife cutting through crap, he introduced the subject of his daughter. At one moment, they had been debating gulab jamuns versus mango ice cream and when Agastya focused next, the moot point had become an attractive, single, young woman with a mind of her own.

'I want her to marry—whoever she wants, but marry. Then she'll stabilize. After which, she can do whatever she wishes—her abandoned Ph.D on the influx into the Punjab of labour from Bihar, her Bharatnatyam—at which she showed promise—even her silly TV job, whatever. She isn't stupid, you know. She's tall, beautiful *and* intelligent, even if it's her father speaking. She was shortlisted for the Rhodes scholarship in her final year in college. At the last interview, at the Golf Club, I'd sat outside in the lobby and prayed that she wouldn't make it, because it would have upset all my plans for her. Do you think I'm old-fashioned? . . . But she's precious, and there's a time for everything in life, a time for fun and a time for responsibilities. I asked her whether she'd like to sit the Civil Services exam; instead, she joined some incredible fly-by-night television production company called TV Tomorrow. It pays her per month more than what I earn per year after twenty-six distinguished years in the civil service. I must say that there are times when I don't understand the economics of the modern age. Nor its outlook . . . We—my wife and I—have built a rather nice house for ourselves in Gulmohar Vihar—do you know it? It's a bit far from the centre of town—fortunately, I say—fresh air and all that, breathing space—but my daughter simply refuses to stay with us for more than the occasional weekend. It's embarrassing in company, she contends, to reveal that one stays in the suburbs *and* with one's parents. To quote her, a total loss, yaar. She's rented a place the size of a paperback novel just off Cathedral Road. I suspect that her rent is paid by her Gujarati venture capitalist friend. Sunita's conduct has made her mother more religious than ever. She's changed her name too—Sunita, I mean—to Kamya Malhotra, after a character in some modern epic or myth, I forget which.'

'Would you still consider me eligible, sir, if I were to quit the government and join a small ad agency as its Senior Vice-President, Public Affairs?'

'You'd be less attractive, but not entirely worthless . . . which organization were you thinking of?'

'Softsell.'

'But the DGP's office reported that after your transfer to the capital, your ardour for that lady had considerably diminished.'

'On the contrary, sir, to cite St Augustine, absence makes the fart go Honda. We're still thick as thieves, a chain gang, Hell's Angels, absolutely.'

As usual, Agastya exaggerated without meaning to. To be sure, whenever he and Daya met, Casper still flew with the old vigour and froth, but because several hundred kilometres now separated them, they simply met less often. They wrote occasionally and frequently wished they hadn't. They were both by nature composed, self-centred and unhappy. They thought of each other only in fits and starts, often guiltily, puzzled at the fickleness of their desire. They would have both liked to return to the old life—the romance by night, the yoghurt with honey at three in the morning, the happy film music through the open French windows—but they—Agastya in particular—were too dazed by the minutiae of their daily lives to act, to move towards recapturing their past. Their letters to each other reflected their sadness and confusion only indirectly, that is to say, they never straightforwardly described their feelings. Daya for example never wrote: 'Look, cut the crap, let's be together because then we both feel very nice, and despite—or perhaps because of—the differences in age, temperament and upbringing, we should give a future together a chance. Therefore, please ask the Welfare State for a transfer back to where you belong.' Her letters instead were altogether of a different style.

August,

That last visit of yours wasn't such a grand success, was it? . . . you've definitely become thinner, weaker and more depressed (oh-oh, she means Thursday night, when she could come just once because I asphyxiated and had a heart attack with my nose in her pussy. How selfish of the darling, how come she hasn't blown me even once, and we haven't fucked—in the sense of in-out, in-out, the earth moves, in-out—even once in all these nights that we've spent together. We've never even met by day. I'm not even sure that she and I can be called an affair. Which modern oracle can I ask?) . . . *Please give me a week's notice of your next trip and I'll set up an appointment with my doctor, a homoeopath with an absolutely luminous intelligence. Yours is a condition that can be corrected. I've read up a bit on your problems and am convinced that Dr Thadani is the person for you. I don't know if you've ever consulted any specialist, but even if you have,* please *meet this luminary. I'll accompany you and if you like, wait outside while you chat with him. Please, August, you owe yourself a chance. Shape up! Why do you allow the inertness of your official life to seep into the personal?*

What else is new? Quite accidentally, I reread Wuthering Heights *last week and was very impressed by Emily Bronte's sexual energy, by its (obvious) transformation into a creative energy and by its transference onto the elements, the very landscape, of the book. Heathcliff is nature's power wonderfully anthropomorphized, of course . . .*

Agastya shuddered at the prospect of their next assignation.

Moreover, she was right; his last visit hadn't been such a grand success. Of the three days that he'd been there, she'd had a female friend—a large, Caucasian Anand Margi whom Daya had addressed as Lazy Susie—staying over two nights and sharing her bed, hai Ram, so what was one to infer? Lazy Susie and Agastya hadn't hit it off. She'd found August, his nickname, rather droll and him in general ill-informed when he, to make polite conversation, had asked her whether she, as an Anand Margi, liked dancing with the skulls of wolves. Later, Daya had told him that Lazy Susie had disclosed to her that the vibrations that she, Lazy Susie, had received from Agastya had been 'cold, sneering and anti-life'.

One of the many things that he'd liked about Daya was that she came from another planet; there existed nothing to connect her with the world of the Pay Commission, the Steel Frame, Interim Relief, Off-White Paper and the Efficiency Bar. With her, therefore, he'd felt less tired, less futile. On his last visit, however, he learnt that he should have known better; the Welfare State was truly everywhere and even those who sneered at its clumsiness condescended to suck at its dugs.

Over mugs of hand-churned buttermilk and tiny Chinese bowls of raisins and blanched almonds, they had been chatting in their usual manner of this and that; Daya had been asking him whether he'd finally succeeded in slipping either a request for a transfer or a letter of resignation past his extraordinary boss and Agastya had been describing how her health food tended to fill him up like a balloon with gas and how therefore it was the one element of his old life that he didn't miss, when she had sighed, tied up her hair at the nape in a bun and muttered:

'As Senior Vice-President, Public Affairs, you'd be the talk of the town.'

'Yes, but what if I quit my job and join you and then you die?'

'Well, I'll try to take you with me, if you like. I mean, really. And don't eat so much if flatulence is a problem.'

In a bit of a huff, she had swished off to the kitchen with the mugs and unfinished bowls. She'd returned, calmer and more determined, to suggest that if he gave her a copy of the letter in which he was going to ask for a transfer, she'd probably be able to swing it through Jayati Aflatoon.

'Oh, I say.'

Apparently, they had been dear dear friends ever since boarding school. Agastya must have looked disoriented because Daya had continued, 'In the few minutes per day that you must take off from gazing at your navel and feeling sorry for it, have you never wondered what takes me to the capital twice a month? Apart from love of you, of course. Those hotel bills and plane tickets—it isn't the hand of God, you know, that pays for them.' But pretty close. Daya had turned out to be the Principal Media Advisor to the Executive Group of the Gajapati Aflatoon Centenary Celebrations Committee. The Executive Group was nominally headed by the Prime Minister but the buzz confirmed that it was his power-hungry, culture-loving wife-of-cousin who actually called the shots.

She had got her friends and lovers into the group—Rani Chandra, Rajani Suroor, people she could work with. Culture was fun—tribal operas, carnivals of ethnic wear—one dressed to kill all the time for elaborate dos—not dreary and dusty like Land Reforms or the Agriculture Census. Her friends of course worked gratis, for the honour (the equity, in Daya's words) and the fun of peeking at the behemoth from up close—and for the pickings that were to be had. Daya for example had an eye on the general elections (God willing) eighteen months away and the ruling party's advertising and publicity plans for it. Jayati would get her cut, naturally, were Softsell to succeed in seducing the party of the Aflatoons into letting the agency manage its fabulous publicity budget. In its high places, the Welfare State could be quite exciting.

And munificent. To celebrate the centenary of the birth of Gajapati Aflatoon, statesman extraordinaire, founding father and Guide of the Nation, the Committee had over a hundred and fifty crores to spend. In Parliament, members of the Opposition, feigning outrage, had yelled and bayed for over four hours (at the rate of fifty thousand rupees per second) on the subject of the gross extravagance of the Centenary Committee. Had the government again lost its mind? Would the Prime Minister care to explain why he had sanctioned ten crore rupees to combat the plague scare in Madna and *fifteen times* that amount to celebrate the birthday of his grand-uncle? Had he any plans for the wedding anniversary of his parents which was just round the corner? Why did the Centenary Committee have an incredible one hundred and fifty members? One fiddler for each crore—was that the idea? If so, why had the government discriminated against the backward castes? Didn't they too enjoy the right to nibble? Why had the recommendations of the Kansal Commission not been implemented in the Centenary Committee? Did the government believe that matters of culture and heritage were above the grasp of the depressed castes? If the Committee truly comprised, to quote the Government Resolution that had announced it, the 'best and brightest of our cultural firmament', then how on earth could one explain the presence in it of Bhanwar Virbhim? And Madam Jayati Aflatoon and her friends? Whatever were they doing there?

The Opposition had indeed enjoyed itself hugely. When Jayati Aflatoon's name had cropped up, Member of Parliament Bhootnath Gaitonde had suddenly jumped up from his bench and baying for attention, stridden down to the Well of the House, waving a document that he'd hollered was the New Charter of Sycophancy of the ruling party. Nobody had allowed him to speak but that had never posed a problem in the House. Shrieking over the tumult, shrugging off the hands that reached out to physically shush him, overriding the commands from all quarters of the hall ordering him to keep quiet and cock up, clambering over the benches, dancing and dodging in the aisles like a football maestro his colleagues and adversaries who rushed up to show him his place, Bhootnath Gaitonde informed the Chamber of the People of the grand plans that the riffraff of the ruling party, led by the redoubtable Nominated Member of the Regional Assembly from Madna, Shri Makhmal Bagai, had chalked out to celebrate in a befitting manner the fiftieth birthday of the Prime Minister's cousin-by-marriage, Madam Jayati Aflatoon.

'Honourable Mr Speaker, sir, with your permission . . . this truly is a season for celebration. Centenaries, anniversaries, birthdays—may I remind the chair at this juncture that mine falls on January 14? Not that far away, particularly when compared to my centenary . . . this document in my hand is an advance copy of a pamphlet that is to be circulated for publication in the major regional newspapers and journals in my dear constituency of Madna. It purports to be the Official Programme of Action for the Fourth of November, the Official Birthday—like many of us in this House, she too has two, one official and another, usually preceding the official by a few years, actual, birthday—of the Mother Goddess of the Future. I skip over the other hysterical appellations bestowed on Madam Aflatoon—particularly since my colleagues in the Treasury benches would've coined some of them and do certainly use all of them in their daily morning prayers—and come to what precisely is going to happen on that glorious day.

'One: The Regional Forest and Transport Minister has announced that the Forest Department will dig fifty J-shaped tanks in various forest lands for wild animals to quench their thirst at. If the tanks by any chance prove to be death traps for some of the larger animals—elephants, for example, his Department, the Minister elaborated, will request the Department of Environment to arrange for fifty mobile veterinary units to visit the tank sites every day.

'Two: The Minister for Urban Transport has proclaimed that fifty women—presumably J-shaped—will be licensed to operate motorcycles as taxis in the regional capital. Men can ride pillion, he stated, on payment of a fixed fare. Any eveteasing will be most severely frowned upon . . . Three:

The high-yielding tamarind trees that the Sapling Research Institute has developed and that produce over two thousand kilogrammes of tamarind per acre, the Agriculture Minister declared, will be rechristened Jayatirind and planted in fifty acres of land in different districts in the region.

'Honourable Mr Speaker, sir, Four: Each of seven unnamed Ministers has promised to publicly eat fifty clay pots filled with mud. One of them, incidentally—the Ministers, that is—has been found to be HIV positive. It is not yet known whether their act of penance on a day of universal festivity will please Madam Aflatoon—or indeed whether it is a true expression of contrition and not simply an irresistible addiction to mud. The official version states that they are sorry—and want to show it—for having earlier celebrated the *actual* birthday of the Protective Angel by rolling down all the six kilometres of Cathedral Road, right up to the Gokul Nath Temple, where they'd had their ears pierced and had prayed for the speedy entry into active politics of the Birthday Girl.

'Five: Ms Kathipalari, a chairperson of a Regional State Corporation, has promised that she will lead a—and I quote—"bevy of naked virgins decently covered with neem leaves"—to the Har Har Mahadeo Temple at the crack of dawn of the fourth of November to invoke the heavens into—and I quote again—"making Madam the permanent Prime Minister of the Welfare State" . . . May we take the last to mean that the palace intrigue amongst the Aflatoons is at last official? . . . Six:—aaaargh!' He had stopped then, using as a pretext the second paperweight that'd struck his shoulder. Clutching it, groaning softly, he had collapsed onto a bench, happy with his performance, quite certain that it would have equally pleased the lobbyists behind it.

Agastya of course wanted coffee and Dr Kapila nothing; while they waited for it, he asked Agastya whether he and

Sunita had met recently. Just checking out the police report.

'No, I don't travel that often. Besides, the Gujarati venture capitalist and all that. I'm of course flattered that Sunita remembers me and has told you that she wouldn't mind meeting me again, but I wouldn't raise my hopes, sir, if I were you. She probably means that it'd be nice to chat over a drink.'

'You drink far too much, if I may say so.'

'Yes, sir. D'you think that it—the booze, I mean—reflects the quality of my life, its quiet desperation, so to speak?'

He hadn't ever regularly drunk in office hours before. He had picked up the habit from Kalra and Footstench who boozed in their office rooms because otherwise dealing with Dr Bhatnagar would have cracked them up. Agastya discovered that they were right; when drunk or stoned, looking and listening to Doctor Saab and his family actually became quite fun. When sober, however, he'd feel depressed at the thought that Dr Bhatnagar, simply by *being* who he was, *qua* Dr Bhatnagar, had ruined and continued to ruin the health of all his office staff. Agastya had even wanted at times to write anonymously to the National Human Rights Commission.

Kalra kept the best booze behind his chair, locked in the official Godrej steel almirah along with the fancy photocopier paper, the extra packets of felt pens, tiny emergency polythene bags of breath-freshening cardamoms and cloves, and spare copies of Dr Bhatnagar's electronically-typed curriculum vitae. Agastya had christened the Godrej almirah the office Efficiency Bar. He had also helped Dr Bhatnagar's cv reach its present form.

'Agastya, in the past few months, you've begun to know me as a man of many interests, not the typical stuffy bureaucrat at all. Tell me, for my bio, under *Hobbies/Recreation/Interests*, how would *you* do justice to my—I'll be frank—myriad-faceted mind? . . . no, no, not immediately . . . here, take a copy of the bio away, reflect on it at home and give me a feedback by Thursday afternoon. Can't be rushed, you know.'

Agastya'd finally come up with: *Reading, Writing, Golf, Walking, intelligent, stimulating Conversation, followed by long periods of reflective Silence*. After *Reading, Writing*, he'd had an urge to add *Arithmetic*, but had sternly controlled himself. Impressed but reluctant to show it, Sherni Auntie had okayed it the same evening.

In the career of the mandarin of the Welfare State, the Efficiency Bar bobbed up at some stage or the other. It had to be negotiated if he wanted an increment in his salary, a promotion—to get on, in short. To decide the matter, Administration usually checked, among other things, his annual confidential reports of the last five years. If the verdict'd been *Good* or above in all five, the mandarin'd cross the bar.

So far so good, except that in the language of confidential reports, *Good* meant *Ordinary/Average/No Great Shakes/Nothing to Write Home About/Hardly Efficient/Barely Passable.* There were usually five categories in which bureaucrats could place their subordinates, namely, in ascending order: *Bad, Average, Good, Very Good* and *Outstanding.* After fifteen years of written debate and counter-comment, Personnel, wishing to be positive, had changed *Bad* to *Poor* and *Very Good* to *Excellent.* Only the brave and demoniacally industrious civil servant, the sort who waded through files even on Sunday afternoons and didn't notice that his children snapped at him—only he ever used the categories *Poor* and *Average* to rate a subordinate, because when he did, Personnel freaked out and, having at last some work in hand, increased fourfold the sod's paperwork. It deluged him with demi-official letters and printed annexures labelled *Secret.* Had he intended his grading to be retributive or corrective? Did he have any objection to the assessee being informed of his superior's estimate of him? Could it be presumed that for the assessee to be rated so, there must have been, in the course of the year, many occasions when he must have failed to deliver? On those occasions, had the demoniacally industrious superior officially informed his subordinate of his disappointment with him? Had the superior kept an official record, minutes of some kind, of all these occasions? If not, had he, the superior, any document or written proof of the year that his assessment was neither caprice nor malice? Personnel had to keep the welfare of its assessed personnel in mind, hadn't it?

To avoid being trapped into an eternal correspondence with Personnel, most civil servants therefore used the standard, unwritten, euphemistic code in writing the confidential reports of their subordinates, by which the slippery performer was judged to be *Good* and the disastrous *Average.* Everybody who spoke the language knew the code, of course, so that when names were being circulated for certain posts, one could insist on—if one wanted to, that is to say, depending on whom one wanted to pick—candidates with five *Outstandings* or above in the last five years. The grade above *Outstanding* did exist to fit into the language of the code those who were, simply, outstanding but who obviously couldn't be described so because—it may be recalled—in the language of the code, *Outstanding* simply meant *Good.* How best to describe the *truly* outstanding civil servant was left to the creative abilities of the Reporting Officer who, to make matters clear, usually began with: *The assessee is more than outstanding*, and then let himself soar, *She is as stainless as steel . . . a veritable lion of the jungle. . . Yours Truly found her more utterly reliable than the Undersigned. . .*

The code also operated to sniff out the odours of corruption. In the confidential report, one couldn't of course record: *The assessee-bugger's been raking it in for years, so what's new?* because then Personnel would make one regret it—at least till one's first crippling heart attack; instead, for the madly venal, like Chanakya Lala for example, those whose improbity had achieved the status of myth, so that one could construct proverbs and maxims around them—in the reports of civil servants like those, in the column marked *Integrity*

(Use a Separate Sheet if Necessary), one was advised to write: *Nothing Adverse on Record*, which, for those who knew the language, meant, *Boy-o-Boy*! For all those bureaucrats about whose honesty one just wasn't sure, one wrote: *Above Reproach as per all reports*. Tradition hadn't bothered to dream up phrases for any other category.

Since the code was unwritten, it could at a pinch be ignored as though it didn't exist, which it didn't, officially speaking, being unwritten. Thus in the case of Dr Bhatnagar, for example, his lobby would interpret his five *Goods* in a row to mean, clearly, that here was a candidate who was rock steady, persevering, not flashy, salt of the earth, absolutely. When valued along with his sound grasp of management techniques and his multidimensional range of Hobbies/Recreation/Interests, his lavish dinners and his generosity with his office organization, staff and services with anyone who mattered—when thus viewed as part of a larger arsehole, his confidential reports made Dr Bhatnagar a sure winner, a pole vaulter above any efficiency bar.

Like other characters of his type, he pounced like a gecko on a moth on any office case that Madam Tina had successfully brought to a close and that was therefore ripe and ready to redound to his credit. She reported directly to him four to five times a week, alone, behind closed doors, in sessions of half an hour each. Agastya didn't think that he pawed her. Kalra confirmed his opinion. 'Too scared, with Sherni just a hotline call away. Can't get it up but he leaks into his pants when he sees Tina and that's enough excitement for the day.'

Dr Bhatnagar liked to listen to good news from Madam Tina, the success stories that could be transformed into a set of coruscating faxes. He left the crap and the bad news for Agastya, naturally, he himself being so senior and all that. Thus, to him she would report, for example, that the Regional

Industries Secretary's Laminated Security Pass for All Central Ministries had been signed just that afternoon and had been collected by her within minutes of its being issued, and that the Foreign Exchange Clearance for the Regional Tourism Minister's trip to the Reunion Islands had been sent by the Ministry of Finance to External Affairs that very morning and that yes, she had procured a photocopy of that confidential letter. For Dr Bhatnagar's office, the most valuable news, naturally, concerned not the doings of the regional government in general but the personal fortunes of its more important individuals.

From the very first day, the office had made it clear to Agastya that Madam Tina was a whore. 'You should be informed, sir,' Kalra had firmly announced the moment the door had shut behind her, 'that she's a P-R-O.'

'Ah, I see, like our colleague with the foot stench, the same Department—though his toejam, I imagine, couldn't be doing very much for our image.'

'No sir, he's our PRO, our Public Relations Officer, but Madam Tina is our prostitute. We have only one. It's a small office.'

'What's her payscale?'

'That of a Senior Office Superintendent. She's received two out-of-turn promotions in the last three years. The rest of the office hates her. You'll receive many phone calls for her at your number. As Deputy, you should put a stop to it. A question of the dignity of office.'

Sure enough, that first afternoon, Agastya had received a phone call for Tina, except that the caller had called her Mona. A harsh and very horny male voice, as though he had his erect cock in his other hand.

'I'm deeply sorry to have to tell you,' Agastya, welcoming a familiar feeling, had intoned, 'that Madam Mona left us this morning . . . no no, for her heavenly abode . . . a sudden heart attack in the room of a Member of the Regional Assembly. She'd gone there for some urgent dictation . . . I'm her ex-boss speaking. We've just returned from the cremation ... the office is closed for the rest of the day as a mark of respect ... yes, so sorry ... as a keepsake, would you like a speck or two of her ashes?...'

Innocent that he was, he'd never actually met a prostitute in flesh and blood before. Of course, he wasn't quite sure about Madam Tina, and the two or three times that they met per week, he certainly didn't expect her to show him some cleavage or let her hair down with a sigh or rub her bum against him or something; in fact, he didn't much mind when she cancelled their meetings because of 'urgent work that she had to chase up'. For one, the files that she brought to discuss with him concerned the headaches stuck in Defence or Industries or the Cabinet Secretariat, certainly not the problems towards solving which he could contribute anything significant. For another, she was cute, well-mannered—she never failed to call him 'sir' with every sentence—she smiled easily, making one want to say stupid things all the time just to see her teeth, she was anything but dumb—in fact, twelve times more efficient than everybody else in the office barring Kalra, and one afternoon, daydreaming behind his desk, Agastya had suddenly realized, while imagining Madam Tina in the nude, astride him, smiling above her shaved pussy and her small brown breasts and still calling him 'sir', that he was getting older and lonelier by the minute, and that maybe he should follow his father's advice and marry before it was too late, because now he knew what too late could mean—a pass at a possible prostitute, for example, made in the heat of the moment and the privacy of his room, would make things too late, wouldn't it, because slipping was so easy and welcoming, and once one had slid, it was too late to retrieve one's place—not because one couldn't but more because one simply wouldn't want to.

'Of course, one should marry in time, sir, there's a time for marriage, and a time for orgies,' thus Agastya to Dr Kapila, to distract him from the intense scrutiny to which he was subjecting their lunch bill, 'to quote Ecclesiastes.'

'This is most embarrassing. Our lunch has turned out to be more expensive than I'd expected—about a thousand rupees more, in fact. It's all that whisky that you drank, I'm afraid. I'll have to borrow some money off you—that is, if you carry that kind of cash around. This is terrible.'

'Yes, it is. It comes of hanging round, sir, all the time in high places. One loses touch with the grassroots. In your case, I'd imagine that the problem's compounded by the fact that you don't drink and that you're a vegetarian. Which is ironic, sir—come to think of it—that you continue to be a vegetarian even after you've lost touch with the grassroots.'

'From your gibberish, I conclude that either you don't have the money or don't want to lend it to me. Well, say it straight out, man! I've handled crises before! What about ideas? D'you have any of those?'

'Well, I've my credit card.'

Dr Kapila transferred some of his intense scrutiny to Agastya, who continued, 'Well, I mean, sir, don't you? I have one in lieu of a bank balance, if you know what I mean. We've rented out part of our ground floor, you know, to the Regional Cooperative Bank—that scam dates from the era of the second Liaison Commissioner. The presence of the bank immediately makes Dr Bhatnagar a landlord and V$^{\infty}$IP in the eyes of its General Manager, who's a twenty-first-century cow-belt Brahmin—download, CD Rom, online and all that—and me a deputy landlord. How much Dr Bhatnagar harassed the GM, poor man, when he first called on Doctor Saab to offer him his credit card gratis—without the annual service charge, we being landlords and V$^{\infty}$IPs, you see. I haven't used mine yet because they always swish off with it somewhere, don't they? That makes me insecure because the waiter leaves me with no receipt to prove that he's taken it. What if he returns, denies that he has it and presents me with the bill again? In our system of things in the Welfare State, one produces receipts and records for everything—to prove when your domestic cooking gas cylinder was last delivered at your doorstep and whom you telephoned on such-and-such date. To mistrust is much safer, more realistic and professional. It doesn't get you very far but all the paper that it generates makes you feel better, illusorily protected from the outrages of Fortune. Even when the records are faked and the receipts counterfeit, one still has a basis for writing letters and rushing off to court, for creating more documents and dusty off-white files.'

Outside the restaurant, while they waited for the chauffeur and car to discover them, Dr Kapila said, 'It's ridiculous that I invite you out to lunch and you pay. I'll write you out a cheque as soon as we return to the office. Or if you prefer, I can add the amount to your dowry. That's why I kept the bill. You have thought of a dowry?'

'Not the nitty-gritty, sir, not yet. But if you've decided to bequeath us your house, I'd be inclined to say no, thank you, sir. I'm not much of a suburbs person either. One always feels a long way from home.'

'I should find out whether there are other contenders in the field for your fair hand. Mrs Bhatnagar reported to my wife quite emphatically that nobody so far's made any alarming moves. Just some postcards in your dak, I gather.'

'Would you like to set up an Efficiency Bar for your prospective sons-in-law? Whoever drinks the largest number of glasses of fruit juice wins. Dals and vegetarian soups will be allowed but soft drink cocktails frowned upon. Look, can you swing for me a transfer back to where the action is? It'll be so much easier then to wean Sunita away from the bosom of the Gujarati venture capitalist.'

'What'll happen then to the BOOBZ programme here? Well, tit for tat, let me see . . . but you haven't answered my question about my competition.'

'It can't be compared, sir, rest assured, to the annual Public Service Commission exam to enrol wise men in the Steel Frame. In fact, there's only one old friend of my father, from his college days in Calcutta, who's been trying for the last several years for either one of his two grand-daughters.'

'Well?'

'As a first step, my father, the grand-daughters and I are waiting for him to die.'

'Here it is. Thanks for the lunch. Can I drop you somewhere?'

'Yes sir. Aflatoon Bhavan, if possible.'

Where the Under Secretary for Demotic Drama has finished his tai-chi exercises and is sitting in the visitor's chair before the desk, calm of mind, gazing at nothing. To his left and slightly behind him stands a suppliant, head bowed like those of the statuettes of the Magi in a creche. He is a Madna type whose face Agastya recognizes but whose name for the moment he can't recall.

Agastya to Dhrubo: 'Why aren't you sitting behind your desk?'

'For a variety of reasons . . . One: it gives me perspective. Two: from here—or elsewhere in the room—on the occasions when I do answer the phone, I can with perfect truth inform the enquirer that there isn't any response from the incumbent's seat. Truth, you know, cannot be achieved by the weak. Three: I'm not sure whether my seat isn't a piles-giver.'

Dhrubo then turned to the suppliant and asked pleasantly, 'Is there anything that *you* wanted to ask me?'

'Yes . . . I wanted to know why the funds that your Department used to give my organization, Vyatha, have suddenly dried up.'

'*Gand Mein!* Vyatha, I see! . . . What are you there?'

'I've become the Number Two in the organization. You must've received from me at least one letter a fortnight over the last two months. My name is A.C. Raichur.'

'In the euphemisms of one's nonage, Number One was pee-pee and Number Two potty.'

'We're still headed by Rajani Suroor.'

'Rajani Suroor . . . He often used to grouse that everybody else in his organization had the capacity of a lazy cretin, that the only thing that all of you were any good at was cooking the books. I suppose I mustn't speak ill of the comatose. Frankly, I don't think Vyatha'll get any more money from us until Suroor wakes up. There's nobody left here, you see, to push and chase your file. I could, I suppose, but I simply don't have the time.'

'But how'll I survive?'

'Would you like some more tea? If you order it in your room, it's more expensive and the service slower, but the tea's better.'

Dhrubo pressed a buzzer on his table. Save for a rack that held six rubber stamps, the table was scrupulously bare. A comradely silence, while he and Agastya gazed benignly at Raichur.

Dhrubo to Agastya, while continuing to look at Raichur, 'So how are things with you, friend?'

'I am being plagued by my neighbour in the Transit Hostel, a Srinivas Chakki, to join him to foment a revolution.'

'Ah yes. The plague. He once used to share this room with us.'

Suddenly the door crashed open, as though it'd been kicked, and a large, bilious-looking monkey squatted in the doorway, right arm extended to prop the door open, munching peanuts with the other.

'Hahn, Boss, three teas please, mine without milk and sugar.' The monkey departed without a word.

'Acute staff shortage, I see, Dhrubo.'

'Yes. A combination of BOOBZ and the Minister's office, which has been gobbling up staff like the giant in Jack and the Bean Stalk.'

'When I was last here, I couldn't help being struck by the

large number of one-limbed, blind and deaf and dumb Class IV staff.'

'Or is it only the lumpen, the Depressed Castes and the backward classes that lose their limbs and their faculties in accidents or at birth? How many one-armed, one-legged, Brahmin senior civil servants do you know? And are they any good? Do they—can they—deliver the goods? Does it matter if they can't? Because isn't it enough that the goal—of having a one-armed senior civil servant—has been achieved? Please don't ask me these questions. Reserve them for the Under Secretary of the Kansal Commission—a Brahmin incidentally, four-limbed but with thick bifocal spectacles, though they haven't yet decided whether they should reserve any Welfare State posts for the myopic. They could, you know, logically. The more sat upon you are socially, the more likely you are to suffer from other disabilities—of education, health, poverty—and surely the State should try to help you to the extent that you are disadvantaged. But if you ask me, we should first pump in all we've got into creating aware minds in healthy bodies, and then give everybody a level playing field.'

Giving up, Raichur meanwhile had dropped into a vacant seat and sighed explosively. His breath carried to Dhrubo, whose nose twitched. A faint grimace distorted his fine features. 'Garlic for breakfast and lunch, I see—and smell. Dragon-like, your breath, absolutely. Probably excellent for your blood pressure and your bowel movement, garlic, but it won't help either you to widen your circle of friends or Vyatha to prise some funds out of us. I should've told the monkey—had I known earlier, had you exhaled those noxious fumes at me in good time—to crush a dozen cardamoms into your tea. He's resourceful and quite helpful when in the mood. He was bequeathed to me by my ex-peon, Shri Dharam Chand, who was a tremendous asset, madly corrupt and madly competent—and had sedition brewing in his head all the time.

'For instance, in one of the General Staff Meetings last year, Dharam Chand startled everyone by wanting to know why Aflatoon Bhavan had separate loos for Women officers and Women Staff, and Men Officers and Men Staff, and why the Welfare State should officially discriminate amongst its citizens in the matter of their bodily functions. I, as Official Spokesman of the Officers' Cadre, had pointed out that from the stink in the entire building, one couldn't really tell the difference between a conference hall and a canteen, leave alone an officers' loo and a lumpen loo—and that the stink was part of the Official Strategy for Equality. Anyone who's visited our men's toilet on this floor would've seen that the number of the Physically Challenged amongst its users is rather high. That is Dharam Chand's doing. Either we have Equality or we have Reservation. So he successfully led a campaign to reserve one lumpen loo only for the PCs. God knows where the non-PC lumpen staff goes for its ablutions—perhaps into the almirahs that line our corridors.' Then, to an agitated Raichur, 'Was there anything else?'

'Sir, I—my family and I—have become beneficiaries—creations of the Welfare State. We—Vyatha—signed an agreement with you to receive a certain sum of money every month. We submit every quarter to you a report of our activities and our accounts. Even though we've been headless for a while, we continue to flap our limbs about on schedule. We've planned our activities for the next six months and sent you a copy for your final approval. We invite the Department—the concerned Under Secretary and above—to all our functions, theatre events, street happenings, protest shows and drama festivals. We also keep you informed of our weekly meetings. So I don't understand why the udder's dried up. Do you disapprove of the programme? We can do a street play around the opinions of Mr Dharam Chand, if you wish. We're already working on one on the life and times of Rajani Suroor—it'll be ready by the time he either wakes up or passes over. We've left the ending open.'

'Who's your Chartered Accountant? I can't quite make

out from the signatures in the accounts. Is it your mother or your wife?

'My mother. I've time and again implored her to use her maiden name but she's both—if you'll pardon me—stupid and obstinate.'

Dhrubo relented only when Raichur began to weep, finally proving himself to be one of the world's losers. 'Stop crying and snivelling, don't be silly . . .' Dhrubo opened a drawer and handed Raichur from it a sheet or two of off-white paper. 'Here, blow your nose, wipe your tears. I'll see what I can do. Deputy Financial Advisor Mrs Tutreja's off to Ulan Bator early next month to coordinate an exhibition on *Gotama and the Non-Violent Tradition*. That's when we'll slip the file through. As a last resort, I'm afraid that I might've to request you to arrange a fire in one of the rooms.'

Patiently, Agastya waited for Raichur to stop blubbering in simulated gratitude over Dhrubo's hands (that he didn't release for close to a minute for fear that he wouldn't appear thankful enough). It never ceased to astonish Agastya that there was nothing in government that could not wait, *nothing*. Whenever somebody pressed for urgency, his hackles rose. Because then there was even more reason to wait. For the urgency was always to warp the rules to do somebody else a favour in return for a consideration or another favour. Be honest, Raichur, change the rules and the game, and redefine discretion to include dishonesty. Our consciences will then rest, our hearts won't go thump-thump each time we note the possibilities of the fast buck in each file, so fewer cardiac arrests, substantial economies in medical reimbursement. Oh how often had he wanted to quit! Except that every time that he'd drafted a letter of resignation, a Pay Commission had been set up to hike his salary up by a millionth of a fraction. A raise, as Jesus said, is a raise. One can't, you know, leave one's mother's lap. The outside world is much less funny and far more wicked. Out there, all of them would trip head over heels over the lowest efficiency bar.

FIREFIGHTING ON A WAR FOOTING

To lessen the awesome amount of paperwork in the Welfare State, as a last resort, one government servant does sometimes request another to arrange a fire in one of the rooms of an office (not in his own, naturally, for that would be conduct unbecoming of him). A great many files are disposed of in this way. Numerous instances of this style of decision-making spring to mind—the Aflatoon Tower blaze of 1973, the Non-Aligned National Centre conflagration of 1977, the Senapati Place catastrophe of the same year, the Millennium Plaza disaster of 1983 and, of course, the Vesuvian eruption at the TFIN Complex that the Welfare State took twenty-one months to recover from.

The burning down of the last was special mainly in the magnitude of the calamity. For the rest, like its predecessors, it provided, while it lasted, terrific entertainment to hundreds of spectators and after it had charred itself out, goaded the government to review for the tenth time the existent firefighting measures in its buildings.

In the corridors of Aflatoon Bhavan, it will not be easily forgotten that to house some of their countrymen who had swarmed into the capital for the event, the organizers of the OYE OYE Happening had finally set up Camp One in the car park of TFIN Complex. Public Works had objected vehemently and recorded in a series of rapidfire confidential exchanges with the Department of Culture and Heritage that the entire happening was a grave security risk to the building.

There were thus some four hundred ringside witnesses to

the conflagration. The chosen visitors who'd never seen a washing machine before hadn't ever seen such fireworks either. They gawked, wide-eyed with wonder and joy, their fireside entertainment abandoned, as the vast electric circuitry of the building gushed, at one corner, a shower of red, blue and green sparks that lasted half a minute, hissed menacingly as the fire careened down its wires and explosively spat out fifty metres away a large gob, a burning ball, that shot up some feet into the evening sky before descending in slow motion to smoulder and trigger off other pyrotechnics. Quite a few of the spectators believed initially that the fireworks were part of the official programme, were more awed by their grandeur than by the sightseeing of the day, were impressed by the thoughtfulness of the organizers and mentally noted that while they were there, they should explore the possibilities of other junkets. A loud collective gasp was heard right across Camp One as, all of a sudden, the windows of the east wing of the ninth floor belched out, alarmingly like a dragon, a huge tongue-like banner of fire. One of the representatives of the district of Madna, none other than A.C. Raichur, who by one of the campfires had been providing a Vyatha play with the background noises of a typically crowded lane of a red-light area the morning after, and who'd been distracted from the production of the sounds of women screeching at their kids by thoughts of Vyatha and how it could be milked—A.C. Raichur was distracted from his reveries by a deafening explosion from somewhere high up in the building that really sounded like one storey collapsing on to another, and that was accompanied by enormous, dense, noxious, infernally hot clouds of smoke and burning debris that whooshed out of the windows like the fallout of a revolution in hell. It impressed him so much that it was only on the day after that the idea popped into his head to include in his repertoire of simulated noises the impressive sounds of the father of all fires eating up a state-of-the-art building.

The thrilled crowd milled about uncertainly, drawn to the spectacle by its grandeur and at the same time repelled, even frightened, by its fierceness. In the glow from the flames, the faces looked aroused, happy, smiling, like those of children in Disneyland. The visitors stole glances at one another, bonded by the shared excitement. Not one countenance expressed shock, horror or sorrow at the awesome destruction of a national treasure. Naturally; it wasn't theirs.

By the time the fire brigade and the police turned up to organize and spoil things, a group of musicians from the eastern region, fired, as it were, by the conflagration, had begun to thump out an irresistible foot-tapping rhythm on their drums, enthusing others in turn to clap their hands, shake a leg and chant along. Thus, for the visitors, the burning down of TFIN Complex became an enormous, memorable campfire experience, for which, at dinner the following evening at the Gajapati Aflatoon Sports Stadium, with giggles and nervous simpers, they profoundly thanked the Prime Minister.

'My God, exactly how primitive are we? Don't we have firefighting systems in our buildings? Alarms, that sort of thing? Or are they all—all those hundreds of them—meant to be ovens? Grill, Bake, Toast and Barbecue? Answer me, c'mon, I'm waiting.'

'You're asking the wrong person, sir.' Even while conversing with the Prime Minister, the Public Works Secretary continued to be as suave as silk, all white coiffure and expensive aftershave. 'It may be recalled, sir, that despite the best efforts of my Department, Routine Maintenance of Welfare State Property has not been centralized with us. It remains the responsibility of the administrative or residing Ministry.'

He was still smarting from his visit to TFIN Complex the evening before. He'd received a confused phone call about the fire from the Disaster Management Cell of Home Affairs at about eight p.m. and'd decided to drive down to the site in his private Maruti car without waiting for an hour for the official white Ambassador. Two kilometres away from the building, the cops'd stopped him and forced him to turn around. Naturally, seeing his car, they'd refused to believe that he was who he was. Dazed and hurt, he'd cruised around for a bit, gazing at the vast glow in the night sky that had looked as though the night lights at the sports stadium had suddenly turned orange, the crowds in the streets rushing towards the spectacle, and had distractedly wondered whether he could get some tea somewhere.

The ancient demand of his Department to maintain all the official property of the government was a routine empire-aggrandizing move to which Bhuvan Aflatoon acceded after the father of all fires'd burnt itself out. In the first phase of its Revised Firefighting Measures Programme, Public Works proposed an additional budget of nineteen crore rupees. After an intense skirmish, Finance sanctioned one and a half.

On the buildings directly under its control, Public Works began the firefighting programme on a war footing. Their manoeuvres looked, sounded and felt like war too. At the Prajapati Aflatoon Welfare State Public Servants Housing Complex Transit Hostel, for example—one of the first to be taken up—work on the alterations to the different wings of the six buildings began within four days of the Prime Ministerial order and actually went on, without pause, day and night, for weeks. The jokers in Public Works said that the Transit Hostel'd been declared Top Priority because the mistress of the Departmental Secretary stayed there, and surprise inspections of work in progress enabled him to officially visit her once a day—over and above, that is, his regular lunch-hour assignations. He was an indefatigable man. It is true that his mistress, a short-haired, short-tempered, widowed Assistant (later Deputy) Financial Advisor, Mrs Minu Tutreja by name, stayed in Apartment C-308, but the real reasons for the choice of the Transit Hostel as one of the first ten properties to be dealt with were: 1) that it was large; lots of money could be shown as having been sunk into it and nobody would notice—this was a crucial factor because the end of the financial year loomed perilously close and they still had this monstrous budget left, and 2) that it was full of people, legitimate occupants even at night; it looked good that the government thought first of the welfare of inhabited buildings.

Fire extinguishers had always—since time immemorial, as it were—hung on the walls of the corridors, unnoticed, unchecked, nooks for geckos, a formal stipulation in some municipal bye-law; they obviously weren't meant to combat anything. The revised firefighting measures were altogether more ambitious. They proposed the construction, beside the veranda of every fourth flat, of a one-metre-wide wall that, from the ground floor, would stretch right up to the eighth. On the outer faces of these walls would be fixed three rows of water pipes that too—naturally—would reach up to the heavens. To these walls—and to all the strategic corners of the hostel—from the six gates of the complex, zig-zagging across the lawns, would be laid lanes of tarmac wide enough for the standard fire engine and for a total length of twelve kilometres. The new walls and pipes would of course be painted and appropriate signs put up.

Ferrying sand, gravel, drums of tar, bags of cement, bricks, pipes and stone chips, trucks roared into the Transit Hostel by day and night, at four in the afternoon and three in the morning, shattering the sleep even of the sozzled. With each arriving lorry, the entire population of some twelve hundred public servant families cocked its ears to wait for the hellish engine to calm down to an idle growl—it was never switched off—and the incessant babble from the everpresent labourers—the shouted questions, hails of greeting, the cries of annoyance and whoops of incomprehensible glee—to again become audible; then the clink, clang and clatter of the sides of the truck being unfastened, followed by the infernal din of drums of tar simply being pushed off the vehicle, or the steam-like hiss of sand streaming down. Even at three in the morning, some families could be spotted on their verandas, breathing deep the fog of dust that hung over the entire complex like a curse in a fairy tale, and dazedly watching the construction simply because they couldn't sleep—not only because of the noise, but also—as February slipped into April—the heat. There was hardly ever any electricity because the contractors'd tapped the mains for their construction work. Besides, the numerous fires that'd been lit all over the lawns to melt and mix the tar, sent up shimmering waves of heat that seemed to drift in through the doorways and open windows to settle on one's wet skin like a warm shawl. Were one philosophical, one would admit that watching the leisurely—but steady—rhythm of the workers was lulling, and that one could rest as in a daze, with eyes blinking and smarting, observing the road-rollers that trundled up, down and all over the lawns with the ponderousness of elephants, like children's cars from some primitive giants' amusement park; the bidi-smoking masons with towels wrapped around their heads, who materialized like magic outside one's sixth-floor bedroom window, stopping their regular slapping of cement on brick to ask—quite politely—the housewife on the veranda for a drink; the buckets of water being hauled up by precariously-knotted rope from the cement tank by the car park; the hammocks made out of old saris in which slept the infants of labourers whose drying drawers, vests, lungis and saris dotted the gardens like corpses after a skirmish.

Before the invasion, the lawns had been fairly green, with lush grass and tastefully-placed bushes of hibiscus and jasmine, ideal for burp-releasing after-dinner promenades. However, save for the occupants of C-401, Dr Srinivas Chakki and of A-214, Agastya Sen, no other inhabitant of the Transit Hostel seemed to really mind—or mind enough—the degradation. Karma, tolerance, maya and all that, no doubt. Some of the residents actually welcomed the change. The eight-to-fifteen age group, for example, obsessed with cricket, went mad with joy at the sight of all those walls coming up, each with three parallel, perpendicular, perfectly-centred pipes and an even asphalted surface leading up to it, to boot. Some of their parents too, tired of squabbling and scrambling for parking niches for their cars and two-wheelers, were overjoyed at the unexpected quadrupling of available tarmac surface. The support systems as well of the Transit Hostel—the vegetable and fruit vendors, for example, who for lack of space had had to park their handcarts just outside and around the gates, narrowing the passageway down to the width of one car, causing unimaginable—but permanent—chaos, resembling a fishmarket set up on a crowded railway platform, only noisier, with angry horns and yelled curses being exchanged like gunfire on the border—they too were happy with the largesse of the Welfare State. Thus, within a matter of a few months, when the walls and the pipes were up and the lanes for the fire engines all neatly laid out, one could glimpse, on a Sunday morning, fierce cricket matches crisscrossing one another, like life on a city's roads viewed from far up in the sky, being played out amongst cars, two-wheelers and handcarts parked all anyhow, sprawled out, as it were, like sunbathers on a spacious beach.

Agastya was an illegal occupant of A-214. That is to say, the flatlet had been allotted to him three years ago during his tenure in the Ministry of Labour. When he'd been transferred out to Navi Chipra, he'd simply forgotten to surrender it to the Commissionerate of Estates. 'Surrender' is the verb officially used to denote the restitution of government property to the Ministry of Urban Affairs. It is in keeping with the idiom of general hostility in use amongst different departments. No one anywhere had noticed Agastya's lapse. The records of the Estates office were at that time being computerized. The consequent chaos had helped cases like his considerably.

Even though he was aesthetically revolted by the renovations to the Transit Hostel, he, being an illegal occupant, felt at the same time a bit removed from all the turmoil of building construction. He was a bird of passage; when things became insupportable, he could always take wing.

'But things became insupportable a long time ago,' objected Dr Chakki to his attitude outside the Mammary Dairy milk booth at six in the morning on a fine day in April. 'What is left of the body politic if its steel frame takes wing? We must fight the rot on a war footing. Prod the middle classes awake.'

'I'm upper middle class, I hope. What about us?'

For them all, as a first step, Dr Chakki wished to spread the word. Firefighting too was best begun at home. Since he was on leave and dangling between two posts, Agastya helped in the drafting.

> *Anyone who's ever lived in this hostel, surely the ugliest building—pure Public Works—in one of the suburbs of hell* (complained Dr Chakki in the letter that he sent to the Minister and to a dozen newspapers, and a copy of which he endorsed with compliments to Mrs Minu Tutreja of C-308, with a humble request to push the plaint with all the clout at her command), *will testify that on the good days, that is to say, three times a week in the monsoon, all the flats on the third floor and above get water in their bathroom taps from six to six-thirty in the morning and from six-thirty to six-forty-five in the evening and in their kitchen taps from five-thirty to six-fifteen in the morning and from four-thirty to five-fifteen in the evening. On the bad days,*

that is, for the rest of the year, the taps of those eight hundred-and-fifty-plus flats are as dry as the mammary glands, so to speak, of an old desiccated male of the species. Those less-fortunate residents have worked out a deal with the inhabitants of the first two floors; they haul buckets of water up in the mornings, when the pressure is strongest, by elevator when they're in working condition, and up the stairs or by rope or knotted saris from their verandas when they're not—which, naturally, is very often, this being hell and electricity being as rare amongst us as statesmanship and honesty. Each bucket of water costs three rupees. It will interest you to know that w.e.f. January 1 next, the rate will be made more specific and scientific, i.e., three rupees for twenty litres of water or, if you prefer, fifteen paise per litre. Payment in kind is officially discouraged because it tends to cloud the clarity of the exchange.

Of course, you're well aware that in most offices and schools, when a latecomer is asked why he isn't on time, his perfectly genuine reason, that he stays on the third-floor-or-above of the Pashupati Aflatoon Transit Hostel and that he spent three hours that morning hauling water up by bucket, is not accepted. This fatheaded attitude of government needs to be reviewed, or water provided to all of us, whichever is simpler.

Our Welfare Association also wishes to propose that our elevators be converted to a manual pulley system that will function exactly like a well and for much the same purpose. I enclose with this letter rough but reliable sketches and diagrams of the minimal changes mooted in the two lifts in each residential block. Their weights—with and without buckets of water in them—have obviously been taken into account in our plans. The counterload suggested is our litter. We consider the proposal a rather fine example of Appropriate Technology, well adapted to need and availability.

Gastero In, Garbage Out.
Blueprint C provides the overview of the plan. It was truly inspired architecture that originally placed the garbage chute of each building right beside the lifts, because now connecting the two will be a piece of cake. Of course, at the moment, the chutes aren't very popular with the residents because they—the chutes—all choked up some five years ago—somewhere between the third and fourth floors in Wing B, that's for sure. A dead body, insist our oldest inhabitants, of a chowkidaar who was far too drunk to distinguish between an open elevator and the chute with its lid raised; of course, to be fair to the dead, one doesn't have to be intoxicated to be confronted with the problem. But he's there, maintains the pro-chowkidaar lobby, because the stink bears him out. Which isn't being fair—again—to the march of time, because—naturally—the chowkidaar hasn't prevented the stuffed polythene bags from landing on him, even though at the same time his stink has deterred some of my neighbours from getting close enough to the chute to open its lid to junk their rubbish. Thus, on each floor, the entire corridor area around the chute has become an awesomely-colourful garbage dump, each plastic sac—if you permit—like a faded, puckered, birthday-party balloon resting on the vegetable scraps and banana peels that have burst their skins of polythene and with time come to resemble the good earth. Aaaaaarrgghhhhhhh, gags the unsuspecting newcomer as he exits from the lift, that is to say: Where in heaven have I arrived? Hell's refuse dump? What this place needs is a bloody sweeping flood.
To which we'll gladly contribute our buckets. Frankly, while on the subject of our water problem, we need to fight fire with fire. Our Association—we have a dream!—would be quite happy to consider your fire engines to be water tankers that will use the new

cricket-stump-pipes of our energetic adolescents to pump water up to our deprived neighbours round the clock—that is, if the fire engines can ever negotiate our gates and the new parking lanes to reach the new walls. As a citizen, I wish to know: whatever happened to the water that was freely available—to return to where we began—at TFIN Complex, *which is just down the road from us and whose rich glow on its last night we sadly miss during the evenings when we lack electricity?* 'Water theft,' *whisper the contractors who supervise here the convulsion of the structure of our lives,* 'in our country, remember, we even sell cowdung.' *Naturally, we've discussed the subject with them in some detail and suggested that they steal some more water, which they can sell to us—we don't want them to lose in the deal, obviously—at a rate less harsh than fifteen paise per litre. Our negotiations have been significantly hindered by the lobby—a wretched breakaway group—of the denizens of the ground and first floors.*

Apart from Mrs Minu Tutreja of C-308, Dr Chakki also presented with his compliments four copies of his letter to Sukumaran Govardhan. That is to say, he pushed them into the letter-box of the guest house of the Regional Potato Research Organization that occupied all the four flats of the top floor of the east wing of the second apartment block. Its letter-box was affixed to the wall beside the stairs on the ground floor. The guesthouse itself was cut off from the rest of the building by an iron gate at the mouth of the corridor that led to its constituent flats.

Contemporary legend had it that Govardhan had a hundred and eight residences dispersed all over the country, that number being auspicious, and that he spent an average of three and a half days in each. No one—naturally—had actually seen him on the top storey of the Aflatoon Transit Hostel but then nobody had spotted him anywhere else in the country either. If anyone had, he, after a few months, had changed his mind. However, the prostitutes who operated out of the guesthouse did confirm that once or twice a year, those of them on duty were asked to pack up and disappear and invariably, for those few days, a handful of new, very young girls were ferried in from some dot on the map.

Govardhan moved about and in and out of the Transit Hostel—claimed the buzz—generally at dusk, when the traffic chaos was maximum. To ease his passage, that he arranged for general power failures in the area was, as was noised about, perfectly possible.

He'd be rather disturbed, wouldn't he, debated the residents of Prajapati Aflatoon amongst themselves, by these firefighting measures, these walls and pipes three feet from his bedroom window? By all reports, the flats of his guesthouse from within were quite posh and tastefully, intelligently and completely illegally inter-connected. After those decades of dealing in sandalwood and ivory, his developed aesthetic sense would surely revolt against government-inspired renovations to any building. Apart from the enhanced security threat, of course.

In the twenty-one months that the TFIN Complex took to recover from the father of all fires and the firefighting measures of the Public Works Department, the happenings of the Welfare State occurred elsewhere, in the sports stadiums, auditoriums and multi-media centres of the city, but not with the old zip and vigour. In that time, Bhuvan Aflatoon successfully fought off a threat to his Prime Ministership from an obscure ghost of the extended family, a virtually-illegitimate pretender of a third cousin who headed a splinter in the party, was a thorn in its flesh (and a bloody prick to boot) and whom Bhuvan Bhai packed off to the North-East Council as its Executive Governor. He wasn't as pleased, however, with the astonishing failure of his think tank, in that year and three-quarters, to come up with a suitable, melodious, pronounceable, Sanskrit name for TFIN Complex. He had received suggestions, certainly—*Srishti, Samvad Bhavan, Varta, Sanchar*—but they'd all sounded unreal and alien, partly because he could barely understand Hindi, leave alone Sanskrit—though doubtless he could hardly have his ignorance of both the official language and its mother bruited about. Till the time that one of the light bulbs clicked on an acceptable name, proposed Rajani Suroor to Bhuvan Bhai, would the PM like to refer to TFIN Complex as P-C-Om? Privately, of course.

In those twenty-one months, one Aflatoon Centenary, a quiet affair in memory of Trimurti, blended into another, altogether more glorious and politically more explosive, that of Gajapati, statesman extraordinaire (to quote the blurb, crafted by him and attributed to his amanuensis, on each of the back covers of his six-volume memoirs), thinker, writer, sage, savant, philanthrope, cricket enthusiast and founding father of the Welfare State—and unfortunately for Bhuvan Aflatoon, only a distant grand-uncle of his. Try as he might, because of a handful of Aflatoons in between, Bhuvan Bhai couldn't quite get the effulgence that the centenary celebrations reflected off the immense bald dome of Gajapati to shine on him. Jayati of course hadn't been born an Aflatoon but she'd become one when she'd married Gajapati's younger grandson, one of the continent's great jerks, a polo player and a lover of horses with the mind of a thoroughbred, haughty, pure and simple. But she herself was Raw Sex Incarnate and Bhuvan felt warm and laughed a lot whenever he was with her. When she'd suggested, smiling into his eyes, that she slip into the saddle at the Centenary, he'd welcomed her with open arms, silently pointing out to himself that he'd credited her with more intelligence. As a strategy for an entry into politics, Culture sucked, and while sucking, emitted wrong signals, because only the closet bisexuals dipped into Culture, didn't they, because Home Affairs was far too sweaty and macho, and all the rest of the junk—Rural Development, Energy, Planning, Industry, Water Resources—simply too dry and unsexy. Well, Jayati'd fit in because the inner circle'd whispered a couple of times that she, to use the phrase that they used to giggle over in school, swung both ways and that moreover, her appetite was that of a corrupt civil servant of the Welfare State, quite bottomless. But man, what a bottom.

To inaugurate the renovated TFIN Complex, a befitting event, it was felt, would be the first full-blown meeting of the Gajapati Aflatoon Centenary Celebrations Committee. To fix a date, the Secretariat of the Committee put up a file through the proper channels—to the HUBRIS Minister, Bhanwar Virbhim, who consulted his astrologer. The eighteenth of November, decreed Baba Mastram. *May kindly see and approve*, pleaded the Minister in a note to Madam Jayati, who did but added, *May we discuss the agenda? I wanted to do something special for poor Rajani Suroor.*

With reason. Much had happened to him—apart from the slide into coma—in the months between the two centenaries. He'd grown in official size, as had his orbit of influence, in keeping, as it were, with the comparative stature of the two Aflatoons in question. He'd also moved laterally from Bhuvan's court to Jayati's, displeasing Bhuvan not just a bit. Old bedfellows and dormitory-mates that they were, he of course didn't stop frequenting the PM's office; he simply began showing up just as often at the headquarters of the Gajapati Aflatoon Centenary Committee, exploiting to the hilt his official post of Advisor there. A busy man, using, with the industriousness of a bee, his clout to push his own theatre group into every nook and cranny of government. His street plays were thus used by Welfare to propagate its new Integrated Female Child Nourishment Project, by Public Health for its Early Plague Detection Strategy, and by Rural Development for its revolutionary Revised Bank Soft Loan Programme. Vyatha, needless to say, performed for a pittance—and rather well. In return for board, lodging, transport and a handful of rupees, its enthusiastic amateur actors successfully concentrated their energies on spreading the messages of the Welfare State. Everyone was surprisingly happy with the arrangement—the Ministries because Vyatha, when compared to radio and TV, to which it was an inconspicuous adjunct, was a damn sight cheaper and far more effective, Suroor because his group gained some terrific goodwill and publicity, and the actors because they travelled to, and performed in, outlandish places.

Like Madna, for example. Being quite a performer himself, Suroor journeyed with Vyatha as often as he could. Street plays helped him to unwind and rejuvenate himself. Of course, after he was knocked about on the head by Makhmal Bagai's hoodlums some eleven months ago, the pace of his life had really slowed down—in fact, virtually stopped. Only his heartbeat and a couple of electronic graphs on spasmodically-functional video screens kept him away from absolute zero. For the entire period, he'd been comatose in Madna and not because of the town. His body had been politicized, for Bhanwar Virbhim, on Baba Mastram and Bhupen Raghupati's counsel, refused to have him shifted out. It was Madna that'd crushed the skull of the esteemed Advisor, declaimed Bhanwar Saab at public forums and whined he before Jayati and the PM, and it should be Madna where he—the esteemed but comatose one—must recover (or rot). For political and personal reasons, Bhuvan Aflatoon agreed to let the brightest of his light bulbs rest in peace in that town. Serve the quisling right, thought he in his black moments, but whenever his heart melted and he missed his groovy, long-haired dorm-mate, he'd helicopter the best specialists out to the middle of nowhere to check on the goodly frame of Rajani Suroor.

After each visit, the specialists submitted to the PM's office an impressive series of documents, reports, assessments, charts, prescriptions and diagnoses and to their own organizations their more modest hotel bills of the Madna International. He's steadily improving, sir, they concluded, jargon edited to suit addressee, the bumps on his head've healed completely, the spinal column now looks terrific, the collar bone, ribs and shoulder are almost as good as new, the last cat scan and cerebral angiography show nothing abnormal, his hypostatic pneumonia's responded very well to our antibiotics and is now a thing of the past, he has the heart and blood pressure—if you permit—of a healthy, happy fifteen-year-old dreaming of a good game of football. All he now needs to do is to wake up. A mystery of science, really, why he doesn't.

'Perhaps he's fed up,' mused Bhuvan Aflatoon, 'and needs the rest.'

Along with Rajani Suroor, the portion of the Madna Civil Hospital that he inhabited, and certain parts of the town, improved too—marginally, fitfully, it is true, but improved, nevertheless. A special cubicle, for one thing, was erected for him in the corner of General Ward Two that stood furthest from the loo. Off-white distemper on its walls, disinfectant, white tiles, new wiring, tubelights that worked, scrubbed floors that'd changed colour like the sun breaking through, electricity available almost—certainly, officially—round the clock, not that he was ever dragged out of his coma by a fan that stopped whirring. Someone declogged the drains, the rat population diminished, the stink lessened. The monstrous garbage dump at the hospital gates was shifted to the lane behind the municipal school, thus, within a week, since old habits die hard, creating two dumps in place of one. Naturally, because of the number of V$^{\infty}$IPs who streamed in and out of Madna to look in on Rajani, the two routes from the helipad and the railway station to his bed were mapped out and cleaned up, up to a point. The bedpans were removed from the corridor, but the authorities could do nothing permanent about the paan-spittle stains on the walls or the hawkers and the cattle in the lanes. Life must go on, they would have argued, no matter who slips into coma.

He was sorely missed, initially. With time, however, because he neither died nor awoke, he became just a bit boring, a fixture of the town, like the new, unfinished boundary wall of the Collectorate. At the same time, the months in a sense augmented his stature—mainly, no doubt, because of the number of his visitors, V$^{\infty}$IP pilgrims at a shrine, and made him, by a mythopoeic process, almost a figure in some hoary tale, dormant till the magic moment broke, perhaps with a kiss or—mindful of the sexual traditions of the country—even a touch, the spell that bound him.

No one, it should be clarified, kissed any part of his body even once in those eleven months. For one, he looked too grey. Besides, he had all those tubes, wires, pipes and bottles attached to him. Jayati and Daya might have, had they visited him inconspicuously, without a cortege. Jayati missed him even professionally. He'd been full of ideas. He'd known the system, where the money was, how to steal—clearly a personality who was going places even after he'd arrived.

'Tell me, Jayati—' to him, she was Madam only in public—'Gajapati Aflatoon officially was a great lover of Hindi, wasn't he? A motive force behind the Our-Own-Official-Language Policy, etc? It's a facet of the Great Man that the Centenary Committee could underline, highlight, whatever, because you could then lay your hands on some of the budget of the Official Language Caucus. Even five per cent would fetch you some crores . . . yes, thanks, it *is* quite a brainwave, isn't it? . . . we wouldn't have to do very much,

I imagine, just copy what each Department does for Hindi every year. Organize a Hindi Week, in fact . . . usually in winter, out in the sun, with a public address system, really quite festive, with vendors of oranges, peanuts and aphrodisiacs mingling with the Section Officers and Senior Assistants . . . all non-Hindi-walas in the central Ministries are invited-coerced to participate in a Hindi essay competition and the winner reads out his entry before his colleagues. Terrific entertainment . . . Under Secretaries rolling in the aisles, clutching their stomachs . . .'

The germ of the idea of exploiting the funds of the Official Languages Wing of the parent Department of the Committee for other, officially-acceptable purposes had infiltrated Suroor rather early in his tenure as Advisor to the Committee. In his third week in his office, he'd been trying to figure out anew the monstrous organizational chart under the glass top of his desk and'd stopped once again at the smiling face of the Director (Official Languages), a pleasant, slippery man who, Suroor knew, reported to him but whose precise day-to-day tasks and responsibilities remained enveloped in a cloud of unknowing. The chart stated that the Director was being paid to implement in the Committee the official language policy of the Welfare State.

'Yes, but what does that mean, exactly?' asked Suroor of his favourite Under Secretary, Shri Dhrubo Jyoti Ghosh Dastidar, who had nothing to do with the subject. 'This Director guy gets up in the morning, drinks two cups of tea, reads the newspapers, maybe uses the office car to slip off to the local temple to pray for his daughter's success in her school exams, returns for breakfast, gobbles up his alu parathas, mango pickle and dahi, and with a mind as clean and quiet as a blackboard on the first morning of the new school term, turns up at nine forty-five at Aflatoon Bhavan to start his day—and then what? He sits at his desk, puts his lunch box on the side shelf, summons his PA to prioritize his personal work—and then? What does he do?'

Sure, he'd asked him directly too. The Director (Official Languages) had been quite taken aback.

'Prepare for our Hindi Week, sir,' he'd elaborated after a minute's thought.

'The essay, the elocution and recitation competitions, a play, film and non-film songs, and a dozen speeches for the Minister, the Chairman, the members, me and you. But the other fifty-one weeks of the year? What goes on in your room?'

'Well, sir, in the time left over from preparing for the future, and analysing the previous, Hindi Weeks, we translate into Hindi the Parliament Questions, correspondence, orders, circulars, resolutions, notes, memorandums and Unofficial References of the Committee.'

They'd been conversing, of course, in Hindi. The Director thought it proper to speak nothing else in office. In a sense, he was being paid, he reasoned with himself, to set an example, to hear himself enunciating in the official tongue. His newly-arrived temporary boss, though a bit theatrical, was perfectly fluent too—with a deep, resonant voice, moreover. They should get together in the after-hours for a poetry reading—rum, cashew nuts, kebabs, deathless Urdu couplets, that sort of thing.

'But you yourself, personally, don't do any translating,' Suroor'd countered, a bit startled by the Director's laziness. Dammit, the bugger doesn't even have the energy to invent a set of tasks for himself. 'I see from this chart here that you have with you two Deputy Directors, four Assistant Directors and six Senior Translators. What do *they* do? Put up for your approval their translations of memorandums?'

'Yes, sir. And their ideas for Hindi Week.'

'Well, I've some too.' Vyatha thus slipped into the programme that year and considerably improved it. Demure, disciplined, it was ready to shoulder all the low-profile, rural, small-town stuff. It was quite welcome, given Rajani Suroor's clout. Equally naturally, once he fell into his long doze, the standing of his troupe plummeted correspondingly, particularly since it'd been at one of its performances that, to use a phrase popular with the coterie, a joker of a happening had snicked Suroor's balls—and cracked his skull.

Headless Vyatha remained, flapping its limbs about in the corridors of Aflatoon Bhavan, wandering around in the dark, stumbling into cupboards and monkeys, looking for direction, succour, inspiration and funds. By the time that the money started flowing again—in a sad trickle, a cruel parody of the munificence of the golden age, barely enough for Raichur's phone bill and petrol costs—a few more months had passed and the drifting about in Aflatoon Bhavan had become habit. Thus, when the Ministry began to warm up for the grand meeting of the Gajapati Centenary at TFIN Complex, and the panic started to set in, and hundreds of hands—and more important, feet—seemed to be needed every hour, to dash off to the printer's, zip down to Jayati Aflatoon's office, run around in circles in the city hand-delivering invitations, careen around in intersecting circles hand-delivering corrigendums, and scurry up to the Zonal Municipal Office for permissions to put banners up across some streets, the headless staff of Vyatha came in handy. They were quite happy to be peons for the Welfare State. They were after all paid for their labours and their routine was unpredictable and undeniably dramatic—hardly routine, in fact.

Thus when Agastya Sen looked in on Shri Dhrubo Jyoti Ghosh Dastidar on official work, the Under Secretary's chamber was crowded with the amateurs of Vyatha waiting to be packed off on errands. They stood and sat about in different parts of the room with professional listlessness, like actors out of work, who'd given up waiting for their cues. Raichur sat opposite Dhrubo, breathing heavily, diffusing garlic into the air. Dhrubo himself was on the phone, strongly advising his auditor against seeing some striptease show.

They were always very glad to see each other. 'I've come with a complaint from Dr Bhatnagar. The agenda that you've sent him for your jamboree-meeting has a pale green cover. He's discovered that you've another agenda—or rather, the same agenda with a yellowish, glittering cover, which is meant for Additional Secretaries and above. He wants that one in exchange. He's very offended.'

'The yellowish cover was supposed to be golden. It was my symbolic protest against the Centenary. All that glitters is not gold, you follow? I told the printer a hundred times, golden, golden, golden—but I hadn't reckoned with *his* symbolic protest. He apparently spends only his spare time at his printing press. His real vocation, profession, hobby and passion is trading in gold, the prices of which've fallen like a diver off a ten-metre board. We are pissed off with his cavalier treatment of us. I've put up a stinker of a note proposing that we blacklist the printer from all future dealings. *Yellow, yellow, dirty fellow*, begins my note. So how've you been? . . . Have you met Raichur-ji? The heart, soul and—I might add—breath of Vyatha. . .'

'Yes, of course . . . How d'you do? . . . your room's a bit too crowded now for your tai-chi gyrations, isn't it? What d'you do nowadays for peace of mind?'

'There'll always be room for tai-chi . . . Tell me, what should we serve at our Centenary meeting? The last circular from the Finance Controller specifies two Britannia Marie biscuits and tea per head if the meeting is chaired by a Joint Secretary or above. Cashew nuts, potato chips and colas are allowed only if the diplomatic missions are invited. We haven't decided yet between Bangladesh and Finland.'

'Cashew nuts are good. Everyone'll turn up if you mention them in your letter of invitation. Dr Bhatnagar, for example, won't have breakfast that morning. An economy measure.'

'Everyone'd better turn up. The invitation in fact is in the form of a veiled threat, phrased in masterly prose, if I may say so myself. You see, the meeting is a grand event for a variety of reasons. One: the re-inauguration of TFIN Complex. Two: the first reunion of the committee under Jayati Aflatoon, her coming-out occasion, as it were. Three: she's planned, with an astrologer's approval, a huge cultural rite, like a religious mega-happening, for Raichur's ex-boss. Therefore, the meeting just has to be held in Hall One, which seats two thousand. It goes without saying that the auditorium has to be packed choc-a-bloc with bureaucrats taking notes, carrying files, ferrying memos; otherwise it'll be a terrible insult and Bhanwar Virbhim, flattened by Jayati's vengeance, will find himself back in Madna, perhaps alongside Rajani Suroor. Whom *haven't* we sent invitations and agendas to, that's the question. Everyone's on the hit list—Energy, Rural Development, Civil Supplies, Defence Production, Parliamentary Affairs, Food Processing, Labour . . . Our own Department's unofficially shut on the eighteenth of November because everyone, absolutely everyone, has to attend the meeting. Even I've had to change the timing of my second tai-chi session to accommodate the centenary. Would you like to be there?'

'Yes, very much. It's begun to sound like our very own Kumbh Mela. I was riffling through the agenda on my way here. A masterpiece of bilge, if I may say so. Superb.'

'Ah yes, that was necessary. The literature simply had to be as weighty as the event—the prestige of the Department's at stake, you follow. The inclusion of the unpublished poems of Rajani Suroor at Annexure B was particularly inspired, you'll agree.'

He would, in general for the entire document. It was a hundred and fifty pages of culture-related information doubled simply by having been made bilingual, a procedure urged by courtesy to the Department of Official Languages, which had agreed to give eight crores, in the first phase, to the Centenary (for a further four crores, the seminal contribution of the terrifically Anglicized Gajapati Aflatoon to the propagation of Hindi as the State's official language would first be concocted, then highlighted). Each left page of the agenda was in English; the right faithlessly translated it into Hindi. Statistics, headings, figures—of expenditures proposed in the next three years on any culture-related matter by any body of either Central or regional government, of costs incurred in the last five years on seminars, conferences, publications, festivals, lectures on culture anywhere in the country—balances, amounts carried over, sums lapsed into oblivion, seemingly-relevant extracts of audit reports—all that, the very stuff of government, its records, its heart, its dugs—were slipped in whenever possible, whenever nobody was looking, as it were. Nobody'd had the time, certainly, to check the senseless repetitions that bounced about on the same page and the entire lists that returned in every other chapter to tease the page-flipper, in passing, with a sense of déjà vu.

Some sections of the agenda'd impressed even Agastya into emitting low whistles. The Central Archives, for example, in assessing its activities in the previous financial year, had submitted that it had prepared for storage 15,612 sheets, bound 4,326 books, supplied 48,623 photocopies to scholars against a demand of 1,37,091 and answered 1,846 queries on the telephone. The printer, in disapproval perhaps at its performance, had printed the entire paragraph that dealt with the Archives upside down.

He'd objected, justifiably, in similar fashion—so Agastya had noticed as he'd browsed through the pages, in a pleasant, drunken haze, in the car that had ferried him to Aflatoon Bhavan from his second lunch with Dr Kapila—to the contents of the last paragraph of the section on the activities of the

National Secretariat Library. Agastya had turned the agenda around to see what he could be missing: *Other recent acquisitions of the Library include Natwar's* Compilation of Medical Attendance Rules, Including Lists of Admissible and Inadmissible Medicines *(With and Without Notes) (Five Copies) and Natwar's* Compendium of Rules and Regulations Regarding Office Uniforms and Office-Uniform-Related Allowances for Permanent Group C and D Employees of the Welfare State *(With Notes Only) (Ten Copies).*

Daya was delighted to learn that Agastya would officially be present at the Committee reunion. They spent the night before the meeting together in her hotel room. They hadn't met for some weeks. She played Heathcliff, he hard to get, she won, hands down and thighs up and all over his face. In the middle of the night, she ordered yoghurt and honey from Room Service while he smoked a terrific cigarette and marvelled at the latest Woman-to-Woman Rani Chandra cassette.

Out of the blue. 'August, would you like to meet Jayati—tomorrow evening, after that chaos finishes? Or whenever you shed your inertia?'

'Is it a roundabout compliment? You give good head, so I'd like to loan you out to people who matter?'

'I've already told her about your luminous intelligence—he has a good head on his shoulders, I said. After you've impressed her with it, I'll suggest to her that we open a mini-Secretariat of the Centenary in what you most appropriately and poetically call Our City, and that we post you there as Officer on Special Duty.'

'Without specifying them—the special duties. Wonderful idea, Daya. But can't you swing it without my meeting Jayati-ji? I feel nervous and small in front of greatness, as under you. Not at all like Charlton Heston when he's dragged before that sexbomb Egyptian queen—quite Jayati-like—in *The Ten Commandments*. But then I have neither his jaw nor Yul Brynner's tits.'

The next morning, TFIN Complex looked like the setting for a modern film epic. Clear sky, clean sun, trees rustling in the breeze, multicoloured flags, bunting and banners brightening up the enormous renovated courtyard, millions of cops just hanging around, dressed to kill in mufti but still looking like cops, harassed bureaucrats tensely waiting for either a heart attack or a flap, whichever was earlier, ghastly instrumental music—the sort that one suffered, sweating, on domestic flights before take-off—from the speakers hidden in the trees. The selection of the music had been a minor point of discord in the Secretariat. Minister Virbhim had wanted a piece quite solemn and epic, the sort that heralds the arrival of monarchs. It was to be played first for Jayati—but naturally—and then, as a sort of afterthought, for the Prime Minister, who'd be inaugurating the event. That—the inauguration—had been a second minor point of discord. The debate—on how best to kick-start the occasion—had revealed deep cultural differences. Minister Virbhim—naturally—had wanted a series of symbolic rites lasting close to an hour—fire, ghee, priests with tits, bells, incense, Sanskrit, dhotis, garlands, spices, more ghee, that sort of thing. Warm but primitive, had commented Dr Harihara Kapila, the recently-appointed Principal Secretary to the Prime Minister, in Hindi, as usual confounding everybody with his mind that truly functioned, simultaneously and all the time, as both razor and corkscrew. He'd won, of course, and the PM would now alight, set free a white pigeon, light one lamp before Payṇchom—miraculously untouched by the father of all fires—a second on stage and leave.

As for the music, soft, sweet if possible, Kapila'd decreed, and unobtrusive, something like a pleasant whine, like a beneficiary grovelling for more with a shehnai in his mouth—and as long as it's switched off before anyone important arrives.

The important numbered almost two hundred. Even Dr Bhatnagar, it will be recalled, with his new agenda, had become one. They'd been given special car passes of different colours and could zoom right up to the grand portals of the main lobby. The passes, like the invitation cards, were numbered, coded and strictly non-transferable—with exceptions, of course, as always in this hierarchy-sensitive system. Even a Private Secretary, for example, was known in an emergency to stand in for his Minister who couldn't make it because he had to go away—officially, of course—to the South, where he'd shaved his head and was somersaulting around the perimeter of a temple atop some hillock to appease or thank one of the gods, their calls being more peremptory than the summons of the Aflatoons. Thus one explained the presence at TFIN Complex that morning of Chanakya Lala, who drove up in a sparkling cloud of perfume and glided his way from the deep aromatic recesses of his Minister's holy-white Ambassador to his assigned seat in the tenth row like a product on a smoothly-moving assembly line, shaking hands with and namaste-ing the waiting bureaucrats who mattered and painlessly slicing through those who didn't. A gentleman to the core of his heart, which was a five-hundred-rupee note neatly wrapped around a Parisian bottle of aftershave.

Almost all the bureaucrats who didn't matter were lowly Escort Officers charged with the responsibility of conducting the members of the Centenary Committee from their cars to their seats, in case they lost their way en route. This reception was in part a warm welcome and in part a security measure insisted on by the police, who naturally didn't want to accidentally rough up a V$^{\infty}$IP, lost and found wandering around in an insecure daze in the vast labyrinthine spaces of the building, stammering before the unspeakable menace of the law, unable to explain who was what and thus being mistaken for an assassin or an arsonist or both. The happier Escort Officers, like Personal Assistant Dharam Chand, were those who recognized their charges. Dharam Chand was to lead the living legend Kum Kum Bala Mali and show her her place. His bum'd been twitching with excitement for a week just at the thought of swaying a foot ahead of the hips of the ex-actress for a full ten minutes.

He'd offered himself for Escort Officer duty and'd specifically asked that the ageing Bharatnatyam wizard—or rather, witch—be assigned to him. Now that he worked as Principal Private Secretary to Baba Mastram, he usually got what he wanted. He was still ascendant and had his eye on nestling up to Sukumaran Govardhan once his surrender was sorted out. His old friend and one-time boss, Under Secretary Dastidar, had suggested to him that since they were running short of reliable staff, could he also escort a couple of other minor headaches, Dr Bhatnagar, for example, whose office plagued him, Dastidar, four times a day to learn whom Doctor Saab should expect to find awaiting him the *instant* he alighted from his Ambassador.

The good Doctor himself had proposed Agastya, who'd parried, 'If you permit, sir, would that be in form? Seeing us together, the other bureaucrats present might construe that you and I—to quote you, sir—enjoy the same juniority.'

Thus freed, Agastya'd hoped to sit beside and savour the meeting with Daya. But that was not to be, at least not initially. She was important enough to be seated somewhere in the first ten rows, whereas to him was pointed out a corner of the twenty-seventh. He didn't much mind, having prepared for the meeting by smoking a killer joint and wearing new wraparound dark glasses to hide his consequent red eyes. 'Conjunctivitis,' he'd smile at anybody who glanced at him, pointing at his goggles, raising the pale green agenda in his left hand to establish his bonafides. Nobody gave a shit.

He didn't smoke marijuana any more before lunch, not routinely. Middle age, no doubt. That morning was special because the night before'd been remarkable, and ruminating Thinker-like on the pot at seven a.m., he'd admitted to himself that he preferred a room, a day and perhaps a life with Daya in them, so how was he going to handle this mid-life crisis? Well, smoke a joint, yes, but after that?

He was surrounded by bureaucrats discussing the latest transfers, their bosses and colleagues, Jayati Aflatoon, Sukumaran Govardhan, the budget of the Centenary and in the agenda before them, a sub-heading that at times sounded like Beyond War and at other times like Bjorn Borg. 'This figure in the second column—is it ninety-seven crores or sixty-seven crores . . .?' asked Agastya's immediate neighbour of the auditorium in general. He wore a brown safari suit and well-scrubbed tennis shoes. He began to riffle through the pages of statistics and figures with professional disdain. '. . . Either way, the numbers are all wrong—they don't add up . . . Last year's expenditure on Beyond War was Plan or Non-Plan?. . .'

'I find that the best method is to take a sip of tea the moment you get the cup, very noisily; then nobody steals your cup,' declared his colleague, seemingly in reply. He was pale, with long, slicked-back grey hair. He was using his agenda as an ashtray.

'I'm quite curious,' confessed the brown suit, 'to see how they interpret these statistics. D'you see? The details, heads and descriptions of expenditure are on the left page, whereas all the columns of figures are on the right; during printing, however, the figures've slipped one—and sometimes two—lines down.'

'Non-alignment.'

'A turdle. Do you know the word? My son taught it to

me. They use it in school quite often. It's short form for tremendous hurdle. I like it.'

A one-armed peon sidled up to Agastya and sullenly pointed out to him a commandingly beckoning Dr Bhatnagar. Tranquil, at rest, sleepily horny and stoned, Agastya didn't in the least wish to struggle up out of his chair and shuffle down to listen to and note down some utter rubbish. Which it would be, as sure as and worse than death, meant mainly to remind Dr Bhatnagar himself in a moment of stress, brought on by the presence of so many V$^{\infty}$IPs who were ignoring him, that he possessed a mind bubbling over with brilliant, viable ideas and that he, for the betterment of the world, continually needed an amanuensis or he would lose it. 'Hahn, Agastya. . .' he would say, looking at him through his nostrils and at everybody else out of the corner of his eye to note how many of them'd noticed how busy he was with affairs of State, '. . . remind me to send a fax to the Commerce Secretary repeated to Industries. . .'

Agastya instead decided to send Dr Bhatnagar a paper plane. He could write on it all the faxes that he wanted and fly it back to him. An economy measure, even though for Agastya, a doubtful career move. He opened his agenda to decide which page to use and was distracted for a while by the wide variety of choices. He finally settled on the Table of Contents but the plane never took off because while he was making it, all of a sudden, the buzz and murmur of fifteen hundred bureaucrats changed to an extended rustle and swish, like a breeze in a forest, for at the entry of the PM and his entourage, the entire auditorium rose.

The cortege was all in dazzling white. Agastya was reminded of the advertisement for Rin, the detergent that washes whitest. Jayati's white sari had a gorgeous maroon border. Clumsily, Bhanwar Virbhim led the PM and Jayati to the tall brass lamp stand at the left of the stage, where waited two nervous young women dressed in glorious, practically-bridal, silk. With the earthen lamps in their hands, they drew concurrent and symmetric circles of welcome in the air before the PM's and Jayati's heads, chests and for some reason, stomachs. With a sudden, convent-school curtesy, they then handed over the earthen lamps to the Aflatoons and hesitantly motioned them to step forward to the lamp stand.

Since all the eyes were on the stage, Agastya used the moment to steal away to the opposite side of the hall and settle down a couple of rows further back, right next to an unimportant-looking exit, to locate him where myopic Dr Bhatnagar, despite his contact lenses, was likely to take fifteen minutes. Ah, what have men not done for freedom? Or for love. He should send a note to Daya—whose perfect, tastefully-grey head he could glimpse, he was glad to note, a few rows ahead of Doctor Saab—informing her of his change of address. The unimportant-looking exit opened furtively and the Public Works Secretary, criminally late and therefore flustered, and not as marvellously coiffured as usual, slipped in and dived, virtually in one movement, like a soldier hitting the ground, into the seat beside Agastya; clearly, the stares of the auditorium were to be avoided like shrapnel.

In Agastya's lingo, a deep-shitter was a person wallowing in it. Recognizing a mega-example in the Public Works Secretary, he smiled at the senior bureaucrat's profile and to make him feel better, took off his own dark glasses. The Secretary continued to vigorously chew gum till he relaxed a bit in his chair, then, without glancing at Agastya, asked, 'We haven't obviously reached Item Number Two on the agenda. Has anybody said anything so far?'

'Not from the stage, sir.' Agastya consulted the Table of Contents. Ah, Item Two was the vexed question of the placement of the statue of Gajapati Aflatoon in the Arabian Sea. He regarded Deep-Shitter's profile with a little more interest. If what he'd done to the file of the statue was any measure, Agastya was in the presence of a bowler of world-class googlies.

For the last decade or so, certainly as long as he'd been in service, the Russians'd been wanting to gift the Welfare State a hundred-metre-high granite statue of Gajapati Aflatoon which they both—the Russians and some of the living Aflatoons—wanted set in the bay just off Bhayankar. When last estimated, the operation was to have cost twenty-four crores. Agastya'd seen photographs of a model of the statue; it'd remarkably improved the original. More hair on the head, an intelligent, handsome expression, terrific shoulders and pectorals under the shawl, right arm raised in paternal benediction—and it had still resembled Gajapati! Great art, except that Public Works—not being confident enough of not fucking it up—simply didn't wish to be saddled with the headache. Permissions from Environment, Defence, External Affairs, Home and Petroleum were sought, the last because it'd nothing to do with the subject and would therefore take the longest to reply, since the file would tour each Department and Section of its Ministry, relayed by one to the other with the terse note: *Not ours. Yours perhaps?* Clearing—and overriding—all those turdles took six years. (External Affairs, for example, had battled as heroically as Porus against Alexander: *This Ministry will agree to this project only if the Russians allow us to gift them in exchange a statue of comparable dimensions, sculpted by one of our best artists, of Lenin or Stalin, that would enjoy pride of place amidst the ships of one of their warm-water ports.)* The Prime Minister's Office and the Cabinet Secretariat then began to lean on Public Works, the only one of the Ministries that hadn't—officially—definitively replied. They both wanted the statue to be in place and inaugurated in the centenary year.

It was then that the Secretary had asked:

> *Is the statue to face the sea* (in a confidential minute in the file) *or the shore? If the sea, we'd be symbolically*

declaring that Pundit Gajapati Aflatoon has turned his back on us. If the shore, are we not in danger of offending our neighbours across the seas by a permanent, grossly material, display of the rear of the Founding Father of the Welfare State? Public Works is not to be held responsible for the international repercussions of this subject.
Secondly: The bay at Bhayankar is one of the prettiest in the country, but its waters have helped the inhabitants of the world's largest slum in their morning ablutions for generations. A view will have to be taken on whether we wish the statue of Pundit Aflatoon to preside every day, till the end of the world, over a million squatting figures and indeed, whether we wish its granite to be washed forever by—well—rather polluted waters.
It is suggested that the entire subject of the statue be placed before the Centenary Committee at its next meeting and a collective decision taken.

The dozen V∞IPs had settled down on their assigned chairs on the stage and Minister Virbhim had placed himself before the state-of-the-art microphone, which was on when he loudly cleared his throat before beginning his welcome address. The impressively-magnified hawking that boomed in the hall—and that sounded like a thousand throats doing their thing in the early morning, in unison, before the sinks of some railway platform loo—served to completely unwind, amongst others, the Public Works Secretary. 'The first sounds from the stage, sir,' annotated Agastya helpfully. His neighbour chuckled and nearly gagged on his chewing gum, which he then took out of his mouth. Agastya noted with interest that it wasn't chewing gum at all but a long, very curly, black, much chewed, nice and wet strand of what was definitely pubic hair. He observed the Secretary's face change and soften with the memory of a recent pleasure as he examined, played with, wound round his fingers, turned over and over, and squeezed for the feel of its wetness the strand before returning it to his mouth, lovingly and carefully, like a gem being re-imprisoned in its safe. Agastya was impressed. This is true passion, honey, he told himself as he watched the Secretary's flaccid jaws begin again their masculation, but this time more rhythmically and contentedly, slowly. Inspired, he decided to write to Daya at once.

I'm here in Seat 2901. Time is running out. Will you marry me? Please?

He folded the sheet of paper twice, wrote her name atop it, changed his mind about the name, scratched it out till it became an illegible mess, waited for the ink to dry, manfully summoned the one-armed peon with a low but carrying *pssk*, explained where Daya was sitting, gave him the note and asked him to hand it to her. The peon hinted at a nod; his half-shut eyes and unshaven, sullen face discouraged all but the essential communication. Agastya watched him go with the tenderness of a father bidding farewell to a son boarding a train or ship to embark on a new life. The die is cast. I'm in your hands, Daya. Be kind to me. Immobilized by a mess of emotions, he observed the peon drift all the way down to Dr Bhatnagar, pass him the note, half-raise his arm to point in Agastya's direction and amble off to lean against a wall from where he could mindlessly gaze at Jayati Aflatoon.

Who rose from her chair in respect as the PM got up to walk over to the microphone to say, to quote Minister Virbhim, 'a few sweet and wise words'. Agastya rose too, to sidle out of the auditorium, wander down, shell-shocked, to the car park, locate the office car, lean against it, roll and smoke another joint, feel better, ramble off to find the driver, run him down finally at the tea stall outside Gate Fourteen, muttering and playing cards, sweet-talk him back to work, be driven off home to pick up his trunks, then to the pool at the Royal Eastern Hotel for an hour's frenzied and graceless, juggernaut-like, tidal-wave-displacing mimicry of the butterfly and the front crawl. When he returned to TFIN Complex, well in time for pre-lunch snacks, things looked better. Dr Bhatnagar and the PM had disappeared, Jayati looked tired, harassed and more attractive, Daya was clearly visible in the seventh row and a new set of more interesting personages—Baba Mastram and the cadaverous, almost-legendary Dr Kansal recognizable among them—had replaced on the stage the old lot. The atmosphere was more relaxed, more governmental, almost chaotic; delegates drifted about apparently without purpose, officials signalled responses to one another across rows, junior bureaucrats huddled in urgent conference in corners. Agastya noticed quite a few vacant chairs—two fortunately on either side of Daya, towards whom he headed with winged feet.

'Where on earth've you been? Your hair's wet and your eyes maroon.' She looked irritable and tense. Without waiting for a response, she continued, 'I'm fed up. Somebody—you, for one, instead of smoking dope and whining about gas in your tummy—could've warned me against how your meetings are run. Poor Jayati's aged dramatically in the last two hours, like a creature out of myth that makes the mistake of coming down to earth. And I'm amazed—why're they serving *food* to fifteen hundred people? I mean, is this a religious feast or the reunion of a committee?'

'I say—what're they serving? Where's your plate?'

'I sent it away, naturally. But don't panic. The bearers'll return, in these ghastly, frayed, off-white, khadi uniforms to show off their victory-tower red turbans.'

Scattered clapping from the bottom right corner of the auditorium distracted Agastya from his intention of settling down to wait for the waiters. Amidst the applauding hands stood the unsmiling speaker, much like a lighthouse amongst circling seagulls. The group was pro- or anti-PM, Agastya'd forgotten which, a set of powerless but noisy parliamentarians and members of various regional assemblies that had slimed its way into the Centenary Committee by sucking up to he'd forgotten whom—Baba Mastram, probably.

'Secondly,' continued the speaker, reading in perfectly-official Hindi, shuffling the papers in his left hand about, 'it is proposed that an extremely popular and as-yet-unnamed road in Lutyens's City be named after Rajani Suroor. I speak of the alley behind the houses on Ganapati Aflatoon Marg, in which reside, among those present here, Honourable Minister Virbhim, Honourable Madam Kum Kum Bala Mali, Honourable Dr Kansal and, when he's in the capital, Honourable Parliamentarian Bhootnath Gaitonde. On that alley—the honourable members mentioned will bear me out—stand a handful of eating houses that were once upon a time the servants' quarters of Lutyens's mansions. These dhabas are illegal, cheap and extremely popular with the less privileged population of the area. Their postal address unfortunately continues to be *Service Lane No 6/North/A/behind GAM*. Nobody here will deny that we all enjoy a fundamental right to a better address. How better to honour the memory of Gajapati Aflatoon than to improve the quality of life in the area around the street named after his elder brother, to make it—the area itself—*sound* better, and then to regularize, to make secure, the lives and vocations of those of our fellow citizens who inhabit that narrow alley, who provide necessary and cheap nourishment to the residents of the area and who are still officially described as "illegal occupants practising an illicit trade"? I therefore propose that the Centenary Committee immediately resolve that *Service Lane No 6/North/A/behind GAM* be renamed Shahid Rajani Suroor Marg.'

Makhmal Bagai paused for the clapping of his myrmidons to subside. 'I take this opportunity to respond to the doubt expressed earlier this morning about the propriety of discussing the institution of some memorials for a martyr who hasn't actually passed away but is merely in the process of doing so.

I'm not surprised at this revelation of a national trait, a cultural characteristic that prefers procrastination to action, and that achieves fulfilment not in deeds done today but in fine-tuning its skills of postponement. "Whatever cannot wait even a moment will unfortunately have to be looked at tomorrow; push the rest into the agenda for next month." Before these brakes on the nation's progress, I plead: let us honour Martyr Rajani Suroor by being ready for him. If he finally decides to stop breathing, how embarrassing it'll be if we *then* assemble to collectively wonder how best to honour his memory! On that occasion, when the nation whips around to ask of us, "Whatever have you all been *doing* these past few months?" we, hanging our heads in shame—and noticing how our paunches hide from view our dirty toenails—will have nothing to say. On the other hand, were Shahid Suroor suddenly to wake up, this Committee would welcome him with open arms and, with tears of joy, as it were, request him to be Chief Guest at the functions that'll open to the public these memorials.

'For we propose—naturally—more than one course of action in remembrance of a multi-faceted, many-dimensional man who was, fortunately, a bachelor. Had he been married, in keeping with the great traditions of our country, his widow would've been rewarded with a fat sum of money. It is submitted to the Centenary Committee that that amount of compensation—whatever it might be, whether symbolic or respectable, and keeping in mind these hard times, anything symbolic'd be a disgrace—be awarded at once to Vyatha, Shahid Suroor's theatre group, that was to him—if one judges by the passion that he felt for it—parent, wife, second wife, child, in-law, neighbour and keep all rolled into one.

'It is understood that the artistic community of the nation has proposed a major cultural happening on the fourth of December, the first anniversary of Shahid Suroor's departure from the conscious life of the country. Our group of young, forward-looking Parliamentarians and elected members of other assemblies strongly supports the event, no matter what the cost. Painters, writers, sculptors, singers, musicians, actors, directors, graphic designers, photographers, poets and other artistically-inclined souls have been invited, by the clarion call of art against politics, to the Pashupati Aflatoon Public Gardens where, from 4.46 in the morning onwards—a time auspicious for starting an invocation to the heavens, suggest the finest astrological minds of our time—they will pray, through the practice of their different arts, for the speedy and complete recovery of Shahid Suroor. That is to say—if the nitty-gritty of the happening is not yet clear to those who perhaps haven't been paying attention—in different parts of the Gardens, all day on the fourth of December, till 7.13 in the evening, when the propitious hours end, singers will sing, painters paint, poets write, sculptors chip away, photographers click, potters—uh—potter about—pot—and gardeners water the lawns. Each act is holy when its impulse springs from the bottom of the cleansed heart.

'This political group urges the Centenary Committee that it be allowed to participate in the happening for Shahid Suroor. We will orate. Politics is the heartbeat both of the nation and of the martyr in question. As an activist, he was unparalleled as a provocateur, as anybody who's watched his plays will know. It has even been suggested that it was their subject matter—and his rejection of the suggestion made by the prominent members of a certain caste in my native place of Madna that they be allowed to participate in his productions—that offended and provoked them into arranging to teach him a lesson in the realities of castepolitik. Whatever be the truth of that theory—it'll of course be improper to anticipate the findings of the Enquiry Commission in this regard—it is a fundamental principle that the repressed castes must not be denied their right to self-expression in any happening, cultural, political, economic, religious or social.

When you suppress their voice, you send the wrong signals both to Heaven and their constituencies—an axiom with which Honourable Dr Kansal up on the stage will agree, naturally. In fact, I should frankly add here that if we aren't permitted to join the anniversary celebrations, we'll consider it to be an insult to the social interests and castes that we represent and—rest assured—we'll respond with appropriate measures. I pause merely to ask Honourable Dr Kansal whether he wishes to comment at this point.'

Reluctantly, Dr Kansal rose from his chair. He was tall and looked taller because he was terribly thin, loose-limbed, with flapping arms and legs in a flapping safari suit. His walk to the microphone was almost directionless, as though, endowed with independent lives, his feet, knees, forearms and elbows wished to shrug off his will and wander off on their own. He was fumbling in his various pockets for inspiration when the collective attention of the bottom right section of the auditorium swivelled to the nearest door to welcome the new batch of snack-laden waiters that entered just at that point. A low, extended rumble of approval moved like a wave across the rows, a growl in the belly of some enormous dormant beast, obliterating from the air any hint of pleasure at—or any thought of—waiting for the wisdom of Dr Kansal. '*Pssst!*' '*Pssst!*' hissed out like the tongues of a hundred snakes from the agitated occupants of various seats nearest the door, commanding the burdened waiters to pivot uncertainly—as a Bharatnatyam danseuse does to convey indecision—not sure whose greed to satisfy first; greed and not hunger, because they'd already served the hissers once in their earlier round, when too they'd intended to begin with the central section of the auditorium and move back in successive trips towards the exit, but had been gobbled up at the start by the wolves at the door, these sea monsters that waited for Odyssean ships.

'Honourable Madam Chairperson, Honourable Minister

Virbhim . . .' started Honourable Dr Kansal in his deep and lethally slow voice, mind milky with fog, till that moment undecided what to say, but tranquilly confident that when he gave his voice the long rope, as he gave his limbs, it would deliver, and the words of wisdom emerge, all in proper order. '. . . Culture has always needed the patronage of kings . . .' The '*psssts!*' '*Hey yous!*' '*Paynchos!*' '*C'meres!*' '*Hurry ups!*' and '*Let them pass, paynchos!*' that'd now begun to pop, like toy pistols aimed at the waiters from different parts of the auditorium, didn't faze him in the least. He *liked* confusion. He'd spent almost forty years in churning his passage of personal advancement through it, freshening and heaping it up in his wake. He pleasantly sensed—though one couldn't be sure—that these excited, peremptory orders being hissed and shouted by his audience were directed not at him but at the bearers, whom he was certain he knew closely as types, even though they barely existed for him as individuals. The decades that he'd spent studying—amongst hundreds of others—their castes and classes, their economic ascent, their lateral movements from village to town to megalopolis, the erosion under pressure of their caste preoccupations—those years'd developed in him an attitude towards his subject matter much like that of a feudal lord towards his lowliest subjects—of contemptuous, affectionate, intimate, paternal and parasitical disdain. Nothing that they could do would ever surprise him; when it did, the act'd be ignored till it was twisted and squeezed to fit theory. '. . .In our time, a painter has as much need of the clout of a Minister as of his brushes and oils . . . Hierarchy is fundamental to our system and even in the Welfare State, it's no surprise that the unimportant are cut dead and trodden over in the race for power and privilege . . .'

Practically supine in the chair alongside Daya, gorging on madly-spicy samosas, cashew nuts and Parle Monaco biscuits, dripping tomato sauce onto the makeshift tray of the open agenda on his chest, about to suggest marriage as soon as he finished eating and the mood of the object of his desire became more receptive to a proposal, Agastya realized, with stoned surprise, that he really didn't want to be anywhere else. For one, the civil war around him was extremely interesting because it was a bitter struggle over fundamentals—namely, over food in a developing country—fought, as in a model case study, under the uncaring eyes of a self-serving elite; he himself'd gained his share by simply marching down to the nearest waiter and snatching two plates off his shoulder, pointing out to himself in the process that he too was merely enacting a basic economic and social law, as it were: however could a member of the Steel Frame become a have-not?

For another, trying to follow Dr Kansal's chain of thought was sure to be intellectually stimulating, like trailing a charged electron as it bounced off the knotty matter of Rajani Suroor, collided with the complexities of caste reservations in the various spheres of government and touched, en passant, the ostensible subject of the meeting—Gajapati Aflatoon and what to do with him. As far as Agastya could sense—and tell from past experience—the last hadn't been discussed at all in the first couple of hours of the day. It wasn't really meant to be; the point was not to exchange views and reach conclusions but to assemble the whole world, like a show of strength, and to allow whoever wanted to, to hold forth on whatever interested him, constrained only by the condition that he should, every now and then, like Formula One cars grazing one another on the track, touch the theme of the centenary. At the end of the day, everyone felt drained and fulfilled, as at the close of a rigorous session of scream therapy, and the implementers got on with whatever they'd decided on beforehand with the figureheads on stage.

Agastya didn't much like an agenda with dollops of sauce on some of its pages. It looked frivolous. He therefore flattened and placed his empty paper plate between the Section on the Archaeological Survey and the Statistics of the Southern States on Expenditure on the Disappearing Performing Arts in the Last Five Years, shut the book with a magisterial hand and exchanged it with its duplicate on the seat two places away, well in time before its possessor triumphantly returned with *his* second plate of snacks.

Magically, abruptly, leaving the very few in the auditorium who'd been listening a little bewildered, Dr Kansal finished and flapped his way back to his chair. Long before the Master of Ceremonies could invite the next speaker up to the stage, and well before Makhmal Bagai could finish stuffing samosas into his mouth and start up all over again, Member of Parliament Bhootnath Gaitonde had reached one of the standing microphones that dotted—more accurately, exclamation-marked—the auditorium.

'Honourable Madam Chairperson, honourable ladies and gentlemen, colleagues, friends,' began he in sonorous Hindi, his fluency in which—it not being his mother tongue—he was quite proud of, 'I'm *not* the next speaker on the agenda. However, even if you don't permit, I *will* present my views from here, this insignificant spot in the auditorium, from amongst the audience—the people, if you wish—for this is where I belong. You would have noticed of course that I haven't bothered either to register with the Committee for an official turn at the mike or to wait for Honourable Shri Makhmal Bagai to finish eating and speaking. The reason is that I simply did not want to waste any more of one of our most precious resources—namely, time.'

With a kind of relaxed, collective sigh, the auditorium settled down to switch off and listen to him. It was both impossible and explosive to attempt to throttle the representatives of the people. They yelled like dementedly-harassed parents at their children if you tried. They scared even the officialdom of the Welfare State—its toughest birds too—the cops, the Income Tax people, Customs. Over the years, Bhootnath Gaitonde in particular had developed a reputation for being one of the fiercest Parliamentarians, a trailblazer, a pathfinder for the protection of their human rights. It was he, for example, who'd institutionalized the practice, sporadically isolated before him, of screaming at any policeman at any airport who, before any domestic flight, dared to frisk his person or his baggage. The argument at the core of his shrieks and threats, naturally, was the grave insult to, the questioning of, the integrity of the people as represented by his khadi-covered belly and his bags.

He was neither a member of the Centenary Committee nor a Special Invitee. Being an elected representative of the people, he was an Official Gatecrasher. They couldn't be stopped. All hell would break loose if they were. Ditto if they weren't. 'On the subject of the proposed wastage by this body of a second precious resource, namely, money, I made clear my views in Parliament a couple of months ago and I won't repeat myself here. Continually keeping in mind the importance of time, I'll therefore restrict myself only to Item Number Two on our agenda, which—I'm ashamed to add—we haven't yet reached even after two-and-a-half hours of debate. The item concerns the installation, at a cost of twenty-four crores, of a Russian statue of Gajapati Aflatoon in the Bay of Bhayankar. Some of you might know that I've my roots there, in Bhayankar. I was born there—and even after I left it to pursue my calling, I've always reserved a special place in my heart for the world's largest slum. It—my heart—has followed with particular interest, over the years, the growth and development, the ups and downs, of my birthplace. It bled, it stopped beating, in 1980 during the communal and caste riots of March there. Do I need to remind my audience of the carnage of Bhayankar? Evidently, yes. Four thousand dead, a few hundred drowned, thousands of children orphaned, thousands more dislocated, crores of rupees of goods and property destroyed—and more than a decade after our very own holocaust, the rate of progress of our rehabilitation programme is almost as horrifying as the original event.

'Do I exaggerate? Is this the right forum where one should raise such issues? Should cultural events be held completely independent of the realities of the time? Must the show go on like a house on fire principally to mirror the conflagration in the audience? I leave your consciences to decide these questions after I read out to you from one of the First Information Reports reluctantly recorded at Bhayankar Naka Police station during those two weeks of 1980. Reluctantly, of course, because the police, as always, were deep in the midst of the riots, churning up as much as calming down.'

Gaitonde paused for effect. He scanned the pages in his hand, pretended to find what he was looking for and continued. 'Just to take an example, the case of Ballibaran, auto-rickshaw driver . . . On March 17, in the afternoon, his vehicle was set on fire, then his hut . . . He rushed out to face the mob—which included policemen, allege witnesses—and with folded hands begged the crowd to spare his family since it was totally innocent of the savage attack the previous evening on the row of huts in the lane behind his . . . the mob hacked off his folded hands, which fell down; it then attacked with iron rods. The family, including the four children between the ages of six and fourteen, was beaten almost to death. When they were all in a coma, they were piled one atop another, doused with kerosene and set alight. The twenty-four persons named in the report danced around the bonfire, gaily spraying the flames with kerosene, chanting slogans to the tune of popular film songs.

'Multiply the example of Ballibaran by seven thousand, spread them over fourteen days and nights, add mothers and children being waylaid and beheaded while trying to escape under cover of night, and decapitated heads being left at doorsteps, and friendly messages in human blood on the walls—and you've a rough idea of what Bhayankar was like that fortnight.

'The horror hasn't stopped. It's merely eased itself up, toned itself down . . . because today, after all these years, it is true that many of the criminals of 1980 have been brought to book and its victims compensated and rehabilitated, but it's even more true—you all know as well as me—that in neither group have we picked the right men and women. Neither the real villains nor the actual relatives of the dead, the actually traumatized, wounded or dishoused. I reveal nothing new: 1980 wasn't the first time that the officials of the Welfare State, out of incompetence or for a consideration, forged entire lists of beneficiaries, inhabitants and voters. A whole new Department has grown up—prospered—around the riots. One Section deals with criminal cases, another with fraudulent criminal cases, a third with Compensation to Riot Victims, a fourth with Proof of Original Rights of Residence, a fifth with Rehabilitation, a sixth with Verification of Lost Assets—and so on. As I said, the horror continues for, say, the illiterate grandmother who witnessed her sons and grandchildren being butchered to death and is now being asked to prove it.

'But whatever has all this—the villainy and the blood—to do with Gajapati Aflatoon? Indeed. But whatever has Gajapati Aflatoon to do with Rajani Suroor? How can you blame me for feeling confused? Am I at the moment addressing the Gajapati Aflatoon Centenary Committee or the happening for Rajani Suroor? And Sukumaran Govardhan? Will he join the select members on stage before or after lunch? After all, they are some of his best friends. Has his official surrender been delayed only because he backed the wrong horse? We all remember that when questioned on the subject of the series of artificial forest fires engineered by Govardhan last month, the Honourable PM had remarked, "We need to implement our firefighting measures on a war footing." Exactly what would that statement imply for the dacoit's political future?

'However, much as though I'd like to pause for some clarifications, I won't because I don't—you'll recall—wish to waste any more time.

'My suggestions therefore to the Centenary Committee. One: forget Rajani Suroor. Learn from his case, but leave him alone. What happened to him makes clear for the millionth time that the Welfare State can never adequately protect its citizens and that, as often as not, whether it be the riots of 1980 or the sad event of the not-as-yet-martyred Suroor, one could argue that it is the State itself, in the shape of its police force or political leaders, that is the aggressor . . . Let Suroor be. He needs no memorials, not yet. Don't forget that he was encouraged by his Prime Minister-friend to become a part-time civil servant and that they, amongst all the creatures on this planet, have the most finely-honed survival instinct.

'My second suggestion: forget the Aflatoons, past and present. The past members of the family were impressive, but they're dead. The present Aflatoons are pretty fossils. Concentrate instead on the needy, the bereaved and the dispossessed; become their voice if they'll accept you. Cultural extravaganzas are meaningless and wasteful and in an officially-poor country, at times like these, when there's more important work waiting elsewhere—they're sinful too. I—'

The protests and expostulations from different parts of the auditorium that'd begun with Gaitonde's mention, in the same breath, of Govardhan and the Aflatoons had now swelled into full-throated whoops, roars and howled exclamations into other microphones. Alarmed, Daya involuntarily cursed under her breath and Agastya watched, sleepily distant, as a handful of agitated members charged up to Gaitonde from the bottom left of the hall, waving their fists and yelling, not—it may be presumed—to ask him the time. Uh-oh, thought Agastya, meeting adjourned till lunch. Time to send that paper plane to Dr Bhatnagar and maybe take wing myself.

OUT OF THE WAY

They had been advised to wear suits after sundown, and sunglasses and their name tags at all times. 'Had we been better-looking and less fidgety,' the Maltese had commented in English to the few who claimed to speak it, 'we could've made a living in a YSL shop window somewhere in the sixième.' For a variety of reasons, none of his audience had laughed.

Every half a minute, as they tumbled, took a header, came a cropper and bit the dust, their name tags flashed like brooches in the hard clean light of the sun. Winded, stunned, flat on their backs in their bright, kindergarten-coloured gear that had cost them a quarter of their monthly stipend, they gazed up into a flawless, deep blue sky, felt grateful for their sunglasses and pined to be immediately transported elsewhere, to a less perfect, warmer, more human climate where one walked, or better still, was driven about in a car. For those of them who declined to stand again on their own two feet till the instructor drew up to prod them with his barks of encouragement, the skyline was spectacular. The chocolate-and-white undulations of the Hautes-Alpes, with their patches of dour, dry pines and their unbearably-white ski slopes, encircled them like gigantic cakes around a group of gaily-coloured ants. The spotless blue of the sky was completed by the immaculate white of the snow; together, with their newfangled shoes, outfits and daily routines, nature itself made them feel clumsy, a bit silly and out of place. Snow was neither their element nor, as it were, their scene.

Fifty-two of them had travelled together by train and autobus across six hundred kilometres to arrive, disoriented, cold and apprehensive, at Puy-St-Etienne on Monday morning. The more conscientious among them had worn their suits for the journey—partly, perhaps, to prevent them from becoming all crumpled up in their suitcases and grips, but more certainly because they wished to impress their Madam Director who headed the team that was shepherding them. She was a formidable personality, articulate, intelligent, not easily impressed. That was why their dear colleague from the African Democratic Republic of Begon had put on a tuxedo and a scarlet silk bowtie for the occasion. But not everybody sought Madame Europe Olympia Grosse-Reynard out. Some of them, in fact, couldn't emit a sound in front of her. They became tongue-tied, as most would when face to face with an arsehole.

She reminded them, four to five times a week, not to forget that they all received fellowships—subsistence allowances, really—from the European Union. She implied, naturally, though she was too well-bred to explicitly say so, that they therefore, while in Europe, were expected to comport themselves like Europeans. Be punctual, for example. Nine-thirty meant nine twenty-nine and not nine thirty-five. Agastya, for whom, after eight years in the Welfare State, nine-thirty meant between ten-ten and ten-forty, had found the initial weeks under Madame Director quite tense-making. In a well-bred way, she'd made it clear to him that if he wasn't punctual, she'd arrange to cancel his scholarship. Truly, it takes a bitch to shepherd black, thick-skinned sheep.

Agastya had almost skiied once before, as a teenager, in Gulmarg and hadn't much liked it. Too alien, too cold. The little that he remembered from his previous experience of it had urged him to choose, on their first morning at Puy-St-Etienne, cross-country over Alpine. He'd thus earned the joshing contempt of the Head Instructor who, in his other avatar, was a Professor of Sport in Paris. Whatever that title might secondarily imply, it primarily seemed to mean a man bronzed for all seasons, square-jawed, laser-eyed with the men and all-a-twinkle with the chicks.

'You don't feel adventurous enough, Monsieur, for some Alpine skiing?'

'Yes, exactly that, you're so correct, Monsieur, thank you,' replied Agastya in his ghastly French. In the eight weeks that he'd spent in Europe, he couldn't remember laughing or smiling even once, so heavily had his exile weighed him down. Because of the circumstances of his departure from his country, he missed Gandhan, Madna, Nirmalgaon—virtually each one of the eight small, hot, messy places that he'd been posted in. Phoning home and chatting with one's near and dear ones was not at all the same thing. For one, phonecalls were expensive in Europe; for another, one had to pay. In none of the four centres of their training programme—Brussels, Luxembourg, Strasbourg, Paris—did they have access to an office phone. Naturally. He'd had to relearn that in the more efficient part of the planet, the State made the ordinary, unprivileged user pay for everything—the loos on the pavement, the photocopier in the library, the coffee during coffee break.

In Europe, he hadn't laughed even once, not *really* laughed, not in the way that he used to back home, above all in Madna, most of all on the phone with Dhrubo, for minutes on end, silently, stomach heaving like an earthquake, crimson in the face, tears streaming down his cheeks, helpless in the grip of Nutsyanyaya. Those calls had almost always been occasioned by matters of official interest and had therefore—but naturally—been official. 'Chidambaram, get me Mr Dastidar, Under Secretary for Demotic Drama, Aflatoon Bhavan.' 'Chidambaram, get me Deputy Chairman, Barren Lands and Disputed Territories Development Corporation.'

That sort of thing.

'Is that you, fucker?' Agastya would ask to establish identity because quite often, it wasn't, but Dhrubo's PAs didn't seem to mind being mistaken for their boss. When at last he'd get him on the line, Agastya, without saying another word, would collapse, like a marathon man who reaches the finishing tape only a step, a breath away from his breaking point. Virtually on cue, just the idea, the image, of Agastya hysterically and soundlessly guffawing away at the other end would trigger Dhrubo off too. For a couple of minutes, any phone-tapper would've picked up nothing save their harsh, periodic intakes of breath and extended, rasp-like exhalations—almost like two members of an obscene-caller club practising their heavy breathing tricks on each other. Just a couple of middle-level civil servants unwinding, having a laugh at government expense. When one began to flag, the other would incite him to continue by reminding him, with a few key words, of some past instance of Nutsyanyaya that had cracked them up. Or one would have a new illustration to share.

Agastya to Dhrubo, for example: 'I've just received a fax from Bhanwar Virbhim's office. May I share it with you? . . . *Enclosed pleased to find Honourable Minister's tour programme for constituency*. Of course, you know that the telegraphic style, the elimination of articles and grammatical rules in general, is an old economy measure. *On 7th instant, Minister desires evening of interfacing with cultural luminaries of Madna, followed by night halt at Circuit House.* I've ordered RDC in writing to round up the cultural luminaries of Madna. Never at a loss, quick as thought, he's come up with A.C. Raichur. I think I'm going to fax back: *All arrangements tied up, including Shri Raichur to the bedpost of the double bed in the master bedroom of the Circuit House, in the raw, with an empty bottle of massage oil over his willy and a full one upright in his left palm, raring to go at Honourable Minister's flaccid, trembling calves. Permission sought to add the cost of the new, wonder-working liquid to the overall expenses of the Ministerial visit under the Given Head of Promotion of Non-Conventional Systems of Therapy in Less-Privileged Areas. . .'*

In Europe, Agastya usually felt too blue to simply step into a phone booth and dial Dhrubo. Everything was efficient, formal, cold and different. One got through immediately, for one thing—quite disconcerting; it left one no time to figure out what one had to say. Then the delay between saying something and hearing a response was impersonalizing and off-putting; instead of participating in a dialogue, one became an auditor of banal phrases recorded in two different voices and played back alternately, off-key and off-cue. So he sent faxes and letters instead, randomly detailing the First-World face of Nutsyanyaya, the omnipresence of which didn't surprise him in the least. Its evidence in fact provided ideal material for picture postcards filled out during a seminar.

We're in the thick of a one-week gabfest on The Optimalization of Human Resources in the Public Sector, nine-to-five every day, of course. Each one of the other participants wears a suit and takes notes with the help of a footruler, a pencil and ballpoints of four different colours. I've spied on my neighbours and learnt that the blue's for the actual stuff, the paragraphs of immortal prose, the green for date and major headings, black for minor headings, and almost everything to be underlined in red with footruler. The pencil is for afterthoughts in the margins. When I shut my eyes, which is often, I hear, beneath the lecturer's voice, the continuous clatter of ballpoints of one colour being dropped on the table in favour of another. When I open them, I'm likely to see one of my colleagues in a suit, in the corner, over the wastepaper basket, with his back to us. It looks as though he's taking a leak but no, he's merely sharpening his pencil—lead pencil, I should clarify, lest you, harking back to the euphemisms of school, suspect something kinkier. Our ages, I should add to give you perspective, vary from thirtyish to that of the E.T. from one of the Francophone Indian Ocean states, who let drop, early in our acquaintance, that he's an ex-Minister. To redress the balance, the less said of what they *think of* me, *the better . . .'*

As a general principle, Personnel tries and packs off abroad, on one training programme or another, at least once in their careers, each member of the Steel Frame. Only a couple of the dozens of available courses are in French, the rest, naturally, being in English. The general principle is rather sound—a break from the grind for the poor sod, exposure, widening of horizons (Hull in the UK), a chance to see the world (Luxembourg, Cardiff, Adelaide), a fulfilment of a clause in some triennial Exchange Programme and the consequent achievement of an annual target for some Ministry, sometimes a smooth exit from the scene for some unsavoury types and on occasion, an award of a paid holiday for a faithful subordinate. Agastya fell into none of the above categories. His foreign training had been a pre-marriage incentive from Dr Kapila. He thus became one of the two civil servants that Personnel had unearthed that year whose cvs proclaimed them to be fluent in French. Their controlling governments recommended them for all courses in glowing terms and pushed with unexpected focus for their departures.

The Institute officials though were neither impressed with his French nor his reasons for being there. 'In your original application form, Monsieur Sen, you'd written nothing in the column marked *Expectations from the Course.* By now, I'm sure that you're clearer about what they are?'

Agastya mouthed some appropriate drivel in reply. He too was too well-bred, of course, to say the truth, namely, that his government had sent him off to Europe for two good economic reasons: one, that it would spend nothing in conveying him there and two, that it wouldn't fork out even a rupee on his upkeep during those twelve weeks. Ditto for his dear colleagues, the rest of the cream of the Third World. If he'd understood correctly, the Institute spent the equivalent of some five hundred thousand French francs per dear colleague per course. A jacket, a tie, punctuality and a willingness to play the game weren't much to ask for in return.

There were times, though, when he found their demands—and the games that they were made to play—just a bit trying. The entire group, for instance, spent the month of January pretending to be the United Nations. The Institute paid a Professor in International Administration and Geopolitics from somewhere in Europe the equivalent of twenty thousand French francs to guide the dear colleagues through their paces. As a first step, he gave each of them three hundred photocopied pages of UN Resolutions to read. As a second, he asked them to pick a country out of his hat, become its permanent representative in the Institute's auditorium for four weeks, nine-to-five, and prepare a twenty-page file on it within a fortnight.

He was bald, save for two silvery tufts that rose like Cupid's wings above his ears, short, fat, with a splendid patrician nose. In his introductory remarks, he claimed that in the course of the past fifteen years, by means of that game that he'd invented, he'd revealed the fundamentals of the techniques of international negotiation and corridor diplomacy to a wide variety of target groups—students, probationary officers, middle-level civil servants and members of the diplomatic corps. All the dear colleagues felt that it was extremely nice of the Professor to have brought along with him about a hundred students from his university, a wonderfully-high percentage of whom were blonde or brunette, long-legged, tight-jeaned, rosy-cheeked, gum-chewing, cigarette-smoking and exhilarating girls. They were needed to flesh out the UN. All at once, January began to look a damn sight better.

Out of the Professor's hat, Agastya picked Russia. To create his file, he polished his black leather shoes and asked his dear colleague from Georgia what 'Let's git the hell outta here' sounded like in Russian. During the first formal session, after one of the Professor's male students, an enthusiastic jerk, Ireland, had been elected President of the Conference, Agastya suddenly took off his shoe, repeatedly banged the table before him with it, delivered his few words of Russian into the mike, added 'Payṇcho' as an afterthought prompted by nationalistic fervour, put on his shoe and, while the lot on the stage was reminding the honourable delegate from Russia that as per Article 27 of the Joint Declaration of the Four Sub-Commissions, the official language of the present UN Conference was French and French alone, left the auditorium, free as a bird for the day.

For two days, because on the third, he was up against Madame Europe Olympia in her posh office. Being intelligent, she first admired his take-off on Khrushchev and then firmly stated that it simply would not do. 'You perhaps aren't aware, Monsieur Sen, that over the years, your country's record, its performance, at the Institute has been abysmal. This year, for example, you began with two of you here, but one returned home within a fortnight—even though your government had specifically signed an assurance confirming that both of you would be available for the full twelve weeks. Well. Now there rests just you. Truly, the less said about you, the better, even though I've much to say on that score. Your attitude is rather similar to that of your predecessors. There's nothing that a course in Europe can teach us. We're untrainable, in short.'

'Ha-ha, that's very witty, Madame, if you permit . . . thank you . . . May I hold forth for a while, Madame, if you permit? . . . thank you . . . It is true what you say, we simply can't be trained. We are as seasoned and hardened as criminals, if you wish. In my world, no one makes it because of the diploma that he's picked up from somewhere fancy. Please don't get me wrong. It's wonderful to spend these months in Europe—particularly Paris—and be paid for it. But as for going back home a changed, more capable, administrator—as Mahatma Gandhi told Jinnah at Bandung in 1944, "In-service training is a science that provides gainful employment to in-service trainers." It—the training, that is—is simple hard, common sense blended in a mixie with some Management jargon, some boxes, arrows, arcs and circles on charts and transparencies with not more than four magnified words per frame. May I digress here, Madame, if you permit, to include an anecdote? . . . thank you.'

Madame Director agreed because she wanted the Third World to remember her as patient, attentive and wise. She also had very little actual work, despite her packed agenda, which mainly comprised interviews (with others of Agastya's kind, all of whom she'd have to bully and harass for one silly slip or the other) and meetings with different officials to chalk out more short- and long-term courses for other Third World types so that the Institute's impressive budget could be justified and—who knows?—perhaps even increased.

'One day, Madame, in my last week as District Collector of a place called Madna, one of my hundred-odd visitors was a spirited, eighty-year-old woman. If you'll permit me to digress for a minute from the anecdote itself, I wish to add here that our District Collectors are a bit like the French Préfets, only younger, in general . . . The woman's name was Saraswati Something-or-the-Other. She asked me whether I'd heard of her. I hadn't. She was a little taken aback by my attitude. So was I, I confess, by hers. Visitors of the District Collector, even at their angriest, do not introduce themselves and then grimace in disapproval because they aren't household names for their interlocutor. Saraswati Something turned out to be one of our Veteran Freedom Fighters. Fifty years ago, she'd been a captain in our Patriotic National Army, Burma and all that, and had even been awarded a couple of medals. Some months before she came to meet me, she applied for a new passport. Her application was rejected, though—naturally—nobody would tell her why. It took her quite a few visits to the Regional Passport Office and a couple of nervous breakdowns before the door of some unheeding official to learn the reason, which triggered off a third collapse.'

My dear Dhrubo, Madame Europe Olympia didn't have as much time as I needed to finish my instructive tale. She dismissed me in mid-sentence quite charmingly and then sent a letter of warning after me, threatening anew a stoppage of the scholarship if I don't in future finish my anecdotes on time. This above all, to thine apportioned time be true. May I therefore, to an old friend, and since I don't like to leave any business unfinished, recount and round off the fable?
Saraswati Something discovered that her name was on the Intelligence Bureau's list of Dangerous Persons. She had to burrow a bit more to learn that whichever cop office dealt with Intelligence work in her home town of Madna hadn't updated its lists for about fifty years, which thus continued to have in them the names of those who'd once posed a threat to British national security.
Which of the principal characters in the above narrative would you choose to send abroad for training? That's the question. I myself would've opted for ol' Saraswati. I've asked Madame Europe Olympia for a second appointment, in which I wish to suggest to her that to prepare us for the UN, she could invite a European Dr Bhatnagar to come and take some classes.

In their course calendar, Puy-St-Etienne had been put down as a study tour to acquaint the foreign trainees—and their numerous shepherds too, no doubt—with some aspects of a typical European mountain economy. The skiing began at ten sharp. Everyone was punctual since none of them wished to be left alone to catch the others up on a pair of skis, to traverse hundreds of slippery metres—half on one's bum, a bit undignified, but safer—to the ski-lift, to board—and later, to descend from—which, under the derisive eye of some lazy, unhelpful operator, would be subsequent nightmares. Since the group did everything alphabetically, Agastya shared his turn on the ski-lift with his predecessor on the course list, an ancient, amiable but taciturn South-East Asian who settled down on the bench as in a lecture hall for an after-lunch snooze, chin tucked deep into chest, one gloved hand cupping his balls and the second hand covering the first. Agastya'd noticed the posture before and had found it oddly moving, elemental; a primal act, of defending even in sleep one's most vital possessions. On the ski-lift, moreover, that position of repose also helped to significantly increase one's chances of losing one's batons, which one left dangling on the edge of an armrest, where they swayed more crazily and clicked against one another the more one mounted. Of course, were they to fall, the disapproving instructor would naturally order one back—on foot, mercifully—to retrieve them, and that would take care of the morning.

Windy, sunny, sub-zero and breathtaking; Agastya could feel the ice wrapping itself around his bronchial tubes and had to remind himself that he still had a few degrees Celsius to descend before he could claim in his postcards home that he'd slipped into an Alistair Maclean novel.

'Your compatriot has missed the experience of a lifetime, is it not? Puy-St-Etienne? She doesn't return or what?' Conversations amongst dear colleagues tended to be in French, straightforward, elementary. For in his sojourn in Europe,

Agastya had sensed, or recognized anew, the obvious fact of the variety of our planet, of the millions on it from whom English was as remote as Spanish, French and Portugese were from him. They embarrassed and saddened him—his narrow Anglocentricity and the insidiousness of all colonialism, by which succeeding generations of the once-colonized too were obliged to think and to communicate in perpetually-alien tongues.

'I've no idea. I received a long letter from her last week which doesn't mention us, the Institute or the course even once. She had to go back for her lawsuit, as you know. That's taken up most of the letter—and her time, I imagine.' At the mention of Lina Natesan, warmth from the base of his sternum had oozed out in all directions, uncontrollable, thick like the sauce of some meat that slowly cooks in its own juices. Man. What a weirdo, with what an arse. All she needed to become divine was a sense of humour. He really should've written to that judge of hers. Me-laard, the case for the defence rests only on the mute evidence of its one witness, on its irresistibility, in brief. Me-laard, I call upon the arse of Lina Natesan to come to the witness box and take the oath. Meanwhile, I urge you, me-laard, to thine own self be true, observe carefully and imagine a piece of a sari, of grass-green georgette, that's stolen into that cleft and that remains there—snug and warm—for minutes on end. Fifteen. Twenty-two. Thirty-seven. *Oh quel cul t'as*! How can anyone possibly resist digging that sari out and, as it were, allowing it to breathe? *Lebensraum*! And substituting for it one's nose? The defence rests its case, me-laard.

Agastya had proposed more or less the same argument to Lina Natesan herself in the one fortnight that she'd spent in Europe. More less than more, to be honest. They would never have become friends in any other place. This had been her first voyage out and since she'd sensed behind it a conspiracy designed to deprive her of justice, she'd found the whole experience of her first fortnight rather trying. In her hour of distress, she'd turned to Agastya only because he always seemed to be there, smiling like the moon whenever and wherever she'd turned around. On his part, he wouldn't have minded much had she—a suspicious type—not swivelled around all the time to see who was following her because man, what an arse. I shall sink my teeth into that mass before the month is out or my name is Anthony Gonsalves, me-laard.

It irked him that she never smiled at anything witty that he said but he'd always find her tittering politely over the Maltese's jokes. Fortunately, he got on reasonably well with the Maltese, who was a couple of centimetres shorter than him. As a rule, he didn't much like people taller, save for Dhrubo, whose case, reasoned Agastya with himself, was special because in school the bugger had been a millimetre shorter till they'd both turned eleven, which is when the bugger had begun jerking off like a monkey and calling him August; both factors had helped him eventually to look up to Dhrubo.

What he, Agastya, dreamed of most was to make her, Lina, laugh so much that even her arse jiggled. Oooooooooh. He was stupefied to learn—and that too from the Maltese—that she was going away.

'Don't be crazy, you can't go back now. You'll cause an international incident if you use your stipend to buy a plane ticket—Interpol and all that. Don't be stupid, you yourself told me that Raghupati has the judge in his pocket peeing in. The game is so obvious that even a retard would see through it. Announce the dates for the hearing a couple of times in your absence, and then especially since you'll be representing yourself, dismiss the case because the prosecution doesn't show up. Look, leave Raghupati be. He'll entangle himself in any one of the thousand intrigues that he's spun in a long, murky career. There'll always be some petty injustices that simply aren't worth struggling against—Oh dear—foot in mouth again. I mean, here we are, in Paris. I love Paris in the summer, when it sizzles—though by our standards, it's mild winter. Oh why oh why do I love Paris? Why on earth do you want to leave the Jardin du Luxembourg and return to see Raghupati! Look around you, Lina, couples kissing on every bench, children playing in the sand, laughing on the backs of ponies, Americans at tennis, lonely hearts soaking in the sun, and you and me, babe. Think of *me*, Lina! How can you leave me alone in the midst of these corny aliens!' He held her by the shoulders and lightly kissed her on her right cheek, then on her left. She didn't freeze, neither did she look him in the eye; she seemed to be biting her lip and to have reddened a bit, so he hugged her hard and while nuzzling her neck, which smelt nice, though he was no bloody good at identifying perfumes, squeezed, in turn, her shoulder, her waist and a fistful of her bum.

A turning point in her life, though nothing changed in her immediate future. She still insisted on returning home to fight Raghupati and on his—Agastya's—not accompanying her to the airport. But it was the first time that she'd liked somebody else's hands on her. Reflecting on the experience on the long flight back, she attributed its strangeness both to their dislocation and to Paris. Call it the warmth of loving human contact, if you will, but a turning point it was, nevertheless, because out of the blue, against all expectations, she won her case. In fact, Justice Sohan went out of the way to ensure that she did. On *his* long flight back from Honolulu, where, at the World Poetry Conference, neither his Urdu couplets nor Punjabi haikus had bewitched either audience or any literary editor, and where everybody else—Z-grade poetasters in Spanish, Arabic and Chinese—had appeared to be drinking tequila, laughing and slapping English-language publishers on their shoulders all the time—on the long flight back, the boorish air-hostesses had refused to upgrade his

Economy ticket to First-Class. His was a Special-Price Concession offered by Civil Aviation to its Sister Ministries in the Welfare State, they'd explained. Not that he'd understood.

'I'm a judge, d'you follow? Do you know my place in the Warrant of Precedence? On this same ticket, how did I travel First-Class on my way out, tell me!'

The air-hostesses had neither any idea nor were they interested. The least blasé of them even fetched Justice Sohan the Flight Complaint-Book *without* his demanding it, thereby infuriating him all the more against Bhupen Raghupati.

Whom he sentenced to one month in prison, a fine of fifty thousand rupees and dismissal from service. The gist of his wordy, forty-page judgment was that the law must come down with a heavy hand indeed on any conduct unbecoming of a civil servant, on crimes against women and on the abuse of hierarchical power and a junior's trust.

'Payṇcho,' a bitterly-amused Raghupati doubtless would've muttered had he been present on the day of judgment and, after consulting Baba Mastram, appealed against the decision. His rights of appeal would've shielded him for a decade or so; after which, he'd have thought of something. How could the struggle for injustice ever end?

He'd intended to be present in the courtroom but wasn't because he hadn't returned in time from the lightning trip that he'd made, on Makhmal Bagai's squeaking-with-excitement appeal, down to the district of Madna, to swing and clinch an earth-shaking land deal of acres and acres for the development of teak farms south of Pirtana. Curiously, on the day after Raghupati's departure from the capital, Dambha, the tribal lackey whom Bagai had recommended for a post in his father's domestic establishment, vanished from

21 Ganapati Aflatoon Marg without a trace, much like an unlucky soldier into a long war.

Or a jeep into a jungle. Raghupati and Bagai were last seen driving off into primeval forest by Assistant Commissioner Moolar of the Revenue Department. 'They were going to inspect some sites, sir,' declared he a thousand times to senior police officials, Intelligence men and buttoned-up civil servants. To further probing, he could only respond by clacking his dentures.

'We should wait, sir, now for the extremists to announce the kidnapping and demand their ransom.'

Which occurred within the fortnight. The Superintendent of Police of Madna received at home an ordinary off-white government envelope containing a cassette tape of the All-Time Classic film songs of Mutesh and two sheets of paper. The first sheet, presumably the proof of identity, was semen-stained and blank. The second was a typewritten note in Hinglish from a hitherto-unknown outfit called the Neelam Sanjeevam Lazarus Youth, or NeSLaY, for short and sweet. It demanded from the Welfare State, in return for the safe release of a representative criminal-politician and a singular senior bureaucrat, twenty crore rupees in cash and the creation of a new regional state for the tribals with Madna as its capital.

'This tragedy would never have happened,' lamented the SP, 'had all officers of a certain level and above been officially allowed to carry mobile phones.'

'Lazarus?' enquired Bhanwar Virbhim, sotto voce, in one of his rare manifestations of speech.

'Apparently after their leader, sir,' explained Principal Secretary Kapila. 'He's an extremely angry tribal teenager who was once a temporary government servant and who's risen quite rapidly in the last few months in Sukumaran Govardhan's army. Into their ears has been dinned some seditious, post-Naxal, neo-Salvationist ideology. You are aware of course that Govardhan is fed up of government inertia on the subject of his coming out into civil society and is planning some alternative strategies.'

Bhanwar Virbhim had reverted to saying nothing. Dr Kapila continued, pausing between phrases to smile, as was his wont, without mirth and principally to disconcert his audience. 'How urgently and how near in the future would you like the captives back? A view could be taken that the event in effect is Phase Two of the OYE OYE Happening and that as desired by the Prime Minister, two town mice have gone off to experience the life of their country cousins. On our stand would depend, sir, whom we nominate as negotiator . . . I personally had in mind a very fine young candidate for the post of Officer on Special Duty in Madna. He's been there before as District Collector and even been trained in its forests. Very fine officer indeed. An Agastya Sen. He is at present in Europe for a prestigious training programme, where he is expected to shine. I also hope to hear from him certain responses to certain career management plans that have been proposed to him. If he does not rise to the occasion, Madna would be an immediately suitable option for Mr Sen. Of course, he'll be provided adequate logistical support. We are lucky in fact to have found a Junior Officer whom Raghupati was rather keen to have in his own team. This Lina Natesan Thomas would, I'm sure, be a perfect Deputy to Mr Sen.'

Who, though confused, didn't really mind swapping Dr Bhatnagar and Dr Kapila's Europe for Lazarus. He was sick of being buffeted around by the government and depressed that Daya hadn't immediately said yes to his offer of marriage. 'Madna again. It could've been worse. Personnel has apparently asked for volunteers for the UN Peace Keeping Force in Kosovo. Some thousands have applied. Perhaps I should make a special effort in gratitude for the Special Incentive Allowance of a hundred and fifty rupees per month that I'm going to get ... But which language, Daya, will I haggle in? An eye for an eye and a choot for a choot. I'd better brush up my trade terminology.'

'Take your time, sweetheart, botching it up. While you unwind in the forests of Jompanna, I'll ponder over and try and decode your offer. It was sweet of you to have made it.'

They were in Agastya's unsightly Ambassador, en route to a Rani Chandra cassette party which, it was rumoured, Jayati Aflatoon would briefly grace. Following Lina Natesan's example, he had decamped from Paris on the preceding freezing, wet and gloomy Monday morning, completely distracted by the first e-mail that he had received from Daya the Saturday before.

You'll be glad to learn that our new Senior Vice-President (Public Affairs) is someone you know. I chose Kamya, among other things, for her good head ...

To Madame Europe Olympia on Monay morning before departure, Agastya, justifying it, said:

'*Mon père est sérieux*, Madame.'

She let him go, partly to avoid having to listen to his French.

For the Rani Chandra cassette party, he would have preferred to travel to those posh suburban farms in a classier, Japanese, chauffeur-driven, air-conditioned, stereo-fitted car arranged for by Daya's office, but she wished to be alone with him.

He was tense because he was driving at dusk in peak hour traffic. Two successive mystifying and enervating road blocks produced by the movements of some V$^{\infty}$IP's entourage had forced him to change routes and soured him even further. Then, just when he was on the edge of the snarl of enraged, uncivil vehicles outside the gates of the Prajapati Aflatoon Transit Hostel, the city lights went off. The volume of the din—the honking, yelling and the invective—immediately increased; so did the collisions in the foglit smog, much like the shows of strength amongst the more macho members of a herd of animals. 'Cool it, honey,' Agastya advised himself and pushed the gear of the Ambassador into neutral to sit the chaos out.

'Dhrubo phoned me yesterday to ask whether I'd like to join this new political party that he, along with another madcap Bengali, hopes to launch before the next general election. I said yes unthinkingly.'

It was doubtful whether Daya heard him. She was distracted and amused by the two motorcycles that in exasperation had mounted the pavement and were chugging their way through the pedestrians, the hawkers with their kerosene lanterns and the stray dogs. Three of the riders were dressed in police khaki. The fourth, riding pillion, was eight-armed, outlandish in a Durga mask and a tight multicoloured jacket from which protruded six stuffed limbs. He carried what looked like a very real AK-47.

The bikes stopped before the gates of the hostel, apparently waiting for the steel-grey Contessa saloon that was emerging from the compound to precede them. As the car inched forward into the muddle, the motorcyclists got off and went up to it. One figure in khaki tapped on a rear window, a second—a woman, with a scar across her cheek—climbed, in two feline leaps, from the back on to the roof of the car. Squatting and leaning over, she, with an iron rod, shattered wide open its rear windshield. Even as she jumped off, the other three opened fire.

For the rest of his life, Agastya remembered that sharp in the headlights of the Ambassador, he had seen the man in the rear left seat of the Contessa—plump, bespectacled, distinguished, with great tufts of hair sprouting out of his ears—duck down and to the right milliseconds before the other three occupants—the driver, a bodyguard and an obese, newly-appointed Personal Assistant—were rocked and bloodied by bullets.

The assassins stopped firing as suddenly as they had begun. They clambered on to their motorcycles and turned into the compound of the hostel. In the ensuing seconds of awesome silence, above the bronchial rattle and wheeze of the Ambassador's engine, Agastya could hear the motorbikes roar away towards the freedom of the south gate. Cautiously, a hawker of wearunders then shuffled forward to the Contessa. He seemed first to inspect the holes in its body and the reddened, spider-webbed shards of windshield before daring to peek inside.

Three dead, with Sukumaran Govardhan wounded but alive when they were all shifted to a van to be ferried to the Chintamani Aflatoon Memorial Hospital. Something however happened en route, for Govardhan was declared dead on arrival at Emergency and the unnamed chauffeur wounded but alive. While the newspaper headlines applauded the event—

> 'END OF AN ERA'
> **'BLOODY DEATH OF LAST EMPEROR'**
> **'GANG WARFARE CLAIMS DRUGLORD'—**

the unnamed chauffeur arranged to slip away from hospital and into oblivion, where, safely out of the way, he had the hair from his ears surgically removed while working out a few deft moves for a smooth entry into politics.

In that hall on the seventh floor of the New Courts, with its defaced tables, broken windowpanes, scarred walls, chipped mosaic flooring and flickering tubelights, Lina Natesan, radiant in a sari of cream georgette, had nobody to share her joy at the judgment of Justice Sohan with save her old neighbour from the Prajapati Aflatoon Welfare State Public Servants' Housing Complex Transit Hostel, Dr Srinivas Chakki. On his part, he was delighted to be present in her hour of need, though he'd been convinced that he wouldn't be able to show up. Ever since he'd been suspended from service for writing articles in various newspapers and magazines that were openly critical of the policies and personages of the Welfare State, he'd become a newer, busier and even more revolutionary man, travelling, writing, thinking, exhorting, curing, debating, making an ass of himself at different forums, not caring because time was still running out at the speed of light, plunging on.

The rules provide a suspended civil servant with half his basic salary, or half a peanut per month for, as they say, a tough nut. While starving his family to death, he is meant, no doubt, to shame himself into joining them. An idealistic vision of the perfect state of things, for shame and guilt are not feelings that he has experienced often since his adolescence, or whenever it was that he lost his innocence. If he has other sources of income, he is supposed to declare them. If he leaves the town or city of his residence, he is obliged to inform the office from which he continues to draw his survival allowance. Contrary to type, as a free man, Dr Chakki scrupulously followed all the rules. To the National Institute of Communicable Diseases, he sent every fortnight an outline of his tour itinerary, attaching photocopies of his second-class train tickets. Of all the stuff that he wrote that was published, and of the meagre cheques that followed months later, he posted xeroxes to his old office, highlighting the passages that he felt warranted careful reading. Never Say Die, Mister Hope, was one of his favourite mottoes. As long as his brain ticked away, there was always a chance that some, or at least one, of his ex-colleagues—fellow-citizens, after all—would arise from his stupor to see the light.

WAKE-UP CALL

On a war-footing, therefore, the Welfare State must encourage our entrepreneurs to make some first-class, hard pornographic films. Nobody who is truly honest with himself will balk at going ahead full steam with this programme, which I have tentatively entitled Operation Bestial, that is, Better Sex for Tuning Into Life. Its acronym is one of the very few aspects of the plan that remain tentative. Indeed, if I may be permitted to say so myself, as time passes, the surer and clearer the future as a whole looks—from my point of view, of course.

It will be necessary to define the programme at length. I have learnt from my experience in bouncing my ideas off Miss Shruti and Miss Snigdha not to abandon even the smallest detail to the imaginations of my auditors. When left to themselves to fill in the blanks, they collapse into endless, low-key giggles. Nothing moves. Bad time management, therefore.

Hence Bestial, first of all, should be seen as part of a larger education policy. It is neither a joke nor a secret that our people need to be told what goes in where. The films will show—in close-ups clear enough to satisfy the most myopic, the dumbest and the most aroused—and explain the acts and processes that are in fact so profoundly moving, so beautiful and fulfilling, but in our country and in the psyche of our countrymen, have been warped and polluted, made obscene, the inspiration for sniggers and lewd, bestial thinking. I speak of terms and concepts like orgasm, clitoris, ejaculation, pubes, erection, cunnilingus, fellatio, ovulation, spermatozoa, fallopian tubes, mammary glands and erogenous zones in general—the bum for some, armpits and all that. Education through positive, wholesome entertainment.

To ensure which will be the responsibility of the new-look, positive, wholesome Cinema Certification Board. All happy endings. Made for Each Other sexual organs live happily ever after. All S & M, under control, positive, wholesome. No debasement of women, no blood, violence or females as sex objects. Just great, inventive sex arising out of love. Above all no film songs oozing sexual innuendo, than which nothing could be more disgusting.

The latest platinum Hindi film hit—which dates from a few months after your time, and which I know by heart because Miss Shruti and Miss Snigdha coo it to each other, across and right through my head, pausing only to giggle, eight hours a day, five days a week—is a perfect example. I translate faithfully from our official to our administrative language.

The rooster-cock of my love
Cock-a-doodle-doo,
Calls to you, my dove,
Cock-a-doodle-doo.
You're very wet, I see.
It isn't the rain, my pussy,
Cock-a-doodle-doo.
Go not away from me,
But cum cum welcome the rooster
Like a virgin bud the bee
For a warm shot of a booster
Cock-a-doodle-doo.

Let me see if I can bring along a tape of it tomorrow. Even your subconscious will revolt against its fat, yellow-fanged vulgarity. And it's one of the better ones! In fact, it's almost redeemed by its infectious, bravely-plagiarized, Latin American rhythm. As for the others! To plumb the depths, I accompanied Miss Shruti and Miss Snigdha to something called Tushun Hi To Hai Darling, Samajh Gaye Na, *universally referred to as* THTHDSGN. *Utterly exhausting. Three hours of spurting blood, bludgeon, thwack, wham, hero indistinguishable from villain, deafening cacophonous music, silicon heroines with faces like powder compacts—where on earth is the romance? I put it to you, as l proposed to Miss Shruti and Miss Snigdha, that you, I and the whole country would be infinitely more fulfilled by a wholesome, hard pornographic movie. Top-angle shot, followed by close-up, of heroine helping hero to correctly slip on his condom. Hero confesses that earlier he'd always donned it on his middle finger, with which he'd then mauled clockwise the nipples of the female forms beneath him. As a contraceptive measure, it hadn't been very successful. Surely you realize the value of the message, the education, that such scenes will transmit into that hot, darkened cinema hall? The possibilities are endless. Vamp has VD, close up, passes it on to villain, who deals in drugs, whose second-in-command mainlines indiscriminately, the dangers of AIDS, and so on and so forth. A good pornographic film would disseminate through tasteful entertainment all the loaded info of the Ministries of Public Health and Family Welfare. At no extra cost.*

On the contrary, while simply raking it in for the Welfare State. Of which more need not be said, save that, to reach out to everybody, I must presume that I'm addressing—begging your pardon—the dumbest of the dumb. It is safe to infer from the last census figures that we have a sexually active and eager population of some seven hundred and fifty million people. Not bad, huh. Tickets will be priced at one hundred and two hundred rupees. The Welfare State itself will take over and run the black market in the sale of tickets outside cinema halls, thereby providing additional employment to thousands, I'd imagine, for whom one may well consider a perk of free entry to the films up to a maximum of ten times per week. At a conservative estimate, I visualize a net revenue of about fifteen crores per film. We are therefore looking at a possible thousand extra crores a year.

Almost all of which will be pumped back into the world of sex. The health of our prostitutes, their housing and hygiene, the quality of their lives, the education of their progeny—their own education too. I mean, what's wrong with power to the prostitute as a welfare policy? Then we'll always need funds to improve the quality of our contraceptive devices—those copper Ts and condoms—and the health of our womenfolk, not necessarily in that order. You know, anaemia, tuberculosis, oral cancer from chewing tobacco, terrible menstrual irregularities, that sort of thing. To any insensitive male pig who objects to this diversion of funds to favour only one sex, we will retort: A healthy woman is the devil's workshop.

My old roommate, mentor and friend, Shri Dhrubo Jyoti Ghosh Dastidar, would require a minuscule fraction of our net profit to fund his research project on the frenetic sexual activity of the mandarins of the Welfare State. I'd be inclined to grant him the amount required for a number of reasons. One: As he himself phrases it in the conclusion of his proposal, if we don't ourselves study our peccadilloes, then sooner or later, a Caucasian European or American academic will slip in and make off with it, and once abroad, squeeze it dry of its richness, its worth, in fifteen papers and four seminars, from which in turn he will wring out two books, which will of course be sold back to us—and indeed—since they'll be on the reading lists and bibliographies of thirty Sociology and Political Science courses here—will become bestsellers of a kind. It is this chain reaction that Shri Dastidar wishes his study to preempt. He sees it as a protection of our cultural heritage. Two: As a long-time resident of the Prajapati Aflatoon Transit Hostel, I myself have been witness to the nuts, screws and bolts of the suggested project. It is an open secret amongst the hostellers that many of our fellow public-servant allottees have sublet part of their apartments to prostitutes, masseurs, computer salesmen, astrologers and barbers.

If I may digress for a minute to elaborate. In your present state, you probably don't recall the PATH—as the hostel is familiarly referred to. Twelve hundred one-room fully-furnished flats, six buildings in all, marvellous location, a minute from the Public Gardens. About five hundred of those flatlets, I'd say, have been sublet. It's easy—undo your pyjamas, and your brother's too—he's bound to be staying with you; back home, all of us have a housing problem—tie the two strings together and hang up a couple of your wife's saris across the middle of your only room—and voila, you've a one bedroom-hall-kitchen-toilet in the centre of town, of which you rent out the portion between sari and balcony for about five times the sum that's deducted from your salary as house rent. Neat. At ten a.m., or whenever the breadwinner departs for the day, an entirely different, parallel life swivels into existence, like a change of scene on a revolving stage. I myself regularly get my hair cut in D-248 and Miss Snigdha, I understand, has her toes done in E-117. After he broke away from Baba Mastram, Dharam Chand first set up shop in B-747, an address, he is quick to point out, numerologically significant for an astrologer of the jet age. Miss Shruti frequently has her fortune told there.

As for the sex, each building of the hostel, like territories carved up amongst the mafia, tends to have its own don of a racketeer. Any one of them, overly venturesome, trying to muscle in on the domain of another, might suddenly one Monday find himself transferred to some dump a thousand kilometres away. Hence they all follow scrupulously the rules of the game. Ministries and Departments too have been parcelled out amongst them. My Under Secretary colleague down the corridor, for instance, covers Home Affairs, Planning, Rural Development, Energy and a handful of others. He's arranged—quite clockwork, smoothly—with the Caretaker of the Commissionerate of Estates to always have at the disposal of the passionate and panting the flats on the ninth floor of our building that are officially designated as the guesthouse of the Regional Potato Research Organization. What Shri Dastidar intends to analyse are the processes and the structures within the system. Can one discern a correlation, for example, amongst the seniority of the concupiscent official, the economic clout of his Ministry and the social class, attractiveness and youth of the service provided? What percentage of the women professionals active in all the six buildings are resident housewives or tenants of the servants' quarters of the nearby Ganapati Aflatoon Marg, all of them terribly respectable middle- and lower-middle-class women who wish to supplement the family income incognito, and who'd be horrified were you to ask them, for instance, in a printed questionnaire:

At what do you play
When your spouse is away?

How many genuine guests does the Regional Potato Research Organization board per year in the capital? Has none of them ever wondered at the goings-on in the guesthouse, at how all its staff seems to comprise painted up, well-turned-out women rather the worse for wear? Is the billing cycle weekly, fortnightly or monthly? Does the don accept payment by cheque and credit card? Do the rates change on religious and government holidays? As you can see, Shri Dastidar has his work cut out for him.

In his approach to the subject of his study, he has, as he says in his Introduction, distinguished two broad categories of male civil servant and one special category of female. He sees one male type as the sort who just can't get it down, exemplified by Shri Bhupen Raghupati, last seen disappearing into the jungles of Jompanna. In contrast, the second male type simply can't get it up, as an example of which, I'm rather surprised to note, he suggests me. Though his illustrations can be—and in one case, certainly is—faulty, Shri Dastidar nevertheless draws interesting connections between the business, the activities, of the Welfare State and the sexual behaviour of its functionaries. It is the mirage of power, he argues, that keeps Shri Raghupati in a state of permanent excitement; and significantly, when he wants to pucker down, Shri Raghupati resorts to reading Cabinet notes, demi-official correspondence, circulars, memorandums and minutes of previous meetings—in brief, to wading through the innards of the Welfare State, the very same stuffing that, whine the male mandarins of the second type according to Shri Dastidar, permanently prevents them from experiencing the joys of a respectable hardon. You'd agree that we should encourage Shri Dastidar to further probe these links between power, documentation and desire.

Operation Bestial will have an interesting spin-off or two. We'll become trailblazers for the International Hard-Pornography Film Festival Circuit, for instance, and when our ageing porn film stars decide to perform in politics, their pasts will help to keep them in perspective.

Dr Chakki's hour was up. He switched off the Walkman, stepped up to the bed and methodically removed the earphones from the head of the comatose Rajani Suroor. He took out of his backpack his sunglasses and his headdress—a Yasser-Arafat kind of thing that he'd fashioned out of a small tablecloth—and packed into the bag the machine, the earphones, his diary, pen and water bottle. As was his habit, he scanned the cubicle with experienced eye—the drips, the ECG, the catheter, the tricky air-conditioner, the voltage stabilizer—before pulling shut behind him the ill-fitting door. Outside in the ward, manfully ignoring the awesome heat, the whirr of the ceiling fans and the reek of disinfectant, he smiled at Miss Shruti and Miss Snigdha, and gave off very good bad vibes. They, simperingly and in a flurry, sat up in the hospital bed that'd been placed beside the cubicle specifically for the guardians of Shahid Suroor and in which they, supine, had been pensively assessing the undulations of their forms down to their painted toenails.

Seven other beds in the ward, six of which were occupied; all six were cases recommended by local V$^{\infty}$IPs, for one still needed clout to get close to Rajani Suroor. In the initial weeks after the attack on him, the cops, adept at bolting stable doors, had cordoned off the entire hall—sanitized it, to appropriate their phrase for a hospital—and hadn't allowed anybody in, not even, at times, the doctors. However, time, the boss that eases up all crises, slackens just as well constables on duty, and thus with its passage, gradually at first and freely thereafter, patients, nurses, sweepers, attendants and visitors wandered in and out of Ward Two.

Since Dr Chakki'd been visiting Rajani Suroor every morning for the last three weeks, he'd become a familiar face at the hospital. Some of the occupants of the other beds in the ward smiled at him as he passed by. The good entomologist had a doctorly word for each one of them. '. . . So, Mr Chidambaram, still feeling nervous? . . . Don't worry, a piles operation is nothing . . .' Another handshake at the next bed, '. . . Well, Raichur, my dear host, the gastero any better? . . . D'you think it's God's way of admonishing you for snacking in the wee hours while officially on a hunger strike? . . . Come come, you'll be out soon, well in time to douse yourself with kerosene and light up at the next auspicious hour and date . . .' Dr Chakki then paused at the foot of Bed One and modulated his voice to sound less pleased with himself and more solicitous of his interlocutor, a blind woman, with a patch over her right eye to boot, who'd been admitted for a dengue fever that simply refused to go away.

Miss Shruti and Miss Snigdha watched Dr Chakki depart with unalloyed joy. Keeping vigil at a bedside was much more fun without his watchful eye on them. On their own tape recorder, they could play for the patient one of Dr Chakki's recorded cassettes and then settle down to concentrating properly on playing their own game of Antaakshari without being distracted all the time by his bad vibes tingling their skins. Of course, Miss Shruti, who was more sensitive, claimed, particularly when she was losing an Antaakshari session, that his bad vibes emanated from his recorded voice too, though—naturally, she acknowledged—not with the same intensity. They'd pointed out to each other countless times, helplessly trembling with mirth at their own wit, that both Dr Chakki's voice and his choices of subject matter were so soporific that a combination of the two would never ever work like an alarm clock, and that Rajani Suroor had surfaced out of coma once, but the bad vibes from the tape recorder had immediately knocked him out again.

It ought to be explained that Antaakshari which, transliterated, means 'Of the last letter', is a game generally played with film songs. One participant sings the first complete stanza of one song, or even just the first couple of lines, provided that they are long enough to convince his auditors that he knows the tune and the lyrics reasonably well. The last letter of the word on which he ends must form the first letter of the first word of the song that the second participant must respond with, usually within a tense twenty seconds. When earnestly played, Antaakshari has been known to be as harrowing as poker in a Western. Miss Shruti and Miss Snigdha, whose knowledge of Hindi film songs is truly encyclopaedic, play with professional single-mindedness, completely blind and deaf to the outside world. Their ne'er-say-die sessions last for hours (no song can be repeated in the same sitting), usually till their next rendezvous with Dr Chakki. Naturally, since they don't wish their surroundings to either interrupt or eavesdrop, they sing only for each other, intensely and softly; correspondingly, one listens to the other with the cocked ears and alert face of a dog sensing a rat.

Thus, there was no way in which they could've either heard Rajani Suroor groan or seen his eyelids flicker. Moreover, he groaned mutedly, respectably, not like a starlet achieving orgasm in a blue film. One must also remember that the ladies sat outside his cubicle, both out of modesty and because neither much liked either air-conditioning or Dr Chakki's cassettes, one of which was playing at that time beside Suroor's pillow. Alas, one will never know whether this was the first time that Suroor had shown any signs of revival or whether he'd stirred and moaned before, but sadly, each time when there wasn't anybody in the cubicle.

Dr Chakki was due back from the Madna International Hotel at two. He'd spend another hour with Suroor and play him one more cassette before tea. He'd recorded all the tapes himself in one of Rani Chandra's studios, complete with different kinds of mindless background music at the beginning, at points of emphasis and changes of topic and as flourishes at the end. Fifteen tapes in all, and that was just the first phase, for he had much to say on the subject of the rebirth of the Welfare State. Unfortunately, since nobody conscious had wanted to listen, he'd been constrained to seek out another type of audience.

The way to Suroor, long and tortuous, had begun with Shri Agastya Sen one rainy evening at the Prajapati Aflatoon Transit Hostel, over spicy samosas and tea. 'He has the right cv for a messiah; he's perfect for a figurehead. He knows the people, he can act, he's performed before them on the streets, he's famous, his resting-place's become a shrine. When he wakes up, it'll be as though Rip Van Winkle'd decided to contest for Parliament. Moreover, Suroor was—is—was—a sort of civil servant, a skilled survivor, he knows—knew—the ins and outs of the nuts and bolts. I think of him as a dormant dragon who needs to be roused into breathing some fire into his fellow countrymen.

'I want to urge him to wake up through sound. Audiotherapy has been greatly ignored in our country. Think of him as a schoolboy determined not to get up on Monday morning no matter what tricks his mother tries. We've nothing to lose, you know, except Suroor. Your Dharam Chand agreed with me. God is yet to take a decision on Suroor Saab's file, but we may issue Him a first reminder, he declared after consulting the stars.

'It's wonderful, Sen da, how you've kept in touch with the influential and powerful. So that's the route that I'd be grateful if you could take for me. Mr Dastidar to Dharam Chand to Rani Chandra to Jayati Aflatoon. Our demands are quite simple. One: No fee. The work is its own reward. Two: My team and I've to be set up in Madna for the treatment, the duration of which I haven't decided on yet. Three: I'm to be placed in charge of Suroor's revival. I don't want any myopic Civil Surgeon breathing dust down my neck.

'I've brought with me photocopies of one of those scripts that later, I'd like to record on tape and eventually propose to Suroor to take up as themes in his street plays. You could present these pages as convincing arguments to both Rani Chandra and Jayati Aflatoon—and in fact to anybody else who you know might want to join us but'd first like to learn what we're up to.'

> *Is it coincidence* (ran Dr Chakki's script) *that in Hindi our official language, Plato the Greek political theorist is called Aflatoon? Three centuries ago, when a migrant family from the North-West settled down at Aflatoonabad, dropped its caste name and picked up another—something less indicative of its social roots and region of origin—it chose Aflatoon. Was that foresight or irony? Or modesty, in that it might've been referring to the incredibly sweet, cloyingly heavy, mildly sickening and slightly lumpen candy of sorts, after which the town of its—the family's—choice is named and for which it—the town—is justly renowned? Succeeding generations of the family—the leaders, thinkers, statesmen, founding fathers and polo players amongst them—have often pontificated on the nature of politics and of the Welfare State, complimented one another on their acuity and wisdom and often recalled in comparison not the candy, but their Greek namesake. He seems a good point, therefore, at which to begin.*
>
> *In* The Republic, *Plato's Socrates states that Asclepius, the son of Apollo and the patron of doctors, believed that 'no treatment should be given to the man who cannot survive the routine of his ordinary job, and who is therefore of no use either to himself or to society'. Plato-Socrates approves entirely of the idea and himself declares a bit later, 'This then is the kind of medical and judicial provision for which you will legislate in your state. It will provide treatment for those of your citizens whose physical and psychological constitution is good; as for the others, it will leave the unhealthy to*

die, and those whose psychological constitution is incurably corrupt it will put to death.' In the perfect state, in brief, imperfection has no place, naturally.
Yes but, I mean, really, I say . . . protests Rajamani Aflatoon, the first founding father of our Welfare State, in the twenty-three volumes of his Complete Works *that've been published so far, and elaborates in his letter to Gajapati from a Swiss sanatorium in 1951, to be found on Page 419 of Volume Fourteen:* Our blemished Welfare State exists, therefore, for all the millions of the imperfect who'll never qualify as citizens of the ideal republic. Like people, like government. The quality of the second can only reflect that of the first. After all, its representatives and administrators are drawn from, and rise out of, them, the different sections of the masses. In fact, to make Plato's monumental meritocracy work, it seems to me that his wise men must first improve the basic stock from which they choose their candidates. In other words, even the perfect state could do with a dose or two of the principles of welfare.
Just as our poor government would fare much better, without a doubt, were we able to put into effect some of the ideas of the first and—I'm sure that our first family will forgive me—the original—Aflatoon. His proposal for the creation of an aristocracy of administrative talent, for example, which is what his rulers become after some decades of training. Well, can we juxtapose against them, even for a minute, our members of the Steel Frame? After all, they too, at the end of their careers, have worked at all kinds of government jobs for thirty-five years. On-the-Job Training, absolutely, and probably more effective than Plato's more formal, academic cultivation of body and mind.
I see at least one more point of comparison. Plato recruits his rulers from all stratums of society, but the

vast majority of them are chosen from the top two layers—principally because they are bred for the job. The cream of the scum, without a doubt. Does one need to underline the similarity with the distorted, top-heavy representation of classes and castes in the Steel Frame that led, almost a decade ago, to the setting up of the Kansal Commission in the hope that its recommendations would redress the balance? The fundamental difference of course is that Plato views this unequable, disproportionate reflection of the people in their administrators as essential to his grand design. The perfect—versus the Welfare—State, no doubt.

After that minute—for the duration of which we compared the two frames, the steel and the Platonic—is over, we can turn our attention to one of the end-products of our deliberations, the civil servant who retires at the age of sixty-two. Sixty-two, by any scientific, physiological, logistical, numerological or astrological configuration, is a mystifyingly insignificant number. Its triviality, its arbitrariness, as a cut-off age is underscored by the fakeness of all our birth certificates. It would be fairly accurate to say that most of our sixty-two year olds are actually between the ages of sixty-eight and eighty. Time being illusion, doubtless. Then why retire our guardians at sixty-two when we can benefit for another couple of decades from the wisdom and administrative skills of a handful of them? Ah, but the problem is—you object—how to select that handful? How to prevent the legendary Dr Bhatnagar—for example—from worming his way into that hand after his return from the UN?

The solution, of course, is to choose your wise sixty-two-year-olds only after analysing the opinions of their subordinates. Pick only those who in all humility have for thirty years sucked below with as much solicitude and nicety as above. Remember that according to their annual confidential reports, they'd all be outstanding.

How then will you differentiate between the matchlessly-outstanding and the a-national-disgrace-but-outstanding? Simple: send questionnaires to—and interview—some of those assistants and deputies who suffered your prospective guardian over their heads in various offices. Ask them:

1) How would you define the term 'outstanding' in relation to the officer in question?
2) Did he get all his promotions on time simply because everyone needs to budge a bit every once in a while, responding, as it were, to a fundamental law of Physics?
3) What degree of relevance to the personage under discussion has the axiom that states that when one removes an officer from his position, one also causes his work to vanish?
4) When his children dropped in at his office to phone aunts in the US and cousins in Australia, did he buy them Pepsis from the Office Entertainment Allowance?
5) At meetings, when his boss dried him up with a look for having brought the wrong papers for discussion, did he hang his head in shame and weep silently like Tom Dooley? Or did he glance at you in such a way, just once, askance, that his boss's ire was deflected onto you fully for the next twenty minutes? While he slumped back in his chair and smirked in witless relief at the others at the table?
6) Did he hang around in office pointlessly, way beyond closing time, only to impress?
7) How skilled was he at leaving his decisions for time—that sage, that overlord—to take care of?
8) Did he usually sit in front in the office car beside the chauffeur either because he wished to show that he believed in social equality or he was gay? Or because in an Ambassador, the front seat is a damn sight more comfortable? Or because he didn't wish to be machine-

gunned down at the back?
9) How hard did he try to scramble into the Intelligence Bureau Endangered List? With what success?
10) Did he regularly sign differently different official papers, depending on their importance and the extent to which he understood them?
11) Did he address village gatherings of the semi-illiterate in English? With a quote or two from, say, Louis Mac Neice? Or did he speak some of our other languages with such perplexing fluency that in a matter of minutes, he'd notice the members of his audience eye one another in polite bewilderment?
12) Did he spit into the urinal while pissing?
13) Or sigh audibly and invoke a god while leaning forward, resting his head against the tiles, gazing down and playing a sort of billiards with the naphthalene balls in the bowl with his jet of urine as the cue?

And so on. The questions that one poses will depend, naturally, on the parties in question, on who is being interviewed about whom for what job. Rest assured that I don't envisage selecting more than a couple of wise guardians per year. They'll of course undergo a series of physical, medical and psychological tests—if a blue flag flapping in the wind suggests a woman drying her long hair on a terrace on a bright Sunday morning, and a glass of cold coffee suggests a middle-class wage-earner contemplating a crime, then what does an empty goods train hurtling through the night signify to you? Confidentially, of course. That sort of thing.
Well, you've selected your SAge-Man-for-All-SeASons and he's distributed his mithai in celebration; what next? Why, he rushes off to his astrologer, of course, to tap the future. Okay, and after? After, you ask him to handle a specific project, keeping in mind the field of his expertise. No macro-level crap. Back to the grassroots. Dump on him acres of wasteland, for

example, to convert into a profitable orchid farm. Let him pick his own team, back him to the hilt, no knives in the back. Give him constitutional and extra-constitutional protection. Tell him to tackle the problem of traffic in your megalopolises. Ban cars completely downtown and wherever else the action is. Update your neolithic buses and trains, and instead of your air-conditioned, chauffeur-driven automobile that inches forward, sleekly and silently, at four kilometres an hour, use the bicycle-car, the manufacture and popularization of which will be given top priority in the new Welfare State. You know, doubtless, what I'm talking about? The cycle-car? With four sets of bicycle pedals, two in front, two at the back, that is to say, one for the driver, three for the passengers, with a steering wheel, a tooter and a set of gears in front? It's either that or the normal, standard bicycle. My sixth sense—or my astrologer, if you wish—tells me that it—the cycle car—will become incredibly popular and will in fact totally revolutionize industry. You see, while pedalling and giving some shape to your leg muscles, you can at the same time bicker with your husband, paw an object of desire, or daydream to a Rani Chandra cassette. No exhaust fumes, traffic jams or parking nightmares because it's half the size of every other car. The country's petrol consumption plummets, its air improves and jet loads of multinationals bid it tearful farewell, only to return by the next flight, in new lightweight suits, with firmer handshakes and different briefcases with state-of-the-art plans for the various components of our cycle car. Rest assured that their modern technology simply won't leave us alone.

Of course, no one, absolutely no one, will be above the law that will oblige the citizens of our cities to park their purring cars far away in some ghastly suburb and use our new trains, buses, cycle-taxis and cycle-cars to get to work. No exceptions, no insidious class

hierarchies or caste reservations. Ministers, terrorists, cops—all equally subject to the new regulations.
Yes the police too. I intend to devote an entire session—for which the script is ready—to the management of the police, so I won't anticipate myself here—not beyond a point, anyway. It is monstrous how we, in our daily lives, continually allow to be flouted and belittled the bedrock-axioms that ensure the health of the state: namely, that the upholders of the law must never be seen to be above it, and that the hand that holds the gun shouldn't sign the order to shoot. When you don't rein it in, the beast goes berserk, and tramples all over your life and mine, and swaggers up to the richer farmers of the north and demands of each one of them a lakh of rupees, or else it'll whisk away, torture and finish off their innocent, full-blooded sons and then congratulate itself the morning after for having wiped out some more dreaded terrorists.
The question that needs to be answered is: Is Operation SAMASAS beyond the reach of the tentacles of the Kansal Commission or not? That is to say, though it is true that the lowering of standards is fundamental to the idea of the accommodation of all imperfection within the Welfare State, isn't it equally important that one mustn't compromise in the least on quality control in certain key areas? That one must not lower one's standards to the point where the rot might start to set in?

The rhetorical questions continued for the rest of the paragraph. Dr Chakki's scripts were best read out by Dr Chakki himself. He thought so too but since Suroor hadn't responded to them with the alacrity that was their due, he had concluded that perhaps they needed to be delivered in a voice more melodious. Miss Lina Natesan's had suggested itself when she had phoned him at the hotel the previous week.

'Can you, Dr Chakki, arrange for someone to receive me at Madna station when I arrive there next Tuesday? My trip is official, so I deem myself entitled to a reception committee. I have repeatedly faxed, telegrammed and phoned the Municipality but have received no firm reply.'

'It will be a pleasure, Miss Natesan. We will recreate in Madna a little of the good times that we enjoyed inside Aflatoon Bhavan and outside the milk booth of the transit hostel. Particularly since Mr Agastya Sen will be here too, fresh from Europe and en route to Jompanna to take up his post as Officer on Special Duty for the negotiations with NeSLaY. May I ask what brings you down here?'

The plague, was her answer. She reminded Dr Chakki that it had always been with them. It had broken out in the national newspapers more than a year ago only because none of them, in the silly season, had been able to bear the agony of waiting for Jayati Aflatoon to grant audience to Bhanwar Virbhim. It had now receded in the main to where it had always thrived, the alleys and drains of places like Madna. It also survived, for a season and gathering dust, in Miss Natesan's thirty-page memorandum on the table of the-then HUBRIS Secretary, Dr Harihara Kapila. He had skimmed through it till page 3 and then given up. However, before he quit his post to climb the ladder, he marked her complaint down to a subordinate with the remark:

May please forward to the Disaster Management Cell in Home Affairs for advice on her and her colleagues. Meanwhile, if she can't be accommodated in one of our training courses abroad, pack her off to Madna.

A.C. Raichur was well enough by Tuesday morning to be ferried off to the railway station with a description of Lina Natesan and a board with her name on it. Just as well, for even those who knew her well would have failed to recognize her when she stepped off the train. In her externals, she had changed but marginally. It is true that her spectacles had been replaced by soft contact lenses that lent a sparkle to her eyes, and her hip-length hair had been pruned to a mannish helmet, but the georgette saris remained the same. It was her demeanour, her deportment, that had been utterly transformed. Inner fire on a war footing, no doubt. Her victory in the court case, her success in Paris, and her recent appointment as General secretary of Tetra Pack had all contributed to give her a sense of purpose and a springy step.

After a few hours of dialogue on the phone, Tetra Pack was the name for their new party that Dhrubo and Agastya had finally come up with. Tetra of course for tetracycline, for the party that would rid the country of the plague.

In the auto rickshaw, the new Miss Natesan's preferred mode of transport, en route to the hospital, she recruited, in her unique mellifluous Hinglish, an awed A.C. Raichur.

'We have to think small. Big is clumsy and slow to move. Once it moves, Big is uncontrollable because of its size. Look at our policemen in a riot, for example, monsters gone berserk. Big is filthy, inefficient, wasteful and *causes* calamities. The hills of garbage in this town that the Municipality leaves unattended is one contributing factor of the plague, isn't it? Remember that over the decades, every single institution, organization, building, agency and establishment that has been taken over by the government has been unsystematically ruined. The State needs immediately to shed weight, you know. It can retain defence, foreign policy, finance, justice and a couple of others but no more, I say.'

She spoke non-stop. The auto-rickshaw reached the hospital, they alit, walked through the corridors, entered Ward Two, greeted Dr Chakki and the simpering Miss Shruti and Miss Snigdha, did a round of the beds and she was still speaking. She had a hand on the door knob of Rajani Suroor's room when all of a sudden, her voice began to boom.

It took Dr Chakki a second to realize that inexplicably, the lone air-conditioner in the cubicle had gone off. He was vexed. It'd never happened before, at least not officially.

Agastya, who was at that time inside the cabin, was not however at fault. He had just that moment managed to prise open the stiff fingers of Suroor's left hand and place in his swollen, livid palm a Yin Yang box full of dope. He then remoulded the fingers tight over the box. 'You look as though you need it, friend.'

Miss Natesan turned the knob and opened the door a fraction when they all distinctly heard from somewhere inside Rajani Suroor a groan. It was a slow, loud and deep rumble of disgust, exactly the sound that one hears from someone who is wrenched out of sleep by the heat. To Agastya, it sounded dreadfully like a long-drawn-out *Pa-yṇ-cho-om*. They were a set of syllables appropriate for the occasion, he felt, a couple to bid adieu to the dead and with the balance, to greet the world of the living.